CROSS INTENTS

THE BIRTH

CROSS INTENTS

THE BIRTH

S.R. WELLS

CROSS INTENTS

THE BIRTH

This is a work of fiction. In some places where the story intersects biblical or historical canon, direct quotes are utilized. References to these quotes are included in the appendix.

Scripture marked NIV from the Holy Bible, New International Version®, NIV® Copyright ©1973, 1978, 1984, 2011 by Biblica, Inc.® Used by permission. All rights reserved worldwide. Scripture marked NASB or NASB(1995) from the New American Standard Bible®, Copyright © 1960, 1971, 1977, 1995, 2020 by The Lockman Foundation. All rights reserved.

The views and opinions expressed in this book are those of the author and do not necessarily reflect the official policy or position of Illumify Media Global.

Published by
Illumify Media Global
www.IllumifyMedia.com
"Write. Publish. Market. *SELL!*"

Library of Congress Control Number: 2021907738

Paperback ISBN: 978-1-955043-04-5
eBook ISBN: 978-1-955043-05-2

Typeset by Art Innovations (http://artinnovations.in/)
Cover design by Debbie Lewis

Sword and shield art by Phil Elsner.
Author photo by Kimby Family Photography,
www.facebook.com/kimbyfamilyphotography

Printed in the United States of America

To the King and to His glory

1

BEGINNING OF THE END

Burial minus 17 hours

*E*lric opened his wings and shot up into the night sky, carving a spiral through the thickening canopy of enemy spirits gathering over the Mount of Olives. He planted his foot on an attacking demon's face, pushed hard, and accelerated his climb. A plasma fireball sizzled in from the left. *Crash!* His shield met the incoming fireball, sending shattered streaks of energy around him. His left arm recoiled against the blow, but his right arm swung his sword upward and sliced through the arm of another vile beast on the right. The injured demon shrieked, and his sword fluttered toward the ground. The demon grabbed his wound with his remaining hand. Sulfurous vapor spewed from the wound. The leathery skin sealed around the cut, and the demon dove downward.

Elric reached his new vantage point. Now to assess the battle. He spun to the left, blocked another fireball, and checked the horizon.

Thousands of incoming beaelzurim raced toward the battle. He spun to the right and sent a small demon careening with the flat edge of his blade. He scanned the horizon again. Thousands more. He turned everywhere, looking for the requested reinforcements.

Where are they?

Most of his angelic team joined him in the air, engaging three or four demons at a time. Skillful and ferocious, these warriors could withstand this present attack. But with the flood of the incoming horde, they would need more help. *We need legions. Where are the legions?*

Elric spun, hacked, dodged, and flipped. His speed and intensity increased with the growing number of attackers. Clashing metal and war shouts filled the spiritual air.

Elric shouted, "We. . ." swing, "will. . ." kick, thrust, "not. . ." spin, "surrender. . ." thrust, "the King."

Still more attackers. *Has every demon in the region come to the fight?* A scream from his right thundered over the din. One of his warriors hung frozen in air with the tip of a demonic sword protruding from his chest. Six demons grappled the angel to the ground and bound him chest to ankles with black cords of pulsing energy.

No! We can't lose a single warrior! Not with all these. . .

Flash! An enemy blade tore through his left shoulder. The world turned white, shafts of light blasted from the gash, and searing heat filled his chest. "Ahh!" His wings faltered. He heaved for breath. He squeezed his eyes tight and gritted his teeth. With light still escaping the closing wound, he clenched his sword handle with his numb fingers and swung around with all his remaining strength. "Arghahh!"

His blade cut his attacker in two. With strength returning, his eyes brightened, and he sent three more demons falling to the ground.

Another anguished cry came from behind. Elric blocked another fireball and spun around. *No!* Another angelic warrior in white succumbed to the overwhelming numbers, shouting and writhing all the way to the ground where enemy warriors bound and immobilized him. Elric looked again to the heavens for signs of deliverance. Nothing—no reinforcements, no mighty ones.

The King! Have any of the attackers reached the King? Below, in the Garden of Gethsemane, the King knelt alone in prayer as the battle raged about Him. *Does He not know the mortal danger? Why does He not call down the legions?*

Elric spotted one of his warriors fighting on the ground near the King. The warrior spun and flipped and bounded from stone to stone, wielding two swords in a blur. Sparks sizzled from the crashing steel. *Timrok, of course.*

Timrok hacked his way to one of their fallen comrades and sliced through the cords that bound him in a single, precise swipe. The warrior regained his weapon and flew over a nearby clearing where eleven of the King's human disciples lay buried in a fog of sleep. *What's that?* A mob of men with torches clamored toward the King through the olive groves. *They're coming!*

Elric checked the horizon again for the main wave of demons. *They're too close!* A demon from below caught Elric's foot and pulled him downward. Elric scanned the sky for help. Still nothing—only the cloud of bat–like wings that surrounded them. *Help is not coming! And the enemy is too strong. My team cannot prevail against this frantic horde.*

Elric batted away four more demons and looked again to the skies. His left eye twitched twice. *This is it—we'll all be captured if we don't pull back and regroup.* He pulled the war trumpet from his belt and sounded retreat. He sliced through the arms of the assailant at his foot and blasted upward as fast as his wings would carry him. On each side, the other streaks of light followed. Behind him came the shouts of victory and mocking from the enemy.

Moments later, Elric's war-battered team rendezvoused in Jerusalem, hiding amongst the stone and mud buildings of the city. Elric and his lieutenants ducked under the cover of a stable for a private council. On dung-laden straw between two dusty cows, Elric planted both knees, crossed his arms, and waited. Jenli entered and knelt beside Elric on one knee. Timrok came into the stall but paced near the entrance and kept watch around the corners.

"Where is Lacidar?" Elric asked.

Timrok checked outside.

Jenli looked to the ground and said with a low voice, "He was taken."

Elric's shoulders slumped, and his arms dropped to his sides. He looked at his remaining two lieutenants. The silence of the moment gathered in his constricted throat.

He swallowed hard and said, "First we lose Zaben. Now Lacidar is taken. What is the status of your teams?"

Jenli answered, "The rest of Lacidar's team is all accounted for. I lost one warrior. Zaben's team lost two, plus Luxor."

"My team is intact," said Timrok. "But the King has fallen into the hands of the enemy! How could we retreat and leave Him there? We are warriors of the Most High. We could have stood against anything they—"

"No," Elric interrupted. "We would have all been taken captive, and the King would still be in their hands." Was he trying to convince himself or the others? The memory of an ancient wound pinched his mind, and his left eye twitched twice. He rubbed his temple and pushed the vision back into the belly of unspoken things without looking around to see if his face had given him away.

Timrok grumbled, "We could have stood. We could have—"

"The captain is right," Jenli said. "There were too many." He looked over at Elric. "Did you signal for reinforcements?"

Elric nodded.

"I don't understand it," Timrok said.

For several more moments, all three looked at the ground in silence. Then Jenli stood up and propped his hand on the end of his sword handle. "What is our next move, captain?"

Elric paused, then answered, "The Sanhedrin. If I am right, that's where they will take Him next. They need the approval of the elders to make their actions legal. Our immediate task is to secure the court and speak to the elders. We still have nineteen of us. Perhaps we. . ."

Elric stopped and glanced at Timrok, who appeared to be only half-listening in the doorway, distracted by something outside.

"Perhaps," Elric continued, "we can achieve His release through. . . what is it, Timrok?"

"You need to see this," Timrok muttered.

A chill dropped like a blanket of invisible terror all around them. Elric and Jenli stood up and joined Timrok. All three rubbed their arms with their hands and huddled at the threshold with only their heads poking out of the cover.

"What is that?" Timrok asked.

They all stood motionless and silent, gazing upward as the chill blanketed them. Thick blackness crept across the sky of the Middle Realm.

Jenli said, "It's like nothing I have ever seen."

The fingers of darkness progressed, and a hollow emptiness replaced the distant stars and cut off connection with the heavens. Isolation! *We're becoming isolated from the King's Realm! But our power comes from. . .* A shockwave of weakness shot through his frame, and Elric crumpled to his knees. Timrok and Jenli fell to theirs.

Timrok struggled back to his feet, and he gasped, "What's going on?"

Elric took a breath and looked upward. "Lord, what is this, and what would you have your servants do?"

He climbed back to his feet, waiting for an answer from heaven. They all returned to their cover in the stable and waited. No logirhim with a message from the Throne appeared. Only a strange and lonely silence.

Elric asked, "Anything?"

The lieutenants shook their heads.

"I have never. . ." Elric's voice cracked between faltering breaths. "Never. . . felt this cut off from the King." He turned to Jenli. "What are you sensing?"

"Nothing. There is nothing there at all. Before this. . . cloud of darkness. . . I was sensing pain—like the pain of a father watching the pain of his son. But now, there is nothing. Is this the enemy, or has the King pulled back His hand from us?"

"The truth is not apparent," Elric said. "I sense no malice in this cloud—only emptiness. One thing is certain—we are alone."

His words carried as much dread as the darkness that surrounded them. Lone soldiers deep in enemy territory. Cut off from their source of power.

"How is that even possible?" Jenli whispered.

They all exchanged blank stares.

Elric dropped back to his knees with his hand grasping his sword hilt. He lifted his chin and said, "This changes nothing. Our mission to protect the King has not changed, and we must move forward."

Timrok nodded once.

"If we fail here tonight. . ." Elric's voice trailed off, not sure how to finish the thought. The very question seemed too unfathomable before this moment. "What *would* happen? What would happen if the enemy destroyed part of the Godhead? Is it possible?"

"If it wasn't, the Lord would not have charged us with this mission," Jenli said. "This is a question beyond comprehension. It is unthinkable."

"You can be sure the enemy is thinking of this," Timrok said.

Elric stood and said, "Then we must not fail. Rally your teams and prepare to advance on the courts of the Sanhedrin."

"Wait." Jenli's arm blocked Timrok from exiting, and Jenli turned to Elric with a grim expression. "There is more we must consider."

"Quickly," Elric urged.

"What if it is actually the King's intent to die?"

Timrok wheeled around. "No! Not at the hands of the traitorous beaelzurim and sinful men."

"We have all heard His own words in these last weeks. He has been very unambiguous," Jenli said.

Timrok stood firm. "Not like this. If the King wishes to lay aside the frail flesh of man and take on an imperishable body to lead us to victory, He will do so in a manner of His own choosing—with honor and sovereign will."

Elric rubbed his chin. "I agree. And if He intends to. . . die. . . why did He not change our orders?"

"How long has it been since we have received word from the Throne?" Jenli asked.

"Not since His entrance to Jerusalem," Elric replied.

"Is it possible the enemy is working to deceive us?" Jenli said. "What if the enemy has intercepted every logirhim message and is setting us up to fight against the King's true wishes?"

"Fight *against* the King?" Timrok said with a voice higher than usual. "We could not be so easily deceived."

"Could we not? How many of us lost close friends to the deception that led to the Rebellion?" Jenli said.

They each dropped their gaze and stared at the straw–covered ground.

"And," Jenli said, "tonight's events were completely unforeseen. We have been blind. And now this. . ." he gestured toward the rolling blackness. "I believe there is much more happening than we understand."

Timrok's tone became low and deliberate. "But if we fight against the King. . ."

"We become His enemy," Elric finished. "We will become one of them."

"Fallen ones." Jenli said. "Cut off from the King forever."

Timrok's hands pulled away from his two swords, and he wiped them on the front of his tunic. Jenli placed both palms on his stubbled head.

"Surely the Lord would not condemn us for doing what we think is right?" Timrok said.

"Be careful," Elric said, "deceiving individuals to do what is right in their own eyes is exactly the tactic the enemy has used since the beginning. The only thing we can rely on is the word from the mouth of the King."

Jenli nodded. "And His words of late to his disciples have been contrary to our current direction."

Elric dropped back to his knees, the full weight of the moment pressing hard on his shoulders.

Alone in an animal shack, surrounded by an unknown darkness, cut off from their source of power, Timrok and Jenli awaited a decision from Elric. They looked at each other with desperate eyes only once and turned their gaze to the straw–strewn ground.

Elric stood and lifted his head. "My brothers, here then is what we have before us. If we do not attack and try to release the King, our mission has failed, and we do not know what consequences that will bring. The end is probably dire. If we do attack, we will likely be walking into a trap, and our chances of success are small considering we appear to be cut off from our source of strength. *And*, if we attack, we could unwittingly play into the enemy's hands and possibly curse ourselves for all eternity."

Timrok took a deep breath and let his hands rest on his sword handles. "We will follow your orders to whatever end."

"We are with you," Jenli agreed.

"How did it come to this?" Elric pondered aloud.

As he searched his heart for the right decision, he couldn't help but think back to when this whole campaign started. His thoughts took him all the way back to the beginning—before the King took on flesh, before this mission of mystery had been given to him.

2

BEGINNING OF THE BEGINNING

Birth minus 2 years

Dusty sandals. Dusty legs. Dusty hair. Eight-year-old Daniel trudged behind his brothers with the large flock of sheep and grumbled, "All I want to do is stop and wash off all this grit." Not that he minded being dirty, but his heels and toes and thighs burned from the chafing. He took several double–time steps. *My legs aren't as long—I have to take twice as many steps as everyone else.*

"Don't fall too far behind," his brother Jesse called back. "And do not let those two strays wander that far off."

I wish Father were here. Just because Jesse is the oldest, he thinks he can take Father's place. Daniel turned toward the straying sheep and daydreamed about the times he shared with his father Jeremiah out with the flocks. He pictured his dad sitting under the shade of a tree, teaching him and his brothers the trade, explaining business and money matters—which he didn't understand at all, and having long discussions about God's laws, the exploits of the forefathers and prophets, and the traditions of their Jewish heritage. He pictured himself lying beside his dad under the piercing stars of heaven, surrounded by the sleeping sheep, and thinking his father was probably the wisest man in all of Galilee. . . maybe in all the world. Someday, he would grow long whiskers and be as wise as his father. *But I would sure rather do something less dusty. Maybe even be a fisherman. This miserable plain—how much longer 'til we reach someplace with water?*

He herded the strays back toward the main flock, coaching them with his stick. "You two don't make this any easier. Three days of this already. I miss Nazareth. I miss Mom. They said we'd find better grazing land this direction, but I sure don't see it. Come on, keep moving."

Ahead, the last of the flock disappeared over a knoll, leaving nothing but a receding cloud of dust. Daniel encouraged his strays forward with his stick and ran to catch up. "Move! I don't want to be alone out here!" Running and running until his lungs burned and his legs screamed, he finally reached the crest of the hill. The two strays continued running. He stopped cold.

Below, on the other side, the flock stood grazing in a lush green meadow. His brothers unloaded their packs under the shade of a small grove of trees, and the hired shepherds spread out to set up a perimeter.

His eyes paused only a moment on the meadow. He looked beyond it and gasped. *There it is. The Sea of Galilee.* It shimmered in the midday sun like a pan full of silver and diamonds. The huge lake lay nestled in the wide, serene valley, and the rolling hills dropped at a steep angle into the blue waters. He pulled off his sandals, stepped onto the cool grass with his bare feet, and drank it all in. *They told me it was beautiful, but I never could have imagined this.*

Transfixed by the unexpected view, his eyes swept up and down the lake—then up and down again. He closed his wide–open mouth, wiped the layer of dust caked around his sweaty neck, and checked to see if his brothers were watching his novice response. They weren't. Jesse and Levi talked by themselves by the trees. Daniel picked up his sandals, strolled up to the shady grove and plopped down for a drink of water. *What I wouldn't give to go down there. I'd jump right in. I'd wash off all this dirt. I'd splash and. . .*

". . . Fish and provisions from that village down by the shore," Jesse's voice interrupted his thoughts.

Daniel jumped up and shouted, "So we are going to stay here for a while? When will you go down to the sea? I want to go! I want to go with you! You have to let me go, too. Please, please? I've never been to the sea. I want to see the water and the fishermen and the boats and the nets. I want to. . ."

Jesse shook his head. His face turned stern. "I don't think it is a good idea. For one thing, I promised Father that I would watch over you. And I need you here to help."

Daniel stormed off and ran toward a small rise facing the great sea, where he planted himself in a huff with his back to his brothers and his eyes toward the unattainable prize.

Levi's voice floated over Daniel's shoulder. "You know, Jesse, I could take care of him. And if one of the older men came with us, I'm sure we would be fine." Levi's sixteen–year–old voice sounded low and grown up. Daniel craned around to see Jesse's answer.

Jesse crossed his arms and looked down at his foot, which cropped the tops of the blades of grass from side to side. He looked up and pursed his lips. Finally, he shook his head again.

"No. It doesn't feel right. Something inside tells me it's too dangerous. He will have other opportunities. Father will take him there sometime."

Levi continued using his grown-up voice. "Look, you can see the village from here. You can see the trail that we will travel. He won't trouble us. And he will be helpful to carry back supplies. You have to give me this chance. . ."

Amos, one of the older hired shepherds, walked into the middle of the discussion. He gave Jesse a smile of experience and offered, "If it pleases my master's son, I will go with them. I'll watch over them both as though they were my own sons. I was a fisherman in my youth, and I am familiar with this port." He pointed toward Daniel with his eyes and said, "I think the boy needs this. It will be a good experience for him."

Jesse's foot went back to work on the grass. He looked from the two sets of eyes awaiting his decision back to the grass. Then, he released his crossed arms and let them fall limp to his sides. "Very well. But you need to take very good care of your brother."

Daniel jumped to his feet. Leaping and hooting and twirling, Daniel almost knocked Jesse over with a hug. Once the initial excitement settled down, they rehearsed the details of the errand and packed some light provisions.

"You need to leave immediately to reach the village before sundown. Eat supper in the village," Jesse advised Amos.

"We'll sleep by the shore," Amos said to Daniel, which brought a full-face grin and enthusiastic nods.

Jesse continued. "In the morning purchase fish at the market, fresh from the night's catch. Fruit and bread. Then come straight back and be here by midday. Everyone understand?"

Heads nodded.

"You must promise to obey Levi and Amos," Jesse said to Daniel.

"I will. I will."

Daniel led the party down the trail with newfound energy, oblivious to the chafing sand, and focused on the adventure before him.

————

The evening bustle of the lakeside town captivated Daniel's imagination as his eyes bounced from one new sight to another. The strong smell of fish filled the air; tethered boats bobbed beside piers; men mended nets for the night's fishing excursion; and squawking seagulls danced on the breeze. Daniel and Levi returned to the pier with hands full of bread, fruit, and water skins, and they approached Amos in the middle of an animated discussion with a weathered fisherman.

The old fisherman's voice sounded low and gruff. "This is a working boat, not a family cruise. I don't have time to watch after children."

"You won't have to watch after anyone. I will see to the boys. They are good workers and. . . oh, here they are. Levi, Daniel, this is Gal of Tiberias. He and I fished together for years before I moved to Nazareth and began working for your father. Gal owns his own boat now. Two of his crewmen are sick today, and he is looking for extra hands. He offered me the job for tonight. For my wages, we can have our fill of fish to take back to camp." Amos stroked his beard and eyed the boys. "The problem is, I can't leave you two alone while I'm out all night. So, we were just discussing the possibility of bringing you onboard." He paused and looked at Gal. ". . . As crewmembers. Hardworking apprentices who follow orders well. You can use the help. With just me, you're still a man down."

The captain surveyed the boys with an upturned lip that revealed neglected, brown teeth. "Fine, I will take the older boy. He looks strong enough. The little one—he stays ashore."

"You know I can't do that. Both these young men come aboard, or we have no accord."

"Humphff," Gal said. He looked toward the sun which had almost sunk behind the horizon. He scanned up and down the docks. He sighed again. "Deal. Go have your supper and stow your gear. Be back here before the end of the first watch to load the boat."

The three turned back toward town. Amos slung his pack over his shoulder and walked with a determined gait. Daniel beamed and skipped and held tight to his groceries.

Levi shuffled to catch up with Amos and said, "Are you sure about this?"

"Of course. It is good work. Good wages."

"I don't think Jesse would approve. And something inside tells me. . ."

Amos stopped and put his hand on Levi's shoulder. "There is no need to fear new things. Take advantage of the opportunities life gives you. This will be great experience for you and Daniel. And we will return with fish *and* the silver in our pouch. Jesse will commend you for your resourcefulness."

———

Thirty miles away from the pier, in the early night, Ruth—a devout woman, faithful to God and devoted to prayer—had already gone to bed for the night. Her husband, Jeremiah, was in Jerusalem for some business deal, and their three sons, Jesse, Levi, and Daniel, were out with the flocks somewhere. As always, she had offered special prayers for her family before going to bed. Safe travels. God's hand of protection. Good health.

She hadn't been asleep long when she awoke for no reason. She rolled over and tried to go back to sleep, but she couldn't. She pulled herself out of bed, lit a lamp, and poured a cup of water from a clay pitcher. She sat alone in the yellow glow of the flickering oil lamp. *My babies are out there somewhere in the night.* They were all so big now, but they were all still her babies. Especially Daniel.

"Lord, take care of my boys tonight." She prayed a while longer, finished drinking the water, and went back to bed. Refreshed and peaceful, she drifted back to sleep.

———

Daniel closed his eyes and listened to the water splashing on the wooden hull and the wind flapping through the sails. *It's like another world—no dust, no wandering sheep, no predators lurking in the shadows.* Only the freshness of the water spray, the laughter of the waves, and the anticipation of a boat full of fish. The rising moon and the lamp swaying from the mast provided enough light for the men who readied the nets. Daniel made his way to the very front of the boat to stay out of the way, but really he wanted to get up close and let the cool night wind blow through his hair and feel the spray of the water from the bow. Levi worked hard as an apprentice-crewmember, taking orders and putting his back into it.

A stiff wind filled the sail, and the boat sped across the white-capped waves. The spray from the water hitting his face made Daniel laugh out loud. Levi looked up and smiled at his little brother. Every time the bow plunged down and sprang back up, Daniel laughed and wiped the water from his face.

"Rough seas tonight," Gal called out from the stern. "Tell your boy to move back off the bow and find a secure lashing."

Daniel pretended not to hear.

"Daniel," Levi shouted. "Daniel, come back here off the bow."

"But the waves," Daniel shouted back. "The water!

"Daniel, do as I say. Come back here now!"

"Ohhh," Daniel muttered. He grabbed the waist–high edge of the boat to steady himself, but the slick wood slipped under his wet hand, and he fell to his knee.

"Daniel!" Levi shouted.

"I'm fine," Daniel called back.

This time, Daniel reached for the edge with both hands. Just before his hands reached the wood, a huge wave caught the ship from the side. The bow pitched downward with a jolt and then heaved back up to the right. Daniel's hands overshot the railing, and the edge of the boat caught him just below his waist, toppling him into the black water.

Shouts rang out and scrambling feet thumped across the deck as the boat passed by him. "Help! I can't. . ." Lake water gushed into his mouth. He sputtered and coughed. He flailed his arms and screamed and kicked with his legs. He gasped for a breath, and a wave broke over him, flipping him once, twice. "Help me! Help. . ." More water shot past his mouth and into his lungs. He coughed and convulsed, but when he tried to catch a breath, he swallowed more water. His lungs burned like fire, and his arms became too weak to fight. Another wave crashed and tumbled him. He kicked and got his head just above water. He sputtered out a feeble "help" and coughed again. *Crash!* Another wave submerged him. Dizzy. Dark. *Which way is up?* So tired. Dizzy. Scared. Tired. And then everything went black.

3

MIDDLE REALM

Birth minus 2 years

More than 150 miles from the Sea of Galilee, at the far southern edge of Israel, two men hurried along a well–worn footpath from Beersheba to a house in the flanking hills.

"Come, come, doctor," said the younger man, "we're almost there."

The older man, grey-bearded and wrinkled with wisdom, huffed and sweated and labored five steps behind. "Yes, Seth," the doctor said between breaths, "I was here just yesterday."

"My father's condition has worsened. I pray it's not too late," Seth said. He glanced at the sinking afternoon sun. "Hurry."

They approached the small family home, where the stone and mortar walls cast a long shadow from the waning sun. They passed a weedless vegetable garden laid in tidy rows. They passed a small stable with three goats and a donkey. Then, with a clatter and final burst of momentum, they passed through the weathered wooden front door of the house.

"The physician is here," Seth announced.

Four women stood in the front room. Two prepared food. One paced. One sobbed behind a hand cloth. All four turned when the front door opened.

"My father is in the back room. Please, come," Seth said, taking the grey-beard by the arm.

One of the women handed the physician a cup of water.

"Thank you," the physician said on his way to the back room.

The woman bowed her head and turned back to her work.

In the bedroom three men stood near the bed. Seth and the doctor took their place next to them. An aged woman seated beside the bed had her slight hand resting in the hand of the old man in the bed.

"He's sleeping," she said.

"It is for the best," the doctor said. "Let me take a look."

The men all made room for the physician, but the lady held her station.

The doctor felt the man's forehead. "His fever is worse. He is not responding to the medicine I gave him yesterday. How long has he been asleep?"

One of the men answered, "Most of the day."

The physician stood up. "I fear there is little more I can do." He rummaged through his traveling sack and pulled out a small pouch of medicinal herbs and handed it to the eldest of the four men. "It probably won't be long now. If he does awake, give him some of this. It will help him rest."

The lady wiped her eyes with a cloth and said, just above a whisper, "Will you not stay and sit with him a while?"

"If I tarry long, I will need to spend the night, for the journey is too far."

"Please stay," the lady said.

"Of course, Hannah. I will stay and do all I can."

———

At first, blackness surrounded dreamless sleep. Then Amichai opened his eyes and sat up. His four sons stood around the room as though awaiting some unwanted visitor. His wife, Hannah, sat with her head resting on the bed beside him. His friend Ezra the physician sat next to Hannah.

"Why all the downcast faces?" Amichai said, jumping out of bed. "I feel great! I have never felt better."

Nobody moved or even acknowledged him.

"Did you not hear? The pain and sickness are completely gone. Hannah. . ."He reached to touch her shoulder, but his hand stopped short. "What are you wearing?"

His eyes drifted toward the man in the bed. *Is that me?*

He turned with a start, and there, just inside the doorway, stood a very large man. The man's eyes stayed fixed on Amichai as though no one else in the room existed.

Amichai looked back at the body in the bed. "Am I. . . dead?" He turned back toward the man.

The man smiled. "I am come to escort you to a place of rest."

"But my wife, my sons. They need me. I can't leave them."

"Your work is complete. It is time for you to enter into His rest. Come, the Lord awaits." The man put his arm around Amichai's shoulder and led him toward the door.

Ezra leapt to his feet. "He has stopped breathing. Amichai! Amichai!" He shook the shoulders of the lifeless body.

The four brothers jumped up and crowded around. Hannah wailed and buried her face in Amichai's chest, "No, no. Oh, Amichai."

Amichai stopped and watched the unfolding trauma, but the large stranger pressed him forward. "Come."

Amichai's feet took the steps, but he continued looking back. The escort stopped and positioned himself between Amichai and the heartache in the bedroom.

"Amichai, son of Reuben. Do you feel the yearning in your heart? The passion of a lifetime bound up and ready to burst?"

Amichai nodded.

"This is the drawing of the Lord. He longs to see you. You. Face to face. These ones who are dear to you. . ." He motioned toward the bedroom. "They will always hold a special place in your heart. But nothing can begin to compare with the fellowship of the Lord Himself."

He put his arm around Amichai's shoulders again and said, "Come."

They passed through the front door and out into the twilight. Amichai turned back and blinked. Yes, he just walked through a solid door. Just outside the house stood another man, his back to the house and his gaze to the north. He stood no less than twelve feet tall with wavy brown hair that just touched his powerful shoulders. His tunic had an earthen color, and his sleeves bore two golden braids. At his side hung a sheathed broadsword and a small silver trumpet. He hummed a tune, somber and regal. *This must be a formidable warrior—more mighty than any I've ever seen.* At the sound of their approach, the imposing warrior turned and surveyed Amichai. His piercing green eyes melted Amichai's strength, and Amichai instinctively stepped back.

The escort stepped forward, gave a respectful bow of his head, and said, "Captain Elric, I present Amichai of Beersheba."

A smile erupted on Elric's face, and he raised his hands like an excited child. "Amichai, servant of the Most High King. I am honored to finally speak with you face to face."

Amichai's mouth hung open.

Elric moved toward Amichai, his entire frame reducing in size with each step. Twelve feet of brawn became six feet of brawn. Amichai now faced him eye to eye. Elric exploded with laughter and wrapped him up in a powerful hug as though they were lifelong friends. After a long embrace, Elric took a step back and grabbed Amichai by his shoulders.

"For years I have awaited this moment. It was my earnest hope to have the opportunity to see you before you departed. I wanted to thank you for your service to the King."

Amichai turned his head toward the escort, then back to Elric. "I. . . I don't understand."

Elric laughed again. "Do you not know what you have accomplished for the Kingdom?"

Amichai shrugged.

"You and your wife Hannah have been valiant warriors—praying for your children, your grandchildren, all your family. And your constant prayers for your rabbi in Beersheba and the priests, the high priest in Jerusalem, the deliverance of Israel from the Romans, the glory of the Lord's temple—these have all been heard by the Lord."

Amichai shrugged. "But. . . the high priest is still corrupt, and the Romans are still. . ."

"Look. Look at what you and Hannah have created."

Elric, still holding Amichai's shoulders, turned him around to face the house and then laughed again at Amichai's reaction to the unexpected sight. There before them stood a fortress. The humble stones of the house remained visible, but the entire building appeared veiled behind a semi-transparent layer of light. Elric walked over to the fortress wall and slapped it with his hand. It made a solid thumping sound.

"Every one of these bricks of light, all the plates of armor—you and Hannah set in place."

"But how?" Amichai approached the wall and tested it with a firm smack of his hand.

"You have many questions. When you see the King, he will instruct you in all things. There is much I want to show you, so I will try to explain a little now. Do this," Elric said. "Speak a word of praise to the Lord."

Amichai cocked his head.

"Anything. With your mouth, speak praise."

Amichai's voice sounded timid but sincere. "Praise the Lord. His mercy endures forever."

The sound from his words rolled up into a small vortex of light that propelled itself into the wall and spread into a thin layer of glowing light on the surface of the armor.

Elric said, "Words, beliefs, thoughts—but especially words—carry power. A word spoken in the Physical Realm may not appear to accomplish anything, but that word enters the Middle Realm as pure energy. Here, that energy can be turned into spiritual matter. Or destroy it. Words are constantly building up or destroying. Words of darkness—unbelief, bitterness, pride—can tear down structures of light and build structures of darkness. After much time and many words, a person can create a stronghold."

Elric pressed his shoulder hard against the wall and continued. "You have created a stronghold for the King. The King and we," he pointed toward the escort and himself, "His angelic host, can operate freely here."

Just then, Amichai's youngest son, Seth, stormed out of the house. He slammed the wooden door and passed through the wall of light and into the front yard. He scooped up fistfuls of earth and threw the dirt into the air. Several times he scattered the dust and screamed. Caleb, his oldest brother, followed him out.

"Seth," Caleb said.

"Why? Why did he have to die? He was such a good man. Does God hate us?" Seth paced and yanked his hair with both hands. Caleb tried to put his arm around his brother, but Seth pulled away. "If there even is a God."

"Now you speak foolishness," Caleb said.

Elric led Amichai aside while the two brothers sparred.

"Do you see how Seth has built his own strongholds?" he asked. The young man appeared mostly exposed but had a thin helmet and breastplate of darkness. "And Caleb his?" He had breastplate of light. "Now, watch."

Amichai stood speechless.

Elric walked over to Caleb, who spoke with a raised voice as he admonished his brother. "Peace. Peace of the King," Elric said. And he touched Caleb's chest. Elric's words and the touch of his finger flashed and then dissolved into the breastplate. Caleb's tone of voice settled and grew calm.

Elric then spoke to Seth and touched his chest. "Peace. Be still." Again, the words became a flash of light, but they bounced off Seth's dark breastplate and dissipated into the air.

Seth continued to rage. "I don't care what you say. It's not fair, and I think. . ."

Elric put his arm around Amichai's shoulder and said, "Let's go inside."

They passed under an exquisite archway of light with intricate carvings and artistic patterns. Then they passed through the unadorned front door. All the people gathered in the back room, and their muffled voices and crying sounded distant as Elric continued to speak.

"Because of the stronghold you have built here, we, the elzurim, have been using this place as an outpost headquarters for years. You are standing in the middle of our war room. Here we devise strategies, receive updates, and direct operations. This is what I wanted you to see."

Elric waved his hand over the ground in a long sweeping arc. A multi-dimensional map of the region appeared and almost filled the room. It stretched as far north as Phoenicia and as far south as the northern part of Egypt. The western edge lay somewhere in the

Mediterranean Sea and the eastern edge extended to Syria. Beersheba, where they were, appeared near the bottom of Israel. He easily identified the cities on the map—as well as the Sea of Galilee in the north, the river Jordan, and the Dead Sea. And he saw thousands of tiny lights, no larger than individual grains of sand. Glowing, iridescent clouds of many colors formed layers upon layers above the ground map. Each layer pulsated and swirled within its own layer and had veins that extended outward, upward, and downward, wrapping intricately within the other layers. Between the colored plasma layers floated black, smoke–like layers. These also had fingers that wove themselves throughout. Occasionally, strange colored geometric shapes appeared in mid-layer. Some glowed for a while and then disappeared. Others blinked. Some moved about. He also saw thousands of black spots of anti-light that spread throughout the map and into the layers above it. Sparkles and endless chaotic movement flashed everywhere. The whole scene appeared like a swirling mass of surging energy.

"This is our war map," Elric said, "a valuable tool in our war against the enemy. You see clouds and colors and lights. I see people, enemy forces, economics, social patterns, weather, physical environments, spiritual environments, education, politics. We use this to see the inter-workings of all the important factors which affect the battlefield."

Elric's voice became higher than usual and he did a small skip as he moved to a region of the map where he motioned to a swirling green cloud.

"Here you see the beginning of Hellenism during the Persian period. Over here you see how it progressed and how it permeated the cities and the daily lives of your people."

He shuffled to another area and pointed to other features.

"You can see the periods of spiritual awakening and then watch them wane. The rise of the Roman empire and the long string of power struggles from one ruler to the next is over here. The drought over there led to a migration of people to this region, bringing with them their mystic philosophies. The greed of this ruler led to increased commercialization. There was an excellent yield of grain from that field that year. A self–serving evil high priest died this year. Over here you can see where the enemy raised up a tyrant who affected generations of people. But there you can see how the King's army turned the situation around and gained additional ground. All these forces and events are working together—each affecting the other."

He stopped and made his way to the far wall where Amichai stood with wide eyes.

"Part of my duty is to devise strategies to affect both individuals and generations. A single event today can have a huge influence on the future. It is delicate work. We can't simply move individuals around like pieces on a game board. These pieces move on their own. And we can't see beyond that which is revealed. The edges of the map are fuzzy, even to me. The King knows what lies beyond the edges and is actively moving the entire scene in the direction He intends, but it is up to each of the individuals, including his warriors, to actually make it happen."

Amichai's mouth hung open and he shook his head. "All this. . . in my home? I had no idea."

"You knew more than you realized. Sometimes during our meetings, you and Hannah would pick up issues and intercede for concerns we had just been discussing. You were partners with us in a war you could not see."

"Are there other war rooms like this?"

"Oh yes, there are outposts throughout the Middle Realm. Each reports to commanders of larger regions. And they report to the generals above them in the King's Realm. The King, of course, issues commands that are relayed to the various levels. But we have authority to make decisions and work for the welfare of mankind in the name of the King. A daily status meeting is about to begin. Would you like to observe?"

Amichai smiled and nodded.

The escort stepped forward. "Captain. . ."

Elric held up his hand and laughed. "The King would approve a short delay. It will please Him to reward my friend with this opportunity."

The mourning continued in the back room, but Amichai hardly noticed. His eyes kept scanning the war map, and his head kept shaking back and forth. *A meeting of angels! Right here in my house. A strategic war room. This is amazing!*

4

ANGEL MEETING

Birth minus 2 years

One by one, the other captains arrived at the war room in Amichai and Hannah's house. Each passed through the front door and contracted his enormous frame down to the size of a man. Each greeted Amichai with great smiles, laughter, and hugs. One broke into song and danced with him. Amichai counted ten mighty warriors with two gold braids on their sleeves. *So much power packed into this room. Their presence is overwhelming. How did I not perceive them before?* Each wore an imposing broadsword which hung ready in its sheath. The sheaths had engravings of elegant patterns—mostly leaves, symmetric geometric shapes, and the words of some beautiful language.

Elric leaned over to Amichai. "We each have responsibilities for different sectors within this region. We all have ten lieutenants who each command one hundred elzurim, but of course our numbers vary constantly as the times dictate. Tonight, we will discuss strategic plans and receive reports from the field."

Elric led Amichai by the arm. "We are pleased that you can finally see the real activities in your home, but we will ask that you stay here in this corner and simply observe. It is important work that we do."

Amichai nodded and backed into the corner. The meeting began.

The strategic discussions included successors for the high priest in Jerusalem and for Herod the Great. The enemy already worked to position men with evil hearts. The captains deliberated over their own potential successors and looked for ways to see them promoted and positioned for the opportune time. They talked about the good that had come from Herod's reign—like the rebuilding of the temple in Jerusalem. They seemed pleased with that successful operation. The King used an evil man and that man's own selfish agenda to advance His kingdom on earth. But overall, this ruler remained a ruthless tool of the enemy and needed to be moved aside. They submerged deep into deliberations over complicated and intertwining issues on the war map for some time before the first lieutenant from the field arrived.

Within moments, a dozen new warriors with single silver braids on their sleeves entered the room, lined up against the walls, and awaited their turn to give their report. One of the captains waved his hand over the map panorama, and it disappeared. The lieutenants had their full attention.

They started with births and the passing of the righteous. Every name reported among the righteous deaths brought cheers and laughter and praises to the King. When a lieutenant announced Amichai's name, they all cheered even louder, and several of the lieutenants closest to him gave him vigorous slaps on the back. Births proceeded the same way—another creation with the breath of life and the hope of a great future. Amichai shook his head. *Never have I witnessed such pure joy and genuine delight. I wish Hannah could see this.*

Next, they moved to the tactical. One of the lieutenant's warriors had a skirmish with a demon who tried to indwell a man in Shechem. With the Lord's strength, the warrior prevailed. A man in Hedera had not been so fortunate. The enemy brought sickness to one family. The host prevented a similar attack on another family. A young couple in Nazareth, Joseph and Mary, just got engaged to be married, as did another couple in Gezer. The lieutenants reported a number of betrothals. This man struggled in his faith. That man drew near to God. This one had become completely bent on evil and had allowed himself to become a puppet of the enemy. And so it went, story after story. *Everything is so clear in my mind! Every detail—I hear it, retain it, understand it. It's like I'm seeing and comprehending the world for the first time. But these captains—they go far beyond this. I can see it in their eyes.* They wove everything together, devised strategies, planned countermoves.

One of the lieutenants, who went by the name Jenli, reported that one of his warriors had had a direct intervention.

"Send for your warrior," Elric ordered. "We would like to hear his account."

Jenli disappeared through the front door, and another lieutenant gave his report. That report completed just as Jenli returned with his warrior from the field. This angel took the center of the room with animated hand gestures and energetic steps.

"Yesterday, Jesse, Levi, and Daniel, sons of Jeremiah from Nazareth, found pasture for their sheep near the Sea of Galilee," he began. "They were trying to decide whether to let Daniel go with Levi to the lake for supplies. The Lord gave me specific direction to prevent this. He foresaw an enemy attack. So, I gave this warning to Jesse. At first, I thought he heard me, but then he allowed Daniel to go anyway."

All the warriors in the room nodded.

"The next thing I knew, Levi, Daniel, and Amos were talking about going out on the lake in a fishing boat. Again, the Lord gave me a strong warning—which I spoke to Levi."

"It is no coincidence that the boat captain needed extra hands last night," Jenli interjected. "Remember that yesterday I reported how the enemy had struck two of the fishermen with a stomach illness." They all nodded and returned their attention to the story. In the corner, Amichai's mouth hung open.

"Levi tried to listen to me, but he didn't have the strength to stand up to Amos. They all went out on the boat. I knew I was going to need help, so I sent a messenger to the house of Jeremiah. Our messenger was successful in waking Ruth and prompting her to pray. In the meantime, I remained in vigilant watch for the enemy. Unfortunately, Daniel had put himself in a vulnerable position. Before I could stop it, an enemy warrior caused a large wave to disrupt the ship, and then it took very little for the vile serpent to send the boy into the water. The enemy flapped his wings all around the boy's head while he tried to swim, and it caused him to panic. I engaged the enemy and drove him off, but it was already too late. Daniel was in the water, in a panic, and did not know how to swim. Just then, a logirhi arrived with orders to directly intervene. I grabbed an end of one of the fishing nets the men were throwing out and positioned it right above Daniel. Then, I dove below him and urged him to try one more kick. When he did, I shot him up about fifteen feet until he reached the netting."

"Did he know it was you who saved him?" one of the captains asked.

"I think not. He was too disoriented. From there, the men were able to bring him aboard. Except for an earful of water, he is doing fine now and has rejoined Jesse and flock."

"A job well done," Jenli said. "Thank you for your report. You may return to your post." They all exchanged smiles. The warrior disappeared through the front door, and Amichai forced his mouth closed.

The lieutenants shared a number of stories like this, and each amazed Amichai. *I wonder how many times an angel intervened on my behalf.*

Then, a different kind of angel appeared through the front door. He had the appearance of a man but had a much slighter frame than the warriors in the room. He carried no weapon or shield, and his movements appeared quick and agile. One of the lieutenants announced, "The logirhim arrive." Bypassing all others, the logirhi approached one of the captains, spoke in his ear, and retreated through the front door. The entire exchange took only a moment. The captain motioned to one of the lieutenants and gave instructions. The lieutenant nodded and departed. Another small, fast angel appeared and spoke to a different captain. Then another appeared. And another. Within seconds, at least twenty of these messengers filed through the room at once. They came and went at a pace that left Amichai dizzy. Lieutenants left. New ones arrived. Captains directed. At one point during the chaos, Amichai caught Elric's eye from across the room. Elric gave him a smile and continued his work. Amichai strained to hear some of the exchanges.

The captain nearest him turned to receive a message. The messenger said, "The Lord has decreed that Benjamin, son of Joel, is to be promoted to Chief Treasurer in Egypt and moved into the proconsul palace."

"Timeframe?"

"Immediately."

The captain nodded. "In His service."

"By His word." And the logirhi left.

"Zaben," the captain called.

A nearby lieutenant stepped forward.

"I have a new mission for you," the captain said. "The Lord intends to see Benjamin, son of Joel, promoted to Chief Treasurer and moved into the palace immediately. You are to provide Bartimus, the current Chief Treasurer, an opportunity to repent from his wickedness. If he does, we will make a way for him to move to a higher position in Rome. If he does not, turn him over to the enemy."

Zaben bowed his head once and joined the stream of warriors leaving the war room.

After some time, the clamor subsided, and the flow of messengers dwindled. Finally, the last logirhi delivered his message. Amichai leaned in close enough to hear.

"The prayers of Elizabeth, wife of Zacharias in Judea, are about to manifest in the Physical Realm. Tell your lieutenant Lacidar to encourage her. She will have a son."

"Are we to confirm with a dream?" the captain asked.

"No. The Lord will speak to Zacharias when the time is complete."

"In His service."

"By His word."

The last of the messengers departed, and the room became still. Only the captains remained, and they each became solemn. Their eyes, which had been full of vigor and wisdom just moments before, now looked grim. One by one, they each called out names. With each name, every captain winced as though pricked by the blade of failure. *These must be the passing of the unrighteous.* Defeat, emptiness, and irretrievable loss boiled in Amichai's belly. Name after painful name cut through Amichai's heart. *Enough! No more names!* The captains dabbed their eyes with their sleeves. Finally, Elric announced the last name. All the captains grasped their sword handles. Without another word, they thundered out like a company of lions, full-sized and larger than Amichai's house could contain.

Amichai found himself alone again with Elric and the escort.

The angel meeting dispersed. Elric composed himself and smiled at Amichai. "I am pleased you were able to see the operations here in the war room. You were an effective servant of the King, and we are all in your debt."

"Can I not stay here and continue the fight with you?"

Elric offered a slight smile and put his arm around Amichai's shoulders. "This is the work of the Lord's elzurim. Your labor is complete. The King awaits, and with Him you will find rest and joy unspeakable."

Amichai looked around the room, now dark in the Physical Realm. His sons and their wives all slept on bedrolls on the floor. He made a motion toward the bedroom. "May I see Hannah again before I go?"

"Of course."

Hannah slept in her bed, and another angel—whom Amichai had not seen before—stood watch in the room. A layer of glowing light surrounded Hannah. Amichai reached to touch her skin, but his fingers passed through the flesh and contacted her spirit. He jolted his hand back.

"She's very strong in the Lord," Elric said.

"Stronger than I was," Amichai replied. He touched her again and let his hand rest on her spirit. He looked up at the other angel. "I believe she will be all right."

The angel nodded. "It is always difficult for a time."

Amichai turned back toward Elric. "I am ready. Will you come with me?"

"My station is here. One day I will return to my former place."

"When?"

"Only the King Himself knows. But one day. . ." Elric's voice cracked and his eyes filled with tears. "One day the King will come physically to the earth, vanquish His enemies, establish His kingdom, and reign in justice." His words became slow, as though each was to be savored. "No more rebellion. No more death. Only peace. . . joy. . . music." He closed his eyes, and he moved his right arm in a fluid motion as though directing some unseen choir through a magnificent score. He smiled and turned his ear with satisfied contentment. After a pause, his eyes popped open and he lowered his arm.

"One day."

5

EXPECTANCY

Birth minus 2 years

The synagogue in Nazareth stood taller than the other buildings in the town, but its stone walls cut from local quarries gave it a modest and earthy appearance. Even though it had a six–pillar colonnade defining its inner space, compared to the temple in Jerusalem, this place resembled little more than a mere outpost. Still, it stood as a preeminent edifice in the village—the center of religious and social activities for many. It didn't have an altar for sacrifices, but it did provide a sanctuary for worshipers to gather and a place for the Scripture to be taught.

An angelic lieutenant named Jenli alighted on the steps in front of the synagogue and met two warriors stationed there.

"Luxor, Deenr," Jenli said.

The two warriors bowed their heads.

Jenli stepped forward. "Report."

"All quiet here, sir," Luxor said. "Avner and Raziel are in a study room. Yadid and Shalev are preparing for the morning service. There are a few worshipers here early to pray. No unusual enemy activity."

"Very good."

"Sir, do you bring any new orders?" Deenr asked.

"Not today. But I will join you for today's service."

Jenli and Luxor stepped inside. Deenr remained at his post outside.

"Let's visit our senior priest," Jenli said. "What is he doing with Raziel?"

"His time with Raziel has increased. Avner mentors him at every opportunity."

"That is good. That is good."

The two angels passed behind the main sanctuary with its tapestries and ceremonial fixtures and into the repository. Here in the warm yellow lamplight, Jenli paused and watched the two scribes hard at work. Stroke by stroke they copied the sacred words from one scroll to another. And then they counted every letter, checked and double checked, then cross checked. Jenli lingered.

"You were a recorder, weren't you—before the Rebellion?" Luxor said to Jenli.

Jenli nodded. "All the details of life. Every word from the King. Everything in the King's Realm, Middle Realm, and Physical Realm. We capture it all. I love how all the details fit together for the glory of the King."

"How much longer do you have on your rotation?"

Jenli's brow dropped, and he pursed his lips. *One of the benefits of being a recorder—our services are still needed in the King's Realm.* Unlike the rest of these warriors, he only had to do 600–year deployments on earth and then he returned to his regular station for 100 years before his next rotation.

Jenli put his hand on his partner's shoulder and turned to leave. "One year."

They continued on to the back study room and found Avner and Raziel meeting in private.

Raziel's words rattled off in quick succession. ". . . exactly fourteen generations in all from Abraham to David, and fourteen from David to the exile to Babylon. And depending on whose line you follow, I calculate fourteen generations from the exile to now. Do you think it means something? Do you think this generation could see the Messiah?"

Avner stroked his long beard. "Interesting. Yes, this is very interesting. It is difficult to understand patterns in the scriptures, especially looking forward. However, I believe it is wise not to discount patterns that present themselves. And forget not the seventy sevens in the prophet Daniel. If the 'sevens' refer to years, we could certainly be in the generation that will see the fulfillment of all things. I have prayed my whole life for the deliverance of Israel. And with the oppression of the Romans, we *all* are heavy with expectancy for the revealing of the Christ."

"Not all."

"You are correct, my apprentice. Beware of the Sadducees. Their doctrine has no room for a messiah. Beware, too, of the Pharisees."

Raziel furrowed his brow. "They believe the Messiah is to come and will restore Israel and will sit on the throne of David."

"Yes, but they are more interested in imposing laws and traditions on the people. They know nothing of love and mercy."

"Yadid and Shalev hold to the teachings of the Pharisees."

"Yes, and that is why I spend my time tutoring you. You have a different spirit. You will be thirty this year and will begin taking a more active role in the synagogue. I am counting on you to help me lead God's people in the direction they should go. We must push beyond the endless lists of traditions and customs—and earnestly seek the life behind them all."

Raziel nodded.

Avner continued, "You continue looking for the Messiah. He will come to save us."

Jenli turned to Luxor and said, "We need more men like Avner. Truly, he is doing the King's work."

"About the King's coming," Luxor said. "We all sense the time is near. Including the enemy. Is there any word from the Throne about when?"

Jenli closed his eyes and shook his head. "The King holds this mystery close. There have been no words. I can usually sense His heart clearly. . . but concerning this, much is hidden."

Avner and Raziel rose and adjusted their ceremonial robes.

"The service is about to begin," Luxor said.

"We should take our posts," Jenli answered.

Jenli scanned the main meeting room of the synagogue in Nazareth from his position next to the Torah ark. Avner and the other three rabbis sat in the places of honor nearest the ark while the people shuffled in and filled two-thirds of the seats. Five demons stood in their places throughout the room. Jenli knew every one of them—and the people who brought them there. He pulled his sword partially from its sheath and let its flash warn the enemy spirits not to overstep their bounds. Each demon sneered and turned back to his human and whispered something. Jenli eyed Luxor and Deenr who stood guard, tense but ready. Three more elzurim entered with individuals, speaking words of truth and faith to their charges. The service began.

At the prescribed time in the service, Avner read from the Torah at the bimah table. The moment the Word left his mouth, thin dark clouds appeared around the humans in the room. Jenli shook his head. *Always a veil.* The Word spoken by Avner entered the Middle Realm and coalesced into a blazing white ball of energy. It pulsated seven times and exploded. Thousands of tiny seeds of light shot outward toward every person. The demons leaped and brandished their swords, intercepting and blocking hundreds of light shards with their blades. The seeds they missed lodged deep in the outer layer of the veil clouds around the people. Every demonic and angelic wing sprang to life. The demons raced from person to person, snatching the embedded seeds and crushing them in their fists. Jenli and his team chased, blocked, and wrestled at a furious speed, driving the beaelzurim back to their rightful place.

Only some of the seeds reached a few of the people. Most were stolen by the enemy or squelched before it could penetrate the veil. *And the people sit in silent reverence, hearing nothing.* Jenli ground his teeth.

Shalev recited the Shema prayer. Like a performer on stage, he made a polished delivery. Jenli shook his head. *Empty and rote.* The words entered the Middle Realm as weak vapors that dissipated into nothing. The heart of the King came crashing through Jenli's heart. Tears filled his eyes until he couldn't see. He dried his eyes with his sleeve, fighting to regain focus, but the sense of sorrow became so strong he had to turn away until he could push the King's sadness out of his head and into his belly.

He turned back around—his chiseled jaw clenched tight—and drew his sword. This time the demons had no sneer. They held their places. *They dare not step beyond.* The service drew near its end, and Jenli marched through the front door.

Jenli stood outside at the front entrance of the synagogue as the service ended. Sword drawn and standing strong, he met each beaelzurim with an icy stare. *One, two, three, four, five.* All enemy spirits departed and went on their way with their human charges. The three other angels also left, and Jenli stood alone again with Luxor and Deenr.

Luxor offered Jenli a hesitant smile and said, "At least the Word was spoken."

Jenli slid his sword into its scabbard with a deliberate *shing* and stepped back into the sanctuary. Luxor and Deenr followed. The men had begun to clean up. Avner handled the Torah scrolls; Shalev put away the prayer scrolls; the others minded the seating areas.

"How many centuries have we watched this?" Jenli asked. "How many more before the King establishes His throne and puts an end to this pretense?"

"One day," Deenr said.

"Yes, one day."

A streak of darkness shot into the room. Then five more streaks of darkness. In an instant, Jenli and the two guards stood surrounded by six demons. *Ambush! These five are at least my equal. This one—a captain.* Jenli lunged at the captain with a spiraling thrust. Halfway across the room, one of the other demons intercepted Jenli's attack with a slice that hacked through Jenli's arm. "Aaugh!" His sword bounced and clanged on the floor. Through squinted, blurry eyes, he fought for consciousness and stayed fixed on the captain. *I'll fight you with my bare. . .* The captain blasted a fire ball. Jenli's left arm instinctively tried to raise his shield. *No strength. . . I can't. . . Zzzz— kapow!* The missile of energy smashed into Jenli's face and sent him catapulting backward end over end. Pain sizzled throughout his entire body. Then, the numbness. Then, darkness.

He blinked. He blinked again. He forced his eyes open. Flat on his back. Cords of energy bound him—ankles to neck. He sat up, shook the dizziness from his head, and looked around. Luxor and Deenr lay bound on the floor across the room.

The demon captain strutted over to Jenli, kicking Jenli's sword aside as he went.

"My master is weary of striving against this man of God," the captain said, pointing his sword at Avner. "I am sent to put an end to it."

All six demons cackled and watched Avner, who continued his work, oblivious to the situation.

Jenli bent his legs and maneuvered for position. If he could just reach the dagger he kept concealed in his soft leather boot.

"And now. . ." the captain announced. He raised his right hand to his mouth and breathed, "Brain hemorrhage." A small ball of plasma formed in his palm. He held it up like a trophy before Jenli and his defeated warriors. He prepared to launch it.

Jenli roared, "No!" and slashed through his binding cords with his dagger. He bounded to his feet and vaulted toward the captain in a single move.

A demon guard met his attack with a decisive sword thrust through the center of his chest. Again—searing pain, numbness, and cords of bondage. The captain gave an unimpressed snort, turned back toward Avner, and gave the fiery dart a dismissive flick.

The energy shot across the room. The man of God had a substantial helmet of light and a partial breastplate in the spirit, so when the fire ball exploded against the breastplate, most of the energy reflected away. But not all. Some swirled around and entered his spirit.

Avner continued his work, talking and laughing with the other rabbis.

"It is done," the demon captain snarled. "Six months and no longer will be the end of his days."

The captain turned and took a step toward the door.

"My captain, what of these warriors? Shall we leave them?"

The captain stopped and paused. Then he wheeled around with victorious pomp. "Normally I would. However, today we have bested a lieutenant. This is a worthy prize, and we are approaching strategic times. Take them. Take them all."

———

Jenli hung in the air by the bindings between his shoulder blades. The tightness of the cords bit into his chest and squeezed out a grimace with every pitiless tug. The demon who carried him labored in his flight, but the earth below still sped by in blur. Jenli checked his right and left. His compatriots also slung beneath their demon escorts in a loose low–altitude formation. No additional beaelzurim accompanied them.

I've always wondered where they take their elzurim prisoners. Now I will know. If taken, they were almost never seen again. Would there be torture? Would there be coercion to turn against the King? Then the most dreadful thought—no matter what awaited him, he would be separated from the presence of the King. He thrashed and twisted against the cords. The striving proved useless, but he continued struggling. The reality of being separated from the King became more inescapable with every passing moment, and despair like he had never known gripped his mind. He fought for hope. *Surely, when the King comes to conquer His enemies, He will loose all the captives. But how long? How long will I be without the presence of . . .*

A flash of light. A crack of thunder. In an instant, the tightness between his shoulder blades released, and Jenli plummeted toward the earth. *What just happened?* He twisted in free-fall and maneuvered to see. An enormous warrior in white had his feet on the back of the demon, and his left hand grappled the demon's left wing.

Whump! Jenli hit ground, still bound.

Above, the two combatants corkscrewed out of control. With one compelling thrust, the angel ran his sword through the dark spirit and left him fluttering to the ground in a trail of yellow vapor.

Jenli's rescuer turned his attention toward him. With three powerful strokes of his wings, he dove toward Jenli. Just before he reached him, Jenli recognized his face.

"Captain Elric!" Jenli shouted. "I am so glad to see. . ."

Elric slit the bindings with his blade. "Quickly, on to the others."

The two shot into the air. They scanned the horizon.

"It's too late," Elric said. "They're gone."

6

EARS TO HEAR

Birth minus 2 years

*J*esse stepped out of the tent in the middle of the shepherd's camp overlooking the Sea of Galilee. It had been two days since Daniel and Levi returned from the errand to the lake, and Daniel had come back to camp complaining of an earache. Overnight, the earache became worse, and now this morning Daniel had a rising fever and pus seeping from his right ear.

"His fever is getting worse," Jesse reported. The tent flap closed behind him. "We need to do something. He is suffering, and this is only going to get worse. I'm going to take him back down to the village and find a physician."

"Shall I take him so you can stay here with the flocks?" Levi offered.

Jesse glared. "I think not. You are the reason he's sick in the first place. If you had been more careful. . . if. . . I should have never let you take him with you." Jesse pulled Levi farther aside and lowered his voice. "I'm scared. This is serious. An earache is one thing, but people die from severe fevers, and his fever is getting bad. If he. . ."

"He will not. He cannot."

"But if he does, you are going to have to explain it to Father." Jesse went back inside where Daniel lay sobbing.

"Daniel, I know it's going to be hard for you, but you and I need to go back to the village. We need to find a doctor. Do you think you can do that?"

Daniel nodded yes—a weak yes, but one that made it clear he wanted to do anything to make the pain stop.

"I will go alone with him," Jesse said to Levi. "You need all the extra hands here with the flocks. There is a good chance we may be gone several days. I will not leave the care of the physician until I'm sure Daniel is going to be well." He stared at Daniel and shook his head. "I don't know how he will make the journey. He looks so weak."

———

The shining elzur warrior kneeling next to Daniel placed his hand on Daniel's forehead. He had been at Daniel's side all night, comforting him and speaking hope and peace into his spirit. The trip to the village would be a hard one and would certainly require him to provide strength directly. He replayed everything from the previous day. Was this infection natural or was there an enemy attack? Besides the event on the lake, there hadn't been any other encounters. It was possible the enemy could have initiated this during the attack. At this point, it didn't matter. Either way, he needed extra vigilance—it would be just like the enemy to make another attack with Daniel in this weakened state. The angel continued ministering to Daniel as Jesse packed for the trip.

Within minutes, Jesse entered Daniel's tent. "Daniel, it's time to go," he said. "I need you to get up."

Daniel tried to raise his head, but dropped back down and groaned, "I can't."

"You have to, Daniel. I can't carry you. You need to get up and try to walk."

The angel spoke the word "strength" into his hand, and a blue ball of energy formed in his palm. He turned his hand over and pressed the energy into Daniel's spirit.

Daniel rose to a sitting position. Jesse held his hand and pulled him to his feet.

"Good, good," Jesse said. "Now let's try to walk."

Throughout the trek, the angel bore Daniel up. Though he couldn't carry Daniel's flesh, he wrapped his arm around Daniel's spirit and provided the inner strength with every step. It didn't take Jesse long to find a doctor, and soon Daniel rested on a mat in a quiet room.

"You were wise to bring him in," the doctor said. "This is indeed a serious fever. I put some medicine in his ear. I have also given him a mixture of herbs that should help with the fever and the pain. Now, we will wait and watch."

The day dragged by, long and difficult. The medicines helped Daniel sleep, but he awoke often from piercing ear pains. The angelic warrior by his bedside continued his vigil. Later in the evening, Jesse and the doctor stepped into an adjacent room. The warrior got up and stood in the door threshold.

"Overall," the doctor said, "I'm optimistic. The fever has stabilized somewhat. It's not going down yet, but at least it isn't rising."

The warrior turned back to check his charge. To his horror, a devious little demon of infirmity had snuck into the room and had one of his foul talons in Daniel's right ear. The warrior exploded upon this presumptuous trespasser with all the fury his blade could marshal. The little demon darted through the wall and took to flight. The angel chased a short distance, but Daniel couldn't be left alone. The warrior returned to his post and found Daniel in the same condition as before—although he couldn't tell what damage had just been done.

More vigil. More waiting. It would be a long night. Daniel tossed in shallow, restless sleep. Minutes stretched into hours.

Then, in the very dark watch of the night, a small light, like a glowing snowflake, floated down from above and landed on Daniel's head. No one else would have been able to see it, but this warrior knew what had just happened. The Lord had just answered somebody's prayers and touched Daniel. It could have been his two brothers' prayers, possibly his mother's, probably all of them. Whoever's words released it—healing would now come. Daniel settled down and drifted deeper into sleep. The angel stood and watched for any more enemy attacks. No more came that night. And from that point on, Daniel rested.

———

The next morning, Daniel awoke to the doctor feeling his forehead. "Thank heaven, the fever is beginning to come down. How does your ear feel today?" the doctor asked.

"It still hurts really bad," Daniel replied.

"I'm not surprised," the doctor said, looking in his ear. "There was considerable drainage and even a fair amount of blood. This was one of the worst cases I've seen. It will probably hurt for a while longer. But the good news is the fever has broken. I think your body is fighting the sickness. You should be fine in a day or so. Here, take some more medicine. It will help with the pain."

The next two days saw encouraging progress. By the end of the first day, the fever had all but disappeared. By the end of the second day, most of the ear drainage had dried up. With Daniel on the road to recovery, the time came to say farewell and return to the meadow camp.

Jesse and Daniel packed their things, and Jesse took the doctor aside. "He says everything sounds muffled in his right ear. I don't think he is hearing very well. Will that get better?"

"Hard to say. He has had significant damage. I wouldn't be surprised if he does suffer some hearing loss. How much is difficult to say. You will have to wait for it to completely heal. It may be several weeks before you know how serious it is."

"What are you saying?" Daniel called out. "I can't hear you."

"Just saying goodbye and thank you," Jesse answered. "Come, little brother. It's time to get back to the flocks."

7

THE CALL

Birth minus 2 years

*E*lric stood alone at the widow Hannah's house, pondering over the war map after the daily regional meeting. He peered deep into the layers of colors and clouds and motion. Something was stirring. Something elusive. Something big—yet too small to see. *If only I could. . .*

"How are they all coping?" a voice from behind asked.

Elric turned. Jenli stood behind him. Elric raised his eyebrows and glanced at the map.

"Hannah's family," Jenli said.

Elric nodded. He turned his focus to Hannah's sons and their wives strewn about the room on their bed mats. "Mixed. Caleb is a rock. He is an honor to his father's name and strength for Hannah. Seth. . . is struggling."

"And Hannah?"

Elric gave a sad smile. "It is as painful as it always is. But she is strong. She leans hard on the Lord, and He is sustaining her."

Elric waved his hand over the war map. It disappeared. He turned to Jenli and crossed his arms. "Why do you come back to the war room after the meeting? Do you have a question about tomorrow's assignment?"

"No, captain. It is a simple two-party appointment. I plan to use the Vanbynian Maneuver."

Elric rubbed his chin. "Good. . . good. Timing can be tricky."

"I just exercise faith and do my part," Jenli said.

Elric nodded and waited.

"About the other day. . ." Jenli began. He kept his gaze on the ground.

"There's no need."

"I have to express my gratitude. If you hadn't shown up when you did. . ."

Elric held up his hand.

Jenli continued, "I've been in many difficult situations before, but this was different. They were taking us. I was moments away from. . ." He stopped. He lifted his head and jutted his jaw. "I actually felt despair."

"Separation from the King can only lead to despair."

"I hope to never know it again."

"It was a regrettable battle," Elric said. "I am going to miss the good work of Avner. And I am wounded over the loss of your two warriors"

"Their pain is with me continually."

Elric winced, and his countenance turned grim. "We all. . . carry the pains of the past."

They each stood in silence, gazing off into the darkness of the past.

Jenli broke the silence. "Thank you. I could have been one of them."

Elric smiled.

"Have you ever known any of the captured to escape?" Jenli asked.

"Only a few."

"What do they say about their captivity and how they escaped?"

"Very little," Elric said. "They never seem to know where they were held. Their escapes are usually due to an oversight or mistake by the enemy."

"What about their experiences in prison?"

"They never talk about that. Never." Elric looked down toward his feet. "It changes them. They are able to continue their work and be effective ministers, but they carry an inner sadness that none of us can know. I think it's the separation from the King that causes the most pain. I cannot begin to imagine that."

Jenli grimaced. "I almost can."

Elric nodded.

"Why are *you* here, captain?" Jenli asked.

Elric's eyes brightened. He waved his hand, and the map reappeared. "I am working on a mystery," he said, peering into the map. "Why do you suppose the enemy took you captive?"

"Opportunity, I presume."

"Mmm. Did the demon captain say anything particular?"

"Only that a lieutenant was a worthy prize. And something about a strategic time. Why?"

"Something is happening. All the Middle Realm can sense it."

"The promised coming of the King?"

"The time is near. I know it. But. . ." Elric's voice trailed off. He strained over the map through squinted eyes.

"But, what?"

Elric motioned with his hand. "There's nothing. No word from the Throne. No specific activities to prepare His coming. At least none that I can see. I know He has to be working—I just need to see it."

"Surely the King would not hide His plans from us?"

"There is much we do not know. I don't know why. . ."

A logirhi and an elzur captain appeared through the ceiling and alighted before Elric.

"Captain Elric," the logirhi announced. "Commander Kai requests a meeting with you immediately concerning a new assignment. This is Captain Byroth. He is your replacement."

"In His service."

"By His word." The logirhi turned and disappeared.

Elric put his hand on Jenli's shoulder and smiled. "My brother, it has been an honor and a joy to have served with you. Perhaps we will work together again in the future."

"Maybe after a hundred years!"

Elric laughed. "That's right, you are near the end of your rotation. Excellent. I am glad for you."

Elric breathed into his right hand, "Strength of the Lord." A small plasma ball formed in his palm.

Jenli created a sphere of energy in his hand with the words, "Wisdom and purpose."

The two smashed their hands together in an explosion of light and laughed. Elric gave a smile and a single nod of his head to Byroth and stepped out of the war room and into the nighttime air.

Elric paused. *The stars look so high and distant from this vantage.* He had been so long earthbound in the Middle Realm that he had grown accustomed to this view. His eyes twinkled. *Back to the King's Realm.* No longer bound by only six dimensions. No longer surrounded by sin and death. His heart continually yearned to be there. He couldn't wait to go, even if only for a brief time to receive his orders. *Orders! I wonder what the new assignment will be?*

Elric unfolded his wings and shot into the air. Upward, upward, until the earth became a blur far below. He folded his wings around himself, closed his eyes, and translated out of the Middle Realm.

Spiritual matter to pure energy, back to a higher spiritual matter—it all happened in an instant. And when Elric opened his eyes again, he stood in Commander Kai's headquarters.

Elric stepped into the commander's war room. A similar war map to the one he used swirled in the center of the room, but this one covered much more area and had even more interwoven dimensions. The weightiness of the responsibility and the raw power that filled this place made Elric feel small.

Kai receives orders directly from the throne room. I can't imagine the duty of orchestrating all the efforts at this level.

Kai gave a motion to the dozen angels gathered around the map. They all nodded and stepped out. Elric and Kai were alone.

Kai had a low voice filled with authority. "Elric, the King has requested your presence at the Throne. He has a special mission for you. Even I do not know the nature of it. The Lord is keeping this mission hidden from all but a very few. You are to devote your full energies to this new task. The Lord has not indicated how long this duty will take or what you will be expected to do. It is of utmost secrecy. You are not to discuss this reassignment with anyone. Go quickly, the King awaits."

Elric dipped his head and turned to go.

"Elric," the commander said, "congratulations on being chosen for this duty. You have proven yourself and have found special favor with the Lord. Do well, my friend."

8

THRONE OF THE KING

Birth minus 2 years

*E*lric stood just inside the gates of the outer court in the King's Realm. He took a deep breath. *It feels so good to be here.* Tall vertical curtains of clouds formed the walls—almost a mist, but deeper and more structured. Their radiance filled the court with warm, white light. The massive white columns lining the walls smoldered with an inner light. His feet and legs reflected off a floor as smooth as polished glass, glowing at one moment white, then pure gold, then like a light blue clear afternoon sky. Everything pulsed with life and light. The palpable energy prickled his skin—like an exquisite song sung at a frequency too low to be heard but strong enough to reverberate through his entire being. A soft mist swirled through the atmosphere, filled with life and energy, and infused with an enchanting sweet aroma. Elric breathed it in. *Like the smell of a delicate flower, but I know of no flower on earth with* *which to compare.* If overwhelming love had a fragrance, this would be its bouquet.

Thousands of angels—warriors, messengers, even some seraphim—filled the court. Each passed through the court with some individual purpose which somehow fit into the King's overall purpose. *I can just picture Commander Kai receiving orders here and bringing them to his war room.* Elric closed his eyes. *Peaceful. Tranquil. Joyful. Clean. Right.* None of the strife and unrest of earth could be found here. He opened his eyes. *I love being here in the outer courtyard with all the others.* He proceeded farther in, passing groups of warriors discussing new orders. These elzurim and logirhim were on their way back to earth. Those just arrived. Many high–ranking generals came and went. Elric shook his head. *I miss this. Here there is only order, peace, and deep purpose.*

Purpose! What could the King's purpose be for me? With each step, the anticipation swelled in his chest until he thought he would burst. His eyes fixed on the inner court, and all the figures around him faded into a blur. The glowing white columns girding the inner court walls towered before him, and light exploded out of its only entrance. The brilliant light surrounding him in the outer courtyard seemed like a shadow compared to the wave of brightness bursting from within the throne room. Long rumblings of thunder from within echoed through the inner court walls and thumped against his chest. Heavy white smoke rolled out of the entrance along the floor and spread like a thin living carpet over the outer court. The layer of smoke now reached up to his knees.

Elric approached the entrance and slowed his pace. He swallowed hard. Of course, the King's presence filled the universe. Of course, the presence of the Lord surrounded him at all times everywhere he had ever been. And, here in the outer court, the King's presence seemed so thick, he felt wrapped in it. *But entering the inner court. . .*

Here, in this most sacred place, the very glory of the Almighty Creator rested in all its fullness. Here, the actual physical presence of the King sat on the Throne. *Of all the thousands of times I have been here, every time seems like the first. I think I shall never be able to fully know depths of His glory.* Breathtaking and fearsome, and yet. . . *I can imagine no place I would rather be than in the presence of the great King.* The one knew him by name and spoke with him like a friend. His body almost wanted to shrink away from the crushing glory and power before him, but he took another step.

He reached the threshold. He stopped, and two seraphim alighted before him. These six–winged beings, charged with guarding the holiness of this place, each had a red–hot coal in their hands. Elric raised his arms.

Without speaking a word, the two seraphim each took their coal and touched the bottom of Elric's tunic, one on the left and one on the right. The tunic erupted in a brilliant blue flame. It started from the bottom and unfolded upward. Elric raised his chin and squeezed his eyes tight shut. *The inner core of lightning can't rival this!* Intense heat consumed everything he wore—the tunic, the boots, the sash, even the sword and shield. The flames subsided. Elric opened his eyes. Everything he carried on earth had been burned away, and a sparkling, flowing white robe rested on his shoulders. With his head bowed, he entered with slow, deliberate steps.

There, in the center of the inner court, sat the Throne. It stood high and massive and glowed with the purest white. Bolts of lightning with deep rolling thunder continuously shot outward from the Throne. The One who sat upon it looked like the clearest brightest light with a man-like form. He wore a robe which flowed out onto the floor, transforming into a shimmering white smoke which filled the inner court up to Elric's knees and rolled out the entrance to the outer court.

More seraphim had positions above the throne. They flew on one set of wings with large, graceful strokes like an eagle soaring on unseen currents. Another set of wings covered their faces, and the third set of wings covered their feet. Continually, they called back and forth to each other, "Holy, Holy, Holy, is the Lord of hosts," with voices so strong and intense that the very foundations shook.

And then, the cherubim. The four cherubim which go before the Spirit had positions around the base of the throne. Huge and imposing beings, the order of cherubim had four wings. They each used one set of wings to stretch up and outward so that their tips just touched the tips of the others' outstretched wings. They used the other two wings to cover their human-like bodies. They had faces unlike any of the other angels—one face like a human, a face of a lion, a face of a bull, and the face of an eagle. Each was covered with darting, piercing eyes—on their bodies, on their wings, under their wings. Like flashes of lightning, they constantly shot to and fro and called out, "Holy, Holy, Holy, is the Lord God, the Almighty, who was and is and who is to come." And among the four living creatures, balls of intense fire continually flashed between them with bolts of lightning bursting from the fire. In the middle of them and below the Throne were the burning coals—blazing, blazing, blazing.

Elric folded his wings over his body, kept his eyes down, and awaited the Word from the King.

A hand touched under Elric's chin, lifting his head. "Come, Elric. Walk with me."

Elric raised his head. *Where are we?* A quiet green meadow. And there before him stood the Lord himself, in what appeared to be a human form. Elric looked around. *I've never seen this place before. This is not earth, and it certainly isn't the throne room.* It did have some earth-like features, though—trees and majestic rock–faced mountains with snow–crowned peaks. To their left, a lively mountain stream with crystal–clear water gurgled and splashed. The meadow had plush grass and vibrant yellow flowers with the same fragrance as the one he experienced in the outer courtyard. His sweeping glance passed over the trees but then stopped. *These are no ordinary trees.* A living green light smoldered from within. And the leaves shimmered and burst with light around their edges. Every tree hung heavy with some kind of succulent fruit—some red, some deep purple, some a blazing orange. *Everything here is completely, fully, absolutely alive.*

And the two of them were alone.

Whatever mission the Lord has for me, it must be more important than I could have imagined.

They walked without speaking. With each step, Elric's stomach drew tighter. They happened upon a small cluster of round, smooth, moss–covered boulders. They stopped and sat.

"Do you know why I have called you?" the King began.

Elric loved the way the King did this. *Nothing is hidden from Him. And yet, He asks questions as if He doesn't already know the answer. He just enjoys having the interaction.*

Elric smiled. "No, Lord. But I can sense that it is very important, and I am excited and honored that you have called me."

"Yes, it is important. This mission is the most important in all of history. I am about to physically enter into the world. The fullness of time has come."

Yes! The tension in Elric's stomach released like a spring, and he fought to stay seated. *Finally!* Ever since the angels' Rebellion—when Lucifer and his rebellious followers were relegated to the earth, and then the subsequent Fall of man—all of creation had been groaning for this time. Finally, the true King would establish His throne on earth, establish justice, and bring all things in line with His perfect will. Mankind would be saved. His enemies would be defeated. There would be peace.

Elric's thoughts raced uncontrolled. *But wait, I am a mere captain. Certainly, the King doesn't need me to lead the campaign? That's the level of responsibility for the archangels, the mighty ones.* He rubbed his forehead. *What task would I be best suited for?*

His eyes widened. *The temple. The Lord needs me to construct the temple to house His throne room.* Elric had been instrumental in the reconstruction of the temple by Herod. He had even been involved in the original temple built by Solomon. But those were simply manmade structures. This new temple could not be built by men. The Lord wanted him to literally build His temple. *Yes, this must be it. How exciting. There is so much to do. First, I need to work through men to clear the current temple site.*

Political, social, and economic strategies flooded his mind. The soonest he could get this first step accomplished would be about five years. Would that fit with His timing? *Hopefully, the timing will be more like ten years. By that time, presumably the main campaign to defeat the enemy forces will be complete, and I will be free to work on construction without having to deal with enemy attacks. If not, the fighting will be fierce. I'll need substantial numbers of warriors to defend the position. . .*

The Lord interrupted his thoughts. "But I am not coming in my full glory at this time."

Of course—He promised to come as a Messiah, born of a woman, to sit on the throne of David. Good, that will give me at least thirty to fifty years to get the temple finished. Still, I need to get started right away.

"And I will make my temple in the hearts of men."

Elric's eyes darted back and forth. If He didn't need him to prepare the temple, what could it be? *Preparation of a palace for His birth! Yes, that must be it. Where? Rome. That's where the grandest palaces are. No, wait. The Lord spoke to prophets over the centuries. He would be born in Egypt—"out of Egypt did I call my Son." Or Bethlehem—". . . but as for you Bethlehem. . . from you One will go forth for Me to be ruler in Israel. His goings forth are from long ago, from the days of eternity." Or Galilee—"He shall be called a Nazarene."*

These can't be contradictory messages, but how do they all play together? Egypt. It definitely has to be Egypt because there are no palaces grand enough in Bethlehem and certainly not in Nazareth.

He stopped. He looked up at the Lord, embarrassed he had let his thoughts run away. The King smiled and waited.

"Lord, I am overwhelmed. This is the word we have all awaited for centuries. What is Your will for me? Why all the secrecy?"

The King's eyes sparkled, and he smiled wide. "Elric," he said, "I am going to become a man. I will fulfill all the words I gave to my prophets, and as a man I will reclaim the authority given up by Adam. However, I am not coming in the manner you think. Instead, I will be born in the most humble place and live among the poor. I will lay aside my glory for a time and live as a man. Men will be able to touch me and see me. I will feel pain and be acquainted with sorrow. I will show them who I am."

Elric blinked. *This is no plan of conquest! The Lord of Creation sneaking into the world as a humble baby? There must be more.*

"I love them," the Lord said. "I long to fellowship with them and to save them."

Everything around them swelled with love. The stream filled to the top of its banks and became a rushing torrent. The fruit in the trees seemed like they would burst. The light within the trees erupted out of the edges of the leaves, and the distant mountains rumbled.

"This is very important. . . while I am there, I will be fully human. I will actually need to eat, wash, sleep and walk. I will have human parents who will care for me and help me grow. I will know only that which the Father reveals to me by the Holy Spirit. I will perform no deeds of power on my own. At the appointed time, my flesh will be empowered by the Spirit, and then I will do mighty works on earth. Before that time, however, it is important that I remain hidden, for the enemy will try to kill me. I will be within his domain, and I will be subject to the all the laws of the physical world."

What? The implications of this. . . Not only would the triune Godhead experience physical separation—with the Father in the King's Realm and the Son on earth in the Physical Realm—but human flesh had the capacity to die. *No, that could never be.*

"And then. . ." Elric said, ". . . then, as a man, you will defeat your enemies and establish your throne on earth?"

A tender yet resolved smile pursed the King's lips. "This is the mystery I have kept hidden since the beginning of time. No creature in heaven or on earth knows the time or manner of my coming. I will reveal to you my deep mysteries a little at a time, but only as you have need to know. For now, I must keep the full plan a secret."

The Lord paused. Elric looked at Him and waited. He felt dizzy.

"This is why I have called you," the King continued. "You are to assemble a small taskforce—twenty-four warriors, including four lieutenants, plus yourself. Your task is to keep me concealed from the enemy until the appointed time. The enemy will be relentless, so you must employ your best strategies to stay ahead of them. I cannot give this mission to one of my generals because it will draw too much attention. There will be no cherubim going before me. There will be only you and your small troop."

"But Lord. . . ?"

"On occasion, should you see the strategic need, I will provide for you additional forces for a single task. I will reveal some of my plan to the highest generals, who will work around the periphery, but the center of the mission belongs to you. You are a master strategist. You are familiar with the forces in the region. I will be with you."

Elric's mind reeled over the heaviness of the responsibility settling upon him. Then the painful memory hit him. His left eye twitched twice, and he rubbed his temple. *Surely the Lord can't entrust a mission like this to me—not after what happened. . . but I dare not question the Lord.* He looked up to find the King smiling.

"Yes, you are the one I have chosen for this task."

Elric swallowed, buried his fears, and focused on the King. *This is a bold plan. The enemy will never expect an entrance like this. If I can keep the Son hidden until the right time, the strategic leverage we will have will be enormous. Then the battle will be swift and decisive. And the King will finally reign from His throne on earth.*

The Lord continued, "The birthplace is Bethlehem. I have already selected the one who will carry me in her womb. You must begin preparing for my visitation to her. The enemy must not know who she is. I will reveal additional details to you as you need them. For now, I will say no more. Go and assemble your team. Be discreet. Speak to no one about this except to your team." He stood up.

Elric jumped to his feet, and the Lord said, "Turn around."

He did as commanded, and the Lord placed a cloak over his shoulders. "I will not be easy to hide," He said. "Men walk around with spirits that are dead due to their sin, but my spirit will be alive and visible to the enemy. So, there will be occasions when you will need to hide me from the enemy. This cloak will help you. If you overshadow me with this cloak, I will blind the eyes of the enemy."

The Lord put his hands on Elric's shoulders and leaned in close. He whispered, "Remember this, Elric, I *am* humble of heart."

Elric felt the waves of overwhelming love and purpose. *I am so humbled to be found worthy of this amazing mission.* He turned back around to look again into the face of Lord, but by the time he turned around, he found himself back in the inner court, standing before the great Throne. Cherubim and seraphim still thundered. Lightning blasted from the Throne. The coals blazed. Elric looked deep into the light on the throne, saw again the familiar smile, bowed low, and backed out of the inner court.

9

THRONE OF PRIDE

Birth minus 2 years

The great demon lord, Marr, landed at the threshold of a small cave entrance in the side of a rock–faced mountain thousands of miles from any civilization. He rustled his leathery wings, and they disappeared into his back. The rest of his entourage alighted behind him. His six commanders and a dozen captains formed a zone around him and pushed the other demons aside. His personal aide, a lieutenant named Luchek, elbowed his way through the parting group in front of Marr.

"Make room," Luchek gruffed. "Move aside for the Prince of Persia."

Marr's twenty–foot frame couldn't begin to fit through the cave opening, but he marched forward with commanding purpose. He passed through the stone constriction and stepped into an immense cavern—high enough that even he didn't need to stoop, and wide enough to contain a writhing mass of thousands of demons. The outer court. He paused. All around, portentous stalactites crept their way down from the wet ceiling. Smaller stalagmites clawed up to meet their mates from above. Across the room, the entrance to the inner court glowed red behind the stalactite fangs. Black smoke rolled out of the inner court and covered hundreds of years of bat guano on the cave floor. The air felt thick and musky.

Marr snorted. "The dark lord summons his mighty ones, and all the worthless dogs come to fight for scraps."

On the left, two lieutenants erupted into a vicious brawl, each jostling for position nearer the inner court. A captain on his way toward the front broke them up and pushed them out of his way. Dozens of fights flared up throughout the outer court. The two enormous guards at the inner court entrance strong-armed the pressing crowd and kept the uninvited out.

A small demon breached the barrier, but one guard snagged him by the back of the neck and flung him back into the outer court. In a flurry of tumbling wings, the little demon screeched, "You can't do that! I am the great Tumur! I deserve entrance! Curse you! Curse you! You can't. . ." A lieutenant pulled him down by the ankle and smashed him to the ground. The other entrance guard ejected another amid shouts and curses. The whole horde strained inward, and a never-ending stream of rejects catapulted back out.

"Hmph," Marr snorted. He started crossing the outer court. Most of the crowd had enough wisdom to give way as he advanced. Those who didn't, he crushed without regard. Marr's entourage pushed and shouted, "Move aside! Make way for the Prince of Persia!" But they became mired in the throng and failed to keep up.

Marr reached the entrance. He scowled and puffed hot sulfurous jets from his flared nostrils. *I hate being here.* He sneered over his shoulder at all the pathetic clawing for position. *And for what? To receive some word from the great dark lord? As though he were a true king. He may have been given dominion over the earth and its kingdoms, but that authority could just as easily have been given to another. Or seized by one with enough power.* Marr lifted his chin and glared at the two guards. They nodded slightly, indicating he was free to enter. He shot out both his arms and seized the two guards—one hand around each of their necks. He lifted both of them several feet off the floor and held them in a crushing dangle. He held them there for a moment and let his rage burn through his eyes.

"The mighty Prince of Persia is worthy of only a head nod?" he growled. "The next time I encounter either of you, I will expect the full measure of respect."

He dropped the two guards like discarded rubbish and stepped into the inner court. Jeering of the guards from the crowd faded behind him.

Though less chaotic than the outer court, the inner court also writhed with strife. Massive brutes maneuvered toward the positions of highest honor closest to the throne. Marr paused only a moment and pressed his way forward. There, centered along the back wall of the cavern, stood a huge throne, elevated and exalted. Marr sneered. The stalactite fangs hanging on either side of it glistened from the throne's red glow. Bolts of fire exploded from the throne like red lightning. Thick smoke formed the ceiling of the room and rolled out along the floor and into the outer court. The throne itself was absolutely black with elaborate carvings—mostly intertwined serpents and dragons.

The edges of the claw–footed legs had gaudy gems of various colors. Dozens of small demons with fast wings buzzed above and around the throne. They darted about, ready to carry out whatever errand might be issued from the throne, which was empty.

Marr glared at it. *That should be my throne. I have as much power as he does. One day, he is going to make a mistake, and I will take his place. I will. . .*

A demon shoved Marr's left shoulder. He shoved back, but the offender stood like a rock. Marr turned his shoulder away, and the two held their positions.

I wonder how he will present himself today. As the great deceiver, Satan often took on many different forms. Sometimes he would be as beautiful and stunning as the host of heaven. Other times he would appear as dark and monstrous as his heart. He could look small and frail. Or he could be as large as a mountain. *Knowing him, he will. . .*

An explosion of fire blasted from the throne, followed by low rumbling and thick smoke which filled the room. The form on the throne became visible through the receding smoke.

Of course, he has to demonstrate that he is the only one of us who was among the cherubim.

The creature's form dwarfed the throne and the room. With two wings, he formed a canopy over the entire inner court. His other two wings draped downward and filled the platform. And there were the eyes. Eyes everywhere on his body. On his wings. Under his wings. He had the face of a lion, fierce and wild. His burning red eyes surveyed his subjects, who had all become still and silent. Then, without warning, his whole body burst with light. The mighty demon generals winced under the dazzling display.

"Do you not bow?" His voice thundered and shook the room. "Where is the honor due your lord?" The blasting light doubled in intensity, and every knee in the court bent to the ground and every head bowed low.

Marr endured the humiliation with gritted teeth.

Another explosion of fire and smoke rocked the room. The light subsided, the smoke cleared, and the form on the platform appeared like any of the other beaelzurim in the room—only larger and more kingly.

We are all very impressed. Now, why have we been summoned?

Satan sat and rested his spiked arms on the high armrests of the throne. "We are on the brink of a new age. I sense the King of Heaven is about to make His long–promised entry into my domain. I have been preparing the battlefield for centuries, and I have created the perfect circumstances for Him to come now."

Marr grimaced. *You created the circumstances? I was the one who brought the Romans—who are allowing the Israelites to practice their own religious laws. I have elevated Herod to his place. . .*

Satan continued, "We do not know exactly where or when He will make His entry, but when He does, we will be ready for Him. According to the words He has given His prophets, we know He will somehow come forth as a man. This is where He has made His fatal mistake. While surrounded by His cherubim and seraphim and all the host of heaven, we do not stand a chance of overthrowing the Godhead. But, with the Son here in my kingdom in a pitiful human body, we will be able to destroy part of the Godhead."

One of the general lords pressed, "Yes, lord, but did not those same prophets also predict His death? Why would He come knowing we would kill Him?"

The dark lord pounced off the throne and wrapped both sets of talons around the general's leathery neck. His size doubled, and giant flames burst out of his arms, neck, and back.

"You dare question my wisdom?" he growled. Flames shot out of his mouth and wrapped around the general's face. "Be gone." He shot the general out of the inner court in a blaze.

He glared around the room, and his size returned to its previous state. He remained standing in the middle of the room. "He thinks that by dying, He will be able to somehow show the depths of His love for man. And He thinks He will be able to overcome the grave. What He does not know is that *we* will choose the time and circumstances for His death. And once He is dead, I myself will see to it that He remains that way. With part of the Trinity destroyed, we will be able to ascend and take our rightful place."

The room erupted in shouts and cheers. The dark lord held up his hand for silence. "It is important that we destroy Him while He is young and vulnerable. You are all to make it your top priority to find Him. Where will He be born?"

"Egypt," called Molech, one of Marr's commanders.

"Bethlehem," called Yarikh.

"Nazareth," came from Asherah on the far side of the room.

"He attempts to divide our attention," the one on the throne continued. "I believe it will be Egypt. There are no palaces in Judea or Galilee suitable for Him. Our next question is what woman will He choose? Concentrate your efforts on Israelites in Egypt who might be associated with the proconsul and who will have access to the palaces. Search the genealogies. Whoever it is must be from the house of David. We shall allow the birth, but we need to kill Him while He is young and has not had time to become known to men."

He made his way back up to the throne. He turned, sat, and rumbled with a low voice, "And if any of you locate Him, you are to notify me immediately. You are not authorized to destroy Him yourself. None of you have the strength to keep Him in the grave. Only I have the power."

He paused and glared across the generals. His eyes locked with Marr's. "Loyalty will be rewarded when I enter my new kingdom. Disloyalty will bring severe punishment." He stood again, took a single step down, and then disappeared in a blinding flash of red energy and smoke.

The room erupted in a frenzy. Generals shot out of the cave like meteors—with hundreds of smaller demons clawing and chasing after them, trying to find out what had just happened. Marr glowered at the empty throne, ruffled his wings, turned, and stepped toward the outer court.

10

GATHERING BEGINS

Birth minus 2 years

The marketplace on the streets of Jerusalem bustled with mid-morning shoppers. The vendors lined up like a hedge of brightly colored flowers while a hive of patrons buzzed from one host to the next. Elric took up a position behind the awning of a vendor cart—close enough to hear the encounter, but far enough away to stay concealed. Through all the commotion, Elric searched for his objective. Several minutes passed.

There he is—a young man, about twenty years of age, weaving his way through the bustling street. He wore fine cloth, looked neatly groomed, and had a Torah scroll tucked under one arm. He smiled, made eye contact with as many as would receive it, and greeted each with pleasant congeniality. He happened upon a street beggar, just two cart-lengths down from the fish vendor. A slight smile pulled the corner of Elric's lips.

The old, haggard beggar sat against a wall with one leg tucked under himself and the other sprawled out in front. The hair on his head and face was matted and full of dust and bits of straw. His eyes were sunken and closed. At the end of his bony arms, he had long skeleton-like fingers with cracked skin and broken nails. He held out one of his hands, limp and shaking.

The young man saw the beggar, stopped, and knelt down on one knee just in front of the man's crusty bare foot. "What is your name, sir?"

The man replied with a broken, raspy voice, "My name is of no consequence anymore. Could you spare a denarius for a hungry old blind man?"

"How long has it been since you have eaten?"

"It has been a long time."

The young man pulled out a small leather pouch and retrieved three silver coins. "Here, buy yourself some food. This should be enough to serve you for a while."

"God bless you, son." The old man gave a tired smile, revealing three rather brown teeth.

"And the Lord bless you, my friend."

The young man rose to his feet, continued to the fish stand, and bought the night's supper. With his fish wrapped, he stepped back into the buzzing street. A man several paces in front of him lost control of his basket and spilled a load of fruit onto the dusty street. Without hesitating, the young man carrying the fish dropped down on all fours, fetching the scattered fruit. It took some time, but eventually between the two of them, they recovered it all.

"I don't know what happened," the older gentleman explained. "Somebody must have bumped me. Thank you very much, young man. What is your name?"

"My name is Joseph."

"Joseph, it seems you are in the habit of coming to the aid of helpless old men."

"What do you mean, sir?"

"I saw you with that blind beggar earlier." They both turned, but the beggar had disappeared.

"Oh, that." Joseph shrugged. "When I see a need, I do my best to fill it."

"This sounds like something my rabbi might say."

Joseph smiled. "I shall take that as a compliment, sir. I devote much time to studying with the rabbis. In fact, someday I hope to serve on the Sanhedrin."

"The Sanhedrin? You, then, are a man of some means?"

"My father is very blessed. I am training in his business and will someday assume his position."

The two smiled at each other for a moment. Joseph fidgeted with his package of fish. The man looked down at his basket.

Elric smiled. *And now. . .*

The older man blurted out, "Would you care to buy some land?"

"What?"

"Forgive me. It is rude of me to impose on your kindness. But I don't often have an opportunity to meet someone who has the means to help me. And our meeting today seems like more than a coincidence."

Elric nodded.

"Help you with what?"

"I was unable to work for a season due to an illness. By the time I was well enough to work, I was behind in my taxes. Now, the Roman tax collector is threatening to take my home. I have a small piece of land just outside Jerusalem that I have been trying to sell. If I could find a buyer, I could pay my taxes and keep my home."

Joseph rubbed the beginnings of his young beard. "Is this land good for crops or grazing?"

"No, that's part of the problem. It is mostly just a garden in a rocky area. But it has a spot which would be perfect for a new burial tomb."

"A tomb? My family is actually from Arimathea. I'm not sure what I would do with a tomb near Jerusalem." Joseph rubbed his beard again. "Still, a piece of land with a tomb already prepared could be valuable. Especially near Jerusalem. I am intrigued—let's go see this land. It might prove to be a good investment. And if it would help you save your home, I might be willing to consider it."

Elric looked back across the street to where the beggar had been. Jenli stood there in the Middle Realm, leaning against the wall with his arms crossed, chuckling at the two men's conversation. Joseph and the older man walked off discussing business, and Elric crossed the street to greet the lieutenant.

"Good morning, Jenli," Elric said. "That was a good operation."

"Captain Elric!" Jenli laughed and stepped forward. "The Vanbynian Maneuver—one of my favorites for a two–party appointment. Do you know why the King wanted this meeting?"

"I only know that He wants Joseph to procure this piece of land. I don't know why."

They both turned and watched the two men pass out of view. Joseph now carried the old man's basket while the old man embellished some story with animated gestures.

Jenli chuckled again. He turned back to Elric. "I'm surprised to see you here. How was your meeting with the commander?"

Elric pulled Jenli aside by his shoulder and spoke in a low voice. "That is why I have come. I must talk with you immediately. And we cannot meet here."

Jenli's jovial face turned serious and he nodded. His eyes scanned the street.

Elric had already been watching for unwanted observers. "Come, we will talk at Commander Kai's headquarters."

The two wrapped their wings around their bodies, closed their eyes, and disappeared from the Middle Realm.

———

One white flash streaked across the late evening horizon in the deepest of the dark jungles of Africa. Elric alighted near a small band of elzurim, huddled together on ledges of a sheer rock cliff overlooking a valley clearing.

Timrok, the lieutenant in charge of the detail, said, "Good evening, captain. You are just in time. You bring a welcome sword."

"Actually," Elric interjected, "I came to recruit *you* for a. . ."

Timrok held up a finger. "Shhh. The time is near. The cup of wickedness is nearly full."

Down in the clearing, a large circle of pointed–top huts flickered in the light of a courtyard bonfire. Its flames and floating embers shot high into the still air and cast an eerie orange glow on the clearing. It looked as though the entire village had gathered for some ceremony. The driving furor of the drums thumped across the valley, and the war–painted dancers with enraged carved masks chanted and shouted. *This is no joyful gathering.* Nearly a hundred people danced in the pulsing crowd.

In the air and mixed among the crowd, twice as many enemy spirits churned up the Middle Realm. The demons swirled around, stirred by the fervor and helping to feed it. The people were in a trance and the demons were on the move.

Elric pressed into the shadows of his vantage point on the overlooking cliff.

"Do you see the chief human, the one with all the extra feathers, bones, and ornamentation?" Timrok asked.

Elric nodded.

"He is possessed by about fifty demons. They control him and use him to command the services of the other demons. Sometimes these meetings result in nothing more than a sweaty dance. The way things are progressing tonight though, unless we intervene, the chief will probably demand the sacrifice of a young girl or will drive his men out on a raid of a rival tribe."

"How do you stop that?"

Timrok cocked his head and frowned. "We attack. If we can disband this party the demons are throwing, we may be able to prevent them from inciting more destruction."

"Makes sense. What is your strategic plan?"

"We. . . just attack."

Elric looked around at the band of warriors on the cliff. Six. Seven counting himself. He looked down at the swarm of enemy forces. He looked at Timrok.

"You do know you are outnumbered at least thirty to one."

Timrok smiled, raised his finger again, and turned toward the commotion below. "Warriors of the King—we must do battle tonight. Is everyone prepared? We can wait no longer. Let's go."

Like gleaming white falcons, blazing wings tucked, diving headlong toward an unsuspecting prey, six warriors launched from the cliff side.

Elric blinked. *I can't believe the audacity of this. . .* He couldn't delay long. His comrades would need the extra sword. In fact, in that split second of hesitation, they had already begun to engage the enemy. Elric pulled his sword and dove toward the fray.

As he began his dive, Elric laughed to himself. Over and over through the centuries, Timrok always seemed to be in the middle of disproportionate battles. He loved the challenge. He loved watching the King provide impossible victories. *This is exactly why I need Timrok for the team.*

Pandemonium broke out below. The host swooped downward into the horde and then shot straight up in an effort to draw as many as possible away from the men. This tactic worked—all too well— more than a dozen furious demons chased each elzurim. Elric joined the fight in the air.

With a powerful stroke of one wing, he spun like a tornado, his sword extended at arm's length. Expanded to the full stature of his class, Elric's size was twice that of any of the attacking beaelzurim, and his reach proved formidable. Demons careened off in every direction from his spinning blade, leaving trails of yellow smoke and squeals of pain. He stopped his spin, swatted one attacker with the flat of his steel, crushed the face of another with his shield, and kicked the sword out of the hand of another. Two attackers lunged from opposite directions. He flipped forward, and the two smashed together and flittered downward out of control.

Between thrusts and kicks and spins, Elric glanced toward Timrok.

Timrok looked like a wild animal unleashed. He carried two swords, and both moved in a constant blur. He roared and shouted "aha" and "ho" and "for the honor of the King." Demons dove toward him from every direction and faltered away with shrieks and wounds.

Elric scanned the battle space for the rest of Timrok's team. They fought with equal success. Most of the demons were small and easily contended, but they were relentless and numerous. For the fraction of a second that could be spared, Elric laughed aloud at the valor and skill of Timrok's team.

These warriors don't need my help here. I'll go after the forces controlling the chief of the tribe. He swatted three more buzzing pests and dove headlong toward the chief. With his sword stretched like a jousting lance in front of him, he flew through the ornate breastplate of the chief. He passed through the man, and twenty demons exploded out with shrill shrieks.

The man opened his eyes with a jolt and looked around. He looked disoriented and weak. Elric turned and made another pass, this time with twenty furious demons on his tail. He passed through the back of the man, and another twenty evil spirits spurted out. The man stood and tried to raise his arms and take a step. Instead, he fell forward on his face—unconscious.

The drums stopped. The dancing stopped. The young men rushed to the side of the chief. They rolled him over.

Elric shot straight up, hacking demons with his sword in one arm and blocking fireballs with his shield in the other. Below, the muffled voices of the men became distant behind the crashing steel in the Middle Realm.

"Is he alive?"

"Yes, yes, step aside!"

"What happened? Why did he faint?"

Six of the men lifted him and carried him past a hushed crowd to his royal hut. Several of the elders stood around the outside of the hut and chanted.

Just above the jungle tree tops, Elric smashed a demon's face with his shield, sending it falling to the ground. To his left Timrok's two swords slashed through four more beaelzurim. They dropped, leaving trails of yellow smoke.

Below, the crowd began to disperse. All quiet now, the people returned to their family huts.

"Success!" Timrok roared over the battle din. "Warriors of the King—withdraw!"

Seven twinkling lights disappeared across the horizon, and a waning bonfire gave way again to the jungle shadows.

In a secret cave some distance from the jungle village, Elric and Timrok's team gathered. Timrok's team formed a wall at the entrance of the cave. Elric drew Timrok to the back.

"Timrok, I need you for a team I am assembling. The mission is of supreme importance and secrecy. If you will accept this assignment, we must leave immediately to begin making preparations."

"What about my warriors? May I bring them with us?"

Loyalty. I admire this soldier. Timrok's width almost matched his height, and he had all the height of the mightiest lieutenants. All muscle. All fight.

Elric answered, "I can't discuss specifics of the mission here, but. . ." He looked around for any signs of the enemy and whispered, "I will ask you to select a team of five to serve under you. You may select whomever you wish."

Timrok smiled—not a happy, friendly smile, but more of a cunning, satisfied kind of smile. "Then I choose these."

11

PROMOTION

Birth minus 2 years

Zaben crept through the open entry and into the long corridor of the grand state building inside the Egyptian palace grounds. The stately alcoves along each side were more than architectural details—they provided stations for hidden guards. But the Roman guards did not concern this angelic lieutenant. *Surely beaelzurim lie in wait.* His golden yellow eyes darted like an eagle's, taking in every detail, seeing past the flickering torch sconces and into every dark corner. He held his sword in an upward position, close to his body. He advanced and ducked into the next alcove. Scanning the area, he couldn't help but admire the artistic details in the building. These grand palaces of ancient Egypt that once knew pharaohs now housed the Roman proconsuls of the far-reaching Roman Empire. *Men and empires pass through, but these stones endure. And so does the spiritual battle.*

Another angel appeared from behind.

"Report?" Zaben whispered.

"The treasury room itself is not much more than a simple square room with no windows and only one entrance." He pointed toward the large double doors at the end of the corridor. "The one you see here. In the room are several tables with chairs and stacks of parchments. At the far end of the room is a single entrance to another room that is twice the size of the first room. This is the vault itself. There are no enemy stronghold structures to prevent access to any area."

"Human guards?"

"Two at the door to the vault and four inside. Four more in the outer room. I count eight hidden along this corridor."

"Beaelzurim?"

"Only one. In the outer room. Not your equal—but strong enough."

"And the chief treasurer, Bartimus?"

"He is there, preparing for the auditor as you predicted."

"Excellent. Tell the others to take up their positions and wait for my signal."

"In His service."

Zaben continued down the corridor, still wary but with a quicker pace. He stood before the thick wooden arched door and expanded into his full ten-foot-tall frame. With his right hand he gripped his sword. His left hand partially hid a sly smile as he stroked his black goatee. Then he stepped through the door.

There at the center table sat Bartimus, reviewing his records one last time. The auditor from Rome was scheduled to arrive tomorrow. Standing over Bartimus, equally interested in the ledgers, lurked the demon Zaben expected. The instant Zaben entered the room, the demon leapt between Bartimus and Zaben with his sword brandished. Zaben stopped, positioned his sword in front of himself with the point touching the floor, and leaned with both hands on the handle.

"Today, I take authority over this place in the name of the King of the hosts," he said. "You have clouded the mind of Bartimus for too long, and this day the King will speak to him without your interference."

"You cannot have him," the demon growled. He lunged toward Zaben, who stood unmoved by his advance. The demon stopped. He paused a moment, glaring at Zaben. "You shall pay for this trespass," he squealed. He shot up through the ceiling, calling over his shoulder, "I will be back."

"I am counting on it," Zaben said under his breath. In a strong voice, he called out, "Warriors of the King!"

Four hidden warriors stepped into the room.

"Bartimus is corrupt and a puppet of the enemy," Zaben said. "He has been embezzling from the state treasury for years. His cup of iniquity is now full, and it is time for him to reap the harvest he has sown. Today we will provide a last opportunity for him to turn around. If he repents and makes appropriate restitutions, we will make a way for him to move to a higher position in Rome. If he continues down his current path, we will have to turn him over to the enemy. But Bartimus is not our primary mission. We must see that his seat as chief treasurer is vacated in order to promote Benjamin. The enemy will surely try to promote Bartimus's close assistant, Festus, whose heart is even darker. Timing is critical if we are to succeed."

"Do you think the enemy will fall into your trap?" asked a warrior.

Zaben's calculating eyes twinkled. "One thing we can always count on—the blinding pride of the enemy. Now, to your hiding positions. We don't know how long we have before he returns."

Zaben turned toward Bartimus. *The Lord has already begun speaking to him.* Zaben bit his lower lip and took a deep breath. Wave after wave of light from the Lord broke upon Bartimus' spirit—pleading with him to turn from his wickedness. But none of the Lord's entreaties penetrated the dark shell he had built around himself. *His heart has become too hard. He has made up his mind.* Zaben shook his head. *I grieve for the destructive path you have chosen. Things are about to be set into motion that will make you wish you could have this moment back again.*

The time for Bartimus ran out. Through the roof of the treasury room burst three demons—the original poacher of the room plus a demon lieutenant and another enemy warrior.

The demon lieutenant announced, "Now we shall see who has authority in this place."

All three demons flourished their blades and advanced toward Zaben, who stood unmoved.

Without warning, four ready–for–battle elzurim emerged from their concealments. One angel released a deafening war shout and rushed the demon on the left. Their swords met and sent an explosion of sparks and energy sizzling through the spiritual air. At the same time, another angel bounded over that demon, executed a tight flip, and landed behind him. In one fluid motion, his sword sliced through the demon's torso. The demon crumpled to the floor. Weak and defeated, the demon lay flat on his back with one angel's foot pressed hard on his neck and the other angel's blade inches above his belly. A residual cloud of yellow smoke drifted up into the ornate chandelier of dripping wax candles.

A sly grin pulled the corner of Zaben's mouth, and he glanced to his right. His other two warriors stood victorious over the second demon.

That leaves. . . He lifted his chin and narrowed his eyes. *Just the lieutenant.*

"You are too late," Zaben announced, still leaning on his tip–down sword. "The Lord is already speaking to our man."

"You mean *my* man," the demon lieutenant shot back. "He has never been your man, and he never will be. If you even try to win him, I will destroy him."

"You dare not. You have no one prepared to take his place. And, with me here now, you cannot touch him."

"Argghh!" The demon's sword made a high arc and whirred down toward Zaben, who awakened his resting blade and met the descending steel. *Crash!* A blinding flash. Their swords locked amid crackling energy. Sparks shot around their faces, now inches apart. Zaben held his face like stone—confident and powerful. The demon's face contorted and trembled.

The demon's hot sulfurous breath shot yellow jets of smoke into Zaben's face. "I will destroy him, and you will not be able to stop me." He snorted out a final puff of yellow smoke, stepped back, and sheathed his weapon.

"We shall see," Zaben replied. He motioned to his warriors, and they released the other two demons. Without a word, the three demons disappeared through the ceiling.

"Let them go. The stage is now set," Zaben said. "Tomorrow the enemy will make their play, and when they do, they will unknowingly accomplish the King's will. I need you two to go as we planned and make sure our package arrives tomorrow on time." And to the other two on his right he said, "You two go with Bartimus. I doubt the enemy will try anything tonight—their best opportunity will be tomorrow when the auditor is here. I will stay here in the treasury."

———

The Roman auditor and his aides began the audit mid-morning in the treasury with Bartimus, along with Festus, the assistant treasurer. Zaben took a position beside Bartimus. Two angelic warriors stood by. The men started with the physical inventory of the coinage in the vault room. By early afternoon, they completed the inventory, and the auditor sat at the main table and opened the ledgers.

"Very good," the auditor muttered. "The bottom lines all seem to be in order and match the inventory. Now, let's examine the details."

Zaben glanced around the room and bit his lower lip. "Come," he called out, "we should check on Festus. Bartimus and the auditor will be busy here for a while."

Zaben and his two warriors stepped through the open doorway into the vault room. Inside, Festus and an aide huffed and sweated as they loaded sacks of coin onto a cart—taxes for Rome. Four Roman soldiers stood watch. Multiple layers of stout shelves lined the walls all the way to the ceiling. On the shelves sat linen sacks filled with Roman coins—the silver denarii; bronze sesterii and dupondii;

copper semisses and quadrans; and even the gold quinarii and aureus. Zaben stood near the open door and waited.

Over the clinking of coins inside the vault, a faint whisper from the outer room drifted in. "How careless of them to leave our man unprotected. Now is our chance. Go! Go, fool!"

Zaben pressed against the inside wall of the vault and motioned for the other two angels to move back away from the door. He held a finger up to his lips. The warriors nodded. As silent as a shadow, he pushed his head through the wall until just his eyes emerged on the other side.

The treasury demon leaned over the auditor at the table, pointed with a crooked bony talon to some figures on a half-covered parchment, and whispered to the auditor, "Look at this. See it."

Zaben pulled his head back. *As expected. Right on time.* He cocked his ear toward the door and waited.

"What's this?" the auditor said.

Zaben nodded, bit his lip, and waited.

The auditor's voice floated in from the outer room. "The main ledger shows LXCVIII as the income from the eastern region. But over here, on the original ledger from the eastern region, the recorded number shows IXCVIII. Somehow, a single stroke has been dropped between the two ledgers, leaving 10,000 denarii unaccounted for."

Zaben's warriors reached for their sword handles, but he held up his hand and shook his head. He pressed his head through the wall again. *Now, will the auditor put it all together?*

"This is interesting," the auditor muttered, scanning all the other individual regional records. "This one is the only one with a discrepancy. But it makes me wonder. Bring me the records from last quarter," he ordered one of his aides.

Bartimus found the parchments for them. He handed them to the aide but appeared reluctant to let them go.

The auditor made a short survey of the numbers and mumbled to himself, "Again the eastern region." He scratched the back of his head. "I need to see every quarter for the last two years."

Bartimus dug out the records in question. The aide reached for them, but Bartimus held them tight. The aide pulled them forcibly from his hand.

The auditor stood and flipped through the pile of records, tracing the figures with his finger and muttering, "He has been doing this for years. How did I miss this before? I must have been blind—it is so obvious."

The demon wrung his hands and shook and cackled.

Zaben pulled his head back through the wall and turned to his two warriors. He nodded once. They drew their swords. "Wait for my signal," he whispered. With his own sword still sheathed, he stepped into the open doorway and sauntered into the main treasury room. Zaben's eyes met those of the demon standing beside the auditor. "What is this?" Zaben growled. He pulled his sword with a dramatic flourish and took one step forward.

The demon lieutenant and four more large beaelzurim emerged from the wall and formed a line between Zaben and the auditor.

"Enemy forces!" Zaben shouted. Zaben's two warriors appeared beside him on either side.

"This time, *you* are too late," the demon lieutenant taunted with a guttural rasp in his voice. "The sins of Bartimus have been found out. Soon he will be in prison, and there is nothing you can do to stop it now."

Zaben and his warriors held their swords at the ready. Silence gripped the Middle Realm in the treasury room.

The auditor broke the silence. "Guards, take Bartimus into custody. I have evidence that he has been systematically embezzling funds. Take him immediately to the prison. The proconsul will determine his sentence."

A guard seized Bartimus's arm, but Bartimus twisted it free, spun, ducked, and bolted toward the exit. He made three steps, but another soldier caught his arm. The soldier overpowered him, flung him to the ground, and locked his neck in a chokehold. Two more soldiers wrestled his arms behind his back and bound his hands with a thick, coarse rope. The soldiers hoisted him up and stood him before the auditor.

The auditor thumped his index finger on Bartimus's chest and barked, "And I can promise you, cases like this are dealt with most severely." He gave a dismissive wave. "Take him away."

Two muscled soldiers dragged Bartimus out of the main treasury entrance, followed by two more with spears at Bartimus's back. The demon lieutenant laughed. Zaben didn't acknowledge the demon's taunts but focused on the waves of light bombarding Bartimus in the Middle Realm. *Even now, during this time of intense distress, the Spirit of the Lord is still speaking to him, calling to him, trying to win his heart. I hope he will hear and respond. . .*

Festus emerged from the vault room. "What is happening? Why are the guards taking. . ."

The Roman auditor announced, "Festus, your superior has just been arrested for crimes against the state. I hereby name you the new

Chief Treasurer of Aegyptus. You may begin your duties by bringing me the records for all the years Bartimus held his position. We need to determine exactly the extent of the taxes he has stolen from the proconsul and the Emperor."

The auditor and Festus dug into the records. Within each record, they found a consistent pattern of fraud. Bartimus would drop a digit when transferring to the main ledger, and he always did it from the eastern region.

"Why the eastern region?" the auditor pondered aloud. "Well, this is interesting—that region has shown a steady growth for the last ten years. Skimming the excess off a growing account would attract less attention. Still, I'm amazed I missed it so many times. The total amount embezzled is very high."

"Ha ha!" the demon lieutenant sneered at Zaben. "You thought you could come in here and take control in my domain. With a snap of my fingers, I have smashed your plan. This pitiful man will soon be destroyed, and I have placed a man even more godless in his place."

Just then, a guard at the main door called out, "Sir, the treasurer from the eastern region has just arrived. He brings revenues and requests entrance."

"Let him enter," the auditor answered.

The guard opened the door and announced, "Benjamin, treasurer of the eastern region."

———

The young Benjamin shuffled into the room with parchment scrolls under his arms and a day's worth of sand and dust on his legs. Two large angelic warriors stepped in with him and readied their blades.

Benjamin proceeded toward the tables and called to the men following him, "Please bring the bags of money into the vault for Festus to count, just as we always do." He bowed to the auditor and said, "My lord, please forgive my tardiness, I know my share was due here yesterday. However, something startled my horse as I traveled, and my chariot swerved off the road and struck a large stone, causing major damage."

Zaben flashed a knowing wink to one of his warriors, who returned a slight, cunning grin.

Benjamin continued, "This prevented my travel until now. However, you will find all my records in order and my inventory correct."

Zaben bit his lip and waited. *Put it together. . . hear what he just said. . . think about it.*

The auditor mumbled, "Yes, yes," and fumbled with the scrolls. He pushed aside the stack of parchments, rolled out Benjamin's records, and checked them.

"You are the treasurer for the eastern region? I see you have had remarkable increases in recent years."

"Yes, the Lord has blessed us."

The auditor scanned with his finger to the bottom–line figure that had shown up as a discrepancy on the main ledger. He paused. He looked up. He cocked his head. "What did you say?"

"Sir, that the Lord has blessed our region."

"No, before that. What did you tell your men?"

"I asked them to bring the sacks of coin into the treasury for counting."

"Yes, and who is the one who counts the money you bring in?"

Benjamin paused and gave a puzzled scowl. "Festus is always the one who does our inventory. He then reports the inventory to Bartimus, who checks it against my records. I don't understand, sir, is there a problem with my records? And where is Bartimus? He is the one I am supposed to turn my records in to."

Zaben smiled. *The turning point!* He saw it in the auditor's eyes when he turned to look at Festus. "Now!" Zaben shouted. The angelic host exploded onto the demonic line. The full fury of the battle filled the Middle Realm. Five angels and six demons lunged, spun, flew, and swung blades of spiritual steel with all their might. Sparks and flashes shot through the walls and ceiling and filled the spiritual air with smoke and swirling vortices.

"Benjamin is a liar," shouted the demon lieutenant.

His words rolled up, burst into flame, and shot like an arrow at the auditor's heart. Zaben sprang toward auditor. Zaben's sword slashed upward and intercepted the words just before they pierced the auditor. The fiery arrow exploded and disappeared in a cloud of smoke. Even though outnumbered, the angels surged with strength and power. They pressed the offensive and had the demonic forces on their heels.

"Festus counts your money, and Bartimus records it?" the auditor echoed. "Guards!"

The guards seized Festus, and with both his arms locked behind him, they pressed him forward until he stood face to face with the auditor.

"The two of you were in this together. Do you deny it?"

Festus pursed his lips and raised his chin.

The auditor snatched a dagger from a nearby soldier, positioned the point against Festus's jugular, and pressed until drops of blood escaped and rolled out onto the silver blade. "Or perhaps Bartimus is innocent and you acted alone?"

"Ten percent," Festus rasped out, without moving his head and neck. "Bartimus gave me ten percent. But he was the one. . ."

"Take him away. Throw him in prison with his companion. They will both pay dearly for this treachery." The auditor stabbed the dagger through the parchments into the wooden table and left it standing there as the soldiers removed Festus from the treasury.

Zaben's sword crashed downward toward the demon lieutenant. The demon blocked the strike with his sword, but blow after blow from Zaben's attack drove him backwards. He stumbled and landed on his back. Zaben swung again, but the demon rolled to his left and bounded into the air.

"Retreat!" the demon lieutenant shouted. "Retreat!"

He and the rest of the demons escaped through the roof and out the walls.

———

The passing of the spiritual storm left the treasury room quiet and still. The auditor slumped in his chair and glanced up at Benjamin, who looked at the closed front door with a blank, confused expression. Zaben stood next to Benjamin while his four warriors moved back to strategic positions. The auditor stroked his hair and took deep breaths. For a long time, he said nothing.

Zaben watched the auditor and waited. *He needs more guidance.* He stepped over and placed his hand on the auditor's shoulder. With a calm, authoritative voice he said, "Benjamin can fill this position. He is blessed of the Lord." His words coalesced into shafts of light that shot down toward the auditor. Most of the light bounced off his hardened, dark shell. *I think some of it reached his spirit.* Zaben stepped back and waited.

The auditor looked again at the ledgers. He looked up at Benjamin. He looked at the ledgers.

"Benjamin. . . Benjamin. Hebrew?"

Benjamin nodded.

"You are a very long way from home."

"I left Israel. . . to start a new life. Egypt is my home now."

"And you have been in your current position for five years now? Your records are very meticulous. And your God seems to be blessing you." He paused again and stroked his hair. "I think it would be in the best interest of Rome if you. . . were to take the position of Chief Treasurer for the province."

Benjamin staggered backward a step. "But sir, I am still young. I have a home, and I am engaged to be married soon. Surely you would prefer a more experienced. . ."

The auditor stood and leaned with both hands on the table. "No. You are exactly the kind of man I want. You are very competent. And you have a reputation of integrity. I need you here. Marry your bride. Move your home here to the palace. This is a major promotion. Will you take it?"

Benjamin stood frozen with the auditor looking him square in the eyes. Benjamin fidgeted and looked down at his feet. Then, under the pressure of the moment, he blurted out, "Yes, sir, at your request, I will serve to the best of my ability."

"It is settled then." The auditor let out a long sigh and sat down. He buried his face in his hands. "It is too bad about Bartimus. A higher position recently opened up in Rome. We were considering him for it. Now. . . well, now. . ." He looked up at Benjamin. "Now we have a more trustworthy steward in place here. You will do well."

As the two men discussed the particulars of Benjamin's new assignment, Zaben crossed his arms and nodded his head. "I don't know what the King has planned for this one," he said, "but we have set him in place. All four of you will stay with him until he is firmly established. I commend you for your excellent service today."

"It was a good operation, sir," one of the warriors said. "Well conceived. You do have an eye for strategy."

"We all have our own strengths, but everything comes from the King Himself."

"Still, the way you used the enemy to—"

"This was a simple one. Remember Esther and Haman in the days of Xerxes?"

"That was you?"

A light flashed through the ceiling, and in a blink a huge elzur captain landed beside Zaben. The captain's wings folded away.

"Captain Elric!" Zaben said.

Elric nodded once to Zaben and smiled at the four warriors. With a sparkle in his eyes, he said, "It *was* him. And the tales you hear do not begin to tell the complexity and elegance of his plan." He placed his hand on Zaben's shoulder. "Lieutenant, we must speak in private."

"Carry on," Zaben said to the four warriors.

Zaben and Elric wrapped their wings around their bodies and disappeared from the Middle Realm.

12

RESONATING PEACE

Birth minus 2 years

Elizabeth sat in a small chair next to the fireplace and prayed her morning prayers in her home in the hills of Judea. Her slender old hands rested in her lap, and tears welled in her half–closed eyes. The angelic lieutenant Lacidar stood behind Elizabeth with his sturdy hands on her shoulders. With a sweeping motion, he brushed his hands outward.

"I remove the weight of this burden," he said.

He put his hands back on her shoulders and repeated another sweep. Ten more times he brushed away the unseen weight. She stopped crying and became still. With his hands still on her shoulders, Lacidar hummed a sweet and peaceful melody—melancholy, yet sprinkled with distant hope.

Elric passed through the front door. "Lacidar, I thought I would find you here."

Lacidar turned and greeted Elric with bow of his head. "I try to spend as much time with her as I can. My heart breaks for her, and she needs the strength."

"How long have you been ministering to her?"

"Over thirty years now. She and Zacharias have been unable to conceive in all that time. And still she prays and clings to hope."

"It is a long time for a person to remain steadfast."

"Her diligence honors the King. I will be here to encourage her until she goes to be with Him."

Elric smiled and put his hand on Lacidar's shoulder.

"What is it, captain?" Lacidar asked. "What brings you here?"

"I received a word from the Throne last week. I wanted to tell you in person."

"What is it?"

"It's Elizabeth. She is going to have a son."

"Ya-ha!" Lacidar shouted. "Whoo!" He leapt so high he shot through the roof. He returned in an instant and ran circles in the room. He grabbed Elric by the hands and danced with his knees almost hitting his chest. The two laughed and danced and shouted praises to the King.

"Can I tell her?" Lacidar gushed. "Can I give her a dream?"

"The Lord is preparing a message to be delivered to Zacharias. You are to simply encourage her until the time is complete."

"Yes, sir. This is wonderful news. I'm so happy. I have a new song to play for her."

Elric laughed. "Play your song. Play it loud." Elric's face turned serious. "And when you are finished here, meet me at Commander Kai's headquarters. I need to discuss a mission. It is secret—speak of it to no one."

Lacidar cocked his head, paused, and nodded.

Elric left, and Lacidar bounded over and picked up his instrument. He pulled up his playing stool, sat down, and strummed the strings. The seven main strings came to life under his fingers while the strings of a separate crystal neck picked up the tune and resonated a joyous overtone. He played no melancholy tune. He played a song full of life, joy, and hope fulfilled. He stomped his feet, closed his eyes, and lifted his head as the lilt of the tune and the richness of the sound echoed in his ears. He became lost in the song, and for a moment, his mind replayed the time he first played on this instrument—before the Rebellion, during the time of joy and peace.

Date: Pre-Rebellion

Lacidar stepped into the artisan's workshop and stopped. His mouth dropped open. He blinked twice. *Look at this place! This is amazing!* The enormous room soared with lofty ceilings, ivory pillars, and elegant archways. Brilliant light radiated everywhere, and the pure clean fragrance of violets filled Lacidar's whole being with warmth. The dizzying beauty on the wall to his left captured his attention. Musical instruments hung on the wall from floor to ceiling. *Heralding trumpets.* Some silver, some gold. All beautiful in form and perfectly proportioned. Dozens of other types of horns, including exotic varieties. *What are these? I have never. . . and back there. . .* Drums of all sizes and timbres sat stacked on the floor along the wall. Stringed instruments covered the far back wall, works of art, every one. *And over here. . .* On the wall to his right—hundreds of disks of assorted sizes. *Cymbals? Yes, but these are ornamental shields.* The shields had exquisite artwork on their surfaces, each unique and breathtaking. Tables lined the middle of the room with pieces in various stages of completion.

Lacidar took another step into the room and cleared his throat. "Is anybody here?"

From somewhere in the center of the room, behind a stout pillar, came the clattering of metal hitting the floor. Then the scuffle of heavy footsteps. Around the pillar appeared a mountain of an angel. He had a barrel chest of solid muscle. His arms were so large they couldn't hang straight down to his sides. His wiry and unkempt brown hair looked as wild as the full beard that covered his face.

"Welcome, welcome," the artisan called out with a low robust voice. "Welcome to my studio."

He stepped forward, and his jolly cheekbones and jovial eyes drew a smile from Lacidar. "Thank you. This is an amazing place. Did you make all these?"

"I did."

The angel approached, and Lacidar pulled his right hand up to his mouth and spoke into his hand: "Peace." A small ball of pure plasma energy formed in his palm and suspended there. The artisan wiped his hands on the front of his smock and spoke into his hand: "Joy" and formed his ball of energy. They held up their right hands and pressed the energy spheres together until their hands touched. The energy coalesced and exploded in a ring of light that filled the workshop.

"These instruments are beautiful," Lacidar said.

"Thank you. I love creating new and beautiful things to honor the King. The only thing that brings me more joy is seeing someone use one of my creations to create something new and beautiful of their own."

"Like music. . ." Lacidar gestured toward everything. ". . . on instruments."

The artisan beamed.

"My name is Lacidar."

"I am honored to have you in my studio. My name is Timrok. What can I do for you?"

"I am looking for a new instrument."

"Yes, of course, a musician. Excellent."

"I was told you were a skilled artisan, but I can see I was not told the half of it."

"Whatever is in your heart, I'm sure you will find the right instrument here. And if not, I will do my best to create it for you. What is it in your heart that needs to come out?"

Lacidar led the way to the back wall of stringed instruments.

"I play strings," Lacidar said as he perused the wall. "May I?" he said, pointing to one instrument.

"Of course, please."

Lacidar strummed it gently at first and then began plucking a beautiful and highly technical melody.

Timrok nodded his head and folded his arms. "Very nice. You are very skilled yourself."

Lacidar returned the instrument to the wall. "That had exquisite tone, but. . ."

"But it doesn't release what's in your heart."

"Yes, yes. You understand."

"I do. Try some others."

Lacidar tried several more instruments. Each time, Timrok closed his eyes and sipped the sound as though savoring a fine wine.

Each time Lacidar put an instrument back, Timrok agreed that it didn't match Lacidar's artistic palette.

"I'm sorry," Lacidar said. "I don't really know what I'm looking for. I play regularly in Lucifer's main orchestra, and I love that. But when I'm alone, I want to play something for the King that has never been heard before. I need a unique sound that I can use to create new music. Something that is all my own."

"I know exactly what you mean," Timrok said. He grinned and rubbed his hands together. "Let me create something for you. I have an idea for an instrument that I've been wanting to make. I think it will be perfect for you. Do you trust me?"

"Yes, of course, if you are willing."

"Willing? I live for this. Come, come. You can watch me work."

"You're going to make it right now?"

Timrok laughed. "Try to stop me."

They weaved around the tables toward the very center of the workshop. Along the way they passed tables with enormous swords lying across them so large they stretched across two adjacent tables. They had the same artisan craftsmanship with beautiful engraving and razor–sharp edges.

"What are these?" Lacidar asked.

"Swords for the senturim. I don't really understand it. But I suppose they *are* guardians for the King."

"I can't imagine what there is to guard against."

"Me either. I am thankful *I* have no need for a sword." Timrok came to a stop. "Here we are."

A large round pedestal stood before them. A massive sphere of plasma energy floated above the pedestal. Its brilliant white core and glowing edges made Lacidar squint. Sparkles of pure energy spun and shot about in tight arcs. The whole thing hummed at a frequency almost too low to be heard.

"Where do you get your energy?" Lacidar asked.

"Archangels mostly. But I always add a little of my own." Timrok held his right palm up until a small sphere of energy appeared. Then he pressed it into the large sphere until it merged with the main mass of energy. "For this project, you should add some of yours, too."

Lacidar created his own ball of energy and incorporated it into the main sphere.

Timrok smiled. "Very good. And now we begin. Energy and matter—you just have to know how to work it."

Timrok thrust his hand into the plasma and scooped out a rough-measured amount. He held it for a moment and pinched off a filament of energy, which he flicked back into the source sphere. He paused again, pinched off a smaller piece, and nodded. He turned and set the working sphere on top of a table. With his hands, he began molding. He breathed into the mass and blew in precise directions. He spoke into it. Lacidar turned his ear. *What is he saying?* Timrok's hands worked with constant motion—shaping, molding, drawing out.

Within minutes, a solid object rested on the table. It looked like the body of an instrument with a rich ebony wood and tight uniform grain. Timrok pulled more energy from the sphere and formed the sounding board, which melded to the body as he worked it. *He pulled that from the same batch of energy, but this has multiple-colored woods. . .* intricately inlaid with patterns of pure gold artistically set throughout. Timrok took extra time with this piece, and when he finished, he looked up at Lacidar with a twinkle in his eye. Next, he fashioned a neck, broad and sleek. *Solid silver with gold frets and an ebony headstock—beautiful.*

"And now. . ." Timrok said under his breath. He formed something new.

What is that? It looked like another neck or bridge running diagonally from the left of the main headstock, across the strings at the body and attaching to the body at the bottom right. It had two bridges that connected to the sounding board. The entire assembly consisted of pure crystal, and it flashed dazzling rainbow patterns from the workshop lighting.

Timrok finished forming the crystal piece and exclaimed, "Ha ha! I believe we are ready for the strings."

He pulled a single pinch from the energy sphere and drew it out to full arm's length. Between his fingers he stretched and twisted the filament until it became a uniform strand. Then he plucked it, listened, stretched, plucked, listened, twisted. Finally, he closed one hand around it and swiped down the entire length of the string. He set it aside and pinched off another filament. Within minutes, he formed seven strings. These strings he set into the main bridge and headstock and tuned each by ear.

Last, he drew out twenty-four more strings. Different from the other strings, these had a thin, flat shape. He set them into the crystal bridge in three layers, tuning each as he went. After the last string had been set in place, Timrok beamed a broad smile, lifted his work of art with his fingertips, and handed it to Lacidar.

Lacidar held it like a newborn baby. "It's beautiful. More beautiful than any instrument I've ever seen."

"The main body plays like any instrument you're used to. But this. . ." Timrok pointed to the crystal bridge and strings. "This is what I call a resonar. You don't play these strings. They pick up the notes you are playing and resonate on their own. If you play something sad, they will create a chorus of melancholy that will make you weep. If you play something happy, they will bounce and dance with all the joy of the Lord. If you press down on this clamp here, it will turn the resonar off. Here, let's turn it off for now and see how the basic instrument sounds."

Lacidar plucked the strings gingerly at first. His smile widened, and he picked up the tempo. He smiled more and cut loose. His fingers flew over the strings, and the instrument filled the room with exultation. Lacidar laughed out loud, playing faster and faster. He stopped suddenly and took deep breaths.

"This is amazing. It plays so effortlessly, and its tone is magnificent. This is far above anything else I've ever played."

Timrok smirked, reached over, and unclamped the resonar. "Now play."

Lacidar started in where he left off—fast and joyful. The resonar erupted with life. It bounced interweaving arpeggios and sang a soaring chorus. Lacidar stopped and cocked his ear.

"What is that?" he said, looking around for the rest of the orchestra.

"That's the resonar. All that sound was coming from you."

"Ha ha!" Lacidar shouted. He started playing again. The melody had a happy lilt, and the resonar filled the rafters with full, rich, complex music. "I've never heard anything like this," Lacidar shouted over the music.

Timrok danced around the room with his hands above his head. "Play something soft and sweet," he called out. "Something from your heart."

Lacidar reduced the tempo, and the tune became melodious. The resonar responded. It sang sweet counter melodies, soft and full. Then, as if responding to Lacidar's emotions themselves, the resonar strings swelled and rang out in triumphant harmonies. And in an instant, they pulled back and whispered a peaceful lullaby. Lacidar closed his eyes and bathed in the richness of the moment. His heart poured out through his fingers while his brain listened. He began to weep. Softly at first, but the swell of emotions rose from his belly and lodged in his throat. He had to stop playing. Through tear–filled eyes he looked up at Timrok. The huge artist wiped his eyes with his smock. They both laughed at each other. At themselves.

"That was the most beautiful thing I have ever heard," Timrok said, still wiping his eyes. "Even Lucifer with all his orchestras and choirs could not equal that."

"Because it is my own song from my own heart."

"And mine. From my heart to yours. From your heart to the King."

"You have given me a great gift," Lacidar said.

Timrok laughed. "I shall call it. . . the Lacidian Resonar."

"No, don't name it after me, you are the one who. . ."

"It is done. This is a Lacidian Resonar, and I shall never make another. You alone will create this sound. Now, play me another tune. Something I can dance to."

———

Elizabeth finished her prayer time, pushed the chair against the wall, and set about her daily tasks. Lacidar stayed in the corner of the room and pounded out a dancing tune on his Lacidian Resonar in sheer excitement over the amazing news from the captain. His instrument sounded as full and rich as the day Timrok created it, and Lacidar had to force himself to keep playing and not get up to dance to his own song. The music couldn't reach Elizabeth's ears, but the waves of spiritual energy soaked into her spirit.

Zacharias returned home and greeted Elizabeth with a well–practiced embrace.

"What's the matter?" Zacharias asked. He stepped back and looked her over. "You seem. . . especially happy. Did we receive good news about something?"

"No. No, I was just praying today. Praying for. . . well, you know. . ."

"Oh, Elizabeth, by now you have to know that. . ."

"I know. It's all right. Today I've had such a release about it. It may not ever happen, but I really have a peace about it. Joy, almost."

Lacidar smiled, wrapped his wings around his body, and disappeared from the Middle Realm.

13

MYSTERY REVEALED

Birth minus 2 years

Elric watched from around a concealed corner among the pillars and lofty arches surrounding Commander Kai's headquarters in the King's Realm.

Lacidar's song for Elizabeth is a long one. But then, I would expect nothing less.

Hundreds of elzurim passed by, all too preoccupied with some business of the King to notice him loitering behind the corner of a side hallway.

Finally, Lacidar appeared. He took a deep lingering breath and smiled.

Elric stepped forward and called out, "Lacidar."

Lacidar spotted Elric, let out his breath, and stepped toward headquarters.

"I have a private room," Elric said.

They moved down several unoccupied hallways to an unmarked door.

They entered the room, small and austere, remote and private. A single table and six chairs occupied the center of the room, which was bright and warm and had no light fixtures, but light emanated from all the walls, ceiling, and floor. The low hum of energy of the King's Realm provided the only sound. In two of the chairs sat the lieutenants Zaben and Jenli, who jumped to their feet. Timrok stood at the other end of the table like a mountain of muscle and hair. Zaben, Jenli, and Timrok formed words of joy, peace, and honor as balls of energy in their palms. Lacidar spoke the word perseverance. The four smashed their greetings together in a shower of light.

Elric motioned at the chairs, and the four lieutenants sat. Lacidar pulled up a chair next to Timrok and flashed him a wide grin. Timrok gave him a playful slug on the shoulder.

"I am assembling a small task force," Elric said. He paused and made sure the door had been secured. "I want to give you the opportunity to be a part of the team. This is not a typical order—I am seeking volunteers."

"What is the mission?" Zaben asked.

"I cannot say until you have committed to it. I will tell you that it is an earth–bound mission, no one can know of it, and I don't know details."

The four lieutenants sat in silence with raised eyebrows.

"Why us?" Jenli asked.

"Zaben, after working with you on the Esther campaign, I am convinced you are one of the most skilled strategists in the Kingdom.

Jenli, we have worked together for a long time, you know all the forces in the region of interest, and you have a great eye for detail. Timrok, you are the fiercest fighter I know. And Lacidar, your commitment to endure under a heavy load is known by all."

Zaben bit his lower lip. Timrok crossed his arms and sat back in his chair.

Jenli shifted in his seat and wrung his hands. "How long is the mission?"

Elric looked him straight in the eyes and squeezed out a conciliatory smile. "At least twenty years. Perhaps as long as fifty."

Zaben didn't hesitate. "This sounds interesting. A secret mission. Multiple years to let a plan unfold. I love a good challenge."

"I am honored to serve," Timrok said.

"Yes, of course," Lacidar said.

Jenli dropped his face into his hands then rubbed the back of his stubbly head. "Fifty years," he muttered. He continued rubbing his head. Finally, he sat up straight and spoke without wavering. "I will do it. The King is drawing me. And I am, above all, in His service."

"Excellent," Elric said. He double-checked the door again. He crossed his arms and paced. *How do I begin?*

"Captain?" Zaben said.

Elric stopped, took a deep breath, and began, "This mission is. . ."

A single thud on the door echoed across the room. Elric jumped and spun around. "I. . . was not expecting. . ."

He opened the door a crack, gasped, flung the door open, and stepped to the side. In walked a chief general, an archangel, dazzling white and monstrous in size. Everything was white—his hair, his robes, his face. His eyes shimmered like silver. He moved with large, commanding motions. Two paces behind him followed a logirhi, small and sleek, quick and darting.

Elric cleared his throat and said, "Master Gabriel!"

The lieutenants all stood at attention. Zaben leaned in and whispered to Jenli, "It's Gabriel! Do you realize what this means?"

"Pardon the interruption." Gabriel's low, booming voice vibrated through Elric's body. "The Lord has sent me with instructions."

Elric fumbled to secure the door.

Gabriel took one step to the side. "I present Grigor."

The logirhi took three quick steps forward and bowed his head once.

"He is your dedicated messenger. He is cunning and stealthy, and among the fastest in the Kingdom. The success of this mission requires utmost secrecy. The King will reveal only the most needful information, and then, only to a chosen few. Receive words only from Grigor or me."

"Yes, my lord."

Gabriel opened the door but stopped and looked at Elric. The enormity of the task and the anticipation of what it could all mean was so thick Elric could taste it. He could sense Gabriel searching for the words to convey how important his role would be. Elric understood.

"In His service," Elric said.

Gabriel smiled. "For His glory."

Grigor darted out behind Gabriel, and the door closed behind them.

Elric turned to find the lieutenants still on their feet and bouncing heel to toe. He stalled in spite of their pleading eyes and took another deep breath. He started to open his mouth but stopped. He ran his hand through his hair, looked down at the ground, and said without looking up, "I must reiterate the importance of secrecy." He raised his head. "This mission must remain hidden from all—the enemy, mankind, even our own. Outside of this team, the only ones with revelation are Gabriel and the messenger Grigor."

They all answered with enthusiastic smiles.

Elric clenched his jaw to suppress his own smile. "I see you anticipate my word. You surmise correctly. It is time for the coming of the Messiah."

Zaben leapt three feet into the air. "I knew it!" he shouted. "I knew it," he repeated over and over.

"Hallelujah," cheered Lacidar, who jumped and spun with his hands in the air.

Jenli bounded about shouting, "Yes, yes, yes! I could tell the time was near."

Timrok stood motionless and dried his eyes with his sleeves.

Eventually, Elric had to bring the room to order. They still had much to discuss. The lieutenants couldn't sit, but they did stop most of their dancing.

"Why us? What is our role?" Lacidar asked.

Zaben said, "A captain and four lieutenants—surely the Lord does not expect us to lead the battle?"

"Why not?" gruffed Timrok.

"There is no battle," Elric interrupted. "Not yet. The King must first be born of a woman."

"Yes, yes, of course," Zaben said.

Elric continued, "And our task is to keep Him hidden until He is prepared to begin His campaign. He will have the flesh of man and will live in the Physical Realm, within the kingdom of the enemy."

The room became silent. Faces turned grim.

"This is magnificent," Zaben said. "The wisdom of the King is matchless. The enemy will expect a grand entrance and will be waiting to destroy Him while He is young and defenseless. Instead, He will stay hidden until He can raise an army. He needs us now because the workings of the chief angels would draw attention to His position before He is ready."

Elric nodded. "You can see why secrecy is so critical. In fact, I know very little about the details of the mission. We will make plans based on whatever word we are given and execute in faith."

A light *tap, tap, tap* at the door interrupted the meeting. Elric opened the door and let Grigor step in. Typical of a logirhi, Grigor spent no time on niceties.

"The word of the Lord—there is a priest, Zacharias, of the division of Abijah in Judah. His wife Elizabeth is barren. But the Lord has chosen her to be the mother of the prophet. Gabriel will deliver this message to Zacharias in the temple two hundred and fifteen days hence. You and your team shall make preparations for this. We must keep this hidden. Also, the Son shall be born of Mary of Nazareth, the betrothed of Joseph of Nazareth. Four hundred days from now is the time of the Spirit's visitation to Mary."

"In His service," Elric said.

"By His word."

Elric closed the door behind Grigor.

"My Elizabeth!" Lacidar squealed. He started bouncing again.

Everyone else stood silent and still. Lacidar's bouncing slowed and stopped. The room became very somber as the weight of responsibility settled on everyone's shoulders.

"We must complete our team," Elric said. "You must each choose for yourselves five worthy warriors. Timrok has already appointed his team."

"Before I release you to find your teams, we should prepare strategies. We now have a basic timetable and key people identified for the initial phase. We also know the birthplace is Bethlehem."

They all moved to the table. Elric took a position at the middle of the table, and the lieutenants gathered around. The energetic meeting proceeded with many ideas and complicated contingencies. Hours and hours of planning passed. Finally, they had a basic plan in place.

"It is settled, then," Elric said. "Timrok—you will take your team to Jerusalem and prepare for Gabriel's visitation. Determine the widest perimeter we can establish without drawing attention. I would prefer to empty the entire temple grounds of enemy forces, but that will probably not be possible. After Zacharias receives his word, he must be isolated from the enemy. It will be difficult to keep his message hidden."

Elric glanced across the table at Timrok. His hair looked big and wild, but his eyes sparkled with eager anticipation. "Yes, captain."

"Lacidar—you will station yourself at Zacharias and Elizabeth's home. Establish a protective perimeter. When Zacharias travels to Jerusalem, you stay with Elizabeth, but send your team with Zacharias. They will supplement Timrok's team in Jerusalem while Zacharias is there."

Lacidar nodded.

"Jenli—your team will go to Nazareth. I will join you there after Gabriel delivers his word to Zacharias. We will work with Joseph and Mary. More importantly, we have to secure a suitable location in Bethlehem for His coming. We have received no word about this."

"Yes, captain."

Elric turned to Zaben. "And you are in charge of the diversion in Egypt. Are you prepared for an operation of this magnitude?"

Zaben chewed on his lower lip, and Elric could see the strategizing wheels in Zaben's mind spinning at full capacity. "This is the Lord's battle. He will provide," Zaben said. "In fact, He already has. The real purpose behind my last assignment in Egypt with Benjamin, the treasurer, is now clear. I am confident the enemy will follow the trail we provide. It is the timing at the end that will be the most critical."

"Agreed. This is the most tenuous part of our plan. Any final questions?"

The four lieutenants exchanged glances and grim smiles.

Elric said, "This is a good plan. Well-conceived. Now you must go select members for your teams. You have three days. We shall meet back here. On the third day, we will assemble the whole team. Stagger your arrivals so as to not attract attention."

One by one, the lieutenants departed the room at random times until Elric alone remained. He pulled his sword from its sheath and laid it on the table. He sat. He lifted his chin and closed his eyes.

14

FORMING THE RANKS

Birth minus 2 years

Fifteen sturdy warriors in neat ranks filled the secret room in
Kai's headquarters to near capacity. They had all arrived at
varied intervals, but some time had now passed, and none of
Timrok's team had appeared yet. Elric paced and shot glances toward
the closed door.

"Where is he?" Elric asked.

Zaben, Lacidar, and Jenli answered with shrugged shoulders and
blank looks.

Elric turned to the rest of the group. "Has anyone seen Timrok
or any of his team within the last three days?"

One of the warriors within the ranks answered, "Sir, I saw him
speaking with Gabriel three days past."

"Gabriel? What purpose would he have. . ."

The door clattered open, and Timrok filled the doorway. He hobbled through, with one of his hands grasping the handle of a large, bulky chest. One of Timrok's team members hoisted the handle on the other end of the chest. The two shuffled in and set the chest down along the front wall with a heavy thud. Two more chests followed, each borne up by the strong hands of Timrok's team.

The last of the three chests chunked into the line at the front of the room, and Elric asked, "What is this?"

Timrok stood up straight and smiled. "These are special gifts. And if it pleases the captain, I would like to present them at the end of this meeting."

Elric crossed his arms and walked over to the chests. He pressed his foot against one. It wouldn't budge. He looked back toward Timrok and said, "As you wish. Have your team join ranks."

Timrok motioned to his team, who had already begun moving into position. Twenty angelic warriors formed a tight unit—disciplined, formidable, and ready for action. Jenli's team formed the front row: Brondor, Jennidab, Jerem, Jessik, and Kaylar. Zaben's team formed the second row: Emms, Lorr, Xarjim, Christov, and Carothim. Lacidar's team formed the third row: BaeLee, Stephanus, Kelsof, Jaeden, and Ry. Timrok's team took the back row: Prestus, Chase, Nalyd, Kylek, and Micah. Elric stepped forward to address the squad. The four lieutenants spread out in a line behind Elric, facing the troop.

"You have all been specially selected for this most important mission. You know the nature of our task, so I need not tell you the significance of every move we make. The enemy will be watching closely. For this reason, we will be isolated and operating without regular direction. Our primary objective, above all else, is to keep the King hidden—which we will do. Today is probably the last time we will be gathered like this. If you have any questions, now is the time."

"Captain," one of the warriors called out. "The cherubim always go before the presence of the Lord's glory. How will we keep Him hidden when the cherubim go forth?"

"There will be no cherubim."

The warriors gasped and looked at each other.

Elric continued. "He will enter the Physical Realm like any other man. We are the only ones who will know of it."

Murmuring broke out within the ranks.

"How is this possible?"

"Will God put on flesh?"

"It *has* been foretold."

"With God all things are possible."

"It is beyond comprehension."

One of the voices rose above the others, "Sir, if He becomes flesh, does it mean that His flesh can die?"

The room became silent.

"He will be subject to *all* the physical laws."

A long breath of silence followed.

Another warrior asked, "Once the King is old enough and our mission is complete, will He bring in the generals to lead His army in the final battle?"

"We know nothing more than this first phase. But we know that the Lord in His wisdom will put in place that which is necessary for the day."

"I am ready for that day," Jenli said.

Everyone nodded.

"A day of judgment," Zaben said.

"A day of peace," Timrok said.

"A day of rejoicing and music," Lacidar said.

Elric held up his hand. "That day is His day. Our day is today. Today we establish a foothold in enemy territory—without him ever knowing."

"In His service," one of the warriors declared.

"In His service," echoed the whole company.

"Are there any more questions?" Elric asked.

The troop stood in their ranks with set jaws and square shoulders.

"Timrok," Elric said, "do you have a presentation?"

Timrok, beaming, gave a little hop and spun on his heels. He opened the first chest and turned toward Elric and the others. "As some of you may know," Timrok said, "before the Rebellion I was an artisan, crafting all kinds of articles for use in the Kingdom." He flashed a glance and a grin toward Lacidar, who smiled back. "In preparation for this mission, I have fashioned some special tools for the team."

Timrok reached into the chest and pulled out a concave disk—a shield, round and functional in size, with leather straps for the forearm. It was made of a burnished silver material that glowed in the light of the room. "This shield is for Zaben." Timrok held it up for all to see. "To honor your strategic vision, wisdom, and power, I have adorned your shield with an eagle."

Elric cocked his head to the side and admired the intricate embellishments in concentric circles around the circumference—vines of ivy around the outer ring, and in the center of the shield, the extruding head of a majestic eagle.

"This is magnificent," Zaben said as he accepted the shield.

"And I have the same design for each member of your team," Timrok said.

Two of Timrok's warriors distributed the shields to Zaben's team. They each fastened their shields to their arm and tested them for weight and balance.

"They are so light," several of them remarked.

Timrok answered, "This is a special material provided to us by the King through Gabriel. It is lighter than common materials we know, and far stronger and more durable. They will serve us well."

Timrok reached in and pulled out another shield. "This shield is for Lacidar. The hard–working bearer of heavy loads, strong in perseverance and faith—the mighty ox. And for your team."

This shield had the same embellishments around the outside and the image of a powerful, composed ox head in the middle. Timrok's team distributed the shields to Lacidar and his team.

The next shield Timrok held up had the bust of a man protruding in the center. "This shield is to honor the strength of empathy, attention to detail, and practical skills of Jenli."

Timrok's warriors handed out these shields, and the room buzzed with energy as everyone admired the artistic beauty and the feel of the material.

Lacidar shouted above the commotion with a laugh, "Where is your shield, master Timrok?"

Timrok furrowed his bushy brows and extended his very hairy chin. "Shields are for defense. I have no need for such a thing."

The warriors erupted in laughter. Timrok turned and pulled another shield out of the chest.

"However," Timrok shouted, "for my team, I have made shields of the lion."

Everyone clapped as Timrok's team took their shields with the head of a regal lion in the center.

"And for the captain?" Zaben hollered.

"And for the captain," Timrok answered while reaching into the chest, "the light of the King shining to guide us through the darkness we must tread. The bright and pure Morning Star."

A four-pointed star embossed the center of Elric's shield. The star had two horizontal arms and two vertical. Three of the star's points had the same length, but the bottom vertical arm was slightly longer. Elric saw only a beautiful artistic rendering of a star and didn't notice it had a vague resemblance to the shape of a Roman cross. Behind the star, shafts of light burst outward in the engravings. Elric admired the workmanship for several moments and then held it high above his head and rotated it for all to see.

"It is truly beautiful," Elric said. "They all are. We will carry these into battle with great humility and honor."

More applause.

Timrok bowed and then raised both hands in the air. "Please, please. I have saved the best for last."

Timrok moved to one of the other chests, and Elric repositioned his head to see. *What other surprise does he have waiting?* The other two crates looked longer and more narrow than the large chest that held the shields. Timrok opened the lid and reached in with slow, deliberate motions. He emerged with a broad sword resting horizontally across his palms. The blade remained concealed in a sheath, simple and unadorned. Timrok turned and held the sword waist high. Everyone strained to see the sword, narrower and shorter than a typical sword.

Elric scanned across the troop. The onlooking eyes showed a mix of anticipation and confusion over the underwhelming sword Timrok held before them.

Timrok's eyes sparkled, and he gave a sly grin. "Few of us have had the honor of experiencing the flame of vengeance—when the spirit of the King comes upon your sword, it bursts into flame, and a strike from it sends the enemy directly to the abyss. The last time I experienced it was in the days of the Nephilim."

Several warriors smiled and nodded.

"There is one problem with the flame of vengeance," Timrok said.

Elric interjected, "It destroys your sword."

"It completely destroys your sword." Timrok continued. "And Gabriel anticipates we may be visited with the flame of vengeance at various times during this mission."

Every warrior smiled and nodded.

"So, the King provided us with another exclusive material and a special design. It is stronger than any steel we know—lighter, and most importantly, it can hold the flame of vengeance indefinitely without any damage. I have forged swords for everyone. Captain, this sword is yours."

Timrok turned and held the sword out for Elric. Elric stepped forward and wrapped his hand around the handle as though greeting an old friend. Timrok bowed and stepped back.

Elric drew the sword from its sheath. He stopped with only inches of the blade showing and gasped. A blue aura of energy glowed from within several slots in the blade.

"What is this?" Elric asked, examining the glowing base of his blade.

"Pull it out. Pull it out," Timrok said, bouncing up and down.

Elric held the sheath in his left hand, gripped the handle of the sword with his right, and pulled the blade out with one swift motion.

The blade rang out with a crisp *shing*.

Everyone in the room gasped.

The width of the blade doubled, and its length extended to the full reach of a normal broadsword. The overall blade had a shape straight and true, and its tip had a narrow, sharp point. Elric held it straight up for everyone to see. The strange glowing slots were not slots at all, but open spaces between individual pieces of the blade. And the open spaces made intricate patterns across the full extent of the blade so that the blade was actually a composite of dozens of individual pieces. Dozens of shining silver blade components, held together by glowing sky-blue energy.

"What is this?" Elric asked again. "I've never seen such weapon."

Timrok bounced like an excited child. "It is a design given me by the King." Timrok stepped up and pointed to the individual pieces. "These are floating blades, bound together by pure energy taken from the burning coals beneath the throne. They form a single blade and are stronger than any blade in the Kingdom."

"Exquisite," Elric said.

"There's more," Timrok said, still bouncing. He pulled one of his own traditional swords and held it outward toward Elric. "Spar with me."

Elric smiled and took a step backward. He positioned his feet shoulder width apart and readied his sword.

"You should take a practice swing," Timrok said.

Elric raised his eyebrows and paused. Then, he lifted his sword and brought it downward in a diagonal arc. As the blade descended, its shape transformed from a straight blade to a complex form. The leading edge curved back in an elegant arc, and the back edge had two small barbs that trailed behind, their size changing with the speed of the blade. It had the shape of a flame slicing through the spiritual air. Elric stopped his swing, and the blade returned to its original form, straight and true.

Everyone in the room gasped.

Timrok laughed. "The floating blades give it the ability to change shape as needed for balance, efficiency, and power."

"Amazing," Elric said as he examined the blade.

"Now, make a swinging strike," Timrok said, holding his own sword out.

Elric raised his sword and brought it down on Timrok's ready blade. Elric's blade flew through the air like a tongue of fire, and just before it struck, two of the floating blades on the leading edge came together to form a wedge. The wedge struck Timrok's blade with a crash and sent sparks across the room.

Elric laughed and nodded his head.

"Now, make a piercing thrust," Timrok said.

Without hesitation, Elric pulled his sword back and thrust it forward toward Timrok. The tip of Elric's blade changed from a single point into three lethal prongs. Timrok deflected the advancing blade just in time.

"Ha ha!" Elric shouted. "Amazing!"

Elric stepped back and took two more swings through the air to see the blade transform. Then he made a series of powerful full-circle arcs. Then he broke into an all-out flurry of sword acrobatics. The blade blurred through the air as it whirled and spun and thrusted. Elric laughed. He continued to laugh when he finished and held the sword up.

"This is the most magnificent sword I have ever handled. The weight, the balance, the feel of the handle. It is perfect."

He touched his thumb against the edge of the blade. With the slightest touch, he cut his thumb. Light burst out of the cut, he jerked his hand back, and he yelped, "Ow."

"It is very sharp," Timrok said.

"Very sharp," Elric agreed. He held the sword up and examined the flat of the blade just below the handle. "And you have engraved the Morning Star on the blade."

"Every sword bears the sign of the team to which it belongs," Timrok said.

Elric put his hand on Timrok's shoulder. "You honor us with your gifts. Your skill as a craftsman is second only to your skill in battle. Thank you. The Lord bless you."

Timrok smiled. "With these tools, we will protect the King and usher in His kingdom on earth. Come, everyone. Receive your swords."

15

SETTING THE TRAP

Birth minus 20 months

Marr tapped his armrest and gazed across his throne room in the old temple in the ancient city of Babylon. The rubble that formed the hull of this old building resembled just an empty carcass compared to the splendor of the old days—days when worshipers would present sacrifices to their supposed idols—sacrifices and worship which he, the great prince, would devour as his own. Marr reveled in the sacred wickedness of this place. The state of ruins only added to the completeness of the destruction that had emanated from this spot for centuries. His seat of power rested here, and from here, he had all his available minions searching for a man and his fiancée who might be the ones chosen to bear the Messiah. So far, he had received hundreds of reports. However, he dismissed most as overzealous half-true possibilities promoted by glory–hungry inferiors. But this latest report showed promise.

"Are you sure?" Marr asked, "You have checked his genealogy? And his betrothed?"

"Yes, my lord," a demon lieutenant said.

Marr sat back and scratched his neck. "Very interesting news from the province in Egypt. Explain again the circumstances of the man's promotion."

The demon lieutenant grimaced. "It is not a report I wish to recount, my lord. However, if I have indeed found the couple being sought by my lord, perhaps my lord might accord me some honor in his domain?"

"You will tell me what I require at my word," Marr snapped. He paused, then added, "If your information proves useful, I may consider increasing your authority in a position I choose."

The hundred demons who were gathered around the throne snarled their disapproval.

The lieutenant scowled and proceeded with an upturned lip. "Without provocation, a high-ranking warrior of the King appeared and claimed authority over the treasury room and the chief treasurer. I was summoned and brought my own warrior with me to drive the enemy from the place. We were then ambushed by at least ten enemy warriors and had no choice but to retreat. I returned the next day to destroy the chief treasurer and install a new one. However, through trickery and pure chance, the enemy promoted their own man. His name is Benjamin. His fiancée is a young virgin by the name of Rachael. She remains in the house of her father in the eastern district. Benjamin has already moved into quarters within the palace. I have double checked—their lineages are suitable."

"Interesting. . . a remarkable promotion which puts their man right in the palace. It is exactly as our lord predicted." Marr tapped his talons on the armrests of his throne.

"And there is more, great prince," the lieutenant blurted out. "It appears an enemy lieutenant named Zaben arrived at the palace a month ago with five more warriors and has extended their perimeter."

"This has to be it," Marr growled through clenched teeth. "They are establishing a stronghold. If I know the enemy, they will continue to bring in forces a little at a time until their numbers are great. They will seal their man in where we cannot reach him. It matters not. We do not need to reach him. Not yet." Marr cackled and sat back on his throne. "The careless fools. They have revealed much, and now we know where to concentrate our efforts."

Marr stood, towering over the company around the base of his throne. "Benjamin and Rachael. These are the ones we have sought. I am so convinced of it that I am going to temporarily move my seat to Egypt to oversee the developments there. You two captains will go before me and prepare a place for me. I need a stronghold near enough to the palace to be able to respond, but not so close as to cause a disturbance. You have one week. I will follow when I finish some affairs here. The rest of you, prepare for our own buildup in Egypt. We should have a year to complete it, so coordinate your entry so as not to arouse attention. None of you are to attempt any attacks on the palace until I give the order—which will not be for a long time. We will wait until the moment is exactly right. Until then, I want to know every enemy warrior who comes in or out of the palace. Once I arrive, I will assign spies to try to penetrate their perimeter to learn all we can."

One of the captains asked, "Lord, shall we send word to our lord Satan about our findings?"

"Not yet," Marr replied with a long contemplative tone. "We shall wait until we know more. We have time."

The lieutenant who brought the news from Egypt said, "Great prince, if I have found favor in your eyes. . ."

"Yes, yes. You have done well." Marr sat forward and rested an elbow on his knee and his chin in the palm of his hand. After several moments, he sat back up. "I shall make you my personal aide. You shall serve me in my court."

Another lieutenant named Luchek who stood by roared, "No! That is my post, and I will not share it with another."

Marr gave a dismissive wave of his hand. "You are correct. You will not share the post. You are released from your duties. I have spoken."

16

PROPHET FORETOLD

Birth minus 16 months

Asmall demon named Tumur slunk around the Jewish temple in Jerusalem during the late–night hours. He controlled every silent breath. Every movement mimicked the mute shadows. Behind him, a raven squawked. Tumur flinched. His eyes darted left, right, up, behind. *Just a bird. Just a bird. Still, there is something in the air. Ever since Marr moved his headquarters to Egypt, the tension has been rising. Four months now. Something big is coming. Something. . .*

Motion in the inner court! He ducked around a corner. *What was that?* With his round bulging demon eyes, pointy ears with tufts of wiry hair, and the one stray fang that wouldn't stay behind his lip, he looked like a small, gaunt dog standing on its hind legs as he spied around the corner. There at the top of the steps leading to the temple, a dozen elzurim had just landed. *Strange, at this late hour of the night.*

He surveyed the courtyard of the priests. Dark, quiet. He turned back to the squad of angels. The largest, probably a captain, motioned with his hand, and without a word, the warriors fanned outward from the temple. One of the warriors, a lieutenant carrying two swords and no shield, flew to the top of the wall that separated the inner courts from the court of the Gentiles. The captain paced on the landing at the top of the temple steps.

Tumur's head made quick jerky movements. *Oh no! They are going to drive everyone out. I need to hide!* There—that raven, on the cleft of a ridge on the wall. *That will work!* Tumur leapt and squeezed his spiritual body into the flesh of the bird. At first, the raven jumped and squawked, but Tumur took control—fully possessing the flesh of his host. The nearest angelic warrior making the sweep turned his way. Tumur hopped in his raven shell behind a stone pillar. The angel moved on, and Tumur used the raven to fly to the top of the wall. His raven claws curled around the edge of the stone block and his head cocked sideways toward the inner courts. *I'll be able to see the whole operation from here.*

Below, one of the elzurim approached a small demon in the shadows. The angel spoke something and motioned with his drawn sword, and the tiny demon flittered off into the night.

The squad's radius expanded as they made their sweep. They cleared all beaelzurim from the courts of the priests and the Israelites, and the court of the women had nearly finished when one of the warriors encountered a demon too powerful to be driven away by the intimidation of a single elzurim warrior. From his perch on the wall, Tumur cocked his crow head and turned an eye toward the encounter below. The big demon in the court swatted the angel's sword aside with his own sword. The demon stood a full foot taller than the warrior in white, and he gave away no ground. He took a step forward and prepared his sword for a fight. Tumur hopped once. *Yes. Don't give way.*

Just then, the angelic lieutenant on top of the wall swooped down and squared up with the demon on the ground. *Oh, no. This is a powerful one.* Tumur couldn't hear the words spoken, but he could see the defiance in the demon's motions. The demon continued to stand his ground until the angelic lieutenant pulled his two swords and stepped forward. The other angel circled around to the side. The demon took two steps backward, scratched his taloned feet across the ground, and flew off. The lieutenant returned to his overlook.

Impressive operation—efficient, quiet, commanding. *But what is this all about?* He looked at the senturim towering at the corners of the temple grounds. These mighty guardians of sacred places struck fear in hearts of even the most powerful beaelzurim, and they monitored every movement within the temple compound. They remained uninvolved in the clandestine sweep, although they watched with wary scrutiny. The inner courts were cleared, and five of the elzurim stood guard around the inner perimeter. The remaining five continued outward. Tumur hopped to the edge of the wall facing outwards to follow their progress. *They're clearing the outer court, too. Why? For what do the host prepare?* A light from over the horizon streaked in toward Jerusalem. *Who could this be?* The angel flew low and very fast over the rooftops of the city. Without slowing, the angel shot through the back wall of the temple grounds and alighted on the steps just in front of the temple door. He greeted the captain there, and with one quick glance outward, he stepped into the temple.

Gabriel! Tumur almost squawked the name aloud. *That was Gabriel!*

———

For all the worshipers and priests, the next day proceeded like any other day in the temple courtyards. The priests presented the sin offerings and fellowship offerings. The smell of roasting flesh hung thick in the air. The priests slaughtered the sacrificial animals, preparing them in a prescribed manner and burning them on the altar. Elric and Timrok stood at the top of the temple steps and watched the production.

"With all my remote deployments, it has been a long time since I have watched the temple rituals," Timrok said. "It is a bloody business."

Elric nodded. "Sin is a serious matter. And death is its only payment."

"Yes, of course," Timrok said. "But the blood of these bulls and goats can never. . ."

"No. No, it's all about faith. It has always been about faith. Unfortunately, most people don't understand that all the laws, all the rituals. . . they were put in place to help man realize his desperate condition, so he would have to put his faith in the mercies of the King."

"At least man has a way to be restored."

A stern grimace fell over Elric's face. "Unlike the fallen ones."

"Mmm." Timrok rested his hands on his sword handles. "The sting of this is strong with them."

"Hatred fueled by jealousy is powerful indeed."

"Captain, the priests are gathering for the casting of lots," Timrok said, pointing to a small gathering.

"Yes, and we have work to do."

They walked down the steps, and Timrok asked, "Who is this Zacharias?"

Amongst the group of priests stood a stately elder. His long flowing beard had long ago lost the black color of youth and grown into a distinguished grey. He spoke with the others with his hands crossed behind his back and years of experience etched on his face.

Elric pointed out the priest and answered, "There he is. The King's word to him today will not be expected."

The gathering of priests turned deathly serious. Together they prayed for the Lord's direct guidance in the choosing of the one who would present the incense offering in the temple. Then, they cast their lots. Just as the lots fell, Elric stepped forward, spoke "Zacharias," and gave a simple wave of his hand.

"Zacharias!" one of the priests called out. "Zacharias will present the incense offering."

Elric smiled at Timrok.

Zacharias stood up tall, straightened his robes, and rubbed his hands together. Then, with pursed lips he began his ritual preparations.

"It is set," Elric said. "Now the difficult part. Once delivered, we must keep this word hidden from the enemy."

Timrok answered, "My team is prepared. We have layers of diversions in place, ready to execute as needed."

Elric nodded, crossed his arms, and scanned the courtyard. A whole multitude of worshipers gathered outside for prayer during the offering.

Zacharias completed his preparations, and he began his slow, pensive steps up to the temple door carrying the incense and fire. Elric followed. Timrok stayed behind.

"Be vigilant," Elric said as he made one last scan over the courtyard.

Timrok's hands rested on his swords. "We are ready, captain."

Elric stepped into the temple after Zacharias. Gabriel was waiting inside, standing just to the right of the altar of incense. Gabriel acknowledged Elric with a single head bow, and Elric took a place near the door. Zacharias went to work presenting the offering.

Once Zacharias finished and as the smoke of the incense rose to fill the room, Gabriel made his transformation into the Physical Realm. He faded in on a mist—quiet, slow, and gentle. His human-like form stood no more than ten feet tall, and he suppressed most of the glow he carried from standing in the presence of the King.

Zacharias hopped straight up like a startled cat, but he didn't land on his feet. He opened his mouth, but no sound came out. Flat on his backside, he pedaled with his feet until his back pressed hard against the side wall. Trembling, he hid his face behind his arms. Elric, who remained hidden, had seen this same reaction from men before, and he gave a slight smile to Gabriel who moved forward to deliver his message. There in the smoky fog of the holy place, a massive radiant spirit approached a frail man cowering in the corner. Elric had to restrain a chuckle.

Gabriel's voice rumbled low, full of authority. "Do not be afraid, Zacharias, for your petition has been heard, and your wife Elizabeth will bear you a son, and you will give him the name John. And you will have joy and gladness, and many will rejoice at his birth. For he will be great in the sight of the Lord, and he will drink no wine or liquor; and he will be filled with the Holy Spirit, while yet in his mother's womb. And he will turn back many of the sons of Israel to the Lord their God. And it is he who will go as a forerunner before Him in the spirit and power of Elijah, to turn the hearts of the fathers back to the children, and the disobedient to the attitude of the righteous; so as to make ready a people prepared for the Lord."

A thick silence fell.

After a few moments, Zacharias looked up and blinked. He struggled to his knees. Elric saw somewhere deep within Zacharias the hope for a child try to reignite, but as Zacharias strained to get his old bones off the hard floor and stand upright again, the reality of his situation choked the small light of hope from his eyes. With a faltering voice, he asked, "How shall I know this for certain? For I am. . ." He finally stood upright. "An. . . old man. . . and my wife is advanced in years."

Elric rubbed his forehead and shook his head. *Always, they doubt the word of the Lord, even when personally delivered by an angel.*

The great archangel's radiance grew until he became a blinding cloud of light. His booming voice echoed off the temple walls. "I am Gabriel, who stands in the presence of God; and I have been sent to speak to you, and to bring you this good news. And behold, you shall be silent and unable to speak until the day when these things take place, because you did not believe my words, which shall be fulfilled in their proper time."

Gabriel disappeared from the Physical Ream like a fading mist. In the Middle Realm, his silver eyes met Elric's. Gabriel shook his head and said to Elric, "This word must not be annulled by this man's words of unbelief." Gabriel approached the perplexed man and touched his throat. Then with a smile and a nod, Gabriel wrapped his wings around his body, lifted his head, and translated out of the Middle Realm.

This is perfect.

Elric passed through the temple door and gave Timrok a hand signal to stand by. Timrok nodded once.

The crowd below looked restless, and whispers shot back and forth: "What's taking so long?"

"It's been too long."

"Did the Lord strike him down?"

A few of the chief priests gathered near the entrance and conferred in a tight huddle.

The temple door cracked open, and then creaked open wide. Zacharias appeared through the entry, weak-kneed and shaking.

Two strong men propped him up and helped him out of the temple.

Voices from the crowd called out: "What happened?"

"Is he okay?"

"Why is he shaking?"

"Did he receive a word from the Lord?"

"What do you mean he can't speak?"

"What is going on up there?"

A raven landed on the stone cornice above the temple doorway.

At the top of the steps, the attending priests bunched around Zacharias. Zacharias motioned to them about something, but they could only determine through his excited gestures that he had seen something and that he couldn't speak a word. Someone brought him a tablet to write on, but his shaking hand could only produce an illegible jumble of words.

The priests examined the scrawling and scratched their heads. "Be a father?" the priests asked. "Elijah? John? What does this mean?"

Elric spoke to the priests. "Move Zacharias to a private place. This is not a word for the masses. Quickly, before the people become alarmed."

The raven cocked its head.

The priests looked down at the crowd.

"We have a most undesirable scene," one of the priests said. "We need to remove Zacharias from before the people."

"But what if he just saw a vision from the Lord? Should he not deliver it to the people?"

"Even if he did receive a word from Lord, he is unable to give it in his current condition. I say we see to this in private."

"I agree."

"I agree."

The priests ushered him to one of the back rooms off the priests' courtyard. Five senior priests and Zacharias went inside. Elric accompanied them.

"Now," said the chief elder, "calm down and start from the beginning." He handed Zacharias the tablet. The priests all watched as Zacharias wrote.

"An angel?" the chief elder said. "You saw an angel?"

Zacharias nodded like a wild man and motioned to his throat with his hands.

"And the angel took your voice?" the elder asked.

Zacharias nodded again.

"What did the angel say?"

As Zacharias wrote, the priests looked at each other with flabbergasted eyes. They crossed their arms, stroked their beards, and raised their eyebrows.

"You're going to be a father. . . Elizabeth. . . in her old age. . . a son. . . John. . . Elijah." The priest's eyes brightened. "You saw Elijah?"

Zacharias shook his head with an emphatic "no."

"Zacharias, you are making no sense," the elder said. "Here, stand over here for a moment."

Zacharias bounced and shuffled in the corner while the other priests gathered in a tight circle. Elric joined the circle.

"What are we to do with this?" the chief elder said to the group. "A notable vision has been witnessed today."

"I think Zacharias is confused," one of the others said. "Look at him. I fear he has gone mad."

"I do not believe that," another said. "He is an upright man, faithful in his duties, and not prone to wild stories. I think he really saw something in the temple. I think he heard a word from the Lord."

"But look at him! Does that look like a sane man who. . ."

The chief elder interrupted. "Let's assume he has not gone mad. What do we do with the message he received?"

"This is not a message for the people," Elric said to the group. His words floated like tiny clouds in the Middle Realm and sank into the men's spirits.

The priests stood in silence.

One of the priests spoke up. "I believe he saw something. But the message. . . seemed to be. . . a personal one. A word for only his family."

The others nodded.

"I agree," one of the others said. "He does not have a prophecy for all the people."

The chief elder crossed his arms and straightened his back. "It is settled, then," he said. "this incident will remain private. We will speak of it to no one, and we will instruct Zacharias to do the same."

Elric smiled. *Perfect.*

————

Tumur hopped from his perch on the doorway cornice and flew back to the top of the inner court wall.

Gabriel. Elijah. A secret message. I have found the prophet! And the man came out of the temple dumbstruck—he must have doubted the word from Gabriel.

He used the raven's wings to fly to a rooftop at the edge of Jerusalem. He then left the bird's body and headed straight for the regional headquarters. *There is sure to be excitement over the happenings on the temple grounds today, but I'll be the only one with answers.*

He entered the room of the headquarters, crammed with dozens of demons clamoring for attention. The captain up front scowled and barked intermittent vulgarities. Tumur smirked. *None of them know anything.*

"I was there!" Tumur shouted above the chaos. "I saw everything. I know what happened."

The captain held up his hand and shouted, "Quiet!" He pointed a crooked finger at Tumur and said, "You! You have useful information for me?"

All the others turned and sneered at Tumur.

Tumur lifted his chin and pulled his upper lip tight, exposing his jagged fangs. "A messenger was sent to give a word of prophecy to one of the priests during the offering of incense."

"Really?" the captain said. "Tell us, little one—what was the message?"

Tumur paused. *Wait! If I tell everything I know, there will be an entire team assigned and I'll be left out.*

"He never delivered it," Tumur answered with a teasing tone.

The captain leaned forward and with an upturned lip said, "The host seal off the inner courts, bring in a messenger, and the messenger does not deliver the message? This is difficult to believe."

"No, the messenger gave the message to the priest. But the priest never delivered it to the people." Tumur paused for effect. "Because just before he could, I stole his voice."

Every spirit in the room erupted in laughter.

"It's true!" Tumur shouted. "The man's name is Zacharias, and he is completely dumb. I was in the perfect position. So, when he came out of the temple, before he could say a word, I struck him."

"And you were able to do this without being seen?"

Tumur stepped up, eyes bulging, and with unflinching grit he answered, "It is my expertise. It is what I do."

The resulting silence proved no one could counter his claim.

Tumur continued, "As it is, the message was for him alone. He wrote on a tablet that he saw a vision that he was going to have a son.

The high priests didn't even have him relay the message in writing to the congregation."

"That is peculiar," the captain said. "Why all the secrecy? The man's woman—is she a virgin?"

"No. They are both old. In fact, they are past childbearing years. I think that is why the enemy took all the precautions. God wants to give this couple a miraculous birth and wanted them to know it was He who accomplished it. Other than opening an old womb, this is nothing of significance. In fact, the messenger who brought the message was not even anybody of note."

The captain rubbed the back of his neck. "Still, I think we should watch this Zacharias."

"No," shouted Tumur. He then bowed his head and lowered his voice. "I mean, my lord, this matter is not worthy of your consideration. It is not significant enough for even one of your line warriors. If it pleases my lord, I shall watch him and see if anything important develops. Spying is my expertise, and you need all your forces for more worthy things."

The captain made a low gurgling growl and stared into space. Finally, he announced, "The matter of the disturbance at the temple today is settled. My spy has uncovered the truth of the enemy's activities. For your diligence, Tumur, I grant your petition. Watch Zacharias and his son. Report to me anything that relates to our primary mission. The rest of you—return to your assignments."

17

HUNT

Birth minus 16 months

The demon lieutenant Luchek, who had been displaced as Marr's personal aide, trudged down the middle of the street in a small village in the eastern province of Egypt, his sword drawn and tip dragging in the dirt behind him. His left eye scowled down the street. His right eye pinched half closed from a disfigured socket.

Marr had no right to dismiss me. He growled and snorted. *I served him faithfully for all those years. And with no regard for my honor, he replaces me with an insignificant underling who failed his last mission. It matters not. I am free now to create real change. While celebrities like him spend generations working to erode a civilization by desensitizing people toward moral depravity, I can be out on the front lines actually doing the work.*

People, oblivious to his presence, passed by him on the street. "Look at her," he whispered to a young man who passed by. "You want her. Undress her in your mind. Release your lust."

The man stopped for a moment, and Luchek's words melted into his spirit. The man gawked at a young woman in the marketplace ahead—lingering, lingering.

Luchek laughed. The man moved on, and Luchek continued walking. *And, while this so–called Prince of Persia plans some long–term strategy for the coming Messiah, I will strike at the heart of the King's plan and become renowned for my quick and decisive action. We shall see then whose honor is the most excellent.* His dark red skin with large black scab-like blotches twitched.

He sheathed his sword and stood by the side at the marketplace. At first, nothing of value presented itself. But then, a boisterous man caught his attention. He appeared to be a customer who had some issue with a vendor and grew increasingly agitated and belligerent. The vendor stood his ground and became angry. Stationed between the man and the vendor stood a small demon with sunken eyes and bulbous ears. His words of poison and self-righteous superiority penetrated both men and elevated the contention into an all–out shouting match.

Luchek nodded his head and laughed. "You there," he called to the demon. "Come here. I have questions for you."

The little demon shot some final words of strife into the two men and sauntered over to Luchek. "What?" he said. His tone dripped with disrespect.

"I seek someone," Luchek said. "You are familiar with this region?"

"I am."

"I seek a young girl named Rachael. A Hebrew virgin betrothed to a man named Benjamin. Do you know of her?"

"Why is everyone so interested in this girl?"

"What do you mean?"

"You are not the first to ask about her."

Luchek balled up his fists. *Others are already at work. I need to act fast.* "My business does not concern you. Tell me about the girl."

The little demon snarled and turned away. Luchek pulled his sword, grabbed the demon by the back of his wiry hair, and swung the sword edge around until it pressed against his bare neck.

"Tell me."

"Yes, yes, all right."

Luchek let down his blade and spun the demon back around.

"As I told the others," said the demon, "she is nobody special. She lives here, just outside the village in a house with her father and grandmother. Her mother died when she was young, and her father raised the children with only the help of the children's grandmother. Rachael is the youngest and the last of the children left at home. She is betrothed to a man named Benjamin, who recently received a major promotion. He plans to move her into the proconsul's palace after they wed."

"Take me to her house so I may see her."

"I can do better than that. That's her right over there," the little demon said, pointing.

"Excellent," Luchek said.

The little demon turned toward Rachael and asked, "Why is this girl so important?"

He turned back to Luchek, but Luchek had disappeared.

Luchek stalked the girl, Rachael, from a distance. *So, this is the girl. So young. So innocent.* He scanned the whole area for angelic protectors. His leathery lips formed a wicked smile. *So vulnerable. I need to find a man if I hope to reach her. I need a human body to indwell.*

He sauntered down the street, eyeing every man. *Not this one. No. Not you. Not you. Definitely not you. You might. . . no, I don't think so. What I need is. . . wait, what's this?*

A man staggered in the shadows of an alley. Drunk, perhaps? More importantly, was he already possessed by some other demon? Luchek stepped up to the man. The man's eyes followed him as he approached. The eyes of men can't see into the Middle Realm—there must be a spirit within. Luchek smirked.

"I have a job that requires the flesh of a man," Luchek said.

The man's head bobbled, but his eyes stayed fixed on Luchek. "I own this man," the man's voice said. His voice sounded low and gravelly—unhuman.

"With your consent, I wish to use him for a critical mission," Luchek said. "We can share the action—and the glory."

"Come in," the demon said through the man's voice.

Luchek smiled and stepped forward. He closed his eyes and entered the flesh of the man.

Luchek opened his eyes and looked out at the world through a human lens. A breeze bristled the hair on the man's arms, and Luchek savored the sensation.

"Tell me your name," the resident demon said.

"Luchek. Thank you for sharing your man. I sense he has a seared conscience, is full of perverse thoughts, and is open to vile suggestions."

"He is easily controlled. We are veterans of many exploits. With a single strike, I can uproot dozens of lives. Anger, hatred, shame, emotional and spiritual scars that never heal."

Luchek laughed. "Today, I give you an opportunity to extend your reach."

"Do you have a special target?" the resident demon asked.

"Yes, one that the King intends to have carry the coming messiah. I have come from the secret counsel of Marr, and we know who she is."

"She must be young and unmarried to fulfill the prophecy."

"And our mission is to spoil her. A plan which will destroy lives, obstruct the King's plan, and bring us great recognition."

"Then I am with you. And my man here can get the job done."

———

The man in the alley could feel the darkness swirling within. That night, he hardly slept. It had been months since his last attack, and he could feel the hunger building. The fitful sweats and waking dreams he had come to know seemed twice as strong as usual.

The next day at the marketplace, his eyes devoured every woman who passed by. *No, I have to wait for just the right one. The right one will come along.* She always did. Without her knowing it, she would call to him and he would know.

The hunger of the morning turned into the frustration of the late afternoon, and he still hadn't found the right one. A few passed by who would do, but something prevented him from following through. He didn't know why, but none of them seemed right. When night came, he gave up the search.

He suffered worse that night than the night before. He found no sleep at all as he replayed his previous conquests and rehearsed his next in the dark dungeons of his mind. Morning brought more frustration. Finally, in the mid-afternoon, a special girl caught his eye—young, very beautiful, and she floated like a princess. Her deep brown eyes had an innocent sparkle that called to him. *This is the one!* He overheard someone call her "Rachael," but her name didn't matter—she was the one. Now, he needed to follow her and watch for his opportunity.

He had no trouble trailing her through the busy city. He bustled amongst the people and ducked behind the buildings and into alleys. It took her some time to finish her daily errands, but he didn't mind. Stalking her through the streets made his pulse race and heightened all his senses. He felt like a giant cobra—silent, undetected, powerful—slithering in the shadows, hunting his helpless little mouse.

He found no opportunity to make a move in the busy town in broad daylight. He would have to follow her home. He had to use more cunning to stay unseen throughout the journey to her house, but for this skilled hunter, the challenge only added to the excitement.

The girl finally came to a small stone and mortar house with a thatched roof and a stable out back. She disappeared into the house and left a new set of questions. *How many others are in the house? Father? Mother? Grandparents? Brothers? Should I dare go into the house? Probably not—too risky without knowing who else might be in there.* He would have to wait and watch.

From his concealed position, he began his watch. Rachael came out a back door and tended to the donkey in the stable. The man snuck over to the stable and peered through the slats of the side wall. Rachael brought the donkey water and straw and spent time stroking its head and neck like a pet.

Take her! Take her now!

Now? In the full light of day?

She's alone! There's no one here to. . .

An older man stepped out of the back door. "Come Rachael. It will be dark soon."

Must be her father. The mighty hunter ducked low. *So, she lives at home with her parents. I have to figure out how to separate her from whoever is in there. I could wait until morning after the father leaves for the day and then catch her on the trail as she goes to town.*

Or, perhaps I could somehow lure her outside into the darkness of the night.

Yes, I like that much better. But how? The donkey. If I could disturb the donkey, maybe she would be the one to come out to settle it down. If the father comes out, I'll just hide and wait for morning. But if she comes out. . . yes. . . it would be perfect.

For now, more waiting.

Someone inside prepared a savory supper, which filled the air with a warm aroma. The man's mouth watered, but his real hunger could not be satisfied by food. Muffled voices filled the evening. Soon lamps inside the house stood watch against the falling curtain of the moonless night.

Eventually, the lamps and the voices went silent and dark. The night settled into pitch black. The mighty cobra slid into place near the back of the stable and waited a while longer. Motionless, his heart pounding, his brow sweating, his hands trembling, the power within continued to build. The time had come—he could wait no more. He took one step forward, and a mere twitch of his shoulder sent the donkey into a restless stir. It acted as though someone, or something, else stood there in front of it.

Why is this donkey getting so spooked? He pressed back into the darker shadows, but the donkey became more and more agitated.

A dim oil lamp flickered from within the house.

Here it comes. . . here it comes. . . please be her. . .

18

FIRST STRIKE

Birth minus 16 months

*L*uchek savored the moment, waiting for Rachael to emerge from her house and into his trap. He snarled again at the donkey and stomped his foot in the Middle Realm. The donkey jerked away and pressed back into the stall until its hind quarters smashed against the back wall.

Funny how animals can sense our presence and men are so blind.

The metal latch of the house back door made a loud *clunk.* Luchek gave a brief glance at the door and jumped back into the man's body hiding in the shadows.

Luchek took a deep breath, and the man's chest rose and fell. *I love being embodied. Seeing through a man's eyes. Adrenaline pumping through his blood. The prickly cool of the night against the flesh of mortal skin. Direct control over a man's body. This man, created by the great*

King, serves as a helpless puppet for me to command. And now, I—the
great Luchek—will use this pitiful piece of flesh against the King.

The back door of the house swung open. A tentative lamp
emerged.

Please be her.

Rachael stepped out, held the lamp up at arm's length, and
squinted past the muted ring of light the lamp made on the ground.
Luchek smiled a crazed, evil smile. His eyes became wide. *I knew she*
would come, and now I will have her.

Rachael stepped toward stable, probing the darkness around
the stable with the lamp. She approached the donkey with soothing,
quiet words. "It's okay, girl. Settle down. What's the matter, Adah?
It's okay. Shhhh." She stroked the donkey and talked to it, and her
calming presence brought peace back to the stable.

Now!

Luchek used the man's body to leap from the shadows behind
her, wrap his powerful arms around her, and cover her mouth with
his hand. He dragged her behind the stable—her legs kicking and
flailing the dust. A perfect attack—not even a whisper of sound to
alarm anyone that she had fallen into his grasp.

At least, not anyone human.

A warrior in white appeared from inside the house. With a loud
war cry, he and his shining sword hurtled forward.

"Finish the job!" Luchek shouted to the resident demon within
the man, and he exploded out of the man's body to meet the oncoming
angel. As Luchek exited, the man stumbled and lost the grip over
Rachael's mouth.

Rachael's horrified scream shredded the quietness of the night,
but the man quickly muffled it. The donkey began to bray and kick,

and in its frenzy, it knocked the oil lamp into a pile of loose straw. A blaze erupted in the dry straw.

The elzur warrior and Luchek met just above the stable and sent spiritual sparks shooting from their crashing steel blades. With a smaller, less powerful frame, the angel's blade yielded ground with every blow. Luchek laughed. *I will have this foe bound and out of the way in short order.*

The angel disengaged and dove to the ground toward Rachael. Luchek sprang downward, landed both feet on the angel's chest, and sent him somersaulting backward. The angel jumped back to his feet in an instant and ducked around the corner of the burning stable. He made another move toward Rachael. Luchek headed him off. Just then, out of the distant darkness, a small fireball sizzled in and smashed into the angel's right shoulder. He spun twice and landed on his face.

Where did that come from? Luchek turned toward the dark field behind the house. From the far tree line, three demon warriors emerged with swords drawn. *Who are these poachers? I don't need their help. And I certainly won't share the glory of this victory with them.*

A flash of light from behind. The angel had jumped back up, and now he dodged through the flames on a path toward Rachael.

First, I need to dispatch this pesky elzur defender.

The other three demons streaked in, and the angel shot upward just as they arrived. *Very well. You three take care of him. I'll take care of the girl.* Luchek strutted over to Rachael and stood over her like a trophy while the man continued his attack.

A heated battle swirled in the air above the burning stable, and the man at Luchek's feet tore at Rachael's clothes. Motion from the house? *Oh no! Rachael's father!*

The father rushed toward them, yelling as he went.

Luchek snorted. *Oh, no, you don't.*

Luchek shouted at the attacker, "Watch out! Use the shovel!" His words shot into the man like arrows of fire. The man's eyes grew wide and wild.

Rachael's father drew within a few strides, and the attacker reached for a nearby shovel. Without losing grip of Rachael, he swung the shovel in a wide upward arc and caught the father on his right temple. The force of the impact lifted him off his feet and sent him flying backward. He landed with a lifeless thud, and a flood of blood soaked into the thirsty dust.

Rachael screamed, "Oh, God, help me. Help me!"

The flames of the spreading fire reached the stable roof. Luchek roared with laughter. All Rachael's hopes of escaping were being consumed like the dry straw in the stable. *Victory is within my grasp.*

———

Night had fallen over Jerusalem, and Elric and Timrok stood beside Zacharias's bed in the visiting priests' quarters near the temple. Zacharias slept hard after a full day of duties at the temple while Elric and Timrok reviewed their progress.

"I am pleased," Elric said to Timrok. "We brought in Gabriel undetected. His message was contained. And the incident in the temple was quickly lost in the busyness of the daily routines. These last two days have been quiet, and in the morning, Zacharias will return home."

Timrok folded his arms and looked down at Zacharias sleeping. "And there were plenty of priestly duties that didn't require Zacharias to speak, so he was able to complete his rotation with the rest of his division."

Elric chuckled. "Did you see him, though? His heart was not here. You could see the word simmering within him. He can't wait to get home to share the good news with Elizabeth."

A light flashed, and Grigor appeared before Elric.

"Grigor! What a surprise."

"A word of the Lord for the captain."

Elric and Grigor stepped aside, and Elric bent down and turned his ear toward Grigor's mouth. Elric nodded as Grigor spoke. Grigor turned and vanished.

"That little one is fast," Timrok said.

"Quickly," Elric said, "gather your team. I have an assignment."

The desert floor rushed by in a blur as Timrok and his team streaked low over the horizon. Timrok outpaced his team. *Can't slow down for them. Every second—so crucial.* With each second that ticked by, he pressed harder and harder. *There it is!* A burning building in the distance. With both swords extended, he began his war shout. Three more wing beats and an enemy target came into view.

Timrok crashed into Luchek like a screaming meteor and sent Luchek tumbling into a nearby field. The smoke from the explosive collision parted, and Timrok stood in a cloud of light with both swords at the ready. A quick assessment—three beaelzurim warriors surrounded him; an elzur warrior lay bound in the dirt; a possessed man was attacking a helpless girl; and another man lay wounded or dead.

Timrok roared, "For the King!" and vaulted upward in a tight flip. He came down beside the bound angel and freed him with a clean slice through his cords.

"You help the girl," Timrok said to the angel.

Timrok lunged toward the attacking man. He drove his sword through the back of the possessed man, and the resident demon shot out with a shriek, spun around, and formed up with the other three demons in a semicircle surrounding Timrok. Together, they raised their swords, shouted, and leapt inward. In mid-leap, Timrok's full team burst into the fray. They smashed the four demons into the ground. The demons scraped themselves up and scattered away like roaches in sunlight.

Timrok turned back to the man, who was rising to his knees with a dazed look and glassy eyes. The angel who had been with Rachael from the beginning knelt beside her and urged her, "Fight him, quickly, now is your chance!"

Rachael drew her knees up to her chest. The angel wrapped his hands around her thigh and spoke, "Strength!" Rachael placed her feet against her attacker's chest and released a desperate kick. The man launched upward—as if kicked by ten men—and stumbled back. Back, back, he stumbled until he smacked hard against the rear panels of the stable.

Rachael scrambled to her feet, but then stopped. The man remained frozen, glued to the wall. He made a low wheezing, gurgling sound and began twitching all over. In the light of the growing fire, blood frothed from his mouth and trickled down his face and neck. The end of a large hook from the back of the stable wall protruded from his chest. As he hung twitching on the hook, Rachael turned and retched.

Timrok knelt beside Rachael's father as the rest of his team watched the attacker's life drain away. The attacker's final strained breath passed, and the angels lowered their heads and all stepped backward and aside, making a path.

From the darkness a large, ominous demon appeared and approached the man through the parted band of angels. They did not engage him but continued backing away and dissolved into the surroundings. The spirit of the man stepped out of his body and stood before the imposing demon. The man looked back at the lifeless shell of his flesh with a perplexed expression.

"What is happening?" he asked the demon. "Am I dead?"

The demon nodded.

"But how can I see myself and be standing here talking with you if I'm dead?"

The demon's gravelly voice had an obvious tone of impatience. "Because you are more than flesh and bone. You are a spiritual being who had a physical body. Your body is now dead, but your spirit continues." The demon produced a pulsing black cord of energy and bound the man head to foot with a single unceremonious whip of the cord. He gripped the bindings between the man's shoulder blades and lifted him off the ground.

"What is this?" The man's voice changed from disbelief to panic. "What are you doing? Where are you taking me?"

"You fool!" the demon hissed. "Did you really think you could live for your flesh and never see the end of your days? You have an entire lifetime to answer for. You have earned your wages, and now you will reap what you have sown. And there is no covering for your iniquities." The demon wheezed an evil laugh. "So, you will have to pay the price yourself."

As the two disappeared into the darkness, the man continued to object. "There has to be a mistake. . . I didn't know. . . it's not my fault!"

Timrok, kneeling beside Rachael's father, stared into the dark emptiness left by the departing spirits. His eyes welled. He dabbed his left eye with his left shoulder. Then his right. He looked over toward Rachael, who stood like a battered reed, wiping her mouth and eyes, and staring at the dead stranger hanging before her. The fire had overtaken the whole stable, and the flames licked at his clothes and skin. The smell of roasting flesh filled the air. She turned her head away from the macabre scene—away from the attacker and toward. . .

"Father!" She staggered over, dropped to her knees, and peeled his blood–matted hair off his face with her fingertips. "There's so much blood. How can this be happening?"

She knelt beside him, sobbing and rocking back and forth. Timrok stroked her hair and spoke, "Strength of the Lord. Peace. Peace. Peace." His words settled like clouds of light over her spirit, but few of them broke through. Several minutes passed. Timrok shook his head. *His time is almost come.*

Timrok bent over and whispered, "Wake up. Open your eyes. You need to say goodbye to someone." He pressed the glowing cloud of his words into the father's forehead with his hand.

The father's eyelids twitched. He opened them halfway. Then he blinked twice and looked up.

"Father!" Rachael squealed. "Oh, you're still here. . . "

With a peaceful smile, he whispered, "Rachael. . ." His eyelids drooped closed, and he took his last breath.

Rachael wailed.

Her father stood up out of his body, and Timrok stood to meet him. Another angel walked up from behind and joined them. The three looked down at the broken figure on the ground. For several moments, they spoke no words at all.

The father surveyed the whole scene. "I'm dead, aren't I?"

Timrok gave him an affirming smile.

"Then am I an angel now?"

Timrok responded with a patient, understanding smile. "No, you are a man, born of the race of Adam. *I* am an angel, a created race in the service of the King. My comrade here is also an angel, and he has been sent to take you to a place of rest."

"But what about my baby girl? What about my Rachael?"

"She is in the Lord's hands. It is time for you to let go now. There is Someone who is looking forward to seeing you face to face."

The father nodded, looked down at Rachael, and nodded again. The escort put his hand on his shoulder. They turned, walked into a cloud of light, and disappeared.

Rachael slumped over the lifeless body of her father while the raging fire crackled behind her. The orange embers of the blaze shot high into the sky.

Timrok said to the angel assigned to Rachael, "Comfort her while I await orders from the King."

Timrok's warriors gathered in a circle around him. He stood with his swords sheathed, his hands across his chest, his head bowed, and his eyes closed. Within seconds and without a sound, Grigor alighted in front of Timrok.

"A word of the Lord," Grigor announced.

Timrok knelt for a private conversation.

"In His service," Timrok said, standing back up.

"By His word," Grigor replied. He unfurled his wings and disappeared.

Timrok said with a tone low and steady, "Go and find the demon called Luchek. He is nearby. Capture him and bring him to me."

Five bolts of lightning shot outward. Timrok glanced at the stable fire, dispatching large glowing cinders onto the thatched roof of the house. Already the house roof began to smolder. *This operation is not done yet.*

Several minutes later his team returned with a writhing demon in their grips. Although bound with glowing white cords of energy, it still took two of Timrok's warriors to handle him. They set him down and pressed him forward at sword-point until he stood face to face with Timrok.

"You are Luchek?"

The demon spit.

"Luchek, your little plan has failed."

"Oh, I think not. I may not have spoiled the girl, but my efforts have left two dead so far, and the night is not over."

"Innocent blood has been spilled here tonight. The ground cries out to the High King. Here is His message to you. Go back and tell your master that because of the innocent blood that was shed here, this has been declared hallowed ground. No demonic force may come within ten miles of this place for seven years. If any dares to approach, he will be instantly cut down and banished to the abyss."

Luchek looked at the fire spreading over the roof of the house and sneered a wicked smile at Timrok. "So what? By the time the sun comes up tomorrow, there will be nothing left here anyway."

Timrok gave Luchek a shove backward and drew his swords. He spun them in wide interweaving arcs—faster and faster until they became a blur of light. He took one step forward.

"What are you doing?" Luchek rasped.

Timrok took another step.

"Stop! You wouldn't attack a helpless prisoner?"

Timrok took another step. The blades whizzed all around Luchek.

"No!" Luchek cried. "No. . . you can't. . ."

Timrok's blades changed orbits and shredded the bindings that held Luchek. Not a single passing blade touched him. Timrok stopped the swords in an instant. And then with a single flick of his right sword, he swung upwards and nicked the side of Luchek's neck.

"Ahh!" Yellow sulfurous smoke escaped the wound.

"Be gone." Timrok said. "Report the message."

Luchek flittered off.

Timrok turned back toward Rachael. She had been weeping the whole time and hadn't noticed how far the fire had spread. A failing beam of the roof snapped. She looked up and screamed. Flames engulfed the entire roof of the house, and thick clouds of smoke belched from the within the house.

She jumped up and screamed again. "Oh, no, Grandmother!" She hobbled headlong toward the inferno.

With every step, the angel called out to her. "It's too dangerous. It's too late. Don't go in."

Timrok muttered, "She refuses to hear."

Covering her nose and mouth with the sleeve of her tunic, she plunged into the thick smoke. Only brief moments later, a horrendous crash rocked the entire house. The roof collapsed under its molten weight. More innocent blood called out to heaven.

19

DUST CLOUDS

Birth minus 16 months

Benjamin strapped on his leather chariot boots by lamplight in the pre-dawn morning inside his home within the palace compound. Humming and grinning, he packed food and water provisions for the day. He stepped out into the cool darkness and took a deep breath of the beautiful, crisp air. He hummed his happy tune in time with his lively steps all the way to the proconsul's livery stables. He came around the corner and found two Roman soldiers already prepared with three chariots ready to go.

"Good morning," Benjamin called out with a sing-song voice. "It is a beautiful day. Thank you for accommodating me on such short notice. I am very excited. Let's get going." Benjamin jumped up into the back of his chariot, still grinning, and snapped the reins.

He drove eastward toward the glowing horizon, flanked on each side by his obligatory team of Roman soldiers. Amid the clattering of the wheels and the thundering of the six horses' hooves, the entourage kicked up a swirling cloud of pale dust. A brisk wind blew through his hair, and he looked back at the receding city through the dust cloud and laughed. "What a day!"

All the times he had made this trip as the treasurer of the eastern region were all business. Today, this trip was personal. *I can't believe the way my schedule opened up so I could make this trip. How did that happen?*

He squinted at the rising sun and gave the reins another snap.

So many exciting things have happened so quickly—chief treasurer, a house in the palace, a wedding in six months—have I stepped into a dream?

The spinning wheels of the chariots rattled, and time and the countryside passed by like blur.

Rachael is going to be so surprised. I can't wait to see her face. I miss her so much. Six months! And then she'll be in the palace with me. Only six months—I have so much to get done. First, I need to talk with the rabbi.

The chariots pressed on. The list of pre-wedding tasks and the list of unexpected blessings mixed into the blur. *What have I ever done to deserve this?* A familiar hill appeared just ahead on the right. *Has it been almost three hours already?*

He gave a little jump in his chariot. Rachael's house was just around that hill. He laughed out loud and gave his galloping team another snap of the reins. It wouldn't be long now. His heart raced as fast at the thumping hooves of the horses.

They rounded the corner, and his racing heart leapt up into his throat. Instead of the welcome sight of Rachael's family's home rising to meet another beautiful day, a smoldering site of ashen desolation lay before them. The stone walls still stood, but the roof and doors were gone, and a few lingering wisps of black smoke rose from what must have been a horrific fire. Angry scorch marks scarred all the walls.

They drew nearer. Tufts of smoke rose from behind the house—even the stable had been destroyed. He pressed his team even harder, racing as fast as he could to the threshold of the house. Pulling his team to a stop, he jumped out of the chariot and stumbled to where the front door used to stand. One of the soldiers joined him. The other began a reconnaissance sweep of the surrounding area, beginning with the nearest side of the house. Benjamin stood dumbfounded, trying to take it all in. From the smoldering embers, it looked as though the fire had just happened. But what caused it? And more importantly, where were Rachael and her family?

He stepped into the charred rubble. Broken pieces of pottery and vases lay half-exposed under the dry black carbon and white ash remains. He took light, slow, and cautious steps. The centurion tromped through with the detached efficiency of a hardened soldier. Benjamin shook his head and covered his mouth with his hand. Everything that could burn had been completely devoured. Things that couldn't burn were either disfigured by the heat or stung by the black tails of the flames.

The centurium called from the back bedroom, "Sir!"

Benjamin quickened his steps. He came around the corner. His heart fell from his throat to the very pit of his stomach. There, next to the far wall of the bedroom, lay three bodies covered by a single large blanket. The blanket, with its bright colors, looked out of place amongst all the black. Whoever laid these bodies here side by side and then covered them must have done so after the fire had run its course.

The centurion stood aside and waited. Tears carved valleys down Benjamin's dust–caked face. Many questions still needed answers, but the one about where Rachael and her family were just became all too clear.

The second soldier burst into the room. "Sir, I found a donkey wandering in a nearby field with a burnt rope. He must have—" His words cut short.

Benjamin didn't acknowledge the news from outside the walls. He stood with his hand over his mouth, holding back the sobs of unbelief and wiping away the flood of tears that blinded his eyes. Finally, he motioned to one of his companions—he had to see under the blanket to know for sure. With respectful care, the centurion peeled back the blanket from one corner until the hidden figures were revealed.

Benjamin gasped at the gruesome carnage. Even the hard Roman soldiers winced. Benjamin lumbered to the far corner of the room and retched. After several minutes, he staggered back to the site. Approaching the three bodies, he dropped to his knees and kept shaking his head. The two bodies nearest the wall had been burned. The one closest to him showed no signs of burns at all.

"This one. . . was my future father-in-law."

He had a horrible gash on the front of his head and blood all over his face and head and neck. Whatever happened to him must have been a violent event. The other two bodies looked like grotesque charred pieces of dry black meat pulled tight over partially exposed bones. Their clothes and hair had been consumed, and their flesh had been roasted down to almost nothing. They were human, but identifying them would be impossible. Through strained glances, Benjamin looked for anything familiar about the two.

"I can't even tell if they were male or female." But his twisted stomach and constricted throat echoed what his mind didn't want to believe. He ran outside and wept from the utter depths of his soul.

After some time, the soldiers joined Benjamin outside. "Somebody knows what happened here," one of the soldiers said. "Rachael's father was obviously laid here after the fire, and somebody covered them. We're going to the nearby houses and see if anyone knows anything."

Benjamin nodded.

The two soldiers headed off in different directions and left Benjamin alone in the dead silence. He crumpled down, leaned his back against the front of the house, and put his head down on his knees.

———

Lacidar stood outside Zacharias and Elizabeth's home in Judea, facing the road to Jerusalem and watching for the telltale cloud of dust from the trail. Zacharias had been away in Jerusalem for a long time, but his rotation finished yesterday, and he would be home today. The rest of Lacidar's team provided escort. Lacidar had stayed alone with Elizabeth.

She had been puttering around the house for days. Cleaning this, fidgeting with that. Today she spent the entire morning preparing Zacharias's favorite meal. All morning she stole peeks down the long path through the Judean hills for the small dust cloud that would give away his coming. One time, she laughed at herself—behaving like an anxious little girl. But that didn't stop her from checking again only minutes later.

Lacidar remained more reserved. However, he too paced. Zacharias carried world–changing news. *To see this family's prayers answered after all these years would have been enough to fill my cup of joy, but for their son to be the prophet that goes before the Lord— it surpasses anything I could have dreamed.* He scanned the horizon again. There! A flash of a blade—a signal from one of his team on the left. Then a flash from the right. Minutes later, the faint fringes of a small cloud of dust from behind the nearest hill. He stepped inside to see if Elizabeth had seen it, too. She had.

Elizabeth's fidgeting began in earnest. She made last–minute touches to the meal, to the table, to her hair, to a dozen things that didn't need last–minute touches. One final check—yes, the cloud had cleared the knoll, and yes, the familiar form of Zacharias walked in the middle of it.

One of Lacidar's warriors stepped through the front wall. A smile and a nod let Lacidar know all had gone well. The warrior stepped back out and stood guard. Several minutes later, when Zacharias came clattering through the door, Elizabeth had her back to it, stirring something over the fire. Two of Lacidar's team entered with him.

"Oh, is that you dear?" Elizabeth called over her shoulder. "Be sure to wash that dreadful dust off your feet and come sit down for lunch. You have to be tired and hungry from the trip. Come, come. How was your time in Jerusalem?"

He crossed the room without a sound. Elizabeth turned and gave a startled hop and slapped him on his chest with a laugh. For a moment, he just stood there. He didn't say a word, but Lacidar could see something in his eyes—more than a twinkle, more than a glow. It was like peering into a wildfire. Then from behind his dusty beard and mustache, he erupted with a full–toothed smile and wrapped her up in a huge hug. He lifted her off the floor and swung her around in circles as she laughed some objections she really didn't mean. With her feet back on the ground, she gave him a tentative welcome home kiss and held him at arm's length with her hands on the sides of his shoulders. She gazed into his eyes with raised eyebrows.

"What is it? What happened?"

He grinned and made some motions with his hands.

"Oh, come on Zacharias, don't play games. Tell me what happened."

He laughed, but no sound came out.

"What's the matter? You're scaring me."

He motioned for her to calm down and sit as he went for a writing tablet. She looked confused.

Lacidar and the two warriors stood with arms crossed. Lacidar didn't even try to restrain his grin.

On a tablet, Zacharias scrawled, "I saw a vision in the temple. The Lord has taken my voice for a time." He looked up at her, and now she looked wild with anticipation, too. They sat with silly smiles—just looking at each other.

"Go wash, you old *dumb* man, and tell me the whole thing while we eat," she said, shooshing him with her hands.

He shook his head. He went right back to the tablet. It took a long time to tell the whole story by pen. He started at the very beginning—the lot had fallen to him to enter the temple to offer the incense offering. Elizabeth jumped from her chair and kissed him on one cheek, then the other. Then again. Then again. These little disruptions didn't make the storytelling go any faster, but Lacidar didn't mind. He would have kissed him, too, if he could have.

Zacharias described the vision he saw. Elizabeth sat with her mouth open. And then, as though he had rehearsed it in his mind a thousand times, he recounted the exact words the angel gave him. And then how he lost his voice. Elizabeth sat back in her chair, and her arms fell limp to her sides.

Lacidar waited to see Elizabeth's response. *Will she believe? Will her age and years of deferred hope prevent her faith from taking hold of this word? Will she. . . ?*

Elizabeth leapt up and danced around the room. "I'm going to have a son! *We're* going to have a son! Finally, the Lord has answered our prayers." She kept repeating, "A son, a son," and half-singing it as she made long graceful twirls. "And—the Lord is going to make him great!"

A sad smile crept out of the corners of Zacharias's lips, and he touched his hand to his throat. But Elizabeth's excitement electrified the room, and he jumped up and joined the dance. The two old grey-heads danced around the room like a couple of young newlyweds drunk on love and too much wine.

"Very good," Lacidar said with a burst of laughter. He hopped to the corner, snatched up his Lacidian Resonar, and played a lively dance tune. He shadow-danced with the couple as he played, matching every turn and step. He called out to other angels in the room over the music, "This is more pleasing to the King than a thousand bulls on an altar. Just look at the waves of worship rising to the Throne."

Lacidar stepped aside and watched them dance. "It has been a long time," he said. He took a deep breath and set his resonar down. "Our work is just beginning. We need to keep the significance of this boy hidden until the right time. Zacharias's muteness will help. Elizabeth, however, is sure to make enough noise for the two of them all over town. This will raise much unwanted attention from the enemy. I have a plan. We just need to wait for the right moment."

The two old dancers had all the excitement of a young couple, but they didn't have the stamina. Their bodies gave out before their spirits did, and they collapsed into their chairs laughing and trying to catch their breath.

"Just imagine," Elizabeth panted, "after all these years, the Lord is going to take away my reproach. *Now* what will the young women say?" She said it with a hint of satisfaction.

Lacidar smiled at his comrades and gave them a wink.

"Yes," he whispered to Elizabeth, "what *will* they say? Are you sure you want to hear it?"

He had planted the seed. He waited to see if it would take.

Elizabeth sat limp, still breathing hard—and then looked up at Zacharias as though a thought suddenly occurred to her. "Hmm, what *will* they say?"

Zacharias held her hand.

"I know what they'll say," she said. "First, they won't believe it. They won't understand what is happening for us. Then they will judge us for having a child at our age. They will say I am too old and feeble to carry him and deliver him."

The excitement of the previous moment turned serious.

"I'm not sure I can stand all the talk. Do you think it is possible to keep this to ourselves until he is born?"

Zacharias placed his other hand on top of hers and gave her a reassuring smile.

The three angels folded their arms and gave each other satisfied smiles.

Outside, a pair of red eyes watched from a distance.

20

RAIN CLOUDS

Birth minus 16 months

In pastureland just outside of Nazareth, Jeremiah and his three sons, along with the hired men, scrambled around the campsite and gathered the provisions into the tents. Daniel lifted the wooden box he had been using as a seat and ran it to the nearest tent. He turned back for another load but paused at the tent opening. Storm clouds hung dark and low over the hills—they would hit camp any minute, though the pastured sheep dotting the hillside seemed oblivious to the imminent downpour. *I used to love the smell of the rain.* He took a deep breath through his nose, exhaled with a huff, and ran for another sack of something.

Motion on the trail in the valley caught his eye. A visitor from town? *Why would anybody want to come out here?* Jesse ran out to meet him. *Of course. Now I have more things to carry in.* Jesse and the visitor met with shoulder and back slaps, and Jesse escorted the man toward the main tent of Jeremiah. Daniel dropped his sack and ran to see.

"Father!" Jesse called out. "Father, look who it is."

Jeremiah stopped in the middle of moving packs into the tent and looked up from his bent-over position. "Joseph?" Jeremiah answered. "Joseph! What a surprise." Jeremiah greeted him with a kiss on each cheek. "It pleases me to see you, son. Why do you come all the way out here?"

Joseph was sturdy young man, a few years older than Jesse. He had shoulder–length dark brown hair with a slight wave. His beard, in its early manhood stage, still looked short and scruffy. He stood straight and tall and replied with his most adult voice, "Master Jeremiah, I am here on business."

A huge raindrop pelted the center of Joseph's forehead. Another raindrop smacked Jeremiah on the top of his head. Dozens of drops splashed all around them.

Jeremiah laughed. "We should move inside."

They all grabbed the last of the packs, and the clouds let loose. The men clamored into the tent, hollering and laughing as they went. They entered a large space—large enough for Jeremiah, Jesse, Daniel and Joseph to stand. They arranged the packs around the tent and started to sit down on them when Levi burst through the front flap, drenched.

Jeremiah chuckled. "It is always a blessing to receive the rain." He reached into one of the packs and pulled out some bread and fruit. He passed them around, beginning with their guest, and sat back down. "Now, Joseph, let us hear about the business that has brought you to our camp."

Joseph finished chewing the bite he just took and then swallowed. "Sir, I am getting married."

"Married? This is wonderful news! Is it Mary?"

"Yes, sir. And our date is set for six months from now. I am beginning to make the arrangements."

Jeremiah smiled and crossed his arms. "I suppose you are looking for a lamb for the wedding feast?"

Joseph nodded. "Just one sheep. We do not expect a large gathering. Unfortunately, I don't have enough money to purchase a whole sheep at market price. That is why I came to you. If it pleases my master, I would like to barter my services for the cost of one of your flock."

Jeremiah leaned back and stroked his distinguished beard. "You have allowed yourself sufficient time to work a fair value. I commend you for your foresight and prudence. However, to honor the memory of your father, I shall give you the sheep you desire without cost."

"No, my master. I cannot accept such a gift from your hand without working for it. Please name a wage that I may serve my master."

Jeremiah pursed his lips and placed his hands on his knees. "Perhaps we could find an acceptable arrangement. You are a skilled carpenter, like your father. There are some repairs for my house— some roof leaks. And a new fence around our stable is needed. If you do these things, you shall have your pick from the finest of the flock."

"My master is too kind. Surely a sheep is worth more than this. There must be more that I can do."

Jeremiah gave a hearty laugh and rocked back and forth on his makeshift seat. "You have not seen the holes in my roof. Our deal is struck." And then in a lower tone he added, "You are a good man, Joseph. It is my pleasure to honor you and your bride. I trust the Lord will bless your marriage and your new family."

Daniel skulked in the corner of the tent. He sat with his good ear facing inward so he could overhear the conversation, but he did his best to appear disinterested. *I don't care about Joseph's wedding. Joseph and Jesse used to play together, and they always thought I was too little to play with them. Jesse has always treated me like a little kid. It's really his fault I lost my hearing. If he would have trusted Levi and me, he wouldn't have insisted that Amos go along, and we never would have gone out on the boat. And ever since the accident, Jesse's really been mean to Levi. Look at him laughing with Joseph like he's all grown up.*

His father laughed along.

Jesse looks just like Father. Actually, he's a lot like Father. Father blames Levi for the accident, too. Maybe Father isn't everything I thought he was. Maybe he's not as wise as I used to believe. Maybe even the God that he's always taught us about isn't even real. If He were, why would He have let this happen to me?

Outside, the rain clouds continued without any sign of letting up any time soon.

————

Benjamin sat outside Rachael's house and stared into blank space. His mind was numb. His tears were spent. There was no sound, no wind, no motion. Nothing for a long time. His empty shell of a body leaned against the front wall of the burnt–out structure—both of them hollow, destroyed, and full of worthless ashes. He forced himself to blink, and it made his gravelly eyes sting. At least some part of him could still feel.

Something from beyond the emptiness caught his attention. Off to the left, a fairly large assembly approached. *Must be a group of people from town.* They drew closer—men with carts, and others, probably city officials and priests. *Word must have made it to town, and these men are coming to take care of business.*

Off to his right, another group appeared—smaller than the first. *Probably coming from a neighbor's house.* Yes, one of his soldiers with about four others. These people might actually have some answers.

The group from town reached the house first. Benjamin dragged his empty frame to the back bedroom with two of the officials and a priest. The other officials sifted through the wreckage out front. Benjamin couldn't face the bodies on the ground in the bedroom but shot distracted glances toward the crunching footsteps and clattering debris out front.

"I arrived here this morning with two Roman soldiers," Benjamin said. He motioned with his hand. "We found them here like this. My Rachael. . ." He wiped his eyes and gasped for a breath. "We were to wed. The other two. . . her father, her grandmother. . ."

A faint female voice from the front room strained across the ashes.

Benjamin cocked his ear toward the door casing. *That almost sounded like. . .* He glanced back at the three lifeless lumps under the blanket and shook his head. His stomach churned. He swallowed hard. "Her grandmother lived with them. She was the nicest. . ."

The female voice sounded again.

His heart raced, and a wave of heat flushed across his face. His churning stomach cinched up into a knot.

"Benjamin," the voice called.

He ran toward the front room and came around the corner. There she was. "Rachael!" he shouted. He grasped the edge of the wall.

"Benjamin!"

"Oh, Rachael, I thought you were. . ." He rushed across the rubble and clutched her in his arms. Together, they held each other up and sobbed.

After a thousand pounding heartbeats, Benjamin loosened his embrace. Wiping her tears with his hands, he said, "Are you all right? What happened here?"

She shook her head and said with a trembling voice, "No. It was horrible." She fell back into his arms and heaved long, silent, weary sobs. He braced her up and held her tight.

She settled down, and Benjamin said, "Tell us what happened. Just start from the beginning."

Nodding, and taking a deep breath, she said, "Some awful man attacked me. Out behind the stable. Father came out to help. But the man. . . he hit Father with the shovel. He killed him, Benjamin. . . there was so much blood."

"You're doing fine. Then what happened?"

"I don't know. It was dark. It all happened so fast. I guess I kicked the man off me, and he fell backwards. He must have. . . the big hook on the back of the stable. . . it was poking all the way through his chest. . . and he. . . oh. . . and then fire started burning him."

"The fire. How did it start?"

"I don't know. Probably my lantern in the straw. The whole stable caught fire. And Adah. . . oh Adah!"

"She's all right. We found her out in the field. What happened next?"

"I went to see Father. I couldn't save him. There was so much blood. That's when I noticed the fire had spread to the house. All the smoke was coming out, and I knew I had to get Grandmother out. I went in to get her, but she wouldn't wake up. I think the smoke. . . I tried so hard. I tried to pull her out, but I couldn't. And then, the roof started crashing in and I was trapped and lost in the smoke and flames. Suddenly, one of these men from the neighboring houses showed up, grabbed me, and led me out the front door."

"We told you, dear, it wasn't any one of us," the neighbor said. "We had just gotten here, and we don't know who the man was."

"Well, whichever one of you it was, you saved my life."

A neighbor said, "We took her to our house because she was hysterical and needed to get away. There was nothing we could do to stop the fire, so we had to let it burn itself out. We couldn't leave her father and the other man lying out there like that, so after the fire, Boaz and Micah moved them both in here and covered all of them until the officials could come."

Two men, standing away from the others, ceremonially unclean, nodded and waved.

Benjamin wrapped his arm around Rachael's shoulders and said, "Let's go outside where we can have some fresh air."

One of the officials said, "We'll stay here and finish our questions with these neighbors."

Benjamin nodded and led Rachael out front.

"Oh, Benjamin. What am I going to do? I've lost everything."

"I thought I had lost you," Benjamin said. "I am so glad you are still here. We're going to get through this together."

"But Father is gone. And I don't even have a place to live."

"I know. I'm so sorry. I wish I could bring your father back." Benjamin held her close. "But as soon as we finish with all the arrangements here, I'm going to bring you back to the palace with me. I can set up a place for you to stay until we can be married."

"I'm so glad you are here." Rachael pressed her face deep into his chest and cried some more.

21

STORM CLOUDS

Birth minus 16 months

The ruins of an ancient temple in Egypt provided an ideal location for Marr's new seat of power. From here he could oversee the palace compound of the Roman proconsul from a distance and still control all the activities in Persia and Israel. This morning, his old aide, Luchek, appeared before his throne.

Luchek did his best to stand in defiance against the raging Marr, but the blast of flames from Marr's roaring mouth sent him tumbling like a dry leaf in a gale. He landed in a heap on the other side of the room. Two demon captains helped him to his feet and propped him up before the great Prince of Persia.

"You did what?" Marr repeated.

Luchek raised his chin, bared his lower teeth, and glared through his one good eye. "I found a weakness in our enemy's plan, and I attacked it. And I was very close to single-handedly thwarting the King's 'great' plan. If not for the legion of enemy warriors who showed up at the last minute, my attack would have succeeded, and you would be praising me right now for my efforts." He gave a little snort of smoke and fire out of his nostrils.

"You fool!" blasted Marr, sending Luchek into a heap again.

Marr didn't wait for his captains to fetch him. Marr stepped off his throne, crossed the room with billowing black clouds under his feet, and lifted Luchek into midair by his neck. He held him eyeball to eyeball, close enough that Luchek felt the heat of his breath, even while he spoke in a low, deliberate tone.

"You almost destroyed *our* plan. Did it ever occur to you that there are larger things in play? We *want* the Promised One to be born. Once He is here in human flesh, we will be able to destroy part of the Godhead!"

Marr tossed Luchek across the room again like a wet rag, turned back toward his throne, and continued. "Fortunately, your reckless actions failed. But what you have done has only served to make our job more difficult. Now, they are moving Rachael inside the palace where the enemy has been building up a stronghold. Now, we will not be able to see her. Now, we can only infer what is going on with her by watching from a distance."

Back on his feet, Luchek's gaze dropped to the floor. *And I still need to give him the message from the King.* He ground his teeth and grimaced. With a cracking voice and eyes held low, he said, "I'm afraid there is more."

Marr responded with a resigned glare. "What?"

"The land surrounding Rachael's house has been consecrated by the enemy. If any of our forces approach it, they will be sent immediately into the abyss."

"You insignificant dog," Marr growled. "I don't care about some worthless piece of land! Our main target has been moved out of our reach. That is the only thing that matters. I would send *you* to the abyss right now if I could."

The heavy huffing of the great demon lord on his dark throne echoed across the dilapidated stone floor. Luchek waited, his head bent low. The demon officers in the court stood by with their arms crossed or fists clenched. Every judging eye burned holes in his defeated pride.

"Be gone." Marr snarled. "I hereby banish you from my entire region. Go find someplace on the other side of the planet to do your work. I never want to see your pathetic face again."

———

Luchek left Marr's headquarters and flew low over the Egyptian landscape. Marr's words "I hereby banish you" gnawed at the core of his being. *He has no right to command where I can and cannot go. I'm free to do whatever I choose. I am free to go wherever I choose.* For the moment he chose to put some distance between himself and Marr's new seat of power.

He flew aimlessly northward and soon reached Israel. Crossing the hills of Judea, he spotted a small squadron of elzurim winging eastward on an intersecting path ahead of him. *Argh. I don't need a fight today.* He dropped straight down, landed, and ducked into a large bush. To his surprise, he found a spirit already concealed there.

"Hey!" came a startled and angry voice. "What do you think you're doing?"

"Trying to hide," Luchek snapped back. "Shut up or you will reveal us both."

The squad passed by, and the original hider whispered, "They're gone. Now get out of here."

"I am Luchek. What's going on here?" He peered out of the bush at the house near their position. "Are you on an operation? Who are you watching?"

"I don't care who you are. And it is none of your business what I'm doing. Be gone."

"I could help. I am a master at lurking and watching. In fact, I just came from an operation where I located the virgin mother of the coming King."

"Oh, really? Then why are you here?"

"I was trying to disrupt the King's plan by spoiling the girl."

"By yourself?"

"Yes, by myself. But at the last minute the operation was broken up by an entire legion of enemy forces. And so, Marr. . ." He paused and clenched his fists. "Marr banished me from his province." He gritted his teeth and shot a blast of smoke from his nostrils. "But he has no authority over me. If I want to continue operations in 'his' region, I will."

"Marr." The other demon sneered and nodded. "My name is Tumur. And I think *I* have found the coming prophet Elijah."

"By yourself?"

"Yes, by myself. But unlike you, I have remained undetected."

"Have you told anyone yet?"

"No, and I don't plan to until I'm sure he is the one. Or until he leads me to the coming Messiah. Then I will be able to deliver Him directly to our lord. I will receive honor surpassing all the mighty generals and regional princes." Tumur scowled and squinted his eyes at Luchek. "You must tell no one," he growled.

Hmm. Deliver the coming Messiah—or even the prophet Elijah— to the lord Satan while Marr watches from the sideline—this would certainly avenge my soiled honor.

"This is too important to keep hidden," Luchek lilted. "Perhaps I could remain silent if I were to stay here and join your operation."

Tumur shook his head and raised his finger toward Luchek.

Luchek gave a wicked smile and raised the eyebrow of his good eye.

Tumur lowered his finger. "Only if you agree to submit to my lead. This is my operation, and I will receive the credit for leading it."

"You are very small to make demands to a lieutenant."

"My lead."

Luchek cupped his hand over his mouth and spoke. "For the fall of the King, and for the humiliation of Marr." A small ball of fire formed in his hand.

Tumur held his hand out like an upward–facing claw. "For the destruction of the prophet, and for my glory." A flaming ball of energy formed in his hand.

The two demons smashed their hands together, and a cloud of black smoke exploded without a sound. The cloud spread across the field and wrapped around Zacharias's house. An elzurim lieutenant outside peered over the area, but Tumur and Luchek ducked low.

22

PREPARATION

Birth minus 14 months

Elric and Jenli stared into the war map in the angelic stronghold at the widow Hannah's house. Night surrounded their little outpost.

"No," Elric said. "A cave is not acceptable."

Jenli looked exasperated. "But captain, there is no place suitable in all of Bethlehem. At least the cave was formed by the King's own hand. Nothing made by the hand of man is worthy to receive the glory of the King. Certainly nothing in Bethlehem."

Elric studied the war map around the region of Bethlehem as Hannah puttered in the background by earthbound lamplight. Jenli alone stood by in the Middle Realm. Elric stepped into the map and paced around the region, shaking his head and rubbing his forehead.

"You are right, of course. But He has spoken that Bethlehem will be the location. We must find and prepare a place there to conceal His arrival."

"Why does He not tell us the exact place?" Jenli asked.

Elric stepped out of the swirling colors of the map and stood beside Jenli. "I have asked this question myself, and I do not receive an answer. I believe it's the nature of our mission. The secrecy demands silence. A single word from the Throne could reveal too much. So, we proceed by faith. He will provide guidance at the necessary time."

They both crossed their arms and stared into the map.

Jenli asked, "Did he say anything to you at your first meeting that might provide a direction?"

"'I will lay aside my glory for a time and live as a man,'" Elric said. He paused and stared off into nothing. "This says to me that He must be born in a manmade dwelling, for this is the way of man. But there must be a place worthy at least for a human king."

They continued examining the map.

"It need not be a palace," Eric said, "just something that is. . ." He stopped and pointed to a spot on the map. "What is this house here?"

Jenli maneuvered around the side and looked closer. "That is the home of Achim, son of Amnon. He is a chief elder of the tribe of Benjamin. A very wealthy man. He spends most of his time in Jerusalem, but he maintains this house on the bounds of Bethlehem."

"Not a grand palace, but it is stately. Do we know its history?"

Jenli cocked his head and smiled. "It was originally commissioned by King Amaziah, who used it as a secret place of safety outside Jerusalem."

"Yes, I remember this place. King Zedekiah used it also. It was mostly destroyed by the Babylonians."

"And rebuilt, and destroyed, and rebuilt, three times over."

"I see the enemy has dominion here. Are there strongholds? Can we take it?"

"This was, in days past, a stronghold of the King. In fact, I have fought from this fortification. But there is only a remnant of these walls left. There are minor strongholds of darkness now, but it is mostly open. We can surely take it."

"Without drawing undue attention?"

"Enemy presence is meager. This place has not been contested for many years."

Elric paced and scuffed his feet along the floor. "A house built by a King as a place to hide. It seems fitting."

Elric's heart pulled against his head. *How could such a meager place contain the majesty of the King's glory? But is there any place on earth that can? Even Solomon's temple was a mere shadow of the King's court. And He chose to fill that house with His glory. But this is no Solomon's temple. But it is the finest in Bethlehem. A house built by a King as a place to hide.*

He rubbed his forehead and grimaced. "We shall not find better. Not in Bethlehem. And the master of the house is often gone." He paused. His arms dropped to his sides. "We will need a human connection for Joseph to gain entrance."

Jenli pulled a small tablet from a hidden breast pocket and thumbed through the pages. He stopped, looked up at Elric, and laughed. "A servant girl in the house is a distant cousin of Mary."

Elric nodded, took a deep breath, and rubbed his eyes.

Jenli continued. "This is it. This has to be it. All we need to do is take the house, arrange for Achim to be in Jerusalem at the time of the birth, and connect Mary with her cousin. Captain? What is it?"

Elric used the edge of his sleeves to dry his eyes. He took quick and shallow breaths. "The thought of the King coming into the world as a baby. . . is beyond my understanding. But to enter through a place as lowly as this is. . . I can't even. . ."

Jenli's eyes filled with tears. "But the strategic value. . . He is wise to hide behind a veil of commonness. This house is the most royal we will find in Bethlehem. Do you wish to keep looking for another?"

"No." Elric composed himself. "No, I believe this is the house we have been seeking." He stood straight and let his hand rest on the top of his sword handle. "It is too soon to make a move against the enemy for the house, but begin making plans as you have said."

"Yes, captain."

"The day for the Lord's visitation to Mary is less than five months away, and all the pieces are in motion as planned." Elric moved to the region of Egypt on the map. "Zaben's team receives more reinforcements every day. Our buildup there is too significant for the enemy to ignore. And see here, we have their attention—the number of enemy forces there grows daily. The premature attack on Rachael was unfortunate, but we can use it to our advantage. We'll be able to hide her under Zaben's canopy. And Timrok's team has secured ground in Egypt which we will hold until needed."

Elric shifted up to Judea. "Lacidar's team has Zacharias and Elizabeth sealed in. Elizabeth is carrying the prophet—and it appears that her pregnancy has not captured the attention of the enemy."

He turned back toward Bethlehem. "And now. . . we have identified the King's birthplace."

Jenli said, "This is the place. All the signs confirm it. We just need to concentrate on its tactical purpose."

Elric forced a sad smile. "How go your operations with Mary?" Elric said, turning toward Nazareth.

"Very well. We become more practiced every day. I'm confident we will be able to divert the enemy away from her when she moves about after the visitation."

"Good. When we finish here, I would like to go and see your team in action."

"Yes, sir."

As if on cue, Hannah blew out her lamp, and the darkness of the Physical Realm settled in around them.

————

Morning in Nazareth brought a cloudless sky and singing birds. Elric hunched low behind the half-wall ledge of the flat roof of Mary's family home. He scanned the nearby houses and trails—no spiritual activity. If Jenli's team kept watch stations out there, he couldn't see them. Some birds to his left fluttered off and caught his attention. He turned back. He waited.

After an hour of waiting, Mary emerged from her home with a warm loaf of bread wrapped in linens and tucked under her arm. A flash of light signaled from behind Elric. A flash from the roof down the street answered. Elric flew from the roof of Mary's house and positioned himself in a concealed place on another roof where he could observe the maneuver unfold.

Mary followed the narrow trail from her house and onto the main dirt street through her hometown. She passed several people and greeted them. No elzurim or beaelzurim in sight anywhere, and everything remained quiet.

A squad of eight Roman soldiers appeared on a cross street ahead. A demon captain and two other beaelzurim escorted the soldiers. *Their paths are going to cross Mary's.* From a nearby side house, one of Jenli's team walked through the front wall and sauntered up beside Mary. He leaned down and spoke to her. Elric could barely hear his words.

"You forgot the water jug," the angel said. "You are supposed to fill it at the well while you're out."

Mary stopped midstride. She slapped her hip as if she just remembered something. She spun around and headed back to her house. Just as she stepped onto the foot trail to her house, the Roman detail crossed the main street behind her and passed by without notice. Seconds later she emerged from her house with a large clay jug on one shoulder and the loaf of warm bread still tucked under her arm.

Elric smiled.

On the street approaching the main section of town, the number of people passing by grew. *This should prove interesting.* He spotted an angel walking with one person. Not one of Jenli's team. Coming the opposite direction walked a man with a beaelzurim companion. The two human strangers passed in the street, and the accompanying spirits eyed each other. But each stayed close to his charge. The man with the demon escort now walked a path that would pass by Mary.

Elric could hear the enemy speaking to the man.

"It's no wonder he's mad at you. You're worthless. You're never going to amount to anything. And it's impossible to change. He hates you. Your whole family hates you. God hates you. And you actually deserve this sickness if you think about it. God is punishing you and. . ."

From out of nowhere one of Jenli's warriors swooped in from behind and clipped the demon with his sword just behind his left knee.

"Augghh!" The demon went down on his other knee for a moment until his wound sealed around the escaping yellow smoke. Then he blasted upward in a rage to catch his hit-and-run assailant. The angel ducked in through the roof of one house, then slipped out and through another. Then he disappeared into another.

Elric watched the demon search house to house until he gave up in frustration. With a wary sword still brandished, the demon returned to the man on the road. Elric looked up the street. Mary and the man had passed each other, and Mary had already turned down a cross street. Elric nodded to himself and flew to a new rooftop.

This street had three beaelzurim that could cross paths with Mary. Just as Elric reached his next observation perch a few roofs away, one of Jenli's team leapt from a side house and thrust his sword into the belly of one surprised demon. The squeal of pain caught the attention of the other two demons, who left their charges and joined the fight. Three angry demons chased the angel straight up, slashing at his heels just beyond their reach. The angel stopped and engaged three furious beaelzurim in mid-air.

Just above the rooftops, a dizzying crash of steel, yellow sulfur, and flashing light split the air in the Middle Realm. On the ground,

Mary passed by unaware of the maneuvers happening all around her. Then the angel retreated over the horizon like comet, leaving the three enemy spirits alone. They congratulated each other on their victory and returned to their humans on the ground.

Elric smiled.

Mary had turned down another street, and Elric lost sight of her. Then he saw a flash of light to his left and another farther into town. He had seen enough. *Jenli's team is ready.*

23

WORD DELIVERED

Birth minus 40 weeks, 2 days

*J*enli stood behind Mary, seated in a chair in Joseph's family home in Nazareth. With the curtains hanging heavy and still, the isolated room had no indication of the bright noontime hour approaching outside. Only the slow cadence of Mary's breathing marked the passage of time.

Jenli rested his hand on her shoulder. *Two days until the Lord's visitation. You have no idea how your world is about to change.*

Mary took her left hand from its folded position in her lap, reached over, and rested it on the hand of the old woman in the bed beside her chair. Over the last two months, Joseph's mother had become more and more frail, and her breathing was shallow and laborious. Her skin pulled tight over her pronounced cheekbones. Years of hardship hung from the dark bags under her hollow eyes.

Each morning, Mary came early to sit with Joseph's mother. While Joseph went out and worked until midday, Mary tended to his mother's needs, brushed out her bed–tangled hair, and sang her favorite psalms. Each day, Jenli stayed close and ministered strength.

The heart of this teenage girl pleases the King. She's new to the cares of adult life, but she is showing herself faithful beyond her years.

Mary stole a glance into the front room. She sighed and turned back to Joseph's mother. She crossed her hands in her lap and glanced toward the front door.

"Strength of the Lord," Jenli spoke aloud. "Strength. Peace. Patience." His words lit the Middle Realm like a warm candle, and they settled over Mary.

A clatter from the front door disrupted the silence. Mary jumped to her feet and reached the bedroom doorway as Joseph stumbled through the front door, nearly dropping a basket of fresh fruit from the marketplace. He pressed the door closed with a careful touch and shut the shining outside world out.

In the front room, Jenli took a position in the corner and waited. He pulled a ledger from his tunic and checked it. *Timing will be important.*

Mary slipped across the room and stood beside Joseph as he washed his calloused hands in the wash basin. "She's resting," Mary whispered. "No change."

Disappointment filled Joseph's eyes from Mary's bittersweet words.

The pain in Joseph's face pinched Jenli's heart. Joseph spent most of his time with his declining mother now. He spent his evenings and nights watching her draw each breath and wondering if the next one would be her last. He spent many hours in lonely prayer, hoping for any sign of improvement.

The King Himself surrounded Joseph with His presence and spoke peace into his spirit. Jenli shook his head. *I can't tell—is he hearing it?* Jenli spoke. "Strength. Determination. Receive it." His words floated like clouds of light in the Middle Realm and tried to penetrate Joseph's spirit. *How many times over the centuries have I shared this difficult vigil with human families? Even with an eternal perspective, I feel their pain afresh every time.*

"The doctor came by this morning," Mary added with an even quieter tone. "He doesn't know what to do for her. He's not optimistic."

Joseph didn't look up from his hand scrubbing. He answered, "God is Jehovah Rophe. He is our healer. I will continue to trust Him until He either heals her or takes her."

A long pause of silence. "And if He chooses to take her?"

"Then He will be to me Jehovah Uzzi. My strength."

Mary smiled.

Jenli smiled. *Faith in the face of great pain. Rare in a young man. This pleases the King. Joseph is the right man for the upcoming task.*

Joseph and Mary shared the rest of the morning's news in hushed conversation, careful not to wake his mother. Mary had fed and watered the lamb Joseph received from Jeremiah's flock several months ago. Joseph had worked on the construction of someone's house and had brought home another family's broken wooden table for repair. Mary planned to spend the afternoon going to the grove to gather olives. Joseph planned to make a lentil soup for supper—always a favorite of his mother's. They shared easy and comfortable small talk. The time came for Mary to go, and Joseph declined her offer to help with the supper preparations before she left.

Mary stood.

Grigor shot down through the ceiling, alighting in front of Jenli. Grigor's sleek wings, which extended upward and outward during landing, pulled in and folded without a sound.

"Master Jenli, there has been interruption to our timeline. You must delay Mary's departure for several minutes. I will signal you when the time is right." Grigor's shimmering wings filled the room and, with one downward stroke, he disappeared.

I need to act fast. No time for anything complicated. He had one simple maneuver that always seemed to work—he would have to use it.

Mary said her goodbye, pulled the linen cloak hood onto her head, grabbed her basket for olives, and headed toward the door. She stopped for a moment, scanning the area around the door entrance.

"What is it?" Joseph asked.

"One of my sandals is missing. I'm sure I left them both right here at the threshold."

"Maybe I accidentally kicked it when I fumbled in the door earlier."

Together they searched. They checked all the obvious places. Nothing. One minute passed. They then looked in less obvious places. Nothing. Another minute passed. They looked in places that made no sense at all. Another minute passed.

"This is frustrating! It has to be here somewhere," Mary said. "Let's start over from the beginning."

Grigor bolted through the ceiling. "Now!"

Jenli nodded. He said, "Eyes open. See that which is hidden."

"Ah, here it is." Joseph announced. "It was behind the wash basin. I must have knocked it over here."

"But I looked there."

"So did I. Oh, well, here you go. Have a good afternoon in the grove. Watch out for the Roman soldiers. There is an extra company of them staying in town for a few days. We think they're on their way to Jerusalem."

———

From his concealed position on the roof of a neighboring house, Elric waited for Mary to emerge. He checked the sun. *After midday. Something must be causing a delay.* He scanned the entire area— rooftops, streets, alleys, window openings, trees. No sign of Jenli's team anywhere. *I trust they are ready. This is a big day.*

The door to Joseph's house opened. Mary stepped into the daylight holding a basket in one hand and shielding her eyes with the other.

Here we go. . . A light flashed on the left. Another light flashed down the street. *Of course they're ready. They have practiced this for months.*

Mary made her way through the streets without an angelic escort by her side. She passed through the network of Jenli's squad, who tracked her every step and handed her off from one stationed warrior to the next. Passing through the western city gate, she headed up the trail leading to the nearby hills. She hummed a melody—a psalm of praise—with the cadence of her steps.

The trail wound into the rock bluffs. Steep rocks rose up on both sides. After some light climbing, she reached a craggy canyon wide enough for only three people to stand abreast. The canyon continued for some distance, and the echoes from Mary's humming bounced off the walls with electrified energy. Her walk turned into a quiet, personal time of worship. Not the flashy or formal kind of thing that might be seen in the temple—just a gentle, unmistakable connection with the King Himself.

Elric walked along the top of the cliff to her right. The sweet incense of the young girl's praises bounced off the stone walls, rose like waves through the Middle Realm, and shot directly into the King's inner court. Elric immersed one hand into the rising waves and smiled. The energy filled him with warmth and strength. *Oh, young Mary, your life is about to change forever. You have no idea about the enormous and daring plan of the King. It almost seems impossible that the most important mission in all history should start here with you—and with only a small band of common warriors. And a mere captain to lead them.* Elric palmed his sword handle.

Mary approached the olive grove. The walls to the left cut away, and a wide opening spread out before her. There, tucked away on a vast field in the canyon stood a sprawling grove of olive trees. Out in the wilderness like this, the grove didn't sit on anyone's property, so the locals who knew about it—mostly the poor and needy—would make the long hike out here to glean olives for free. They would then press them for oil or sell them on the market or cure some for table use.

A dozen women and a pack of exuberant young children already filled the grove. Mary greeted most of them by name and went to work filling her basket.

Elric stood at the base of the cliff on the right. He pulled his sword and leaned against it with the tip stuck into the ground in front of him.

After several minutes, two Roman soldiers approached from the opposite end of the canyon trail, led by three boisterous demons.

Elric held his station and gritted his teeth. *Right on time.*

A deathly hush fell over the gleaners. The children scampered and hid behind their mothers and the trees. The soldiers taunted the women and made threatening gestures, but the three demons froze. They stared at Elric, fidgeting their feet and twitching their hands and shoulders. Elric remained stone cold.

"What are you doing way out here?" one of the demons hissed.

All three drew their weapons, stepped away from the men, and advanced toward Elric in a semicircle.

"Watching over these women," Elric replied without lifting his sword or his voice.

"Just keep watching," the demon sneered. "These men are going to take one of these women, and you are not going to be able to stop it."

"*I* will not need to."

Jenli's team stepped out from behind the trees. Five disciplined elzurim flashed their brilliant blades.

"Enough talk!" the demon shouted at the soldiers. "Attack!"

The demon's words twisted up like a tiny tornado and spun apart, shooting fiery darts into the soldiers.

In the Physical Realm, the soldiers lunged toward the women and children, who ran screaming in every direction. In the Middle Realm, three demons and five angels sent flaming sparks into the air as their blades met with thunderous crashes. Elric stood by with a watchful eye always on Mary.

Roman soldiers lumbered after the nearest women, cursing as they went. Some of the women with children in tow scrambled to the path that led out of the grove. Four others were trapped, including Mary.

Two demons fought back-to-back, fending off three angels. They matched each thrust with lightning–fast parries. The third demon escaped and fled southward, never looking back. Jenli's team pressed in on the remaining two. At the last possible moment, the two demons blasted straight up, abandoned the grove, and took their defeat over the horizon.

Very good. Now we can work directly with these Roman soldiers.

Jenli's team helped three more women squeeze around the soldiers and out to safety, leaving Mary cornered and alone. One of the soldiers closed in from the left while the other advanced from the front. Mary made a slight fake to the right and caught the front soldier off balance. She slipped by him and broke into a full run. Her maneuver didn't fool the soldier on the left, though, and he jumped to within a fingertip's reach.

Elric sprang forward. In a blink, he moved beside the pursuing soldier and, with an arcing sweep of his sword, he translated the sword tip into the Physical Realm, flipped a dead tree branch upward off the ground, and tripped the soldier. The soldier careened headlong into the other soldier, knocking both of them into a tangled heap on the dirt. One of the soldiers' brandished dagger slashed the other soldier's arm, leaving a nasty gash.

"Mary! This way!" Elric shouted, heading back toward the rock valley wall.

Mary reacted on pure instinct. Like a frightened deer, she bounded toward the cliff face. Her desperate eyes darted back and forth, and her hands groped the rock face for a place to hide.

"Here," Elric prompted as he led her to a cleft in the wall. "Hide behind this."

Mary ducked into the crevice.

"Farther back, keep moving," Elric urged.

She squeezed between the rocks. She disappeared into the shadows. A soft thud echoed from within the cleft.

Elric nodded his head, positioned his sword tip down into the dirt again, and lifted his chin. *All the women and children have escaped.* The soldiers argued with each other while one bandaged the other's wound. *The soldiers are preoccupied. And they didn't see Mary's hiding place.*

Jenli's team returned to their concealed positions behind the trees.

Now it was Gabriel's turn to work.

———

Mary looked back for only a moment. One soldier had tripped and landed on the other. *Now's my chance!* She spun around, desperate for an escape route. *The trail is too far. I'll never make it there in time. The canyon wall—it's close. Maybe I can find a place to hide.*

She bounded to the cliff and slid along the rock face, feeling with her hands. *Here! A crack—an opening. I wonder if I can fit between* . . . She turned sideways and squeezed behind the wall face. *Yes! But am I far enough in that they can't see me?* She felt with her hands, and the fissure continued inward. Farther, farther. Inching sideways, the cleft drew narrow, too narrow for a bulky soldier. *Even if one of them saw me come in here, they'll never be able to reach me now.* Another sidestep and the wall opened up behind her. She fell backwards, tumbling into pitch black. A cave? The blackness provided a welcome shield. She lay still—as still as her heaving breath would allow.

The soldiers outside cursed and argued with each other. *They seem so close. I'm going to stay hidden here a long time—until I'm sure they're gone.* She rose to a sitting position. *I'll stay all night if I have to.*

The darkness filled her with an unusual sense of peace—like a warm blanket that wrapped around her very soul. *Thank you, Lord, for protecting me against these men.* She settled against the wall. The voices still echoed in from outside. She took a breath, closed her eyes, and rested.

Alone in the dark, time became blurry. *How long have I been in here? Did I doze off?*

All of a sudden, a voice shattered the fog in her mind. "Greetings, you who are highly favored! The Lord is with you."

Mary opened her eyes and gasped. A brilliant blue-white light illuminated the cave. The stone walls did more than just reflect the radiance—they looked alive with dazzling dancing light. Mary squinted and peered into the light.

A man stood before her, clothed in a shimmering white robe, with snow–white hair, a chiseled jaw, and piercing silver eyes. The man had a stature larger than any she had ever seen, filling the space of the vaulted cave ceiling. The terror of the moment lumped in her throat. She swallowed hard. *"Highly favored?" What could he mean. . .* She struggled to find her breath, and she pressed her back against the cave wall.

"Do not be afraid, Mary, for you have found favor with God."

Her flesh trembled—but it wasn't fear. It was the raw power of this being. An angel? He emanated intense energy filled with peace and purpose.

The angel continued, "You will be with child and give birth to a son, and you are to give Him the name Jesus. He will be great and will be called the Son of the Most High. The Lord God will give Him the throne of his father David, and He will reign over the house of Jacob forever; His kingdom will never end."

What? This is wonderful! I'm going to have a son. And He will be . . . wait. "How will this be," she asked, "since I am a virgin?"

"The Holy Spirit will come upon you, and the power of the Most High will overshadow you. So the Holy One to be born will be called the Son of God. Even Elizabeth your relative is going to have a child in her old age, and she who was said to be barren is in her sixth month. For nothing is impossible with God."

This is amazing. Why would I be chosen for such a thing? I'm just a regular girl. I don't have any special talents, and I certainly don't have any material means to accomplish anything. But if the Lord has spoken it. . .

Mary spoke out loud. "I am the Lord's servant. May it be to me as you have said."

The great angel smiled, knelt down, and brushed the edge of her hair with his finger. He disappeared like a fading mist, and the room became pitch black again.

Mary sat alone in the darkness *What just happened?* The only sound was the sound of her own breathing. She cocked her head toward the cave opening—no sound. *Maybe the soldiers are gone. I should try to get home.* She inched her way back through the cave entrance and peeked out from behind the rock.

No sign of the soldiers. Everything appeared still, and the grove looked abandoned. The sun still shined, but dusk approached. *I need to hurry, before night falls.* She found her basket still half-full of olives, gathered it up along with a small pile that had spilled out, and made her way down the canyon trail.

24

SEED PLANTED

Birth minus 40 weeks, 1 day

The sun had not yet risen in Egypt when an angelic general, four commanders, and twenty captains filed into the outer room of the proconsul's treasury house. They marched with quick steps, full of purpose, and the group of commanders and captains standing around Zaben's table parted to make way for the incoming general. Zaben jumped to his feet.

"Ready for battle and awaiting your orders," the general said to Zaben.

Zaben fidgeted and caught eye contact for only a moment. "Thank you, General." He paused to look over the rest of the detail. "I shall never get used to issuing orders to my superiors."

The general locked eyes with Zaben and rested his hand on his sword hilt. "As site commander, you carry the word of the King. We are all *His* servants."

"Do you know why you are here?" Zaben asked.

"To prepare for a battle. This is all we know."

Zaben smiled and crossed his hands behind his back. He had the privilege to deliver the good news yet again. If only he could tell them everything about the plan. If only *he* knew everything about the plan. He glanced at the veterans in the room who each prompted him with huge smiles and head nods. He explained what he knew of the mission with businesslike efficiency and waited for the inevitable celebration that accompanied the news whenever he shared it.

After the exuberant dance and spirited song finally finished, the general turned to Zaben and asked, "Why are we here in Egypt? Does not the King enter by way of Jerusalem? Are we staging here until He is ready to begin His campaign?"

Zaben gritted his teeth. *Now the part of the news I always dread to tell.*

"He is not coming in the manner you think. He is to be born of a woman, as foretold, and will live as a man. I am part of a small detachment whose mission is to keep Him hidden until He is ready to begin His campaign."

Silence fell over the room.

"We are here because it's where the enemy expects us," Zaben continued. "We *will* do battle, but only to hold the enemy's attention."

A cunning smile lit the general's face, and he nodded.

Zaben asked, "When you arrived, did you come by the secret path?"

"Yes."

"Did the enemy see you?"

"I think so. But we made every effort. . ."

Zaben stopped him with a raised hand. "This is by design. We want them to think that we believe our build-up has remained secret. A hidden treasure will draw many."

"Your strategy is working," the general said. "There are thousands surrounding you. Tens of thousands."

Zaben smiled.

"I am to tell you that we are the last complement you will receive," the general said.

Zaben nodded. "That is because tonight is the night. Tonight, we will give them the show they have been waiting for."

"Do you have sufficient numbers?"

Zaben bit his lower lip and took a deep breath.

————

Morning arrived at Mary's house without fanfare. Birds twittered, leaves rustled in a gentle breeze, and the silent sun made its regular appearance. When Mary returned home the night before, she had set her basket of olives just inside the door, intending to press them for oil. But after dinner and clean-up, she fell asleep expecting the events of the day to fade like a distant dream.

Now sunlight poured in through the window, and Mary awoke with a clear head, feeling refreshed. Yesterday's meeting in the cave burned like a wildfire in her mind. It was no dream. She had a real encounter with an angel. And every word the angel spoke seemed as clear today as the moment he spoke it. Something amazing and marvelous was going to happen, and it would surely change her entire life. *But when will it happen? How will I know when it does? How can*

I explain it to my family? What about Joseph? Why was I the one chosen? What am I supposed to do next? Should I tell my family now? I need time to think. I wish I could get away for a while until I knew what to do.

Just then, a thought bubbled into her mind, as though whispered from an untouchable well within. *The angel said my cousin Elizabeth is pregnant. I should go and stay with her in Judea. I could help with the pregnancy and the birth. At Elizabeth's age, she could use the help. And it will give me time to figure things out. It will be a long trip. I'll need to make many arrangements.*

She gathered some things and rushed off to Joseph's house.

As she spent the morning tending to Joseph's mother, Mary made plans and lists of things she needed for the trip. When Joseph returned from work that afternoon, Mary appeared quiet and ready to leave.

"Is something wrong?" Joseph asked. "You seem preoccupied. Must you leave so quickly?"

"I'm sorry. There are many things I must do in town today, and they fill my thoughts. Everything is fine. But time is short, and I really have to go."

She could see the disappointment in his eyes, but she said goodbye and wished him a good evening.

The remainder of the day went by in a flurry. It surprised her how all the pieces fell into place for the trip. It felt almost as though someone had gone ahead of her and prepared a great many details. By the time she returned home that evening, she had accomplished all the things on her list.

Convincing her father to let her leave for an extended period took some doing, but by the time they finished supper and Mary settled into bed, all the arrangements were set. She still hadn't told her family about the message from the angel. That would have to come later. All that remained was to tell Joseph.

She would have to face that task in the morning. She lay on her back and grinned in the dark as she thought about all the unexpected adventures that awaited her.

———

While Mary slept in Nazareth, Marr studied the late-night horizon from his headquarters in Egypt. Darkness spread across the moonless sky. He couldn't see all spirits at his direct command, but the mass of evil collected around him intoxicated his mind. He sat up straight on his throne, closed his eyes, and breathed it all in. Engorged with power, he let a long stream of smoke escape between his teeth.

"They have no idea what stands against them." He laughed and leaned back. He toyed with a fiery energy ball between his fingertips. "These puppet angels think they were hiding their numbers," he muttered. "But I saw every one."

He squashed the fire ball inside his fist. "Just look at them. They only do what they are told—they have no imagination at all. It's not until you are free that you really begin to possess true knowledge and understanding. We know every elzur inside that perimeter. We also know the time is close for the incarnation because they have doubled their buildup. We may be partially blind to the activities of the young girl, Rachael, due to the blundering folly of Luchek, but I know the King plans to visit this girl any day."

"Then can we finally attack?" said a bloodthirsty spirit with a guttural voice.

"No! Fool! There will be no attack yet. We must continue to wait until the baby is born. Then, we will go in with force." He stood and stretched his crooked black scepter over the commanding officers. "Be sure to control your forces. There will be no attack until I give the word."

He sat back down and brooded over the palace silhouette jutting up from the murky horizon. *I have complete control. This is why I am the established prince over all Persia. Eventually, I will need to alert lord Satan, but I'll wait until my trap is fully set. Then, I will deliver the prize. My wisdom and power will certainly earn me. . .*

A massive disturbance around the palace walls cut his thoughts short. An entire legion of elzurim leapt over the walls and took up positions surrounding the palace perimeter. Next, a thousand captains established positions atop the thick stone walls. Finally, an inner perimeter of commanders and generals took to flight and hovered just behind the walls, above and behind the captains. All the host had swords drawn.

"I was right!" Marr roared. "This is it! Everyone stay down and keep out of sight. Next, we should see the. . ."

Cherubim—descending from the heavens. Their eyes of fire darted to and fro like lightning, almost daring anyone to challenge the holiness of the Great King. Their wings made an unmistakable roar as they descended and landed on mortal earth. The presence of these creatures could mean only one thing—the glory of the King would be there. For several minutes, the cherubim fell out of sight. The rings of angelic warriors remained poised for battle, and the entire valley became silent.

Then, as steadily and purposefully as they had descended, the magnificent guardians of the holy place rose from the palace and ascended back into the heavens. It was an eerie, awesome spectacle. *The last time I've seen this was at the dedication of Solomon's temple.*

For several moments, stillness hung over everything. Then, hundreds of demons—mostly small brash insubordinates—from all around the perimeter exploded inward toward the palace in a desperate assault. The demon commanders snagged many of the imps and wrestled them down in a writhing mass. Several dozen of the quicker demons made it to the outer line of angels. The angelic line dispatched them with ease, and an uncomfortable quiet resettled over the whole area.

Marr sat on his throne, slowly tapping one of his talons on the armrest. *Everything is going exactly as I planned. Now, we will wait.*

———

Elric stood outside Mary's house in Nazareth and looked southward toward Egypt. *At this very moment, the cherubim are making their flight. Every beaelzur eye will be on them.* Here, in Nazareth, the Middle Realm had nothing remarkable to see. Jenli's warriors stood at hidden posts around Mary's house, and Jenli hid on the roof. They had no enemy presence within their peaceful, quiet boundaries.

Elric stood outside at the front door. He pushed his head through the wall and checked inside. Several members of Mary's family lined the walls of the main room, sleeping. It appeared dark and normal— just another sleepy night in a simple house in a small desert town. Elric returned to his post outside.

And then, without even a whisper, a pure white light appeared from inside and spilled out between the cracks around the door. It began to glow like a candle and then grew until it became an intense blast of light bursting from within.

Human eyes can't see that, but anyone in the Middle Realm. . . With a clenched jaw, he clutched his sword handle and scanned everywhere. All remained quiet.

As he and his team guarded the secrecy, the great King—the creator of everything, the one who sits on the awesome Throne in the Holiest of Holies—spoke the Word into the fragile shell of a mortal—a seed that would become His own Son.

Elric shook his head. *It is too astounding to comprehend. The firstborn of all creation is now going to become the firstborn of a mere woman. This is a bold plan indeed.*

After a few short moments, the light faded, and the room returned to its comfortable darkness. Elric peeked in. Mary still slept. The rest of the family slumbered, unaware of the visitation they had just encountered.

It is done. This changes everything. There is no turning back now. Our job just became infinitely more difficult. And infinitely more important.

25

A MOTHER'S EYES

Birth minus 40 weeks

*E*lric's large muscular frame filled the entire corner of the room of Mary's house as the next morning unfolded. He crossed his arms and took in a deep breath of the new day, full of freshness and anticipation. The humans were just waking.

They have no idea. They perceive nothing unusual about this day. If only they knew that the sun has just risen on a new age. Right there, in a sleepy bundle, is the secret miracle of eternity hidden within a young girl. How is it possible? We all know the King's great love for mankind and how He desires to reestablish fellowship with them, but to literally become one of them—it is beyond understanding.

The room was so. . . typically human—mud–plastered walls, dirty clothes, clay vessels, an old wooden table, a cooking pot, a half–filled basket of fruit. *All the times I have stood before the King in the great throne room, and now. . .* He looked at Mary. He shook his head and took a deep breath. *And now here I am, standing alone at the center of this great secret plan. Not only do these people have no idea what is happening, neither does anyone else besides a handful of common elzurim.*

He took another breath.

If nothing else, I shall be glad when the secret is revealed. It seems wrong for this to be known to only a few. How is it that the stones themselves don't cry out? How can we possibly keep this hidden from the enemy until the proper time? What will happen if we aren't able to. . .

Mary rose. Elric's eyes followed her. *I wonder if she can tell.* She went through her morning routines, and every move hinted that she knew something. With a slight knowing sparkle in her eyes, she appeared lost in introspection as she brushed out her long black hair. She finished her hair and rubbed her belly. *She does know! I'm not surprised.*

Mary prepared to go Joseph's house as usual, but this morning she packed several large bundles. After breakfast and some prolonged goodbyes, she left the house with her packs and her sister, Salome. Mary still hadn't told her family anything about her encounter with Gabriel.

She's too frightened, too confused. I am pleased she responded to my promptings to go and stay with Zacharias and Elizabeth. The time away will be good for her. And the danger here is too great.

Next, they needed to get Joseph to release her. It would not be easy.

Mary moved through town, and Jenli's team exercised their network, clearing a path and making necessary diversions. Elric followed from rooftop to rooftop. They had practiced this hundreds of times over the last several months, but things were different now. Even though veiled by an unlikely layer of human flesh, a spark of Divinity now made its way through the dusty streets, and any spirit looking for it would certainly see it. They had almost reached Joseph's house when the girls passed an alley where an unkempt vagrant sat in a sprawled half–drunken stupor. He looked up at the girls, looked again, and then called out to them.

"Hey! What's this?" His voice sounded gravelly and almost inhuman. The man tried to climb to his feet and catch up with the girls, but he couldn't even stand in his impaired state. The girls picked up their pace without looking back. Elric drew his sword but stayed out of sight.

The demon spirit within the man left the man's feeble flesh unconscious in the alley and moved on without him toward the girls.

"Enemy contact with Mary!" signaled a silent flash from a rooftop angelic blade. A dozen covert signals flashed. Jenli's team maintained their discipline and kept an inconspicuous distance while diverting other enemy forces away from the area. Elric tightened his grip on his sword. *Maybe this one will not notice.*

The demon approached the girls from behind. He kept a cautious distance and looked confused. He craned his neck and squinted at Mary. He continued examining her from a short distance while shooting nervous glances at the rooftops and around building corners. He started to move in closer.

He can tell!

A blinding flash of lightning struck directly in front of the demon and stopped him cold. Elric stood in the middle of the smoke, sword drawn and eyes ablaze. The smoke cleared, and Elric squared up with the demon.

"What. . . is that?" demanded the dark spirit pointing at Mary. "Is that girl carrying the Coming One?" His face looked shaded and leathery, contorted by evil and scarred by hatred. His eyes were sunken and devoid of light or mercy. He continued to examine Mary over Elric's shoulder. His bony fingers had large protruding knuckles and short conical claws.

Elric gave no response.

The demon's pointed finger rolled into a tight fist. "She is! My master must be made aware of this at once!"

He unfurled his bat–like wings, but before he could flinch, Elric made a backhanded slash with his sword and caught the demon mid-torso. The sword became engulfed in scintillating blue flames as it swung, and it cut the dark spirit in half, leaving nothing but a small sulfurous cloud of yellow vapor. The encounter happened in less than a blink and without a whisper, and before the wisps of smoke dissipated, Jenli arrived and stood next to Elric.

Elric held his sword up to examine it. The flame dissipated, but the emblem of the morning star engraved on the blade still glowed a bright blue. The glow subsided, and he slid his sword into its sheath. He turned a stern face toward Jenli.

"We cannot send every suspecting enemy to the abyss. We must do a better job of keeping the King hidden."

"Yes, captain." Jenli took flight.

Mary had just reached Joseph's house.

———

Elric entered Joseph's house, stopped, and took in a long, slow breath through his nose. *How I love the sweet fragrance from the King's courts. The presence of the Holy Spirit is strong here this morning.* Waves of peace and comfort settled in the Middle Realm on the old woman in bed. *And He is ministering to Joseph's mother.* Brondor, one of Jenli's warriors, stood beside her. Elric moved into the room and stood beside his companion. Joseph's mother's eyes followed Elric, and without a word, and it made the sick old lady smile.

"She sees?" Elric asked.

Brondor nodded. "We have been talking all morning."

The love of the King wrapped around the old lady like a blanket. Elric knelt beside her and touched her spirit just inside her hand. "It is a special gift—to perceive in the spirit," he said. "The Lord loves you very much."

She closed her eyes and pressed her thin lips together.

Elric took another deep breath of the sweet fragrance and let it out. His gaze started tender at first, but then it became resolved.

"I'm going to tell her," he said to Brondor.

"Captain. . ."

"I know it's a risk. But I sense the Lord wants to give her this special gift. And I think she can help us."

Elric spoke her name and she opened her eyes. He drew close and spoke into her ear. "Today the Lord is blessing you with another gift. Today. . . your eyes shall see the mother of the promised Messiah."

Joseph's mother's mouth fell open and her eyes widened.

A side conversation between Joseph and Mary interrupted their discussion.

"You're going where?" Joseph asked Mary in a hushed exclamation.

"Judea. My cousin Elizabeth is old and expecting a child in about three months. I need to go and help take care of her."

"But what about my mother? I need you here. I can't do this alone."

The pressure and stress welled up in Mary's eyes and dripped down her cheek. "I know, and I hate to leave—especially right now. But I have to. I'm so sorry. I have to go. . . I need time to. . . Elizabeth needs me."

Joseph looked shocked and confused.

Mary looked conflicted and scared. She grabbed her sister's hand and pulled her forward. "My sister has agreed to come and care for your mother in my place. She is very good. You can trust her."

"But. . ." Joseph started to counter.

"Is that her?" his mother asked.

Three simultaneous responses came back to old lady in the bed.

"Yes," replied Joseph. "Mary is here to watch over you while I go to work today."

"Yes," replied Mary. "This is my sister, Salome, who will be taking care of you for a while."

"Yes," replied Elric. He smiled and looked into her tired eyes. "Mary is already carrying the Messiah. He will deliver Israel and sit on the throne of David. Your mortal eyes will not see the final deliverance, when the King vanquishes His enemies and rules over all the kingdoms with justice and power, but you see now the beginning of the fulfillment of your blessed hope."

She propped herself up as much as she could.

"Please. . . come here, my child," Joseph's mother said, motioning to Mary.

Mary came and knelt beside her with Salome and Joseph close behind.

"May I touch her?" the mother asked Elric.

"Of course," Mary replied with a puzzled expression.

Joseph's mother didn't move her hand, but waited for Elric, who smiled and answered, "Yes, the Son of God is come to be touched and handled."

The instant her hand touched Mary's head to stroke her fine black hair, Joseph's mother was filled with the Holy Spirit and prophesied. "The Kingdom of God is upon us. This child will be called the Son of the Most High. He will extend His reign forever and ever, and every nation will bow before Him." She lay back down with a tired smile and closed her eyes.

Mary pulled back, turned, and looked up at Joseph. She glanced at Salome. They both looked stunned and perplexed. Mary opened her mouth and paused, as though searching for the right words.

"I fear I'm losing her," Joseph whispered. "She has been talking gibberish all morning. She keeps talking to someone, but nobody is there."

"Our own little Mary," his mother rambled. "Who would have thought it could be possible. And my Joseph?"

"Yes, Mother," Joseph answered.

Elric answered, "Is not the father. The Son of Man has been conceived of the Holy Spirit as foretold by the prophets. But Joseph will care for the boy and be as a father to Him."

"I'm so proud." She beamed as she held Joseph's outstretched hand.

"There is a small matter for which I could use your help," Elric said to her.

"What is it?"

"What is what, Mother?" Joseph said. "What do you see? Can I get you something?" The three humans standing around the bed looked down at the old lady with a wince of pity in their eyes.

Elric continued. "Our enemy seeks to destroy the child. I need to move Mary to a place where I can better protect her for a short while. She has received instructions to go to Judea immediately."

"What can I do?"

"Nothing, Mother," Joseph said. "You just need to rest. Mary and I will take care of whatever you need."

Elric smiled and continued. "Convince Joseph to let her go. He is very concerned for you and is reluctant to release her on your account. You will be unbound from this body of death soon, and it will be a difficult time for Joseph. However, it is important to God's plan for Mary to be in Judea right now. She will return after a time and will wed Joseph as planned. But for now, I need to move her."

The frail old lady smiled a peaceful motherly smile and nodded. "Joseph?"

"I'm here, Mother."

"Joseph, Mary needs to go to Judea."

Joseph turned his head and whispered to Mary, "She must have overheard us talking." Returning to his mother, he said, "We are still discussing it, Mother. You need not worry about it."

"No, you don't understand." She propped herself up again and addressed him as only a mother can. "It is the Lord's will for her to go."

Bewilderment spread across Joseph's face.

She continued, "Sometimes we need to simply trust and set our own desires aside. Don't worry about me. The Lord has already given me a great gift." She smiled at Mary and turned back to Joseph. "And He is giving you a great gift also. Please do as I ask and release her with your blessing." She leaned back onto her bed and took both of Mary's hands. "My daughter, I release you. Go in peace, you who are most favored of God."

Joseph scowled back and forth at Mary and his mother.

Elric spoke to Joseph. "Be strong. Trust the Lord. Let go of your own plans."

Joseph gritted his teeth, turned, and left the room. Brondor started to follow, but Elric stopped him with a head nod. Several minutes passed before Joseph returned. He stood beside the bed with shoulders slumped and sadness on the lines of his face.

"As you wish, Mother," he said with a slight bow. And then he turned to Mary and said, "Mary, go with my blessing. But please return quickly and remember your vows."

———

An hour later, a group of merchants gathered near the center of Nazareth, preparing a caravan for a trip. Mary and Joseph stood in the middle of the group. Elric and Jenli stood near. Elric only half-listened to the humans. His attention stayed fixed on the area around them and the nearby horizon. *We're too exposed. We need to move now.*

"Are you sure about this?" Joseph asked one of the merchants.

"Of course, of course," the merchant said as he cinched up a pack on the camel. "We'll pass right through the hill country of Judea, and one additional traveler is no burden at all."

At least twenty men hoisted large sacks, bundles, and wooden chests onto camels, donkeys, and carts. The commotion jostled Joseph and Mary, who struggled to keep out of the way. The apprehension in Joseph's eyes grew with each bump and push.

The merchant pulled Joseph over close to his cart. "I have known Mary's family for years. She's like a sister to me. And I know Elizabeth. I think it is a good thing that Mary does by going to her. It's too far a journey to make alone, but she will be safe with us." The merchant finished one pack and began working on another. "It's an amazing coincidence that Mary found me yesterday," the merchant said to Joseph. "We have been preparing to leave for a week, but things kept preventing us. Then, Mary showed up yesterday. The day before we set out. Amazing, isn't it?"

"Mm-hm. How long will the trip take?"

"Several days to Judea. The rest of us will travel on much farther after that."

One of the other merchants pointed toward the western sky. Huge dark storm clouds piled up over the horizon and crept toward them. "Are you sure we want to leave today?"

"We have no choice. We are already late, and we cannot have any more delays." Then turning to Joseph, the merchant said, "Don't worry. We will care for her well on the trip. In fact, as you can see, I have prepared a small shelter here on this cart for her."

He had a two-wheeled cart with long pulling poles attached to the harness of a donkey. On its flat bed, bundled packs stacked up to form a wall at the front. A triangular makeshift tent formed from wooden poles and thick fabric ran the length of the cart.

"It's no palace, but it should keep the rain off," the merchant said.

"You are very kind," Mary replied.

Elric's eyes continued probing for enemy presence—left, front, right, back, high, low. "It's too dangerous having Mary out in the open like this," he said to Jenli. "I am anxious to get the caravan moving."

"It looks like we're close," Jenli said. "The people are saying their goodbyes. Lacidar's team is in position and ready for escort."

Elric scanned the perimeter for the four concealed warriors of Lacidar's team but didn't see them. "Good. Are you and your team prepared for your next task?"

"We are. The Lord will surely give us success."

Two demons approached on an erratic line overhead near the edge of the caravan. Elric's hand moved to his sword and his eyes tracked their path. The demons passed by without noticing them, and Elric's grip on his sword relaxed. He looked to the natural sky. The storm clouds drew close now. The rain should start soon. *Perfect.*

The troop began its march. Dust rose, beasts bellowed, carts rattled, and the rumble of hooves shook the ground.

Elric turned to Jenli and called out, "Send word of your progress in Bethlehem."

Jenli nodded.

Elric walked with Mary. She started out walking beside her beast of burden, but before they reached the end of the street, the rains started, and she tucked away under the cover of her tent. The caravan reached a steady, plodding pace, and the men of the caravan pressed forward through the rain. Mary stayed hidden and dry under her tent. Elric sat on the back of the cart with his feet dangling off. He rode in full view, but the other four warriors fanned out to scout and keep watch over the perimeter.

The rain lasted for hours. Several small groups of beaelzurim passed overhead early in the journey. With each passing enemy, Elric tracked their path with his eyes only, never moving his head. A quick peripheral glance confirmed Mary stayed concealed under the tent. *Thank you, Lord, for the rain.*

26

TWO HOUSES

Birth minus 40 weeks

Around midday at Achim's house on the outskirts of Bethlehem, Jenli and three of his team crouched low behind a half-wall of an ancient stronghold with its jagged edges and bricks of light strewn in loose piles of rubble—reminders of battles long past. Jenli poked his head over the top of the wall and surveyed the house, which was large and stately for a home near Bethlehem. The tall white marble columns at the entry looked like something from Rome. *This is definitely the best we will find in Bethlehem.*

A fourth member of his team, Jennidab, crept up from behind. He knelt on one knee next to Jenli and kept his voice low. "Two beaelzurim. Both in the inner foyer. One is a lieutenant."

"Good," Jenli replied, still examining the battlefield. "This should be a simple operation. We will take them inside where we can remain unseen."

Jenli pulled back down behind the wall. "We'll use the Jerihämer maneuver. Jessik and Kaylar, you two take the north side and hit the lieutenant—blindness. Jennidab and Jerem, you have the other one from the south—confusion. I'll be the focus. Wait for my signal."

All four nodded. Jenli motioned with his hand, and they all moved out.

Jenli stood tall, expanded to his full ten-foot height, drew his sword, and walked toward the front of the house. He maneuvered around barricades of darkness, probing around every corner. He stopped at the front door for only a moment, then passed through into the inner foyer.

The two demons startled and spun around. They each drew their weapons.

"You are mistaken to enter here," the demon lieutenant growled. "This is my domain."

"My captain requires it," Jenli said. "You may surrender it, or I will have to take it by force."

"You have no rights here!"

"I will give you three counts."

"I will not surrender ground that is rightfully mine."

"One. . ."

The demon lieutenant expanded to his full size and snorted smoke through his flared nostrils.

"Two. . ."

The two demons lifted their swords above their heads and stepped forward. The demon lieutenant roared and leapt toward Jenli.

"Three!"

In mid-lunge, a ball of plasma from the side of the room smashed into the side of the lieutenant's head, sending him flailing sideways.

A second blast of energy sizzled in and threw him into a spin that dumped him flat on his back on the floor. The second demon turned toward his lieutenant, and two balls of energy shot in from the other side of the room, hitting him square in the back. He crashed facedown on the floor.

Both demons squealed, jumped back to their feet, and held their swords outward.

"Blind!" shouted the lieutenant. "I can't see!" He swung his sword with wild, aimless gyrations.

The second demon stood for a moment, blinking and shaking his head with erratic, jerky motions. He looked at Jenli, who remained motionless. He looked back at the demon lieutenant who drew closer with each blind swing. The blind demon lieutenant swung again, and the second demon lunged forward and slashed him just above his knee. The lieutenant shouted, and yellow smoke spewed from the wound. He fell to one knee, bringing his sword down in the direction of his unseen assailant. The blade caught the smaller demon across his shoulder, sending him reeling backwards.

His wound sealed, he regained his strength, and he re-engaged the lieutenant with an enraged war cry. Still swinging a furious blind blade, the demon lieutenant fended off three strikes, but a fourth thrust from his confused companion pierced the lieutenant clean through his chest. The attacking demon held his blade in place and the lieutenant dropped to his knees, gasping for breath. With an unexpected burst of energy, the lieutenant made a wide vertical arc with his sword and brought it down on the head of the second demon. The blade sliced from the top of the demon's head all the way through his torso, and the two rent halves of his spiritual body fell together to the ground where thick clouds of sulfurous smoke belched out until the laceration sealed back over. The demon lieutenant yanked the embedded sword from his chest with a shriek and tossed it across the room.

Jenli stepped up and put his foot on the back of the smaller demon's neck and pinned him to the ground. Then, with one simple slice, Jenli hacked through the forearm of the lieutenant, and the demon's sword clattered to the ground. Jenli motioned to his team. They sprang forward and bound both demons head to foot with cords of white energy.

"Bind their mouths, also," Jenli said. "The blindness and confusion will wear off soon, and we do not want to listen to their blasphemies."

Jenli spoke a word and formed a large ball of energy. With his hands he rolled the energy into long poles. They solidified into stout posts of light, and he embedded them vertically into the ground. "Tie them to these posts. We shall keep them prisoner here until our task is complete."

Jenli breathed a long sigh. *The King's birthplace has been secured.* Now for the remaining details. He pulled out a tablet and scrawled notes. He inspected every room. He examined all the spiritual fortifications. He finished an initial assessment of every person in the house. There was no detail too small to record.

"Bring word to the captain," Jenli said to Jerem. "Achim's house is ours."

The warrior nodded and disappeared in a blink.

Jenli called Jessik and Kaylar aside. "You two will keep this place. Guard the prisoners. Hold this ground."

"In His service."

"I wonder how Zaben's mission proceeds," he said. "The evil surrounding Zaben must be oppressive. I can only imagine the heavy load on his shoulders."

————

In the center of Zaben's stronghold in Egypt, the wedding celebration of Benjamin and Rachael marked a sharp contrast to the looming darkness in the Middle Realm outside the palace grounds. While tens of thousands of demonic warriors gathered and prepared for a siege, a human band played happy music with a dancing beat for the guests of the wedding party.

Zaben laughed as he finished a triple spin with a flourish. He lowered his shoulder, slid to his left, shouted "ha" with each of eight crisscross foot stomps, locked wrists with another dancing warrior, spun twice with high steps, and launched his dance partner high into the air, laughing all the while. The music from the band rang out with jubilant energy. The people had high spirits, and Zaben couldn't help but celebrate with them. Benjamin and Rachael had a beautiful wedding, and while the young couple honeymooned, the wedding feast continued. Here in the palace, they had plentiful food and drink, and the guests enjoyed a grand party.

In the midst of all the complicated events of the times, it felt good to stop and enjoy a time of pure celebration. And for the next few days, Zaben intended to do just that. Even though besieged on all sides by a wall of darkness, he would laugh and dance for a while with the humans who rejoiced on this little island of blessing.

During the lulls in the celebration—usually when the partiers rested after a hearty dance—the people and talked and shared happy stories. Zaben listened for information from outside their walls.

"Have you noticed how. . . nice. . . things have been within the palace over the last six months?"

"It's very strange. People seem to be less cross with each other. Things just seem to be working without extra effort."

"I've noticed it, too. And there hasn't been as much sickness. It's as though we are under a shadow of blessing. It's a completely different feeling from the marketplace on the outside."

"And it's not just us—the Romans are sensing it, too. The soldiers, the officials, even the proconsul has been almost congenial"

"I heard his wife is expecting."

"I heard he is having a crown of gold made for the baby."

"I heard old man Isaac over here has a new song he wants to sing."

"Let's hear it! Pour some more wine. Go ahead Isaac. . . sing your song!"

For days the celebration continued. And for days Zaben stood in the middle of it all, soaking up all the joyful life. This kind of innocent exuberance honored the King, and Zaben enjoyed watching the waves of unspoken praise wafting into the heavens. Eventually, Benjamin and Rachael reappeared from their time alone and sparked a whole new round of renewed celebration.

No one could see it, but Zaben knew a surprise awaited Rachael. Sometimes it pleased the Lord to open the womb of a new bride during the honeymoon. They had more to celebrate now than even they knew about. Yet.

27

JOURNEY TO JUDEA

Birth minus 40 weeks

The merchant caravan plodded southward to Judea. Elric stayed close to Mary, making sure she remained concealed whenever enemy presence drew near. The weather had been inconsistent, and Mary spent as much time under the cover of her simple cart shelter as she did walking.

After two days on the road, the afternoon sky became dark once more—more ominous than any before. A fast-moving cloud approached with a darkness deeper than a typical water-heavy thunderhead. The men watched the swirling shadow advance from the south with uneasy glances. They braced for a strong downpour. Mary ducked under her cover.

Elric palmed the handle of his sword and stayed seated on the back of the wagon. *This cloud carries more than rain. There must be at least a thousand beaelzurim.* They flew low under an actual storm cloud like a massive congregation of bats, and Elric remained motionless as they passed overhead. Their piercing eyes probed the caravan and dared him to try to engage. *If any of the enemy comes down to challenge, Mary will almost certainly be discovered.* Even if the four hidden elzurim at the perimeter came to help, they would be no match for a company this large. Every fiber of his being pulled tight.

The enemy made their erratic flight paths, and Elric remembered with sadness how they used to look—beautiful in appearance, graceful in movements, a reflection of the King's glory. Now, wretched in appearance, they were difficult to behold. Ever since the Rebellion, they had become as dark in form as their hearts. The wings, once a lovely translucent white, had become leathery, black, jagged, and rough. These wings used to provide flowing, effortless flight through the Middle Realm. Now their flight looked laborious and unstable. Eyes that used to glow with sparkling blue, green, or brown had become hollow black nulls encircled with evil red. These beings were altogether devoid of goodness, and as Elric watched them, he could find no pity for their current state. Their treason was too unspeakable.

If I just appear undisturbed and unthreatening, perhaps the caravan will go unchecked. A minute passed. *Keep going. Keep going.* Then, one of the dark spirits broke away from the cloud and made a large swooping arc downward toward him. *Oh, no. . .* The demon, a hulking commander, stopped in front of Elric and hovered just above his reach. Elric jumped up and took a defensive stance on the back of the wagon with his shining sword positioned diagonally in front of him. For a prolonged moment, they surveyed each other without speaking a word.

"What is the purpose of your travels?" the dark commander demanded.

"These men are carrying cargo and goods, and I am here to ensure their safe passage."

"This cargo must be of some value to warrant a captain for an escort."

Elric didn't flinch. He remained stone-faced and cold.

"But," the demon continued, "not as valuable as the prize I seek. What is your destination?"

"Certainly nowhere as important as yours," Elric said. "Where are *you* going that requires such a company?"

"Ha!" The commander laughed. "You puny, obedient servants are so predictable. Guarding your little cargo. Trying to gather information. What would you do if I told you? Attack? I think not. I know what you would do. You would stay with your little caravan because those were your orders and then report your findings to your superior at the end of your tasking. You don't have the freedom to execute your own will the way we do. That is why in the end, we will be victorious. It's not until you break the chains of bondage that you can truly experience your own power from within yourself."

The demon commander drew closer until he hovered face to face with Elric. The commander's chest swelled, and he exhaled a hot stream of sulfur into Elric's face. Elric remained unmoved. He didn't blink.

Out of the corner of his eye—movement! Mary poked her head out from behind her tent flap. Only a sword's length distance separated her from the demon commander, and there was no way to drive her back under cover without giving her away. Mary emerged even farther, exposing her head and shoulder. *She might come all the way out. How has the commander not noticed her already? I need to draw him away without leaving Mary unguarded.* Elric drilled his gaze into the eyes of the commander. *Must command his attention.*

"You are afraid to tell me your mission," Elric challenged. "You hide your fear behind your pride."

The demon snorted. "Fear? A mere captain? I shall tell you my objective. There is nothing you can do to counter us." He turned toward the passing horde and lifted his chin. "We know the Coming One has been conceived here on earth. In fact, we have Him surrounded in Egypt."

A clap of thunder shook the natural world. The animals all jumped, the men ducked, and Mary retreated behind her tent flap. Elric fought back a smile.

"You have seen Him?" Elric said with a surprised tone.

"Not directly, but we know He is there. Still, my master has concerns about some prophecies concerning Nazareth and Bethlehem, so he has dispatched my company to Nazareth and another to Bethlehem to be sure. We are going to search those little towns. If the mother of the Messiah is there, we will find her. We will search two or three months if needed. Your King has made a fatal mistake by coming into our domain. Once he takes on the body of flesh, we will tear Him to shreds."

We knew the enemy would be bent on destroying the Son of Man, but hearing it spoken by one of them. . . His inner being shuddered. He tightened his jaw and stared at the commander without emotion.

The demon gave a sneering laugh. "You are as weak as you are inhibited. Guard your insignificant little caravan, captain. I have more important business to attend to." With a dismissive flick of his wings, the commander sheathed his sword and made a slow sweeping pass over the caravan on his way toward the passing shadows.

The demon skittered past the line of travelers, and an eerie chill swept through the natural air. The men's eyes darted about into nothingness. They rubbed the prickly hairs on their arms and necks. The animals' steps stuttered. Then the chill passed, and the troop plodded onward into the menacing thunderstorm. The rain started.

A brief shower fell, and the dark cloud moved off to the north, sinking over the horizon. A small break in the clouds appeared overhead, and rays of golden sunlight beamed through the canopy. Elric took his seat again on the back of the wagon. Mary peeked out of her shelter.

Birth minus 39 weeks

Elric hopped off the back of the cart. *Judea. Finally, we can get Mary indoors and out of sight.* He examined the area all around. All looked quiet. He covered the short walk to Zacharias's in a blink and met Lacidar outside the front door.

"It is good to see you, captain," Lacidar said. "How was your trip?"

"Very good. The Lord has given us success. Is your perimeter here secure?"

"Yes, sir. We have walled in the prophet and have been preparing for your coming. There are no enemy forces within our boundary."

"Good work."

Mary approached with two men carrying her packs.

Lacidar smiled with his hands on his hips. "I've been waiting to see the look on Zacharias's face when he first sees Mary. He doesn't know her condition, but it has been several years since he's seen her. This will be a great surprise."

Mary knocked on the door.

The door cracked open, and Zacharias peered out. His eyes grew wide. His mouth dropped open. He flung open the door and wrapped Mary up in a huge hug, then pulled her into the house and motioned to the men—all without a word.

Elric smiled at Lacidar and nodded. "Surprised indeed. We should go in. I'm excited to see how Elizabeth reacts to Mary's news."

———

Outside Zacharias and Elizabeth's house, two sets of glowing red and black eyes spied from their concealments as a captain and lieutenant of the host entered the house.

"A captain and four warriors escorting one girl?" Tumur whispered to Luchek.

Luchek nodded. "There was something most interesting about that girl. From this distance, I couldn't be sure what it was. But there was definitely something. . ." Luchek picked at a yellowed fang with one of his grimy talons. He turned back to Tumur and asked, "What is our next move?"

"I don't know yet," Tumur said. "For now, we should focus on this young girl and learn all we can. Eventually an opportunity for action will present itself." Tumur peered out from their hiding spot and scanned the perimeter. "Get back to your post and continue the surveillance. Do not try anything brash."

———

Mary and Zacharias bustled into the house followed by the two men carrying her packs. Elric and Lacidar took positions beside the front wall in the main room, which rested in quiet stillness, neat and tidy, with no signs of the disorder children bring. The men placed Mary's bags just inside the threshold and excused themselves. Mary gave them quiet thanks and bade them safe travels.

"Who was that at the door, Zacharias?" Elizabeth called out from the back room.

Zacharias motioned to Mary about his inability to talk. Then he smiled, rolled his eyes, and shrugged as if to say, *She knows I can't answer her.*

Mary muffled a laugh with her hand and called back, "Hello, Elizabeth! It's Mary! From Nazareth."

A startled yelp came from the back room. Zacharias and Mary jumped. From the sound of Elizabeth's voice, it sounded like she might have fallen, but there was no crash on the floor. They rushed in, followed by Elric and Lacidar. They found her standing, hands on her pooching belly, and looking flushed. She trembled and glanced around the room with wild eyes.

Elric and Lacidar stood by with wide silly–looking grins.

"The Holy Spirit just came upon Elizabeth," Elric said.

"And I think she is about to prophesy," Lacidar added.

Elric chuckled. "This should be good."

Elizabeth's eyes met Mary, and she quickly averted her eyes downward. In a loud voice she exclaimed, "Blessed are you among women, and blessed is the child you will bear! But why am I so favored, that the mother of my Lord should come to me? As soon as the sound of your greeting reached my ears, the baby in my womb leaped for joy. Blessed is she who has believed that what the Lord has said to her will be accomplished!"

Elric and Lacidar both laughed aloud.

"That *was* good," Elric said.

Zacharias stood with his silent mouth wide open.

Mary took a step backward, covered her mouth, and muttered to herself, "I have told nobody. First there was Joseph's mother—that could be explained as ramblings of an old woman. But this. . ." She shook her head and continued to mutter. "Not only did she know I'm carrying a child, but she called me the 'mother of my Lord!' She believes this is the Son of God Himself!"

Mary's hands fell to her sides. "This is really happening," she said. She repeated it louder. "This is really happening." In the Middle Realm, a warm shower of light flooded over Mary.

Lacidar said, "She's going to prophesy, too. Isn't she?"

"I believe so," Elric said with a smile.

Mary's voice rang out, and her words filled the Middle Realm with scintillating light. "My soul exalts the Lord, and my spirit has rejoiced in God my Savior. For He has had regard for the humble state of His bondslave; for behold, from this time on all generations will count me blessed. For the Mighty One has done great things for me; and holy is His name. And His mercy is upon generation after generation toward those who fear Him. He has done mighty deeds with His arm; He has scattered those who were proud in the thoughts of their heart. He has brought down rulers from their thrones, and has exalted those who were humble. He has filled the hungry with good things; and sent away the rich empty-handed. He has given help to Israel His servant, in remembrance of His mercy, as He spoke to our fathers, to Abraham and his descendants forever."

Zacharias stood with his silent mouth wide open.

"Mighty deeds," Elric said.

"Rulers from their thrones," Lacidar said. "I live for that day."

Elric nodded. "It is near upon us."

The humans prepared and ate supper, and Elric and Lacidar soaked in a cloud of the Lord's presence. The sweet aroma of the Spirit filled the air in the Middle Realm. Lacidar stood in the corner and plucked a triumphant new song on his resonar while Elric closed his eyes, hummed along, and directed an absent choir with his right hand. Elric kept an ear toward the humans' conversations.

They shared a flurry of stories. Elizabeth couldn't get the events of their experience out fast enough. Mary recounted all that had happened to her. Zacharias couldn't get a single word in, even if he could have spoken. They carried on as if all three had some enormous, marvelous, outrageous secret bottled up and were bursting to tell someone who might understand and believe it.

With his eyes still closed, Elric smiled when they realized the connection of their stories. One carried the Messiah; the other carried the prophet who would prepare the way for the Messiah. Here sat two simple women carrying sons who would change the world forever.

Elric lifted his left hand and then with both hands found the downbeat and directed the music with grand, sweeping satisfaction.

28

TWO CITIES

Birth minus 38 weeks

Two large demons landed outside the house of the shepherd Jeremiah at Nazareth. A smaller demon met them at the threshold and refused them entry.

"Move on," the small demon demanded. His slight frame and insignificant size couldn't begin to match the two beaelzurim brutes who overshadowed him at the threshold.

"Our master requires we search every house in Nazareth," one of the large demons sneered. "We will search this one."

The small demon had an oversized head and bulging eyes. His hairless skin looked smooth and ashen. He crossed his spindly arms and scowled. "I have seen the scourge of this horde. You have all the subtlety of a firestorm. I have a sensitive meeting in progress, and I will not allow you to spoil my work."

"We seek. . ."

"I know what you seek. I can tell you of certainty, He is not here."

"But we. . ."

"He is *not* here."

"You would swear before our master?"

"Yes, of course. Now move on. I have work to do."

A young boy, Daniel—the youngest son of the shepherd Jeremiah, stepped through the meeting of demons, opened the front door, entered the house, and closed the door behind him.

The two demon brutes stole glances into the house through the open door.

"My meeting does not wait," the little demon said.

"Very well," said one of the brutes.

The small demon watched the two warriors lumber off to the next house. He lingered a moment. Then he turned and slunk through the front wall of Jeremiah's house.

He stepped into a thick and smoky atmosphere. Candles and incense burned on the table, and their tireless columns of swirling smolder climbed upward, creating a heavy layer of haze just below the ceiling. The man of the house, Jeremiah, and three other men—distinguished, grey-bearded, and learned—all reclined on large pillows in the center of the room and engaged in important discussions of politics and religion. The boy, Daniel, tossed an extra pillow next to his brothers, Levi and Jesse, who leaned against the back wall. He plopped down and listened to the banter of the elders.

The demon skulked in the shadowy corners, concealing his presence from the senses of the men. No bristly necks or unexplained chills. No sensation of unseen watching eyes. If he did his job right, no one would know or even suspect his presence.

He sneered a satisfied smirk. *How I love my mission*—injecting long–term and malevolent, clandestine, subversive, slow–acting poison into the hearts of men. *Unlike those boorish thugs who wanted to enter my space. . .* he shook his head and snorted a puff of disgust, *. . . I don't need to possess a man or do battle or inflict pain and infirmity. I need only to plant words into the air*—seeds consisting of lies, tiny kernels of deceit wrapped in hulls of truth and fertilized by intellectual reason, whose fruit ripens into confusion, division, and sometimes open warfare. *I can be more effective by turning people's eyes off of the King than by dispatching ten thousand angels.*

He licked his wet lips and watched the three elders talk. They suited his mission perfectly. Educated and religious.

"But what about the promises of the coming Messiah?" Jeremiah said. "Most of the teachers of the Law agree that we should be expecting a King to arise who will defeat Rome and deliver us from its tyranny. In fact, many believe the time is close."

The demon shot a quick response. "Pharisees! You can't believe them!" His voice sounded smooth as liquid, and even though no physical ears could hear them, his words pierced through to the spirits of the men and into the minds of those who would receive them.

"These are teachings of the Pharisees," one of the men said with an understanding and coaching tone. "You need to be careful of these men, my friend."

"What? These are among the most respected men in the synagogue."

"Yes," another of the three men picked up, "but there are some good reasons to question their teachings. We Sadducees believe that the only true authority for religious and civic law is the Law of Moses. Do you not agree that the Torah ought to be our fundamental guide?"

The demon leaned back and smiled. *This will work. Appeal to men's intellect and desire to believe the right thing, and then use it against them with a simple twist of the truth.* He snickered at the irony. The Sadducees were far more secular than the Pharisees—more concerned with worldly success than the spiritual dimension of their faith. *And to think, somewhere else in a similar meeting, other demons slander the Sadducees to a different set of listeners.*

"Yes, of course the Torah is our primary source," Jeremiah answered, looking a bit muddled.

"The Pharisees do not believe this. They hold a large body of codified oral traditions to be sacred and of equal authority to the Law of Moses. How can you tell what is really true if they mix what is revered as sacred with that which ought not to be?"

The demon spoke. "You can't believe anything the Pharisees say." His sulfurous breath wheezed noxious vapors that swirled out and mixed with the layer of haze in the room.

Jeremiah fidgeted and scratched the back of his neck.

He is sifting through his basket of beliefs, trying to figure out what he knows to really be true. Perfect. The poison of division and doubt is injected—now it's time to plant a lie. "There is no Messiah. . ." he puffed into the smoky atmosphere.

Jeremiah sat back and stroked his beard.

The third man then offered his wisdom. "Now, concerning this concept of a Messiah. . . waiting for some savior to come along and do battle for us would be naïvely trusting in fate. We prefer to take our destiny into our own hands. We are free agents to choose and to act according to the way we see fit."

"According to the strict letter of the Torah, of course," his companion interjected.

"Of course. But how do we deal with these Roman oppressors? By waiting for fate? No. By forming treaties and alliances. By commerce and trade."

"By open revolt if necessary," came another interjection.

"Yes, but only if truly necessary. There are Zealots who advocate a more aggressive rebellion. The key point we want you to see is that trusting fate to provide some kind of liberator king is illogical, especially when we have the power to create change ourselves."

"You are powerful. And wise. You don't even have need of a savior," crooned the demon spirit. The lie settled like a thick blanket over everyone in the room.

The conversation concerning the Messiah devolved into an intellectual exchange about the differences in doctrinal beliefs between the Pharisees and Sadducees and even the Essenes. It progressed exactly how the demon conspirator intended. As long as he could keep men focused on laws, differences of opinions, and each other, he could keep them blind to the true, unseen spiritual kingdom.

The conversation took a new direction. "But if what you say is true," Jeremiah said, "what of eternal rewards, or punishment?"

"Ah, yes," the third man said as he sat back with a knowing smile, "a byproduct of another doctrine of the Pharisees—resurrection of the dead. They actually believe in the persistence of the soul. But we know that, in reality, the soul dies with the body. So then, what is the value of piety you may ask. The rewards are temporal. If you live righteously, you reap the benefits of good things here in this life. If you are wicked, evil will befall you. It is to your advantage, therefore, to follow the Torah; but there is no afterlife."

The demon echoed this new seed, just to make sure it found root. "There is no afterlife. All you have is here and now. There is no spiritual kingdom. In fact, there are not even any spiritual beings. Angels do not exist. Demons do not exist."

The first greybeard added another piece of wisdom. "This brings up another fallacy perpetrated by the Pharisees. They try to scare people with their made-up concept of angels and demons—spirits out there helping you or trying to cause you harm." He paused a moment. "Have you ever seen an angel?"

"Well, no, but. . ."

"They simply do not exist. You will not find them in the Torah."

Daniel, who had been listening to all this debate, became more and more fidgety. At this statement, he jumped up and shook his head. "What about the angels that visited Lot in Sodom?" he blurted out.

Jeremiah turned and gruffed, "Daniel, keep your place!"

Daniel scowled, but the three visitors laughed.

One of the men gave Jeremiah an agreeable slap on the shoulder, "It's okay, Jeremiah. The boy asks a good question. I'm glad to see a young man thinking for himself. This is actually a question that comes up often."

One of the other Sadducees said, "If you examine the passage carefully—as we have—you will notice it says they were 'messengers.' In fact, in most of the references to them, it describes them as men. Now, the Pharisees would have us believe that these were some kind of special spirit beings with wings and everything. However, nowhere do you see the mention of wings. Also, they came into the house and ate supper. Now I ask you—how could it be possible for a spirit to eat worldly food? It doesn't make sense."

The third greybeard added, "It is simply a ploy of the Pharisees. They want you to accept their concept of the persistence of the soul. They claim men have eternal spirits, so they invent these fictitious beings to somehow support their claim."

The demon said, "He's right. There are no angels or demons. You do not have an eternal soul. There is no judgment waiting for men."

Daniel, still standing, shook his head. His shoulders dropped, he turned, and he stepped outside. The demon followed and walked close beside him.

Daniel muttered to himself, "No afterlife? No Messiah? But father has taught us this my whole life. Could he be wrong?"

The demon whispered into Daniel's ear, "These men are very wise—wiser, in fact, than your father."

"Is he wrong about other things, too?" Daniel wondered out loud. "Wrong about God? Maybe God doesn't even exist."

"Look at the world around you," the demon said. "There certainly doesn't appear to be a God. There is so much injustice and brutality and hardship. How could a God allow this?"

Daniel made his way out to the flock and sat amongst the bleating sheep. He picked up a stick and threw it.

The demon smiled and returned to meeting inside.

———

Jenli stepped through the front wall of Achim's house in Bethlehem with Jerem, Jennidab, and Brondor close behind. Jessik and Kaylar, who stood guard in the main foyer, moved from their posts near their two demon prisoners and met the team.

"Lieutenant Jenli," Kaylar said, "it is good to see you. Have you seen. . ."

"Yes, they're everywhere—both here in Bethlehem and in Nazareth. It is at least as bad as Zaben predicted. That is why I have brought the rest of team. We must hold Achim's house until the hordes give up their search."

Jenli's team huddled in one corner of Achim's main foyer. They kept their voices low, and each made careful scans of the room as they talked.

"Sir, six of us cannot hope to hold off so many," Kaylar said.

"With the Lord's strength, we can hold off twice as many. And if we are given the flame of vengeance. . ."

They all reached for their sword handles with smiles.

"But I have another plan." Jenli glanced over at their two prisoners, still bound and tied to stakes. He lowered his voice even further, and the huddle drew in closer.

"The horde is not here to do battle and gain ground. They seek the girl who carries the seed of the King. We need only to hide these prisoners and remain out of sight. The enemy will come through, conduct their search, and move on. They may search this place several times over the next few months, but once they are convinced their prize is not here, they will return to Egypt. If we are successful, we will never have to fight a single. . ."

Two surly beaelzurim warriors entered the front of the foyer.

"Sir!" Brondor called out. All six angels drew their weapons and jumped to defensive positions. The two demons disappeared back through the front wall.

"Did they see the prisoners?" Jenli asked.

"They saw," Brondor replied.

"They will be back," Jenli said. "And they will come with reinforcements. It appears we will have to fight after all."

The team moved to the center of the room and formed a defensive circle with their backs to each other, swords drawn and shields up. Silence filled the room like a rising tide until its choking presence reached their necks. They each swallowed hard. Muscles drew tight. Eyes fixed outward.

Jenli whispered over his shoulder to the team, "We will stand until we can prevail no longer. It is important that we are not captured. We will retake this place later if necessary, but we must not fall into their hands."

Jenli looked down at his blade, hoping to see the spark of a blue flame. He saw nothing but cold steel. More tense minutes passed. Jenli's jawbone pressed outward against the tight skin of his cheek.

Boom! The room exploded with red fire. Hundreds of searing energy balls blasted in from all sides with a roar. The plasma spheres all reached Jenli's circle of warriors at the same time. The angels' skillful shields deflected or absorbed every one. Through the smoke, fifty demons bounded into the room, swords drawn for battle. They surrounded Jenli's team.

The demons closed in and laughed with each step.

"Now!" Jenli shouted. His team leapt outward, and the clash began. Clanging steel and war shouts filled the room. Sparks flew from crashing blades, and the air became rank with sulfur and smoke. Each angel fended off ten raging demons, but they lost ground with each passing moment. Jenli kept reaching for untapped strength from the King, but he found none. He kept trying to will a blue flame to his sword, but it never came. *Without additional strength, we will not win this battle.*

"Arggh!" Jenli heard over his shoulder.

Jennidab had been struck and fell face down on the ground. Two demons grabbed him by his ankles and dragged him outwards. Jenli jumped over and pulled his arms. They remained locked in position.

The attackers began to overwhelm the rest of the team.

"Retreat!" Jenli shouted over the melee. "Retreat!"

As they all took wing upwards, Brondor swooped down and sliced through the arms of demons holding Jennidab's ankles. Jenli yanked Jennidab's arms and bolted upward. In an instant, all six shot through the roof and flew away in a low, tight formation.

Jenli scanned the horizon for a safe passage away from town. Enemy squadrons filled the sky in every direction. He examined the ground below.

"They're everywhere," he called out.

"Lieutenant!" one of the warriors shouted, pointing toward a pack of demons flying in their direction.

"We must get out of sight," Jenli said. He searched the ground again. *There!*—a small animal shack behind an inn. He aimed his sword toward it and shouted, "There! Quickly, before they see us."

In less than a blink, all six angels disappeared within the shelter. They reduced their frames to fit within the confined space, and they stood in silence with their swords drawn and their attention focused outward. One minute passed. Two minutes. After five minutes Jenli lowered his sword and whispered, "Our presence is not known."

The team sheathed their swords and turned their focus toward Jenli.

"This is intolerable," Jenli said with gritted teeth. "Warriors of the most high King, surrounded at every side, hiding in a stable." He looked down. "Ankle-deep in animal dung." He rubbed the stubble on his head and chin. "And we lost our objective."

"We'll retake it, sir," Jennidab said.

Jenli's lips drew tight. "Yes, yes we will. We must. The success of our mission depends on it." He took a long, deep breath. "First, we need to get out from beneath this curtain of evil. We will each leave in different directions at various times. Avoid contact with the enemy at all costs and rendezvous at Archer's Cave in the hills. Do not go near Nazareth."

The five warriors nodded.

Jenli tapped one on the shoulder. "Go."

The warrior folded his wings around his body and closed his eyes. A small flash of light lit the inside of the stable, and there on the ground stood a mottled grey pigeon. The pigeon bobbed out between the planks of the door and flew off.

Jenli pulled out his writing tablet and began scrawling notes. After several minutes, he nodded to the next warrior.

29

THE PROPHET COMES

Birth minus 37 weeks

The regional meeting of angels at the widow Hannah's house finished for the day, and Elric and Jenli now had the war map to themselves. The two pored over the war map in silence. Elric stood with his arms crossed while Jenli paced and rubbed the back of his head. They both focused on the thick carpet of darkness smothering Nazareth and Bethlehem.

Elric shook his head. "I should have seen this coming. We knew they would search Nazareth and Bethlehem—that's why we moved Mary to Judea. But I underestimated their numbers. We should not have taken Achim's house so soon."

"We can take it again, after the hordes return to Egypt," Jenli said.

"Yes, but it will not fall as easily as it did the first time."

Jenli covered his mouth and nose with his hand. The swirling evil clouds on the map engulfed the landscape. His eyes filled with tears. "Look at them," he said.

Elric's face became stern. "The day is coming," he said with a low rumble. He drew his sword. "And on that day. . ." He slashed his sword through the black clouds in the map. ". . . I will be riding with the King." With his other hand, he motioned downward, and the map faded away. He put away his sword, closed his eyes, and became very still.

Then, like the sun in the morning after a dark night, a smile dawned on his face. Eyes still closed, he directed an unseen choir with subdued gestures. He opened his eyes and looked at Jenli. "That day *is* coming."

Jenli smiled.

"But first," Elric said, "we must fulfill our mission."

Jenli nodded.

Elric crossed his arms behind his back. "I have a new assignment for you. You can't return to Nazareth or Bethlehem while the horde is there. But having your team free for other duties will work to our advantage. I need you to go to Rome."

"Rome?"

"And infiltrate the inner circle of Caesar's court."

Jenli raised his eyebrows and rubbed his chin.

"It will be a delicate operation," Elric said. "But you have two to three months to complete it."

Jenli stood straight and lifted his head. "I am in His service. What is your plan, captain?"

Birth minus 28 weeks

Nine weeks later, Elric and Lacidar were studying the war map at Hannah's house when Jenli returned from his mission in Rome. They turned and greeted Jenli with plasma spheres of joy and peace.

"It is done," Jenli announced.

"He has issued the decree?" Elric asked.

"No, sir, not yet. But the seed is planted and has support. It will come to pass."

"Timing?"

"Four to six weeks. It has the support of the senate."

"Excellent."

"What is the status here? I have heard nothing since we left," Jenli said.

"Zaben is surrounded by the largest army I have seen since the Rebellion," Elric answered. "Timrok still stands guard over Rachael's land."

Lacidar shook his head. "He must be aching in his heart—not being in the center of the action."

Elric smiled. "He is a good warrior. Faithful to his duties."

"Bethlehem and Nazareth?" Jenli asked.

"Still occupied," Elric replied.

"Judea?"

"Ever since his experience in the temple, Zacharias has spent his days searching the Scriptures for all references concerning the promised Messiah. He does his best to share these with Mary, but it is difficult because he can't talk, and Mary reads very little."

"Elizabeth helps," Lacidar said.

Elric nodded. "Together they have carefully reviewed Mary's genealogy and were able to trace her line all the way to King David.

They found that Joseph's lineage tracks to David, but through a branch that has been cut off from the promise. But they were excited to find Mary's line is admissible."

"The prophecies. . ." prompted Lacidar.

"They are most excited about the prophecies. A miraculous virgin birth."

Lacidar jumped in. "And a prophet to call for the people to turn their hearts toward the King."

Elric laughed. "The more they study, the more their faith grows. It has been an excellent time for Mary. It's a safe place for her—a place where someone else understands and believes what she is going through."

"She has been a blessing to Elizabeth, too," Lacidar said. "Elizabeth is near full term, and she has been confined to bed, so Mary has been serving them around the house."

"What is next for my team?" Jenli asked.

"Return to Judea with us. But keep your distance and don't be seen. After the prophet is born and the enemy moves out of Nazareth, we will need to move Mary."

Birth minus 26 weeks

After a long, hard night in Judea, dawn came with an air of expectancy inside Zacharias's home. Minutes of breathless quiet passed before Mary emerged from the back bedroom with a tiny blanketed bundle in her arms. She had tired, puffy eyes and bedraggled hair, but she had a huge smile on her face. She came to Zacharias, handed him his new son, and spoke in a broken voice. "Elizabeth is doing fine."

Elric and Lacidar stood in the middle of the room, beaming.

Zacharias looked into the face of his only son for the first time and erupted in a flood of tears. An entire lifetime of deferred hopes gushed out of his eyes until he couldn't see. He kept blinking as the river ran down his cheeks onto his old grey beard. He held his boy up triumphantly to the neighbors and relatives in the room and laughed a long silent laugh.

The room erupted in applause. This startled the little one and made him cry, which made the room laugh and cheer all the more. Zacharias carried the bundle back to Elizabeth and laid him in her arms. He knelt down and put his arms around his wife and baby, and the two of them wept for joy for a long time. Mary closed the door and joined the party out front.

Lacidar said, "It was a long night, but it is a very good morning indeed." He picked up his resonar and began to play.

The next week brought a steady stream of visitors, happy well-wishers, and deliverers of food. Mary didn't need to prepare a single meal because of the generous neighbors and relatives. It felt like a week–long celebration. With every passing day, though, Elric could sense Mary's growing apprehension.

"She knows that soon she will have to go back home and face her family—and Joseph," Elric said to Lacidar.

Lacidar nodded. "It won't be easy."

On the eighth day, the rabbi came to circumcise the child. The family and friends all crammed into the house, laughing and talking.

"A special day," Elric said over the commotion. "Today the boy joins the house of Abraham. And receives his name."

Lacidar replied, "Have you heard all the relatives talking? They are sure he will be named Zacharias, after his father. There is great pressure here from the family."

"We shall see if Zacharias and Elizabeth are obedient to the word of Gabriel," Elric said.

The time for the ceremony drew close, and the chatter about "a young Zacharias running around" came from everyone's lips.

Elizabeth overheard the chatter, and she shouted, "No, no." She waved her arms to quiet the room. "No! He is to be called John."

"What? John?"

"Not Zacharias?"

"There is no one among your relatives who has that name."

"This can't be. This isn't done!"

"Zacharias, come over here. Do you hear what your wife is saying? She must be mistaken. Tell us—what shall be the name of your son?"

Zacharias motioned for a writing tablet and he wrote, "His name is John."

A collective gasp hung in the air.

Elric smiled and nodded to Lacidar, who reached up and touched Zacharias's throat.

Zacharias moved his tongue around in his mouth. He made a light humming noise—and sound came out. He rubbed his throat and grinned. Then, with a bold voice, strong and commanding, he spoke. "Praise be to the Lord, the God of Israel, because He has come and has redeemed His people. He has raised up a horn of salvation for us in the house of his servant David, as He said through His holy prophets of long ago, salvation from our enemies and from the hand of all who hate us—to show mercy to our fathers and to remember His holy covenant, the oath He swore to our father Abraham: to rescue us from the hand of our enemies, and to enable us to serve Him without fear in holiness and righteousness before Him all our days. And you, my child, will be called a prophet of the Most High; for you will go on before the Lord to prepare the way for Him, to give His people the knowledge of salvation through the forgiveness of their sins, because of the tender mercy of our God, by which the rising sun will come to us from heaven to shine on those living in darkness and in the shadow of death, to guide our feet into the path of peace."

Elric and Lacidar laughed.

Mary rubbed her belly.

The family and friends looked at each other with mouths wide open. "What then is this child going to be?"

30

A TIME TO MOVE

Birth minus 25 weeks

While one–week–old baby John slept in the back room of Zacharias's home, Mary, Zacharias, and Elizabeth sat around the table and talked. The single candle on the table provided a warm glow on their faces and cast dark shadows into the late–night room. They gathered close and spoke with low voices.

"I'm confident in the thing the Lord is doing in me," Mary said, "but you know they will never understand. Girls don't just miraculously show up pregnant. What do I say?"

Elizabeth patted Mary's hand. "Just tell them the truth. It will sound outrageous to them, but it is the truth. Maybe your family and Joseph will believe you and share in your joy."

Zacharias shook his head. "It's more likely, though, that you will be disowned by your family and divorced by Joseph."

"Zacharias," Elizabeth scolded.

He continued. "Engagements are legally binding, and if the bride-to-be is found to be with child, the groom has legal rights to divorce her in a most disgraceful public way. In the absolute worst case, she could be delivered up to be stoned to death. The dangers are real."

The fear in Mary's wide eyes glowed in the candlelight. "Maybe I could just stay here."

Elizabeth shook her head. "As much as we love you and want you here with us, I don't believe that's the right answer."

Zacharias leaned back and stroked his beard. "Neither do I. You have a promise from God. You need to trust the Lord to see His plan through. He wouldn't have brought this gift to you just to see you stoned by a mob. He will certainly protect you—if for no other reason than to bring His promise to fullness."

"I know, but. . ." Mary covered her face to hide the tears.

Elizabeth dabbed Mary's eyes with a cloth. "You can do this. We don't have any promises that it will be easy. And you may face disgrace and trials, but you do have a promise that you will have a son, and He will be the promised Messiah." Elizabeth paused and lifted Mary's chin with a tender finger. "Any amount of trial is worth seeing this promise fulfilled."

Mary stiffened her lower lip and nodded.

Zacharias leaned forward again. "Yes, you need to go back to Nazareth. How and when isn't clear. We will wait and trust the Lord to provide."

———

From his headquarters in Egypt, Marr sat forward on his throne and leered beyond the rubble of his temple to the canopy of light surrounding the Egyptian palace.

"I need more proof," Marr snarled. "Is the Coming One nesting under the strong wing of this angelic stronghold? How can we know for sure? We have been unable to penetrate their defenses, and we are blind to their activities within."

A commander approached the dark throne. "My lord, the girl Rachael has not left the shelter of the palace grounds since she entered there. However, my spies in town have been able to ascertain that she is three months pregnant."

The corner of Marr's lip turned upward, revealing two yellow fangs. "Have you been able to confirm the report?"

"I have received word from three independent sources at different times under separate circumstances."

"Good," Marr said. "It is just as I anticipated. Things are progressing on schedule."

"It also appears Benjamin and Rachael have wed," someone from the inner council announced.

"Not unexpected. Give me something more."

"Master," another commander grunted as he stepped forward from the group of hulking evil, "*I* have news that I believe you will find *most* interesting."

"Speak it, fool."

"I have received word that an artisan in town is currently working on a golden crown with settings for precious gems."

"So? Why do you waste my time with useless information?"

"It is a size fit for an infant. This is a crown of royalty being fashioned for a newborn!"

"Really? This *is* interesting. Do your spies know who ordered it? Who is it being made for?"

The puffed–up commander lowered his gaze, "No, master, I'm afraid it is very secret, and nobody is talking."

"A secret crown being made ready for a coming king?" Marr leapt to his feet and raised a fist toward the palace. "Our enemy has gotten careless. Good work, commander. Now I know for certain that we have indeed located this coming King, and we are more than ready for Him." He turned to a messenger and barked new orders, "Go to Bethlehem and Nazareth and tell the commanders there to return here with their warriors immediately. Those locations were diversions, and I will need all our forces here when the time comes."

He sat back down. The smirk on his lips accented his air of assurance. *I am the one in control here. And everything proceeds according to my design. Lord Satan, absent as usual, will have to bow to me when I crush the King.*

Unannounced, a small demon snuck from behind the throne and slithered up onto the armrest of Marr's throne. The little spirit looked small and insignificant, smooth and sly. He had the form of a small snake with a viper's head and ridged eyes with vertical slits. His eyes revealed an unsettling depth of wisdom, but he had a puny, weak form. Marr dismissed the spirit with a simple flick of his mighty wrist. In a wink, the snake returned.

"What?" charged Marr with a gravelly annoyed tone. "What do you want?"

The snake's voice flowed out smooth and clean as fresh honey on a hot day. "I am a traveler gathering news from all over the earth. This news of yours is most interesting."

"It is more than interesting!" said the great prince. "It is the most important development since creation. And I, the exalted Prince of Persia, am on the brink of mighty exploits never before seen."

"You are truly wise and powerful. Do you wish me to pass this information on to our great master?" the snake offered with a smile.

Marr's hand shot out and wrapped around the snake's neck. "You will say nothing of this to him!"

"But, lord, you dare not hide this from him. He would be most displeased."

"I will tell him when I decide the time is right. In the meantime, I command you to speak of this to no one."

The snake poked out his forked tongue, "By your command, my lord."

Marr released the snake and continued with a lower tone, "So, *traveler*, if you are one who collects information from everywhere, tell me of news from other regions. Give me something useful if you can."

"My news only confirms your great wisdom. I have been throughout all Israel and Egypt and have found nothing that compares with what you have found here."

"I know everything within this region, fool! What about other regions?"

"There is no activity that indicates the coming of the King in any other region. In fact, the other regional princes are most envious of your key strategic position."

"Ha! Good. Let them envy. Soon they will all see why it was me who was chosen to be Prince of this most important region. Now, be on your way, small one. If you do hear something of use to me, be sure to return here and report it to me. And remember, I will deliver this prize to our lord in due time, so if you see him, you are to say nothing."

With a few short bursts of his little black tongue, the snake made its way down to the floor and disappeared into the shadows.

Birth minus 25 weeks

The regional angelic meeting at the widow Hannah's house drew near its end, and Elric stood in the background, listening to the reports and awaiting his turn with the war map.

The reporting of the passing of the righteous had almost completed when one of the lieutenants brought in a warrior who could hardly wait to share his news. He stepped forward and spoke with a quiver in his voice. "There is a young man in Nazareth named Joseph whose mother just passed today. I was there to escort her to the King. All the while she kept babbling about 'getting to see the promise' and 'thank you for the amazing gift' and how she 'knew the Lord would answer the cries of Israel.'"

The four captains each stood upright, crossed their arms, and looked at each other with raised eyebrows. The lieutenants lining the walls darted glances at each other.

"And as soon as I presented her to the King, He silenced her. She was escorted to a private place, and I was dismissed."

The room became dead silent. No one moved. No one blinked. Then, all together, the entire assembly turned and looked at Elric standing in the corner.

One of the captains broke the tension. "Captain Elric, ever since you left, there have been many strange developments throughout the region. There is an unprecedented buildup down in Egypt. Most of the beaelzurim that are normally active in our regions have moved south. And then, for the last several months, a massive influx of the enemy in Bethlehem and Nazareth has been suffocating. Then, as quickly as they came, those forces just left. Now, this report. This report sounds like. . . like. . . surely the Lord would not make His entrance without announcing it to the host of heaven? If there is a secret mission taking place outside our sphere of authority, we would certainly not speak of it, but is there anything you know that you can tell us?"

Elric took a deep breath and grimaced. "The idea of the King entering mankind is a marvelous mystery, and we have all longed to look into it since the Fall. I can tell you this—you are all involved whether you know it or not. There are many pieces that need to fit together, so you must continue your operations and execute whatever orders come to you. When the time is right, our King will reveal His full plan. Until then, we proceed by faith, as always."

The captains nodded with pursed lips. The lieutenants turned back toward the map with resigned eyes and drooped shoulders. Several moments of silence passed.

"Who's next?" one of the captains said. "The passing of the righteous."

A lieutenant stepped forward. "From my region, I am pleased to announce. . ."

The meeting continued. Elric stepped back and enjoyed the conference from the far corner. *It's like being in the comfortable living room of a former residence. I love this place.* After the business completed and the local lieutenants and captains left, he stepped up to the map and spent several hours studying the present and upcoming landscape.

He finally moved back and made the map disappear with a wave of his hand. *The time has come to move Mary back.*

31

FIVE RIDERS

Birth minus 24 weeks

lric and Jenli stood outside and leaned against the stone wall of Zacharias's house as the red glowing horizon swallowed the sinking sun. A light breeze danced over the hills and carried the coming chill of night. Down the dusty trail from the house, they watched one of Jenli's warriors on a walking patrol.

Elric looked at Jenli and said, "I am going to move Mary tomorrow. You proceed to Mary's home and make sure it is secure. I shall use four of your warriors during transit and the fifth to act as a scout for our party." Elric kept his voice low. He turned toward the road and saw the scout on patrol kneel down, looking at something on the road. Elric touched Jenli's forearm and pointed. "Who is that warrior kneeling there in the road?"

Jenli smiled. "His name is Jerem. One of my top warriors. A skilled scout. He would serve the scouting mission well."

"Very well. He goes undercover tonight. He will lead our party and will need to remain unseen for the full journey. I need you to gather six horses after night falls. They should be swift and hardy—we will be moving fast. Questions?"

Jenli shook his head and disappeared into the waning sky.

Elric turned and went back indoors.

———

The demons Tumur and Luchek spent another uneventful night watching the house of Zacharias. For fifteen weeks now they had watched for some kind of sign that might tell them something about the mysterious girl who stayed with Zacharias and Elizabeth. From a distance, they had observed that the baby John had been born, but they still had no information about the girl.

After weeks of seeing nothing, morning brought a surprise—a fast-moving cloud of dust and a low rumble of horses' hooves from a rarely traveled trail behind Zacharias's home. Tumur and Luchek spied from their strategic vantage points, and they soon had full view of five mysterious riders on horses at a full run. A sixth horse without a rider strode amidst the troop with lively high steps. All six horses were magnificent Arabian stallions—spirited, proud, and snow white. The riders wore pale linen cloaks that hid their heads and faces.

The group stopped abruptly at Zacharias's house amid a swirl of dust. While the horses stomped and snorted and flipped their great manes, the five men dismounted and left them in the side yard. They walked to the front of the home and paused at the door. Zacharias greeted them and spoke with one who appeared to be the leader of the group. Then all five disappeared behind the thick, rustic, wooden door.

Luchek and Tumur looked at each other with wild eyes and smiled.

In a low whisper, Luchek said, "Could it be that we are in exactly the right place at the right time?"

———

Zacharias held the door for five hooded strangers who marched into his house like an unexpected whirlwind. Mary and Elizabeth jumped to their feet with tentative stares. Elizabeth, holding baby John, shot Zacharias a disapproving glance. Zacharias shrugged.

I'm not sure why I just invited these men into my home. A group of strange men unannounced at my door—it is not customary. But there is something different about them. Elusive. And yet, they feel. . . safe, trustworthy.

Zacharias closed the door, and the strangers removed their hoods. The men had swarthy skin and brown eyes, but they didn't look Hebrew or Samaritan—or Roman. They had a layer of dust from their journey, and yet somehow they didn't appear dirty. They had sharp, knowing eyes and robust, commanding statures.

The leader of the group spoke first. "Master Zacharias, priest of God, greetings. May peace be upon you and your household." He bowed and looked at Elizabeth. "This must be your wife Elizabeth. Blessed are you among women. The Lord has done great things for you." He smiled and paused a moment. "And this little one is John?"

Elizabeth rocked John in her arms and turned aside.

Zacharias raised his eyebrows. "How do you know. . ."

"My name is Elric. These are my companions, Jennidab, Brondor, Jessik, and Kaylar."

Zacharias fumbled out, "Those are. . . interesting names. You are not Hebrew. . ."

Elric continued with a steady efficient tone, "We are not from this country. We are on an errand of great importance and urgency." He turned to Mary. "Mary, we have come to escort you to Nazareth and ensure your safe passage."

Mary fidgeted upon hearing her name.

Zacharias stepped forward and positioned himself between Elric and Mary. His stance made it clear that he stood as the authority in the house, and no one would take Mary anywhere without his consent. His long grey beard reached almost down to his folded arms, and his unflinching eyes constricted with a stern gaze. "Who has sent you on this errand? And how am I to know the intentions of your business?"

Elric smiled and nodded as though pleased with Zacharias's response. He bowed his head again in respect and then continued speaking to Mary with a steady tone.

"You are Mary, daughter of Eli of Nazareth. You are betrothed to a man named Joseph, son of Jacob, a carpenter." He waited a moment. "Please have a seat. I regret to say that I bring tidings of deep sorrow."

Mary sat quickly. A look of dread spread across her face. Zacharias took a seat beside her. Elizabeth continued rocking John and held him closer.

"I am sorry to say that Joseph's mother has passed on. The illness finally took her."

Mary's eyes filled with tears and she gasped for a breath. She buried her head into Zacharias's shoulder. "I knew it! I knew I should have never left. I should have been there. I could have. . ." Zacharias propped her up with his arm around her shoulder.

Elric interrupted, "No, Mary. There was nothing you could have done. It was right for you to have been here during this time. But now, there is mourning in Nazareth, and Joseph needs you at home. We have come in haste on horses and have brought a horse for you to ride. We are prepared to leave immediately and bring you to your home as quickly as possible."

He stepped back and paused. He bowed to Zacharias again.

"My men and I will wait outside and give you time alone. I urge you to pray and seek the Lord's counsel. We cannot transport Mary against your will."

The men replaced the hoods of their cloaks over their heads and filed outside one by one.

Zacharias held his arm around Mary. Elizabeth stood near Mary's chair, one arm holding the baby, one hand stroking Mary's hair. Zacharias prayed, *Lord, is this your provision? What is your will? Am I to trust these men? Please give us a sign.* He waited. He heard nothing. No sign appeared. He waited some more. *I need an answer. What should we do?* Still no voice, no sign. Then, without a sound, a warm sense of peace percolated up from his belly. It filled his chest. His racing pulse slowed, and his breaths became controlled and easy. *These men mean no harm. Why would they come here and specifically ask for Mary by name unless they were sent?* A calm assurance settled over his mind. He waited still longer. *Lord, I believe this is from you. I am willing to trust you.* The peace turned into resolve. His muscles tightened with the strength of a young man. He lifted his chin and nodded. *Yes. Yes, Lord.*

Mary's sobbing subsided enough to have a conversation. Zacharias squeezed her tight and said, "I believe this is the Lord's will. Remember, we decided to wait and trust for Him to provide a way home for you and to reveal the proper time. I believe these men are the answer to our prayers. I don't know who they are or where they came from, but my heart tells me they are God's provision."

"These men are complete strangers," Elizabeth said. "We can't entrust Mary to them."

"They are strangers to us, but we are not strangers to them. How is it that they know our names and all the details about Mary? They must have been sent by someone in Nazareth. Perhaps Joseph. We asked the Lord for provision. What did we expect, a band of angels and a chariot of fire?"

Elizabeth shook her head and looked over to Mary. "Mary. . . what do you think?"

Mary wiped her eyes and tried to catch her breath. "I don't know. They seem to be telling the truth. There is something about them. I think. . . I think I trust them."

"They are the answer to our prayers," Zacharias said.

Elizabeth rocked John with a nervous cadence. "At least ask them to have a meal with us so we can know them better."

"Yes. Good. I agree."

Zacharias stepped out the door and found Elric with his hood on and his face turned toward the house. Zacharias met him with a sad, flat smile. "I have decided to release Mary into your charge and to trust you to deliver her directly to her home."

"Your faith is great," Elric replied. "You have heard the direction from the Lord correctly. He who trusts in the Lord will not be disappointed. In order for you to have peace in this matter, I will send a messenger to you after Mary is safely home, so you may know the success of our task."

Zacharias nodded.

Elric straightened his back and clapped his hands once. "Now, we must not delay. Mary needs to gather her things—we will set out immediately."

"First, let me feed and water your animals and prepare provisions for your trip."

"No. Thank you, but this is not necessary. We are traveling light and have all the provisions we need. The horses are already prepared."

Zacharias said, "We have not even had a meal yet. Surely you cannot expect Mary to begin a long journey like this without a proper meal? Please, you would honor me and my house if you would stay long enough to share the midday meal."

"Very well, my friend." Elric bowed. He called out around the corner of the house, "Men, our gracious host insists we come in and have a meal before our journey. Come, let us share his most kind hospitality."

———

"What's going on down there?" Luchek said to Tumur. "And who are those men?"

"I can't tell. Their cloaks hide their faces and they never turn for us to see them. I'm not even sure they *are* men."

"From the looks of their horses, I think they are here to escort Zacharias somewhere."

"Or the girl," Tumur said with an uplifted eyebrow.

"The girl?" Luchek scowled and scratched his neck. "You could be right. That would make things very interesting indeed. You don't think she might actually be the one we seek?"

"I don't know." Tumur said. *I doubt it. The enemy would never make it that easy. It would be too obvious. But this may be an opportunity for me to unload some competition.* He eyed Luchek and continued, "But I think there is a good chance that she is. In fact, I don't think we can afford to let her leave without one of us following them."

He paused for dramatic effect and squinted his big bulgy eyes. Then, his wiry eyebrows changed from excited to worried. "No, on second thought, if she really is the one we are looking for, it would be much too dangerous for either of us to shadow her alone. *I* certainly would not dare to take that risk."

Luchek shot a quick reply, "Maybe *you* are not up to the task, but *I* am certainly not afraid."

"No, it is too risky. I will not allow it."

"You have no authority over me," Luchek growled. "If I choose to go after this girl, there is nothing you could do to stop me. Furthermore, I think—"

"Fine. Fine. Have it your way," Tumur said. "If these men leave here with the girl, you go with them, but I get to stay here and continue my watch over the prophet."

Luchek snorted.

"It's definitely her," Tumur said. "Remember—follow her, watch her, try to find out if she is the one. If you discover anything, come back and share your news. And above all else, do not reveal our operations to anyone until the right time."

Luchek glared at Tumur through tightened eyes.

The rumble of twenty-four hooves shook the ground. A large cloud of dust leapt and bolted in the direction opposite the main road. It moved out over an unused trail, and it moved fast.

Luchek snuck away like a shadow, and Tumur found himself alone on the quiet Judean hillside, watching an old priest, his wife, and their new son go back into their house. This had been a nice turn of events. He had the prophet to himself again. Perhaps he would sneak into town later today and listen to the talk of the people and see if he could learn anything new about the boy.

He smiled a wicked, satisfied smile.

———

On day two of the ride home, Mary's horse held a tight position behind Elric's steed, pressing forward at a full run. Jessik rode at an arm's length to the left, Kaylar to the right. Jennidab and Brondor followed close behind. Without warning, Elric pulled hard left, and the whole formation tracked in unison. Mary braced to stay upright. They bolted down another uncharted path through some obscure valley.

Mary craned around in all directions, but nothing looked unusual. *It feels like we're trying to avoid something, or someone. I sure hope they know where they're going.*

Late in the afternoon, they approached a crescent–shaped alcove with a barrier cliff on one side and an open plain on the other. Elric pulled his reigns, and his mighty stallion reared its head back. The troop came to an instant stop. Elric spun his horse around, examining their perimeter with a stern gaze. He spun back around again.

"We will camp here tonight," Elric said.

All five horsemen dismounted and proceeded with silent, efficient movements. One helped Mary down, another built a fire, two others set up Mary's tent, and Elric stared off over the plain. Mary stretched her legs and unstrapped a pouch from her horse. Dropping the pouch by the edge of the growing campfire, she rubbed her lower back and turned toward the setting sun. With a tired sigh, she pulled the hood of her cloak off and let it drape down the back of her neck.

"Here," Elric said, touching the back of her shoulder. Mary turned. Elric handed her a small loaf of bread. "You need to keep your strength up." He held out a fistful of dates in his other hand.

"Thank you." Mary sat on her pouch and arranged the food on her lap.

Kaylar handed her a water skin and dragged a boulder up beside her. The other horsemen joined in a circle around the fire. With the crackling fire providing the only sound, Mary took a bite of bread. She smiled at Elric, who smiled back and nibbled a date. Brondor smiled from across the flames and took a bite of bread.

These men eat very little. In fact, it almost seems like they only eat or drink when I'm looking.

She took another bite. Elric nibbled his date.

"It's funny," Mary said. "Zacharias was worried that riding a horse. . . in my condition. . . would be hard, dangerous. But I've been amazed at how smooth the ride has been. It's like the horse's feet hardly even touch the ground."

Elric nodded. "These are fine animals."

The conversation remained sparse and centered on the day's ride and the things they had seen along the way. Mary finished her food as the campfire waned.

Looking up at the rising moon, Elric said, "You should get some sleep. We will be home tomorrow, but we still have a hard morning of riding."

Mary nodded and strained to stand up. Kaylar jumped up and lifted her with one hand under her arm and the other around her waist. "Thank you," Mary said. "Good night."

"Good night," replied all the horsemen.

Hours later, in the dark of the night, Mary awoke. *Are those voices outside the tent?* She peeked out. There was Elric, alone, gazing off into the distance. *He is still awake at this late hour? And where are the others? What were those voices?* She surveyed the campsite. Nothing but a lonely, dead campfire pit. *These are strange men, indeed. They hardly eat, and I haven't yet seen them sleep.* She let the tent flap drop closed, rubbed her eyes, and went back to sleep.

Mary awoke in the morning to scuffling feet and anxious hooves in the dirt. She ate a light meal, and they started traveling again before the sun broke over the horizon.

"A short riding day," Elric announced over the rumble. "Soon, our trip will be complete."

Home. It would be good to have this journey behind her, but difficult days loomed ahead. *I wish I could have just stayed with*

Zacharias and Elizabeth. They understood. I was safe there. At home I have to face Father. And Joseph. . .

The horses pounded onward.

Morning sped by like the passing bushes, and the rising dread of uncertainty grew heavier with each passing moment. *How will I ever explain this? How can I. . . hey, this place is starting to look familiar. I know where we are. The village should be just over that ridge.*

Just before they crested the final hill, Elric stopped. He wheeled his horse around and dismounted in one fluid motion. "We will finish our journey on foot so as not to attract too much attention. It would be unwise to come galloping into town on these horses."

The other horsemen dismounted and untied Mary's bags from their animals. One of them helped Mary down.

"Master Elric, what does it matter if we attract attention?" Mary asked.

"It. . . would not be prudent." Elric spun around and handed his reins to Brondor. "Brondor, please return these horses and bring word to Zacharias. Tell him the Lord has given us success. Mary is home this day."

Brondor mounted and headed south at a full run with the small herd of horses in tow. The other three horsemen hoisted Mary's luggage onto their backs, and Elric crossed over the top of the hill with a commanding gait. Mary ran to catch up, stopping only a moment at the top of the hill to take in the familiar sight of her village. Her heart pounded, and she made lively steps. The final leg of the trip would be done soon.

They reached Mary's house, and she said, "Please, would you come inside and meet my family? We will prepare a meal, and . . ."

"No, thank you," Elric said. "Our task is complete, and we must proceed to another assignment."

Mary nodded. "I thought you might say that. Will I see you again?"

"I don't know."

Mary nodded. "Here," she said, twisting to remove her tunic. "I won't be needing this now."

Elric flinched and shot startled glances all around. Kaylar, at one corner of the house, nodded to Elric once. Jessik, on the other corner, nodded once. Elric smiled, took the tunic, folded it, and packed it into his side-pouch. "You are most favored," he said. "You must remember this. You carry the promise of salvation. The zeal of the Lord of Hosts will surely perform it."

A warmth flushed Mary's cheeks, and she dipped her head with a sheepish smile. "I don't know what. . ."

"Take courage. Be strong." Elric touched her shoulder and gave a gentle squeeze.

A wave of warmth, starting from her shoulder, washed throughout her body and filled her with peace.

Elric turned, walked toward Jessik, and the two disappeared around the corner. Mary looked to the other corner of the house. Kaylar was gone. Jennidab was. . . *where is he? I don't think I've seen him since he dropped off this bag.*

Mary stood alone at her front door, her bags at her feet. *What just happened?*

She waited another moment, took a deep breath, opened the door and called out, "Mother, it's me—Mary. I'm home!"

33

THE HIDDEN TRUTH

Birth minus 23 weeks

Jenli entered the synagogue in Nazareth and took a long, deep breath.

"Lieutenant Jenli," an elzur warrior called out from across the room. "What a surprise."

"I always loved the smell of this place. It is exactly as I remembered it."

"Change does not come quickly here. We haven't seen you in. . . how long has it been?"

"About a year and a half."

"That's beyond the end of your last rotation. Shouldn't you be. . ."

"I'm on a new assignment."

"It must be an important one to prevent you from returning to the King's Realm."

Jenli raised his eyebrows and rubbed the stubble on the top of his head. "How is our senior priest, Avner?" he asked, stepping further into the room.

"His work is finished. He rested with his fathers about a year ago."

Jenli grimaced. "I'm sorry I wasn't here to see him at his transition. He was an effective soldier in the Kingdom. How did the others react?"

"It was difficult. Most difficult for Raziel. They were close."

Jenli nodded. "How is Raziel now?"

"A new senior priest has been installed—a strict Pharisee. His name is Zeev. Yadid and Shalev are finding a common bond with him, but Raziel is. . . less conforming. As a result, he carries very few teaching responsibilities. He is consigned to mostly civic duties— marriages, funerals, Bris Milahs."

Jenli took a moment and scrawled some notes on his tablet. He put his tablet away and looked up. "Very good. If everything goes as planned, I will bring in a young man named Joseph very soon."

"Joseph, yes of course. His mother just entered the King's rest."

"Yes. And he should be here looking for a priest for a wedding within. . ."

"A wedding? Is Mary finally back? You do know she has been gone for several months."

"Yes, Mary is back. And I expect Joseph to come in here within the next several weeks."

An excited interjection just reached the tip of the resident angel's tongue, but Jenli cut it off with an uplifted hand. "And, this is very important," Jenli said. "We must see that Raziel is the one Joseph talks with. He must be the one to do the wedding." Jenli spun and took a step toward the front entrance.

"Yes, sir. And, lieutenant. . ."

Jenli stopped and turned his head.

"Sir, has there been any word about the two warriors who were lost in the battle here before you left?"

Jenli's chin sunk to his chest. He muttered low, "Watch for us. Remember, Raziel is the man we need."

———

Elric sat with a stone, sharpening his blade while Mary's family reclined around their table, eating bread with date relish. He made a long, precise swipe with his stone and glanced up at the bright eyes and wide smiles of Mary's father and mother and sisters. They listened to her story of travel, starting with the day she left Nazareth.

"And I spent most of the trip inside the little tent he built for me on the cart because the weather was terrible," Mary said. "It was dreadful almost the whole way. The rain, the wind. It seemed like it would never stop. But we found their house without too much trouble, and. . ."

Elric took another swipe with his stone. *Mary is home and safe. For now. When she reveals her secret, it's hard to know how her family will respond, how Joseph will respond. She needs to do it soon. It will be easier if she tells them before she is found out.*

Jenli entered the room with a tight jaw and concerned eyes. "Captain, Jerem's report is confirmed. The tail we picked up in Judea is still with us. A single beaelzurim lieutenant."

"Has he made any advances?"

"No, sir."

"Has he sent word to any superiors?"

"No."

Elric laid his sword in his lap and crossed his arms.

"Captain? Shall we drive him off?"

Elric paused a moment longer. "No, not yet. Continue to watch him. Do not allow him to report to anyone. But let's permit him to operate within a safe distance."

"Do you have a plan for him?"

"The best course of action is not yet clear."

"Yes, sir."

Jenli disappeared through the wall. The humans in the room gasped, and Elric looked inward again. Mouths hung open and eyes grew wide as pomegranates. Everyone looked at Mary.

"It's true!" Mary said. "An actual angel of the Lord appeared to him in the temple. He said that Elizabeth would have a child—and he would be the prophet of the coming Messiah! Zacharias didn't believe him at first, so the angel struck him dumb. You wouldn't believe all the marvelous things the angel said. . ."

Elric smiled and took another swipe on his blade. He spoke into the air. "Tell them what the angel said to *you*."

His words swirled through the room and found their mark, but Mary continued her story of Zacharias and Elizabeth. *How will the family respond when Mary shares her news? It's easier to believe when the miraculous happens to someone else.* He scanned the faces around the room. They certainly appeared to be believing this report. Faith was building in the room, and words of the coming Messiah filled the room with warm sweetness. Elric closed his eyes and breathed in the energy swelling into the Middle Realm. *Mmm. The coming day of the Lord. For so long we have awaited this.* The thought filled him with strength. It filled him with hope. It filled him with music. He cocked his head to one side and let the symphony in his heart play out in his ears. He sat this way for a few minutes. The refrain drew to a close, and he opened his eyes.

Mary continued, "And after Zacharias confirmed John's name, his voice immediately returned. He began to prophesy and. . ."

"Now, Mary, now," Elric said. "Tell them *your* prophecy now. There is faith here to receive it."

Mary continued on with every detail of John's birth. Elric smiled, closed his eyes, and directed another verse of his symphony. When he turned his attention again to Mary, she still spoke of her journey to Judea.

"And they were the strangest men I've ever seen. We had no idea who they were or where they came from, but Zacharias was sure they were the answer to our prayers. Somehow, they knew about Joseph's mother, and they hastened to bring me home."

Elric spoke the word "courage" into his hand, and a small ball of energy formed. He released it toward Mary and said, "Tell them now." He watched and waited.

Mary's lips drew tight, and she swallowed hard. She glanced at her father. She looked down at her trembling hands. She sat on them. She looked back up, tears filling her eyes. "It is true, then? About Joseph's mother?" Mary asked.

"I'm so sorry, dear," her mother said.

"I should go to him."

Her father reached across and held her shoulder. "There will be time for mourning. Today my daughter is home, and our hearts are filled with joy with the news you bring. Stay here today. Let us be thankful for your safe return. Tomorrow, you may see your Joseph. Come, come, help your mother with the meal."

Elric shook his head, repositioned his sharpening stone, and took another swipe. *Oh, Mary, your best opportunity to share the most important news has just been lost.*

———

Draped in the traditional mourner's black garb and veil, Mary stepped out of her house the next morning. From his concealed rooftop perch three houses down, Elric examined her for signs of the Spirit. Good. Her hood and veil blocked all but her eyes. And those were only visible from the front, and. . .

Motion on the street! One of Jenli's warriors shot into the air and away from the area, followed by two angry beaelzurim. Across the street, a flash of light from an unseen warrior. Down a side street, another flash answered. Elric just caught a glimpse of another one of Jenli's team passing from within one building to another. Elric glanced over at Jenli, who peeked over a rooftop ledge across the street. Elric nodded. Jenli leapt from his rooftop to the next and ducked behind its ledge.

Hmm, what's this? A lone demon lieutenant. *He must be the one who followed us from Judea.* The demon slinked around a corner and melded into the shadows. He stayed a safe distance away from Mary, and his eyes never stopped scanning the streets, the sky, the rooftops.

Elric looked back toward Jenli, pointed at the demon lieutenant, and shook his head. The shadow whisked forward to the next building. As silent as vapors, Elric and Jenli advanced. All the pieces moved with silent precision toward Joseph's house.

Birth minus 23 weeks

The strong morning light made Mary wince behind her mourner's veil. *That sun!* She pulled her hood forward. *It's just as well. I don't want anyone to see these red, puffy eyes.* She stopped and took slow, deep breaths. *Will Joseph ever be able to forgive me for not being there when his mother died?* An aching cramp seized her stomach. *And how are we going to carry on without that dear old lady? How do I fill this hollow emptiness? Somehow, the amazing promise of the Messiah doesn't seem to help. Especially when I can't even find the strength to tell my family. I think it makes it worse. And what if I can't find the courage to tell Joseph?* She took another deep breath, wiped her eyes, and started walking.

She trudged through the lonely streets. People passed by on every side, and some even shot fleeting glances, but no one spoke to her. None of them knew. None of them understood. *Surely the Lord knows what I'm going through, right? Why does He seem so distant? Can anyone even see me? I don't remember this walk to Joseph's house being so long.*

Mary approached the small group of mourners gathered outside Joseph's house. Their wails filled the morning air and left no doubt that this house had been stung by the dark finger of death. Mary pressed past them and into the house.

She spotted Joseph, and her heart sank. His eyes were swollen and tired, his lips dry and cracked, and he had deep valleys of pain carved down his cheeks. A volcano of emotions erupted from the pit of her belly. She broke down and sobbed with deep heaving breaths.

Joseph's eyes met Mary, and a spark of fresh life washed over his dark countenance. He pulled her through the door and clung to her with all his might. Together they wept a long time without speaking a word. Finally, they caught their breath and collapsed into chairs facing each other.

"Joseph, I'm so sorry. I'm sorry I wasn't here to take care of her until the end. I wish. . ."

Joseph gave her a sad smile and shushed her lips with his fingers. "Don't be sorry. I missed you terribly, but there was nothing you could have done. In fact, she didn't even need any extra care after you left."

"What?"

"It was very strange. Almost like a miracle. After you left, she started feeling a little better and stronger. You could tell there was still something wrong, but she had this joy that seemed to be bubbling up from within. After a week, your sister didn't even come over anymore because there was nothing for her to do. Mother kept going on about having gotten to see the promise, but I could never understand what she was talking about. She continued like that for the full three months. Then, last week. . ." he stopped and struggled for a breath. His eyes welled up again. "Last week, without any warning. . ."

Mary started crying again. She gave his hands a reassuring squeeze.

"She just never woke up. I found her in the morning." Joseph forced a slight grin. "She actually seemed to have a smile on her face. She looked so peaceful."

They both cried some more.

"But, enough of this," Joseph said. "Tell me, how was your trip?"

Mary just shook her head. "Oh, I. . . not now."

"Please, I would love to hear something from the outside. I need something to help me take my mind off everything."

Though reluctant, she told some of her story again through broken sobs. This time most of the details seemed insignificant and never made it to the surface. And the amazing miracle of Zacharias's and Elizabeth's child, though nice, seemed thousands of miles removed from the reality of the moment. Still, the happy story brought a welcome breath of hope in the midst of a dark place. More of the story needed to be told, but Mary couldn't bring herself to tell it.

———

While Joseph and Mary wept in the Physical Realm, a blanket of sorrow hung heavy in the air of the Middle Realm. Elric and Jenli spoke words of peace and encouragement, but the weight of the blanket smothered every word they spoke. The strong presence of the King hovered in the room, but His words, too, could not be received.

"How many thousands of times have we watched people go through this?" Elric said. "Joseph's mother is in the presence of the Great King. This should be a time of celebration—but their eyes do not see."

"Do you ever wish you could open their eyes to see into the Middle Realm?" Jenli asked.

"Sometimes. But then, no. It would go against the very nature of the King. It is faith that He wants to see in His children. And it's in these valleys that faith is demonstrated."

Jenli nodded and stroked Mary's hair. "Still," Jenli said, "there are times. . ."

"I know," Elric said as he put his hand on Joseph's back.

Birth minus 22 weeks

At Hannah's home, the regular complement of elzur warriors gathered for their daily regional meeting. Elric, with Jenli and Lacidar, stood out of the way in the back corner of the room, waiting for the meeting to finish. In the middle of the meeting, a strange movement developed in the map.

"Look," Elric whispered to Jenli and Lacidar.

A hush fell over the room. The four regional captains stopped and watched the war map with mouths open. The lieutenants standing around the periphery crowded forward. Elric, Jenli, and Lacidar strained over everyone else from their position in the back corner.

There, from the center of Rome, something that looked like a fluorescent yellow river sprang up. It spread like blood vessels, branching out in all directions. It reached up through multiple layers of the map and touched many dynamic features. In some places it turned pale blue, in other places bright red or pink. In many places it caused swirling clouds and a spectacular mixing of layers. Political powers, economic environments, social climates—it touched almost everything.

Everyone in the room turned and looked at Elric.

Elric gave a sheepish smile and stepped forward. "Behold the power of mere words, my friends," he announced with his arms crossed across his chest. "Some weeks past, I dispatched Jenli and his team to Rome. His mission was to infiltrate the palace of Caesar and plant a seed. He was not able to reach Caesar himself, but he did speak to some of his advisors. We were confident his pride and his lust for power and control would cause our seed to bear fruit, but we did not know the hour. We needed Augustus to call for a census of the Empire. A census will help him quantify the extent of his influence, help him plan the positioning of his legions, and potentially open up new tax revenues. But it will serve other purposes useful to the King. As you can see, this decree has just gone forth. It will affect all of you, but it is necessary for a larger purpose."

The warriors all turned back toward the map. For another few moments, they watched in silence. The captains began pointing here and there and conferring with each other. Then, they turned and issued orders to their lieutenants, and the normal pace of the meeting continued.

Elric stepped back with Lacidar and Jenli. Grigor alighted in front of Elric, and the four gathered in the corner.

Hannah poured herself a cup of water and sat alone in her empty house.

34

THE REVEALED TRUTH

Birth minus 21 weeks

Two dark weeks passed since Mary had returned home. Daily she sat with the mourners and Joseph and returned home at evening time. And daily it became harder for her to find the words she had rehearsed for her parents while in Judea.

Standing in the back bedroom of her home, she prepared for bed after another somber day. *I should have told them right away—when I told them the exciting news about Elizabeth. Now,* she stroked her belly and sighed, *it will be even harder.* She removed her mourner's cloak. *And the problem gets worse every day. I think I'm almost five months now, and I don't know how much longer I can hide this.* She reached for her bed clothes. *At least these shapeless clothes make it easier.*

Passing by, Mary's mother paused and said, "Mary! You look like you have gained. . ." She stopped, and her mouth dropped open. "Mary. . . are you. . ."

Mary felt all the blood rush from her face. *Oh, no! I didn't want it to come out like this.* The shock on her mother's face sent a shudder through her frame. *This is it. Just get it out there quickly.* She took a deep breath, perked up a smile, and blurted out, "Yes! And it is the most exciting, amazing thing."

"Exciting? Mary, you are not married yet! Is Joseph the father?"

"No, and that is the exciting part. . ."

"Oh, heaven help us. What are we going to do?" Mary's mother paced and wrung her hands. "You. . . finish getting dressed and stay right here. I must get your father."

Mary pulled her robe over her head and collapsed onto a bed. *This is what it feels like to have your life spin out of control*—like being strapped to cart pulled by a team of unrestrained horses racing to some unknown destination. On the one hand, she had the most incredible promise in the world. On the other hand, she had to face her father. In either case, she could do nothing to rein in the horses. Things would start happening fast now—the secret had to come to light.

Her mother returned with her father in tow. She pushed the front door closed with him only halfway through it. Mary rose and met them.

"What is all this?" her father huffed.

Her mother said with a distressed voice, "Mary is expecting a child! Tell him, Mary."

"It's true, Father. The most incredible thing has happened."

"Joseph! I knew you should not have been spending all that time with him. I would have thought he would have had more respect."

"He is not the father," Mary interrupted with a strained tone.

"What? Oh, Mary, how could you?" He buried his face in his hands. From behind his hands he asked, "How far along?"

"Almost five months."

"Five months?" He paused and counted on his fingers. "Then this happened while you were in Judea?"

"No, just before."

"So. . . this is why you left in such a hurry."

"No. I mean. . . oh, I don't know. Elizabeth really did need me, and I just needed time to think."

Her mother gasped and grabbed Mary's hands. "Oh, Mary. Were you violated by some terrible man? Did he hurt you?"

"No, please—let me tell you what happened. Sit down, sit down. It's the most unbelievable thing."

Stunned to silence, Mary's parents sat holding hands and looking at her as though no possible good could come of this.

"It all started when I saw a vision of an angel in a cave."

Her father and mother glanced at each other with incredulous eyes.

"The angel told me I would be the mother of the coming Messiah. He would be conceived by the Holy Spirit, and he would be called the Son of God. I have not been with any man. It was this same angel who told me about Elizabeth. That is why I knew I had to go and see her. And when I saw Elizabeth, the baby in her womb leapt for joy. And everything I told you about their son John was really true. Our stories are intertwined. Is it not exciting?"

Her father sat motionless with his mouth hanging open. Mary held her breath several long seconds, waiting for him to say something.

"There is only one way that a girl becomes pregnant," he said, rising to his feet. "Why would you concoct such a wild story to try to hide your disgrace? This is serious, Mary. A betrothal is legally binding. If Joseph is not the father, he has every right to put you away. And if he chooses to do that publicly, your very life is in danger. Do you understand that? You could be stoned! No matter what happens, this matter will bring great shame to our whole family."

"But I'm telling the truth! You have to believe me."

He stared at her with a sad, vacant expression. "We will have to call Joseph in. It will be up to him to decide what happens to you now. Until then, you are to stay inside this house. You are not permitted to expose your shame in public." He turned toward the younger children who huddled in the back corner. "Salome, come here," he said.

Mary's younger sister stepped forward.

"Salome, go and find Joseph. Bring him here immediately. Do not speak of this matter with him. Just tell him I must see him. Go. Go quickly."

————

Minutes later, Joseph arrived at Mary's family home and walked into a room of icy faces. The tension of the silent room squeezed tight against his chest. *Whatever this is, I don't think it's going to be happy news.* He looked from face to face for answers.

"Thank you for coming, Joseph," Mary's father said. "Please come in. Here, have a seat."

The shuffling of feet and chairs disturbed the quiet, but the uneasy silence settled back in like a heavy blanket. Joseph looked around again for answers.

Mary's father cleared his throat and said, "Mary is with child."

The words hit Joseph like a punch in the stomach. He tipped backward from the force. He couldn't breathe. He couldn't move. He didn't know what to expect from this meeting, but this was more than anything he could have imagined. He had loved Mary for years and had always dreamed of starting their life together. It had been hard enough losing his mother, but now these four awful words shattered his entire future. His eyes glassed over. Everything went numb.

Mary's father continued, "She claims you are not the father. From your reaction, I assume this is true."

Joseph half nodded.

"Stop it!" Mary shouted. "You make it sound like I have done something wrong. I told you what happened. It's a miracle! It's wonderful! It is the most incredible news on earth. I have not been with *any* man. This is the work of the Holy Spirit!"

Mary stood and moved close to Joseph. Even face to face, her words garbled together as though she was under water. She went on about some message from Gabriel, and a prophet named John, and strange horsemen who brought her home. She said something about the strange things Joseph's mother had been saying and that, somehow, she knew the truth. Through it all, Joseph's mouth never closed. He struggled to breathe. His heartbeat throbbed in his ears. Straining to hear, straining to understand. . .

Oh, no—silence. Mary had stopped speaking. He blinked and looked up at her.

"Well? Say something," Mary said.

More silence. Joseph swallowed hard and said, "I. . . don't know what to say. This is too much—I do not even know what to think."

Mary's father reached over and put his hand on Joseph's knee. The warmth of his hand and the firmness of his touch cut through the cloud of disorientation. This turn of events was real. This was really happening. With a steady, controlled tone in his voice, Mary's father said, "Son, you know your legal options. You are under no obligation to accept a soiled bride. If you choose to write up divorce papers, we would certainly understand. You should go home and spend some time to consider your path. Take your time. Come back and let me know what you want to do next. But, please, speak of this to no one, out of respect to me. Mary is my daughter, and I do not want her to be put into any danger."

Joseph nodded.

Her father stood and ushered Joseph to the door.

Mary called out to him, "Joseph. . ." He turned to look at her pleading eyes. "It is the truth. You have to believe."

He dropped his head and stepped into the darkness outside.

———

Joseph trudged toward home with limp steps, as if every ounce of life had been drained out of his body. Elric walked alongside Joseph but then motioned for two of Jenli's warriors. They arrived at his side in a moment.

Elric said to the warriors, "Kaylar, Jessik—prop him up and give him the strength to make it home. This is a crucial night for us. I am going to go directly to his house and prepare for a special messenger."

Kaylar and Jessik positioned themselves, one on each side, with an arm around his back as if carrying him. Elric nodded. *He has no sensation of their touch, but their strength will keep him walking. More importantly, the King Himself is dealing with his shattered heart. These warriors can provide strength and speak encouragement, but only the Holy Spirit can do the transforming work from within.*

He was there, and He was working.

———

Joseph approached his house, now dark and quiet. No mourners remained. The house looked like a dark, empty hull. Empty, lifeless, alone. He reached the front door and turned back toward the trail he had just traveled. He had no idea how he had made the walk, how he found the strength, how he even found his way. Everything seemed like a blur. He opened the door, lit a lamp, and shuffled back to his bedroom.

He put on his night clothes, blew out the lamp, and collapsed into bed. He lay in the dark with the room spinning around him. A swirl of emotions—betrayal, sadness, anger, confusion, fear, emptiness, pain, hopelessness, isolation—choked his mind and made it difficult to concentrate—and impossible to sleep. The night stretched out, and his emotions became numb. But his thoughts continued to run out of control.

I can't marry her. The thought of her with another man will always haunt my imagination. And the child—it could never be my own. A child of promise. . . with Jehovah as the father. . . what kind of a story is that? What if her story is true? No, it just couldn't be possible. But what if it is? And if an angel actually came to Mary, why didn't one come to me, too? Do I not deserve the same announcement she's been given? Or have I received a message and somehow missed it? No, the story can't be true. Why would the Lord choose Mary and me for such a monumental task?

A sinking feeling of inadequacy came swirling into the mix.

No, it's too unimaginable. Even if it is true, no one else would believe it. And, if I were to marry her, everyone will think I'm the father. Then all the shame will fall to me. Am I willing to bear that scar? Could I stand all the talk, all the looks, all the whispers behind shielded hands? All for a child that isn't mine? But what about for Mary—would I do it for her sake?

From somewhere in the core of his being, the faltering flame of love for Mary tried to shine through. For a couple of heartbeats, he almost felt like he could carry the shame for her sake. But then all the other emotions came crashing back down again and shook him back into reality.

No, I simply can't marry her. I will have to give her divorce papers. As painful as it will be to lose her, it would be even more painful to take her now. Tomorrow, I will put her away.

But how?

If I do it publicly, it will be a huge disgrace to her and her family. In fact, she could be stoned for infidelity. Oh, no! I could never allow that. No matter how much pain I feel, I would never want to see her hurt in any way. I will do it privately, as quietly as possible. And then just walk away.

Why is this happening? Yesterday, my world was full of hope for the future. Now, everything is lost.

————

Gabriel and Elric stood in Joseph's bedroom and watched him flop from side to side as though wrestling some monster. Words from the King rained down into Joseph's spirit, but he could hear none of them.

"Enough," Gabriel said to Elric. "This is going to go on all night. It seems the whole thing is too much for him to believe. I am going to have to speak to him openly to make him understand. Help him go to sleep."

Elric stood over Joseph and covered his eyes with his hand. He spoke the word "sleep," and a soft blue light glowed from his hand. Within minutes Joseph settled down and slipped off to sleep.

"Thank you," Gabriel said, nodding to Elric. He turned and stepped up to the foot of Joseph's bed. Gabriel began to glow like a smoldering coal. The intensity grew until he blazed as bright as the sun. Elric squinted, anxious for Gabriel's message. Gabriel stretched his hands out toward Joseph, and brilliant shafts of light shot from his palms into Joseph's spirit.

"Joseph," Gabriel said. The word entered the Middle Realm, spun like a tiny tornado, and traveled down the shafts of light. "Joseph, son of David, do not be afraid to take Mary home as your wife, because what is conceived in her is from the Holy Spirit. She will give birth to a son, and you are to give him the name Jesus, because He will save His people from their sins."

Gabriel's glow subsided, and the shafts of light retreated. Gabriel smiled to Elric, wrapped his wings around his body, and disappeared in a blink. The sweet fragrance Gabriel had carried from the inner court of the King's Realm still lingered in the air. Elric crossed his arms, breathed in deeply through his nostrils, and waited for the remainder of the night to pass.

————

In Judea, Tumur crouched low within the thick brush—close enough to watch Elizabeth take the baby John for a walk in the morning sunshine, far enough away to remain undetected. *After all these months, I've still learned nothing new about this prophet.* He snorted, and the puff of yellow smoke swirled through the branches of the shrub. *And still no word back from Luchek. How many years of stalking will it take before I discover any worthwhile clues about the coming One? Will I be able to identify Him when He is a child, or will I end up waiting until the Son of God is grown? I hate this waiting. I should just attack the prophet now and thwart the King's plan. No. No. The prize it worth the wait. I alone have the key to. . .*

A small spirit with the shape of a snake slithered up from behind and stopped right beside him. The snake had a smooth, soft voice and a black, forked tongue. "This appears to be a long–term surveillance. What is the object of your pursuit?"

Tumur jumped and snapped back, "Quiet! Do you want to expose us? Go away, there is nothing of interest for you here."

The vertical red slits of the snake's eyes dilated. "Of course, your business is your own. I am just traveling through. Still, I perceive that you must possess some unspoken wisdom to be entrenched here watching some woman and a baby while the rest of the kingdom is gathering in Egypt for a battle over the coming Son of Man."

"Wisdom? What do you mean? Why would you say that?"

"You obviously know something that is more important than even what the Prince of Persia knows. Otherwise you would be in Egypt with everyone else—not here all by yourself."

"That's right, as a matter of fact. I have definitive news about that child right there," Tumur bragged with a pointed finger.

"He is not the Christ, is he?"

"No, of course not. But he is. . . hey, your trickery will not cause me to reveal my secrets."

"Hmm. Even wiser than I thought. Whatever it is, you are most shrewd to keep it to yourself. That way you can reveal it at the most opportune time and collect all the glory for yourself."

"You are an astute little one yourself. Then you understand my position."

"Of course. I will be on my way. I hope your mission goes well."

"Be sure not to tell anyone about my operation here," Tumur warned with a stern voice.

"Why would I? And who would I tell? I answer to no one. I simply travel around alone and do what I can. Look at me—do I look like one who is after glory or power? I am so insignificant, nobody listens to me anyway. Even if I knew your secrets, they would be of no value to me."

Tumur looked at him with a hollow, superior kind of pity and couldn't help but boast about his findings—especially considering the unimportance of this little belly crawler.

"Yes, I suppose you are right. It is big news, though. If I were to tell you, would you promise to keep it to yourself?"

"Who would I tell?" His black forked tongue darted in and out.

"Do you see that boy right there? His name is John, and he is the prophet foretold to come before the Christ. I have found him myself and no one else knows."

"Are you going to attack him?"

"No, I am going to use him to locate the Christ. If by some chance they are all wrong down in Egypt, I will have the best opportunity to locate Him since I have the prophet. Eventually, I will sow thorns in his path, but for now I am simply watching."

"This is big news. Congratulations on your good fortune. You are truly wise and powerful. This will be a most coveted prize to our lord when you deliver it."

"Remember, do not tell anyone."

The snake poked out his forked tongue, "Not a single hiss." He slithered off without a sound.

Joseph awoke with a start and sat bolt upright. *Morning. What a night.* He rubbed the sleep from his eyes.

"That was the most amazing dream I have ever had," he said aloud.

He looked around the room. Nobody there. *Sure feels like somebody. . .* He rubbed his eyes and plopped back down on his back. *The dream felt so real, I would have sworn I'd seen it with my own eyes.* There was someone dressed in dazzling white, and he could remember every word the man had said. He'd said that Mary's baby had been conceived by the Holy Spirit and that he should not be afraid to marry her.

So Mary must have been telling the truth after all.

Wait. Was the dream really real? Maybe my mind is playing tricks on me because, deep inside, I'm not really ready to let her go. It sure seemed real. How can I know?

The man in white said the child's name—Jesus. Did Mary mention this name? No, she never said anything about the child's name. Was she given a name by the angel?

I need to see Mary.

He jumped out of bed and shouted, "Mary!"

35

WEDDING PREPARATION

Birth minus 21 weeks

*J*oseph stopped to catch his breath after the sprint to Mary's house. His urgent knocking at her front door broke the calm morning silence. Mary's father met the knocking with questioning raised eyebrows.

"Good morning, sir," Joseph panted. "Is Mary here? I need to talk with Mary."

Mary appeared in her night clothes from behind her father. Joseph shot out his hand, grabbed hers, and pulled her out the front door, leaving her father standing in the threshold. Joseph ushered Mary around the side of the house where they could talk alone.

"Mary, I had a dream last night. I think I saw a vision of an angel. He told me the same things you said that an angel told you. But I need to know for sure. Mary, did the angel tell you the name of the baby?"

Mary looked puzzled. "Yes, he said I should give him the name. . . Jesus."

"Jesus!" Joseph shouted. "That's the same name I was told!" He stumbled backwards and let the wall of the house catch him up as he leaned against it. "Do you realize what this means? This is incredible! It is a miracle! It is completely impossible, and yet it is actually happening! This is really happening!"

He wheeled her back around the corner where her father still stood in the doorway. He shuffled Mary past her father into the house, drew her father outside, and pulled the door closed.

Then gathering himself the best he could, he lifted his chin and spoke with confidence, "Master Eli, I am *not* going to divorce Mary. I believe what she has told us. I am going through with the wedding."

"Joseph, I appreciate what you are trying to do, but it really is not necessary. We will bear the burden of the shame."

"No, sir, I really do believe her. There was no other man. I love her and am ready to accept this child."

"Do you realize what this will do to your reputation? You will be the one that ends up. . ."

"Yes, I have fully considered all this, and I am prepared to pay whatever price needs to be paid. Please inform my bride that her bridegroom will be coming for her soon."

He bowed, turned, and ran toward town. He had to see a rabbi about a wedding.

———

Jenli stood near the main entrance of the synagogue in Nazareth when Elric flew in at street level and alighted in front of him.

"Are we prepared?" Elric asked Jenli. "Joseph is close behind."

"Yes, captain." Jenli answered. "Zeev, the new chief priest, is in the back preparing a teaching. He will not be bothered with so lowly a task. Shalev, too, avoids most of these duties. Almost all the civic ceremonies are accomplished by Yadid and Raziel now."

Elric and Jenli stepped inside. Elric scanned the sanctuary. Shalev and Raziel stood alone, offering prayers. "And where is Yadid?" he asked.

"He received an urgent call from someone and is out in the hillsides."

Elric smiled. "Good work."

Just then, Joseph clambered into the quiet room. He waited several moments for his eyes to adjust to the candlelight and his lungs to catch up. With his hands folded in front of him, he took quiet, respectful steps toward the front. Shalev rose and met him halfway.

Joseph bowed his head. "Master, I seek a rabbi to perform a wedding ceremony," Joseph said.

Shalev answered in a hushed, pious tone, "Rabbis Yadid and Raziel do most of our weddings. I'm afraid Yadid is out at the moment. Raziel is here now if you would like to speak with him."

"That would be very kind, thank you."

With hand motions from across the room, Shalev summoned Raziel, who made his way over and met Joseph. The two retired to a private room, followed by Elric and Jenli.

———

Raziel led Joseph into a back room, square and austere. The furnishings consisted of a simple wooden table and four chairs. A single wall sconce cast a dim glow on the two hanging tapestries and the shelves containing stacks of rolled parchments. Raziel offered Joseph a seat and closed the door behind them.

"Rabbi," Joseph began, "I need you to perform a wedding right away."

Raziel took a seat beside Joseph. "Right away? Why the hurry?"

"The story is long. . . and a difficult one to believe. We have been engaged for over ten months now, and. . . it is time."

"I love long stories. And I should prefer to know you two better before I agree to do the wedding. This is not something to rush. Unless. . . is she. . . I mean, does she have a condition that we need to talk about?"

Joseph's face flushed.

Raziel saw Joseph's apprehension. "I am not here to judge. But it is best I understand your circumstances."

"You will never believe it."

"I have heard many things. There is nothing new under the sun."

"This is like nothing you have ever heard."

"Start from the beginning."

Joseph started from the beginning and told their story. He explained all the details and left out nothing. He told about the angel that appeared to Zacharias and the miracle surrounding the birth of John. He told about Mary's encounter with an angel—and his own. He told how he confirmed his dream by the name, Jesus, given independently to Mary and him. He spoke as fast as he could, as though he had to get it all out before Raziel stopped him.

Raziel had no intention of stopping him. He remained unshaken by even the most remarkable components of the story and kept his eyes fixed on Joseph's with genuine interest. Even though he had seen some curious things over his short number of years in service, he had never seen an angel before. He had never even heard of someone who had. He knew the stories in the Scriptures, but those happened to the great patriarchs, not to ordinary people from Nazareth. But something within his spirit burned as he listened to the incredible story. He had been looking for—praying for—the coming Messiah for years.

Could this actually be the One we have been looking for? The Son of God was prophesied to be born of a virgin. The story of Zacharias and Elizabeth and the birth of the prophet seem to fit.

"Tell me, what is Mary's lineage? Is she from the line of David?" Raziel probed.

"Yes, so am I. Why?"

"Oh, nothing. Just curious. This is interesting—very well, I am willing to perform this wedding. And I agree, under the circumstances you describe, we should proceed right away."

Raziel's heart blazed within. He couldn't wait to see what might become of this child. He would marry Joseph and Mary and then do his best to stay close to the family and continue to watch the one they would name Jesus. "I would advise you, though, that you should probably not tell this story publicly. I do not think people will be ready to hear it. We should wait and see how things develop."

Joseph nodded.

"When would you like to do the ceremony?" Raziel asked.

"I need only a short time to prepare. Can we do it two days from now?"

The two men then spent another hour going over logistics and details for the ceremony. They agreed that a small private wedding would be most appropriate—just the immediate family and close friends. When Joseph left, he looked giddy with excitement.

Raziel reached for some scrolls to search the Scriptures for more prophecies.

36

WEDDING DAY

Birth minus 20 weeks

lric stood beside Jenli outside Mary's family home on the day of her wedding, the driving rain passing through their tense frames. Each had his weapon drawn.

"Not exactly what Mary envisioned for her wedding day," Elric said.

"No," Jenli said, "she always dreamed of a huge, beautiful wedding outdoors under the sun. Instead, the ceremony will be small and almost secret due to her condition."

Elric smiled. "And this rain will force everything indoors. They will never know the amount of protection this affords us."

Jerem flew in from the other end of the street and alighted in front of Elric. "Captain," he said, "the groom and his procession approach."

Joseph and a group of a dozen people ran through the rain toward Mary's house. Men blew the shofar trumpets announcing the arrival of the groom to steal away his bride. The procession reached the door, and they all piled through to get out of the rain.

Jenli said to Elric, "Joseph and Raziel set up the chuppah in the synagogue due to the weather. We have searched the synagogue for enemy forces, and all is clear. My team is ready for the transit from here to the synagogue."

"Very good," Elric said. "Stand watch. I am going inside for the veiling ceremony."

Elric stepped through the front wall of Mary's house into a roomful of wet people. Mary stood in the center of everyone's attention in her beautiful wedding dress and veil. Elric smiled as Joseph approached Mary and tenderly lifted her veil. Mary's beaming face glowed. Joseph and Mary's eyes met. A spark, a twinkle, an unspoken connection. *These two share a secret faith—an anticipation of what the Lord is doing in their lives. None of these others understand.* He glanced over the rest of the guests and family. They all smiled and nodded. Someone behind him whispered their amazement that Joseph would still go through with the wedding. *They still don't believe Mary's story.* Elric turned and stepped back outside.

"Almost time," Elric said to Jenli.

Jenli nodded.

A moment later, the door flew open and everyone ran out into the rain. Joseph and Mary led the procession toward the synagogue, laughing and splashing as they went. Jenli's warriors went to work. The distraction of the heavy rain helped, but it took all their best efforts to clear a swathe through town. Their well–practiced maneuvering, though, ensured the enemy forces saw only a wedding procession, not the unborn firstborn of the King within Mary. Elric flew ahead to the synagogue.

Elric took a station beside an enormous senturi at the entrance of the synagogue and waited. Elric stood eye-level with the senturi's knees. "Remember," Elric whispered upward to the senturi, "do not bow. There are eyes watching, and none can know that Mary is carrying the King."

Minutes later, the procession arrived. Jenli took a post next to Elric, and Elric smiled as the people scrambled in out of the rain. A wiry black demon with dark red blotches mottling his leathery skin slinked into the procession from around the corner of a nearby building and reached the entrance amid the crowd.

Elric's jaw clenched. *I see you.* Elric stepped forward with his sword tip pointed at the demon's chest. "You have no place here today," Elric said.

"Authority is not yours to prevent me," the demon snarled without missing a step.

Elric edged his blade forward until the tip touched the demon's chest. "Be gone," Elric commanded.

The demon reached for his sword.

Not today. Elric ran his sword through the demon's chest in one swift thrust. The demon squealed and collapsed backward. Elric withdrew his sword, and yellow smoke belched from the wounds in the demon's chest and back. "Bind him and take him away from here," Elric said to Jenli.

Jenli bound the demon with white cords of energy, hoisted him up from the bindings around his back, and flew toward the hillsides outside of town.

Elric scanned the area again. *All the people are inside. None of the enemy made it in.* He turned inward toward the synagogue and said to the senturi without looking up, "Allow entrance to none."

Elric stepped inside. All five of Jenli's team had stationed themselves in defensive positions, one in each corner and one hovering near the ceiling. They would be unseen from the exterior, but if an enemy somehow got past the senturi outside, he could be dispatched in short order. The wedding ceremony had already started, and Elric moved in and stood near Mary.

All the elements of the ceremony slipped by as a background shadow for Elric. Usually, the tears of joy from family and friends made him shed his own tears, and the praise and honor for the King contained in the rituals usually made Elric dance. Not this day. This day he stood like a stern statue, his weapon drawn and his eyes darting in every direction.

I don't like Mary at the center of attention. Too many opportunities for the Light within her to be spotted by the enemy. He tightened his grip on his sword. *We are too vulnerable.* He probed the room with intent eyes. He waited. The front door—all quiet. The ceiling—nothing. Back wall—*is there something in that back corner shadow?*—no, nothing. Movement up front! *It's Jenli, back from his errand. Good.* The ceiling—all quiet. The wedding guests—*every eye is on Mary. How do they not see the light of the King?* The back wall—

Crunch!

Elric spun and leveled his sword toward the sound. Joseph and Mary laughed at the shattered wine glass under their feet. *Yes, the traditional breaking of the wine glass. Ceremony is over. Time for the next phase.* Elric nodded to Jenli. Jenli motioned to his team, and they all disappeared through the nearest wall.

The humans bundled back up and made the sloshy run to Joseph's house for the wedding feast. Again, the human entourage laughed through the rain while unseen warriors in white cleared a path. At Joseph's house, Elric took a post at the front door. People crammed into the small house—more than it should hold.

"Come in! Come in!" Joseph called from inside the house. "I'm sorry it's so cramped, but I can't control the weather. We're going to have to do everything inside today."

Elric smiled and whispered, "Thank you, Lord, for the weather."

He remained at his post outside while Jenli and his team kept a tight perimeter. Inside, the wedding feast commenced, prepared with the lamb Joseph had received from Jeremiah's flock. Elric kept his eyes drilled outward and his ears turned inward. The festivities and joyful noise continued throughout the afternoon. Then, the music started. It took all Elric's discipline to not leap into the air and join the dancing and laughter. Instead, he tapped his toe and looked stern. The party lasted long into the night, and so did the rain.

The rain finally stopped, and the clouds parted to unveil a clean, clear sky. One by one, the friends and family offered their blessings and good wishes and trudged out into the muddy darkness while the stars winked down at the sleeping young children slung over their tired parents' shoulders. From somewhere out of the darkness, Jenli appeared and approached Elric.

"Perimeter is secure, captain," Jenli said. "All is quiet."

"The newlyweds are alone," Elric said. "We should step inside."

Elric and Jenli moved inside to the middle of the room. Elric crossed his arms. Jenli's eyes darted all around the room.

"Besides the prophecies concerning the virgin birth," Jenli said, "there needs to be no doubt that Joseph is not the father. Somehow, we need to be sure these two do not. . ."

"Look," Elric said, "the Lord is already speaking to them."

Waves of light from the Throne pulsed through the room and wrapped around Joseph and Mary.

Elric gritted his teeth. "It's hard to tell how much they are hearing."

"Look here," Jenli said, pointing at a precariously placed pot, ready to crash.

Elric nodded.

"And here," Jenli said, pointing at glowing ember in the fireplace that could pop onto a nearby linen and create a small fire.

"Good," Elric said.

"And I noticed a pool of water on the roof that can turn into an all-night cleanup and repair project," Jenli said.

Elric nodded again. "All mere interruptions—which we will use if necessary—but we need the Spirit to speak to these young newlyweds. Stand by."

Joseph held Mary's hand, and they walked back to the bridal chamber. They paused just inside the doorway and, for the first time that day, they stopped and hugged. They tried to hold each other close, but they seemed to be very aware of her protruding belly.

"They know," Elric said. "You can see it in their eyes. They can tell Someone else is there between them."

Joseph backed away, still holding her hands by the fingertips. He turned and lit several candles. Mary sat on a chair.

The thick, sweet fragrance of the presence of the Spirit filled the atmosphere in the Middle Realm. Elric took a deep breath and sighed. "The King is reaching their hearts," he said.

"Mary," Joseph said just above a whisper, "I do believe you are carrying the promised One. I believe what the angel told me in my dream. More importantly, I believe the things you have said. I can't begin to understand what it all means, and I don't know why the Lord has chosen us. But I do believe there is something happening here that is bigger and more important than the two of us."

He paused and gazed at his new bride—glowing in the warmth of the candlelight.

"I think that for the sake of His purpose, we cannot share a bed until after the Child is born."

Mary placed her hands on her belly and nodded. Together they sat without saying anything for several minutes, listening to flames of the candles dance. Joseph got up, went to the main room, and drew two cups of water. He adjusted a pot that appeared ready to fall off the stove. As he returned to the bedroom, the last ember of the fire turned black and cold. He handed a cup to Mary and pulled up a chair beside her.

He said matter-of-factly, "What do you think He will be like?"

The two then spent the rest of the night talking about the baby. They tried to imagine what He would look like and how He would behave. Would He be gleaming white like the angels they had seen? Would they have to teach Him things? They tried to dream about what He would accomplish. How would He defeat the Roman Empire? How old would He be when crowned King? Would they end up living in a palace when He took the throne?

"Not exactly what Joseph envisioned for his wedding night," Jenli said.

"What *will* He look like?" Elric pondered out loud.

"What?"

"I have only ever seen His physical presence in the King's Realm. Can you imagine the great King confined to human flesh?"

"No. I don't even know what to expect."

"I have always pictured Him as the conquering King, full of majesty and power, with all of us riding behind Him as He crushes His foes. But picturing Him as a simple baby, I just can't. . ." Elric's voice trailed off as he stared into the dark room.

Jenli nodded, pulled a ledger from his cloak, and scrawled notes in silence.

———

The next morning, Mary woke Joseph with a kiss on the forehead. "Good morning, my husband, are you hungry?" Mary said.

Joseph rubbed the sleep from his eyes and smiled. "Good morning." He sat up from the mat he had laid on the main room floor and looked around. The mess from the party the night before still covered everything, but Mary had cleared a spot at the table. He got up and joined her at the table. He looked at the small loaf of bread and bowl of fresh grapes. "Thank you," he said as he sat down.

"Did you sleep well?" Mary asked.

"Not really. I spent most of the rest of the night thinking about the baby. And about you."

Mary gave a sheepish smile and took a bite of bread.

Joseph continued, "And about what we're supposed to do next."

"What *are* we supposed to do?" Mary asked

"I don't know. But I do think. . ." Joseph paused. "Please do not be offended."

"What?"

"I think that you should stay out of public as much as possible until the baby is born."

"Did you have another vision?"

"No. Nothing like that. There's just something deep inside that tells me it's the best thing for you—for the baby."

Mary took another bite and nodded. "I agree," she said. "I sense the same thing."

"I also think," Joseph said, "that we shouldn't tell everyone our story for now. Let's just wait and see what the Lord does."

Mary nodded.

Joseph continued, "And until we hear something else, I will just work and do what I know to do."

37

CENSUS COMPLICATION

Birth minus 4 weeks

*G*rigor finished delivering a message to Elric just before dawn at Joseph's house.

"In His service," Elric said to Grigor.

"By His word," Grigor replied. He vanished before Elric's next breath.

Elric stepped outside and gazed upward. The pre-dawn sky looked enormous with its black curtain sprinkled with radiant jewels. He could almost hear the stars shouting the magnificence of the King. He admired Saturn and Jupiter, vivid in the eastern sky. He had been to both these great giants, but here from this vantage, their sparkle felt almost magical. *Just imagine the magical effect they must be having on any men who might be tracking their movements.* In particular, he just learned of three men in Persia who would be watching. Elric wouldn't send any of his team to Persia to work with these Zoroastrian magi, but somehow these men would have a part in the unfolding plan. *I wonder what they might be thinking as they watch Jupiter make its flight.*

Against the dark backdrop, motion caught Elric's eye—a light from the south, flashing low over the horizon. Jenli flew in, alighted, and stepped forward next to Elric.

Without taking his gaze off the great expanse, Elric said to Jenli, "Is there any word on when the decree will reach Nazareth?"

"No, captain. These smaller settlements are the last to be reached."

"Every day that passes makes our task more difficult. Even now, it will not be easy to convince Joseph to bring Mary."

"Yes, sir," said Jenli.

"What is the word from Bethlehem?"

"Mary's cousin, the servant in Achim's house, has heard of her pregnancy. She will be open to receive her when they arrive unannounced. The master of the house is scheduled to be in Jerusalem throughout the week of delivery. It is not possible to prepare the room while the house is under enemy control, but there is ample space."

"What is the current fortification?" Elric asked.

"The same original three beaelzurim who were there before."

"I don't trust them. It feels as though they were left there as bait."

"I have surveyed the whole area. I see no reinforcements," Jenli said.

"Keep looking. We cannot afford to step into a trap. We have no other place for the birth, and the delivery will not wait. By delaying as we have, we will have only one opportunity. Everything depends on this."

Birth minus 8 days

Joseph had just finished a job at a house in Nazareth and started toward home with his handcart full of tools when he heard a commotion coming from the city gates. He wanted to get home to check on Mary, who was due to deliver in about a week, but he couldn't ignore the sounds of the crowd. He paused a moment and looked toward home. Then he pushed his cart off to the side under a tree and jogged toward the noise.

Joseph reached the periphery of a large mob assembled by the city gate. He nudged a man standing at the outside edge and said, "What's going on?"

"Caesar has decreed that we must all register for a census."

"A census? What for?"

"So Rome can take more taxes—what else?"

A loud animated man on a platform by the gate shouted some muddled rant, and the crowd erupted in angry shouts.

Joseph raised his voice to be heard over the mob. "Are we all required?"

The man nodded. "They say additional Roman soldiers will be coming through to make sure everyone complies."

"Where are we supposed to register?"

"They have set up key cities, and you are supposed to go to a specific place based on your lineage."

The crowd raised their voices again. Many shook their fists in the air.

"I am from the line of David," Joseph shouted near the man's ear.

"Then you need to go all the way down to Bethlehem in Judea, the city of David."

"How soon are we supposed to have this done?"

"By the end of the month. You should go read the notice yourself. It's posted at the gate."

"Thank you, I will. Who is the man shouting up there?"

"His name is Judas of Galilee. He has started a new sect called the Zealots. He is against this census and is calling for people to resist. In fact, I think he is looking for enough support to lead an open revolt. I'm not prepared to fight Rome, but there is much truth in his message."

Joseph turned his attention toward the man who shook his fist toward the great Roman Empire.

"Listen, men of Abraham!" the man shouted. "Israel has no ruler other than the God of our fathers. These Roman oppressors have no right to impose their rule over us! Caesar is not our king! Herod is not our king. We owe no taxes to these heathens. And now, they want to take a census. There can only be one reason for that—more taxes! I say it is time we stand up and say no! No, we will not be counted! No, we will not pay your taxes!"

I surely don't want to be mistaken as being part of an uprising. I need distance myself from this crowd as quickly as I can. But first, I should see this decree. He pushed his way to where the decree had been posted. The actual proclamation, written in Greek, hung on a large wooden post by bulky, square–headed nails and bore Caesar's official emblem. A companion scroll hung beside it with Aramaic and Hebrew translations. The men who grouped around the decree stood shoulder to shoulder, jostling to see the words. Joseph pressed in closer, read through the document and found that, yes indeed, he and Mary would need to go to Bethlehem or face serious consequences.

Joseph elbowed through crowd. The man near the back caught Joseph and asked, "What do you think? This man is a powerful leader. I wonder if he could be the deliverer we have been waiting for."

Joseph gave a polite smile and replied, "I think I am not ready to die by a Roman sword today. And I do *not* believe this man is our deliverer. But I *do* believe our deliverer is coming."

Joseph didn't stay to debate the matter. He ran back toward his tool cart. He needed to get home and tell Mary.

———

Elric watched Joseph and Mary discuss the Roman census in their home. In the Physical Realm, it looked like two isolated people trying to figure out an unsolvable problem. In the Middle Realm, the real battle of thoughts and words swirled in the air. Words from the Throne rained in like sheets of light toward Joseph and Mary. Words of direction from Elric shot like darts of light. All the answers Joseph and Mary needed filled the room and tried to penetrate into their minds, but the dark clouds surrounding their spirits blocked everything. Elric frowned. They had allowed their circumstances to turn into fear, fear that crushed his words—and the words of the Spirit.

"What are we going to do?" Mary said, pacing a short line. "There is no way we can get to Bethlehem and back by the time the baby is due."

"I know, but we dare not ignore the decree. I cannot care for you and the baby if I'm in prison—or worse."

"Maybe we could postpone it and go in two or three months."

"No, the decree was issued several months ago. It took that long for the news to reach us. The registration books will be closed at the end of this month. That gives us about three weeks."

"But I'm due in a week!"

"I know, I know."

"What are we going to do?" Mary asked. She eased onto a chair, one hand on her belly.

Joseph collapsed into a chair beside her and buried his face in his hands. "I don't know."

Both of them sat in silence searching for some kind of solution.

Elric repeated his solution. "Pack her up and go to Bethlehem. The Lord will provide for you there. Take Mary to Bethlehem."

"I have an idea," Joseph said, sitting upright in his chair.

Elric nodded and crossed his arms. *Good, he heard me.*

"What if I go by myself and register for both of us and come straight back? I could travel much faster alone—I could make it back in time."

"No," shouted Elric.

"But what if the baby comes while you are gone?" Mary said.

"We do still have your family. Surely they would be willing to help you."

"Joseph, you know they have not spoken to me since the wedding. They still don't believe, and they cannot get past the shame. All my friends are too embarrassed to be associated with me. We have the midwife, but we do not have anyone else."

"I'll rent a horse from someone. It would cut my travel time in half. We would still be taking a chance, but I'm sure I can make it. I know a man in town—I have done some work for him. He is wealthy and has several horses. I will barter some work for the use of one of them. He is a reasonable man, and I think he likes me and my work. If I explain our circumstances, I know he will be willing to help."

Mary remained silent.

"This will work," Joseph said. "It's the only way."

Mary paused but then nodded in agreement.

Joseph hurried out the door.

Elric stopped pacing and looked at Jenli, standing in the corner, writing on his ledger.

"This is not good," Jenli said.

Elric shook his head and rubbed his brows. "The decree came too late. They should already be in Bethlehem by now. This week, we would connect them with Mary's cousin. The following week, we would move her into Achim's house." He rubbed his brows again. "Now we need a new plan to get Mary to Bethlehem in time."

"Is there no word from the Throne?"

Elric shook his head. "Nothing. As we approach the day, I suspect we shall see even less of Grigor."

Jenli groaned. "Once Joseph leaves, it will be very difficult to move Mary."

Elric looked toward Heaven. He remained silent for several minutes and stood like a stone statue with closed eyes and a raised chin.

"One day," Elric finally said. "One day the King will be on His throne on earth, and all this striving will cease." He drew in a deep breath. "We must not fail." He turned to Jenli. "Mary's family is from the line of David. They must travel to Bethlehem, too."

"Yes."

"This is our solution. We must convince them to insist Joseph and Mary travel with them."

"Their hearts are hard."

"It is our best option. Send one of your team immediately."

"Yes, captain. I'll send Jerem."

"Wait. The time is very close now. We must secure Achim's house. Without it, we have no place to send Mary. Are you prepared to take it?"

"Yes, sir, but I recommend we wait until after tomorrow morning. Achim leaves for Jerusalem in the morning, and one of the three beaelzurim will go with him. Possibly two."

"You are sure only the three are there now to defend it?"

"Yes."

"And can you afford to make your attack without Jerem?"

"We can surely take it."

Elric crossed his arms and locked his jaw. "Tomorrow is our day. We will have the birth location in our hands, and Mary's family will convince the couple to travel with them before Joseph leaves. Another day closer to victory and peace."

38

PLAN CHALLENGED

Birth minus 8 days

*J*ust before sundown, Joseph returned home with a stout stallion as the shadows crept up the valleys. From a concealed position by a nearby house, the demon lieutenant Luchek watched through his one good eye.

"What is this?" Luchek whispered to himself.

Joseph lashed the reins to a post behind his house and went inside.

This horse is an interesting development. A poor couple like this can't afford this magnificent animal. They must be borrowing it for something—something like a speedy departure—like the way Mary left Judea. That's it. The elzurim are planning on moving her quickly. But to where? And why? He needed to get some answers.

For months, Luchek had been watching from a distance, learning what he could about this young girl. He had only discerned that she and this man named Joseph were married and that she was with child. She had no regular visitors and she rarely came outside—and when she did, she always seemed to be blocked from his view by a warrior of the host or some coincidental circumstance.

He examined the surrounding area. None of the elzurim team who usually kept a loose perimeter around the house seemed to be there. He waited until dark. Then he advanced toward the house and ducked behind a neighboring shed. He surveyed the area again. Still no sign of the angels. *They must be off preparing a way for her flight.* He slunk closer and stopped again. His red eyes peered through the darkness for signs of defenders. *This is the closest I've ever gotten.* He whisked up near the back of the house. Still no defenders. *This is my chance. I'll slip in and take a quick look inside the house. I'll learn what I can and retreat to the shadows before anyone even knows I was here.*

He approached the back wall and prepared to press his face through it. The horse raised its head, snorted, and shuffled its feet. Luchek drew back and slid farther down the wall away from the horse. He stood as still as a shadow and waited for the horse to calm down. He waited several minutes more.

Then, he melted through the wall, face first.

———

Elric stood beside Mary's bed and listened to the sounds of the night. Jenli's team had deployed to Bethlehem, so they couldn't provide the usual perimeter, and Elric's hand hadn't left his sword hilt all evening.

The horse out back stirred, and Elric's sword came out with a flash. Poised, ready, holding his breath, he waited. The horse became quiet, Elric exhaled slowly, and the sword went back into its sheath.

Several minutes of silence passed. *Something is not right. It's too quiet.* He drew his sword—slow, deliberate, without a sound. *I sense. . .*

Without warning and without a sound, a demon head melted through the back wall, face first.

"Ahhh!" Elric shouted. He slashed his blade down and sliced through the demon's neck. The strike severed his head from his body with a sharp sizzle and left a cloud of sulfurous smoke.

The demon dropped to the floor and twitched until the wound sealed. He lay motionless for several moments. Then, with a shout, he bounded to his feet. He reached his sword, but Elric lunged and kicked him with both feet square on the chest and sent him cartwheeling into the back yard. Elric followed.

"You have no authority here. I command you to depart this place and never return," Elric boomed with a stern and forceful voice.

The demon replied with a defiant tone, "You are not my lord. You have no right to command me. What are you hiding in this house?"

He feigned a quick motion to the left and shot toward the house on the right. Elric met the advance, and the two launched into a duel of crashing swords. Sparks flew and lit the back yard with dazzling flashes. Their swords locked, and the two stood face to face. Elric paused.

"Luminir? Is that you?" Elric said with a puzzled gaze.

"I am called Luchek now, my old captain." Luchek pushed away and held his sword forward while making tiny circles with the tip.

Elric winced at the wretched frame that stood before him—blotchy red skin and half–closed eye. "But you used to be so. . ."

"Oh, I am so much more now. I no longer have to serve man or the King. Now I am free to serve myself. I have my own power. I have authority over men."

Elric shook his head. "Until the King crushes you beneath His feet."

"Unless I kill Him first!" Luchek lunged with his sword. "Who is the girl?"

Elric's sword crashed against Luchek's. "Someone you shall not approach."

For several minutes, the fierce battle sent sparks shooting into the dark sky. Then, Luchek leapt high out of reach and alighted on the other side of the horse. Trapped between the two spirits, the horse kicked up dirt and jerked at his reins.

"What is the purpose of this fine stallion? You are planning on moving the girl?"

"It is not for you to know. Leave here at once."

Luchek pressed his eye shut and squealed between bared teeth. "Tell me about the girl," he growled. "Tell me now or I will destroy this animal."

"Stay away from the horse."

"Tell me what I want to know, or I will spoil your plans."

Elric shouted and lunged toward Luchek with a sweeping arc of his blade. But before Elric could reach him, Luchek sprang into the horse. The horse's eyes glowed red, he raised up on his hind legs, and he bolted forward with an explosion of power. The reins snapped like thread, and the frayed stubs of rope that remained swung down from the post.

In an instant, the horse approached the eastern gate of the city wall. Elric shot after him and matched him stride for stride. Elric glanced backward toward Joseph's house. *I have to do something before we cover too much distance from the house.* He wrapped his right arm around the horse's neck and locked his left hand to his right from below—and squeezed. His arms passed through the flesh of the horse and took hold of the evil spirit within.

With a mighty heave, Elric peeled Luchek out of his equine shell, and the two tumbled to a stop in the dirt as the horse continued to bolt. Elric stood up with his foot on the back of Luchek's neck. Elric spoke a word and produced glowing binding cords of light.

"I don't understand you," Luchek stammered. "You're better than this, you know. Why do you continue to serve this pathetic race of mankind? A being with your kind of power. . ."

Elric cut off his rant when the bindings reached his mouth.

"I used to love the sound of your voice," Elric said as he cinched up the last of his bindings.

Elric turned and looked out the wall gate for the horse. With one thrust of his wings, he rose high over the wall. With another he covered the distance of the small field outside the city perimeter. There he alighted at the edge of a high sheer cliff. He stood atop the rocky brow of the hill on which the town had been built and looked to his left and right.

I don't see the horse anywhere. He slowly peered over the edge. *Please, no.* There, dashed on the rocks far below, lay the lifeless form of the once magnificent animal. Elric's chin dropped to his chest, and his arms fell limp. He turned and walked back to Luchek.

Without speaking a word, Elric hoisted Luchek by the back of the bindings and flew to a nearby cave and stuffed the demon through the opening.

"You can stay here until I decide what to do with you," Elric said.

Elric returned to his post beside Mary's bed and listened to the sounds of the night, his hand on his sword hilt and sadness in his eyes.

39

PLANS FAIL

Birth minus 7 days

*J*oseph stepped out his front door carrying a heavy pack laden with a week's worth of provisions. The pale blue morning had not yet seen the fingers of the sun, and Joseph moved as though he raced against it. Mary stood in the doorway. Elric took a position between Mary and the outside world, his keen eyes scanning the area.

"Everything is all prepared," Joseph reassured Mary. "The midwife will check on you several times a day until the due date draws near. Then she will come and stay with you full time. But don't worry—I should be back by then. I have the fastest, strongest horse in town." He kissed her on the cheek and rounded the corner with his bag slung over his shoulder.

Joseph stopped cold. Elric shook his head.

"What is it?" Mary called out from the doorway.

Joseph stepped back and looked around.

"Joseph? What's the matter?"

"The horse. He's gone."

"What?"

Joseph's pack dropped to the dirt and he shuffled toward the post where the horse had been tied. Mary followed. So did Elric. Joseph grabbed the limp ropes dangling from the post and inspected the frayed ends.

"He broke the ropes," Joseph said.

"How is that possible?"

"He broke the ropes and ran off."

"He must be close. He wouldn't have gone far. We just need to find him."

"Follow the tracks," Elric said, hoping his words would penetrate. "Mary, you should go back inside."

"Maybe he ran home," Mary said.

"No," said Joseph, inspecting the ground. "The tracks lead off in this direction." He started walking, following the tracks. "I'm going to try to find him. Go on back to the house."

Mary tried to pick up Joseph's pack on the way into the house, but she couldn't lift it. She dragged it through the dirt into the house and closed the door. Elric stood outside the door with his arms crossed, waiting for Joseph to inch his way toward the eastern gate. He shook his head. *There is pain at every turn.* He felt it. He felt Joseph's apprehension. More than that, he felt the pain that awaited Joseph at the end of his search. *One day, all this pain will. . .*

Jerem alighted in the front yard and approached Elric. "Captain, my mission has not been a success. Mary's family will not receive any word from me. Their hearts are hard with unforgiveness. They plan to travel to Bethlehem this week, but they will not be asking Joseph and Mary to go with them."

Elric shook his head again. "At every turn," he said.

"Captain?"

"The horse Joseph borrowed is dead. Killed by the enemy last night."

They stood in silence. The morning birds twittered in the distance. The sun began to peek over the horizon.

Jerem said, "This means Joseph will not be traveling without Mary today."

"Mmm," Elric replied, nodding. He rubbed his chin and tight jaw. "It means much more. Joseph has no way to make reparations to the owner. He could end up in jail until he can repay the debt."

Elric walked around the corner of the house to check on Joseph. Joseph's search had taken him outside the town wall. Elric walked back.

"What is your word for me, captain?" Jerem asked. "Shall I return to Mary's family?"

"No. Go to Bethlehem. Check Jenli's status and then bring me word."

"In His service."

Elric walked back around the corner. Joseph was following the tracks across the field toward the cliff. He made slow progress, and the tension built with each passing step.

"Captain," a voice called from behind.

Elric turned.

Jerem landed and ran toward him. "Captain, they have been captured. Jenli and the whole team."

"What?"

"The whole team has been captured. The enemy has them bound and tied to stakes outside Achim's home. They are mounted in the courtyard like trophies!"

"Quickly, go to Judea. Bring me Lacidar and his team. Leave one warrior there with John."

"Yes, sir."

"Then go to Egypt and bring me Timrok. His team must stay in place. But I am going to need Timrok. Quickly. Time is short."

Elric paced and waited. *The loss of Jenli's team is unacceptable. They must be freed. Then we need to take Achim's house. With the additional swords of Timrok and Lacidar's team, we should be able to overcome. How many of the enemy are there? There must have been enough to capture Jenli. It doesn't matter now. The only thing that matters is freeing Jenli's team and securing that house.*

Joseph ran past Elric and went into the house. The door slammed. Raised voices and crying came from behind the walls. Mary's strained voice sent a shudder through Elric's frame. *Mary! I still need to get Mary to Bethlehem. This will be difficult if Joseph ends up in jail. All our plans are coming unraveled. The situation couldn't get worse.*

Five lights streaked low over the horizon. In a flurry of wings, Lacidar and four of his team landed in the yard and stepped forward to Elric. With grim faces, they spoke no words. Lacidar stood beside Elric, and his team formed a tight line and stood at attention. They all waited in silence.

Several minutes later, Timrok appeared. With both swords drawn and his wings folding into his back, he approached Elric. "Captain," Timrok said. "Lacidar."

They both nodded to his greeting.

Jerem arrived.

Elric motioned for Jerem and said to him, "Stay with Mary. Under no circumstances allow the enemy near. This is a vulnerable time, and you will have no reinforcements. It is best if you keep her here out of sight. I will be back shortly."

"In His service."

Elric called over his shoulder to the assembled troop. "Achim's house. Let's go."

Seven lights shot low over the horizon toward Bethlehem.

————

Elric peered over the crest of the hill overlooking Achim's house. Six mighty warriors crouched low behind him. There in the front courtyard of Achim's house, five angels bound from foot to chin with black cords were mounted on tall stakes with their feet dangling above the ground. The stakes had been arranged in a semicircle to display the vanquished. No beaelzurim visible anywhere.

Elric pulled back and whispered to Lacidar and Timrok, "At least they didn't take them away to their prison."

"Captain, this feels like a trap," Lacidar said.

"It is most certainly a trap," Eric answered. "But we have no choice. We must free our comrades. And we must take this house. This is too vital a task for us to fail. The Lord will surely give us the strength we need to prevail."

"What is your plan?" Lacidar asked.

"We will set our own trap. They are expecting someone to attempt a rescue. Let's give them someone. Then, when the enemy comes out of hiding to capture him, we will move in and take them. Now, I need someone crazy enough to walk into a trap and be our bait."

Elric looked at Timrok. Timrok erupted in a huge grin.

"You will be hopelessly outnumbered," Elric said.

Timrok pulled one sword from its sheath with a flourish. Then the second.

"Give us time to surround the place," Elric said.

Timrok nodded.

Elric motioned with his hand, and the team fanned out in opposite directions without a sound. Elric watched from the top of the knoll. Timrok made it to the edge of the courtyard undetected. Five flashes signaled from around the perimeter.

Timrok made his move. He shot like a silent arrow to Jenli's stake and slashed through his bindings in an instant. As Jenli's feet hit the ground, he whispered, "It's a trap!"

Timrok handed Jenli one of his swords and smiled. "I know. And we're doing the trapping."

Six demons exploded from within the house and advanced toward Timrok and Jenli.

"Right on time," Timrok said.

Fierce fighting erupted, but Timrok and Jenli stood their ground. Elric held up his hand. The rest of the team stayed hidden. Timrok fought his way toward one of the other prisoners, dueling with multiple attackers. He drew close—almost to the stake. Ten more beaelzurim bounded from behind the rubble embattlements and joined the fight.

Elric dropped his hand, and five bolts of lightning struck the middle of the courtyard. Elric rushed into the fight with a mighty war shout. All around him—the clanging of steel, the smell of sulfur, and the heat of the enemy's fiery breath. He surged with strength and swung his sword in a blur. He blocked an attack on one side with his shield and ran an attacker through with his sword on the other. It would be a tough fight, but they could surely win.

Like a crackling fire combined with a fierce wind, a deafening roar filled the air. Elric spun around. From every direction, thousands of fire balls blasted in on him and his team.

Just as the plasma reached him, he ducked his head and shoulder behind his shield and set his feet. *Smash!* The shield did its job. *How about the rest of the team?* He lifted his head, and a shockwave of searing pain shot through his chest. He gasped for breath. He glanced down. The tip of an enemy sword protruded out of his chest. He fell to one knee. The sword retracted, and light spewed from the hole. Weak and out of breath, Elric raised his head just in time to see the knees of an enormous demon captain. He looked up farther and saw the captain raise his massive broadsword.

Captain Khilaf? Not again. . .

Everything went black.

40

EYES OPEN

Birth minus 7 days

Elric opened his eyes. Birds chirping in the trees? A happy sunny morning? No! Pain, hard to breathe. Bindings cut into his chest and shoulders. He looked down. He hung suspended high above the ground on a thick post. He pulled against the constraints. The bindings constricted everything all the way down to his ankles. He turned his head as far as the bindings would allow. His entire team was mounted on posts in a circle in the courtyard with him in the center of the circle.

His left eye twitched twice.

Failed. We were this close, and my mission failed. There is no way our small team can take Achim's house. The enemy is too strong here. Now, we have no place for the King to be born. It matters little because I can't get Mary out of Nazareth anyway.

His head drooped to his chest. He closed his eyes.

For an hour he hung in silence. Not struggling. Not thinking. Not planning.

Will the King send a new team to pick up the task and finish the mission? The mission could not stop now. Nature would run its course, and the King would be born. Soon. He would have to send somebody else.

Then he remembered the words of the King to him at the very beginning: "The center of the mission belongs to you."

Belongs to you, Elric repeated to himself. *The King would never go back on His word. That means I have to finish it. It also means the King has already given me everything I need to finish it. What, then, am I missing? I've been so focused on seeing the King establish His kingdom on earth that I must have missed something. What was the last thing the King said to me? "Remember this, Elric, I am humble of heart."*

The words rang in his head like cymbal. *"I am humble of heart." "I am humble." "I will show them who I am."* A flood of love washed over Elric as the light started to dawn within. *The King is not entering the world as a humble baby for strategic leverage. He is coming this way because that's who He is. It never occurred to me. . .*

Since the dawn of time, he had only known the King in His glory. *I have been clinging to the honor of His glory.* Achim's house was the *best* he could find in Bethlehem—the most worthy place for a king. Then he remembered other words of the King. "I will be born in the most humble place and live among the poor."

This is the wrong place! And. . . this is the answer to getting Mary to Bethlehem.

He pulled against the cords. They didn't budge. He tried to reach the dagger tucked into his boot. He could barely move his fingertips. He thought for another minute. Then he smiled.

At full volume, with a tone as clear and beautiful as he could create, he sang. He sang a chorus of praise to the King as though he stood in the very throne room. Before he could finish the first phrase, several of the other captives joined his song. Before they completed the second phrase, the entire circle of angels sang at the top of their voices.

The two guards in the courtyard covered their ears, winced, and doubled over. The dozen demons hiding behind the battlements covered their ears and peeked over the rubble shouting, "Stop. Make them stop."

A lieutenant jumped over the battlement with his hands over his ears and commanded the two guards, "Make them stop now. Go bind their mouths, you fools."

The two guards took a few steps toward Elric, but then backed away—and flew off.

The demon lieutenant ran for the house and emerged with the captain. The captain stepped out with his hands over his ears and roared, "Stop this at once."

Elric stopped long enough to answer, "Captain Khilaf. We meet again. We cannot help but to sing praises to the great King. For He is worthy of all honor and glory and. . ."

"Arrgg," screamed Khilaf, tightening the grip on his ears. "What do you want? What will make you stop?"

Elric became quiet. The others followed his lead. The demons all lowered their hands.

Elric spoke with an authoritative voice. "Captain, we concede this ground. It is yours and we will not try to take it. Release my warriors, and we will not trouble you for it again."

"Ha! You are in no position to make such demands. What is so important about this place that you attack it these three times?"

"Its strategic position no longer has value."

"I think it does. We will stay here. And you will remain my bait for the next insignificant team that tries to test my resolve." Khilaf spun around and marched toward the house.

"There will not be another team," Elric called out. Khilaf continued walking without looking back.

Elric began to sing again. The others joined. The demons all squealed and covered their ears. The captain wheeled around and launched a small fireball at Elric. Wrapped up and helpless, Elric clenched his jaw and squeezed his eyes shut tight. The plasma sizzled in and smashed into Elric's face. His head whipped backward against the post and then dropped limp. The other angels fell silent. After several seconds, Elric shook his head and opened his eyes. He lifted his chin.

"A challenge, then," Elric said, his voice weak and strained.

Khilaf laughed.

"I will fight you. If I win, you release my warriors. If you defeat me, we will stay here and we will remain silent." Elric's voice gained strength with each word.

The captain laughed again. "I have already beaten you. Your warriors are already mine." Khilaf turned and gave a dismissive wave of his hand.

"You did not best me alone. It took a whole troop to stop me and my team. Just like last time. Fight with me alone."

Khilaf answered over his shoulder as he walked, "Your power is no match for me. I have nothing to prove."

"But you do," Elric called back. "You know it and so do your troops. Why are you here, captain? Why are you not in Egypt with the rest of Marr's army? And why is a warrior of your stature a mere captain?"

Khilaf stopped.

Elric continued. "Is it not because you were deemed unfit for the coming battle? Is it not because you lack the power necessary to defeat even a captain? Is it not because—"

Khilaf thundered, "Enough!" He spun and launched a large plasma sphere that blasted Elric's whole body. The binding cords melted away, and Elric fell unconscious to the ground. Khilaf picked him up with one hand and held him at eye level. Elric opened his eyes, and the demon growled, "You have your challenge. Prepare yourself." Khilaf dropped him.

Elric landed on his feet, still weak and dazed. He stumbled to the middle of the space between his stake and the circle where their swords all lay in a pile. He pushed several aside until he found his. He looked at the insignia of the morning star on the top of the blade and gave a slight smile. His strength grew with each breath. He stepped over to the pile of shields and pulled out his. He ran his fingers over the morning star on the shield, smiled, and looked over to Timrok. He strapped the shield to his left arm and stood up straight. He turned to face the demon captain.

Khilaf stood on the opposite side of the courtyard. Almost as large as a commander, he had twice the height of Elric. He wielded a broadsword as wide as Elric's arm and longer than his whole body. All the demons cackled and jeered while the angels remained silent and watched. Khilaf stabbed his sword into the ground and left it standing in place. He held out his hand, and a large ball of flaming energy formed in his palm.

Elric smiled and sheathed his sword. In a low voice, he whispered "Liberty to the captives" into his right hand. A plasma ball formed there.

The two stood motionless. Tension gripped the atmosphere. The demon onlookers chanted and became louder, louder, louder. Then, with a booming shout, Khilaf launched his flaming missile at Elric.

In the same instant, Elric threw his ball of energy. But instead of launching it at the captain, Elric spun in a circle and squeezed as he threw. The ball burst into shards of energy that flashed between the fingers of his fist and shot outward toward the circle of staked captives. Eleven balls of light blasted toward Elric's team members. Elric finished his spin just in time to raise his shield and block the incoming ball of fire from Khilaf. The energy deflected off the shield and dissipated into nothing. At the same time, all of Elric's missiles hit their marks. The binding cords on the angels dropped away, and all the warriors in white jumped free.

"Go!" shouted Elric.

All but three of the angels blasted straight up and away. Timrok, Jenli, and Lacidar joined Elric in the center of the circle.

"We will stand and fight with you, captain," Timrok said.

"No," Elric replied. "We do not fight today. Gather our weapons and shields and go."

Khilaf roared. He pulled his sword from the ground and leapt toward Elric. The three lieutenants snatched all their teams' gear and scattered in different directions. Elric lifted his sword above his head to meet the giant blade descending on him. He braced for impact. Both he and the captain shouted.

Crash!

Sparks shot everywhere, and the sound of colliding steel filled the air.

41

NEW PLANS

Birth minus 7 days

*A*rcher's Cave, the pre-established rendezvous point for Elric's team, looked abandoned and quiet from the outside. Inside, eleven warriors in white gathered in silence. The muted clanking of metal provided the only sound in the Middle Realm as the three lieutenants redistributed the recovered implements of war.

Timrok handed a sword and ox–head shield to one of Lacidar's warriors with a grim smile. One of Jenli's warriors already had his shield. Timrok gave him a sword. Lacidar picked up a sword with bust of a man on its base and handed it to Jenli, who passed it to one of his team members. No one said a word. Everyone moved in slow motion. Their defeat and the loss of their captain weighed heavy on their shoulders, and their eyes looked dim and distant.

Timrok leaned over, reaching for another sword, and stopped. Something in his peripheral view just moved at the entrance of the cave. With his head still forward, he continued reaching for the sword. He wrapped his hand around the handle and took a breath. In one fluid motion, he sprang up, swung around toward the cave entrance, and leveled the sword at the intruder.

"Elric?"

"Elric!" the others shouted. They all erupted in applause and laughter. Elric stepped in, laughing, and lifted a hand to quiet the cheers.

"Captain," Jenli called out over the noise. "How did you survive the attack?"

Elric pulled out his sword and held it high. "Timrok's steel. Khilaf's sword shattered when it hit mine."

The warriors in the cave burst into applause again. Timrok stood tall with his arms crossed and his face beaming.

"Enough of this," Elric said, still laughing. "We have work to do, and time is very short."

The three lieutenants gathered close to Elric while the rest of the warriors sorted through their weapons.

"How are we going to take Achim's house now?" Jenli said. "We need much more. . ."

Elric stopped him with an upraised hand.

"Why is the Lord entering this realm as a humble baby in the humble little town of Bethlehem?" Elric asked.

The lieutenants looked at each other.

"Because it is the last thing the enemy will expect," Timrok said. The others nodded.

Elric shook his head. "We are so used to seeing Him in His glory, we all missed it. This is not a ploy. He *is* humble. It's part of His nature. He is demonstrating to man who He really is."

Timrok, Lacidar, and Jenli stood silent with their mouths open.

"Of course," Lacidar said.

"And Achim's house," Elric continued, "was the very *best* we could find in Bethlehem."

The lights went on in Jenli's eyes. "It's the wrong place," he said.

"It's the wrong place," Elric said. "We need a place that is truly humble. Not just humble compared to the King's Realm. Some place that will demonstrate the King's love and true humility. Don't think in terms of strategic leverage."

They all stood in silence. Jenli pulled out his ledger and flipped through it.

"I have an idea," Jenli said. "There was a place we hid while all the hordes were scouring Bethlehem. It was an animal shed. A stable behind an inn. It would be large enough. It is certainly humble. And there are no enemy defenses anywhere near it."

"A stable," Elric said. "That could be it."

Elric paced for minute, head down, rubbing his chin. Then he stopped and looked up.

"Jenli," Elric began, "send your team back to Nazareth to protect Mary. They will travel with Mary on the road to Bethlehem. You and I will go see about a stable."

Jenli nodded.

"After that, I need to hurry back to Nazareth. I need to keep Joseph out of jail and get Mary to Bethlehem."

"Lacidar," Elric continued. "Leave one of your warriors with John, but you and the remainder of your team go to Bethlehem and make sure Joseph will not be able to find a place to stay."

Lacidar nodded.

"Timrok," Elric said. Timrok's face lighted up. "Thank you for your valiant help today."

Timrok nodded.

"You are free to return to your post in Egypt." Timrok's face fell. Elric smiled and slapped his shoulder. "Let's move. Time is short."

Birth minus 6 days

An hour later, Elric and Jenli approached Joseph and Mary's house from the direction of Bethlehem. They alighted in the front yard and walked toward the house.

"It will definitely work," Elric said to Jenli. "Now we must get Mary to Bethlehem."

"Do you have a plan?"

Elric raised his eyebrows and stepped into the house.

Joseph sat slumped over in a chair. His voice sounded desperate and defeated. "Getting to Bethlehem for this ridiculous census is the least of our problems now."

Mary got up, walked around behind Joseph, and rubbed his shoulders.

Joseph continued, "Since the horse was in my care when he died, the man is holding me responsible. He is demanding compensation, and he has the legal right to do it. I have no way to pay that kind of money. It would take at least two years of my wages to pay that debt. If he wants to press this, I could end up in prison until I can pay the full amount. We will lose everything!"

He paused with his face in his hands. "I don't understand why all this is happening. Do we not have a promise that this baby is the Son of God? Why would the Lord want His Son to be born to a destitute couple with an earthly father in prison? This is the greatest event in all history, and look at us! This should be happening in the finest palace with a royal couple and all the people of the world summoned to greet Him. None of this makes any sense."

"I don't understand it, either. But we have to believe that the Lord will provide a way for us."

"How? We have nothing. It is all I can do just to pay the taxes and keep food on the table. If I end up in prison, they will eventually seize the house and property, and you will end up with no place to live."

Elric smiled. *Yes! Here's my chance.* "The property! The property has value," he whispered to Mary. "Sell the house and move on."

Mary stopped rubbing Joseph's shoulders and stood upright. A spark of light twinkled in her eyes. "We do have the house and property."

"Yes, so?"

"So. . . what if we sold it now to pay the debt?"

"But where would we live? You are almost due to deliver!"

"I know, but. . ." Mary paused. Then a new look of resolve washed over her. "But I'm not worried about that. The Lord will provide something. This would not only take care of the debt, but it would give us a chance to make a new start in another town. We could make the trip to Bethlehem together, take care of the census, and then settle some place in that region. Maybe even stay in Bethlehem. Things here are such a mess. My family and friends have mostly disowned me. There will continue to be talk for years, and I would rather not have to be ashamed in public for a wrong I didn't do. We could start fresh someplace where nobody knows us. It would be better for the child, too."

"But you are due in less than a week. There is no way we will be able to make the trip and find a new home in time."

"It will be fine. Who knows, maybe we will end up in a palace in Jerusalem. Like you said, this is the Lord's child, and He should be born in a palace. Maybe all this is happening just so He can move us to a palace. Stranger things have already happened."

"I suppose."

"This is the right answer. I can just feel it. You should go back to the man and offer to sell him the property. It is worth much more than the horse. See if he will deduct the price of the horse and give you money for the remainder. We could then use that money to live on until you can find steady work."

"Are you sure about this? I don't mind making a move, but I am worried about you. It will be a hard journey in your condition, and there is no telling where we will be when you go into labor. And we won't have a midwife."

"I am sure. In fact, I'm excited. We should do it. Do you think the man will be willing to buy the property?"

"I don't know. He certainly has the means. And he has to know that it is the only way he will get any recompense from us."

"I believe he will do it. In fact, while you are gone, I shall start packing. If things go well, we could be ready to leave town by tomorrow or the day after."

Elric crossed his arms, looked at Jenli, and smiled.

Elric stood outside Joseph and Mary's house with his arms crossed and waited. Then, silent as a breeze, Jenli flew up and alighted next to Elric.

Jenli nodded to Elric. "It is done."

"Good work," Elric said. "This is not easy for them. And my heart aches for them."

Jenli said, "Mine too. The King's, too. I sense He feels their pain more than we. It would be easier if they could only see."

Jenli stood beside Elric and turned back toward the trail to town. "Here he comes," Jenli said. With evening approaching, Joseph came trudging up the path, leading a donkey with a sizable cart.

Mary swung the door wide and stepped out of the house. "What is this?" she called out to Joseph.

"We should go inside," Elric said. Jenli leapt to the roof and stood watch.

Joseph lashed the donkey's rope to the backyard post.

"Let's go inside, and I'll tell you the whole thing," Joseph said.

Once inside, Joseph dropped into a chair and shook his head. "It's unbelievable."

"What?"

"He agreed. This house and property now belong to him. He didn't have enough money on hand to pay the full remainder, so he included this donkey and cart. I figured we would need it anyway to carry our belongings."

"How much money did he offer?"

"We have about six months' wages. He gave us a fair deal. I'm surprised how easily and quickly it all went. We even went and had all the official paperwork done. Everything is completed."

Mary eased into a chair and took a deep breath. "It's really happening."

"I'm much less worried about the trip now that we have this donkey cart. I'll be able to lay out a bed mat in the center and then stack boxes and crates and bags along all the edges of cart railing. It's big enough for all our belongings. Then we can use blankets to make a tent roof so you can be protected from the sun and weather. You will be able to ride the entire way."

Mary smiled and rubbed her belly.

"All my work tools will fit on my hand cart. Tomorrow we will load the carts and say goodbye to everyone. We can be on the trail first thing the next day."

"How long will the trip take?"

"Four or five days. It will be very close."

42

HOMELESS

Birth minus 10 hours

Daniel sat with his back to the high afternoon sun and watched across the valley as the other shepherds worked the flock up the hillside. His father, brothers, and he had brought a portion of their main flock to these hills just north of Bethlehem to sell to some men who were now driving their new acquisitions eastward. The rolling hill before him looked like a tan smiling cheek poking up from the face of the land sprinkled with dirty white freckles. The shallow valley between him and the departing flock had a dusty road winding through it—a main artery, well-traveled. Earlier he had seen a small company of Roman soldiers making a southward march with clanging gear and heavy feet.

He sat watching the afternoon and the sheep slip away, and then he noticed another traveler heading south on the road—a man pushing a hand cart and leading a donkey with another cart. *Can't see the man's face from here, but from the looks of it, he probably has all his worldly belongings on those two carts.* For a moment, a dull stab of pity for the poor nomad pinched his stomach. While Daniel spent much of his own life in tents and under stars, at least he had a home where they always returned. *That man probably has no home.* Daniel watched with mild interest as the man plodded onward. *I wonder if he's going to Bethlehem.* With the town only a few miles away, he would probably make it there before sundown. Daniel and his family, on the other hand, would spend the night here in the hills before making their way back home to the north.

The traveler in the valley passed, and Daniel caught a glimpse of what looked like feet in the center rear of the donkey cart—perhaps the feet of a lady lying down the middle of the cart. Just the feet and ankles. *I wonder why she's lying down, all boxed in that way. Maybe she is old and frail. Maybe she's deathly sick. I wonder what their story is. I suppose I will never know.*

————

Luchek stole up over the hilltop and paused next to where Daniel sat. *It looks like Joseph is taking the girl to Bethlehem.* He paused there to make sure no elzurim would notice him tracking the couple, and for several minutes he surveyed the horizon. The only warrior anywhere in sight was his old captain, Elric, who sat on the back of the donkey cart. *You thought you were done with me, leaving me in that cave. Luckily for me, one of our warriors happened along. Now, I'm free, and you have no idea. I will discover your secrets.*

————

Daniel suddenly got an eerie chill and a deep unsettled feeling in the pit of his stomach—as though someone had snuck up from behind and stood over him, looking at him, preparing to unleash some unspeakable terror upon him. He turned with a start. Nothing there. The hair on his arms and the back of his neck prickled up. For several minutes the feeling lingered, and Daniel continued to look over his shoulders to see nothing at all. Finally, the travelers in the valley passed out of sight, and the unexplainable sense of dread feathered away into the wind.

Birth minus 8 hours

The number of people teeming through the streets of Bethlehem amazed Joseph. *I knew there would be a lot of people in town for the census, but I didn't expect this many. Oh, no, with all these others in town, it might prove difficult to find a place to stay.* At first, they had planned to register at the census quickly and proceed on—maybe to Jerusalem. But they arrived too late, and the registration center had already closed for the night. They would need to find a place to stay and then register the next morning. He found a spot to park the carts.

"You're sure you will be all right?" he asked Mary with clear reservation in his voice.

She sat up at the back of the cart. She nodded. "I'm sure. Go ahead. You will be able to cover more ground without all this baggage."

"I should only be gone a short while—I'll be right back."

Joseph spent an hour in his quest for a room. In that hour Joseph heard many stories.

One man had not planned on spending the night. He waited several frustrating hours in the registration line late in the afternoon.

Then, right when he reached the front of the line, the man at the books announced that he was closing for the day. Despite desperate pleas, he refused to take even one more person and sent the man and the others away. The man hurried off to the first inn he could find and got the last room available. He took it as a tremendous stroke of good luck.

One family had spent the previous night at a different inn and had completed their registration that day. But by a wild coincidence, they ran into some long–lost relatives from another town, and both families decided to stay an additional night so they could spend some time together.

One innkeeper couldn't believe his bad luck. Right here in the middle of the busiest season the town had seen in a long time, a freak accident took out two of his boarding rooms. Some careless man let his donkey get spooked at something and thrash into an awning beam connected to part of the roof—sending a large portion of his roof crashing in. Luckily, no injuries occurred, but it would be several days before he would be able to get the roof fixed and rent those rooms again.

Inn after inn, Joseph heard the same story, "Sorry, nothing available." In every case, he heard about some amazing coincidence or unexpected change of plans that filled every potential vacancy. Joseph returned to Mary and the carts discouraged and exasperated.

"There is nothing open anywhere in town. If only we had gotten here just a little earlier. It seems like everything is working against us. I'm really sorry. We should just find something to eat and go camp just outside of town for the night. We spent the last week under the stars. Another night. . ."

Mary winced and sat upright, grabbing her lower back and reaching deep for a breath.

"What?" Joseph said. "What is it?"

"I'm not sure. It's a sharp pain—almost like somebody squeezing around my back. It was short. I am fine, it has only happened a few times."

"A few times? Mary! You are going into labor! Oh, no, what are we going to do? We can't go back out to the hillsides now. I have to get you into some kind of shelter right now and find a midwife! Right now! Oh, no, oh, no!"

Two men, tall and hooded, passed by, talking with each other.

Mary stared at them in the waning twilight and cocked her head. "Jessik? Kaylar?" she called out from their secluded alley.

"Mary? Is that you?" Jessik answered, leaning against his walking staff.

"Yes! What a coincidence! Joseph, these are two of the men who helped me on the trip back home from Elizabeth and Zacharias's house. What are you doing here?"

"Oh, we are actually just passing through. We are—"

Joseph interrupted, "Yes, very nice. I don't suppose you men have a room in town tonight? We could really use a place to stay."

"No, there is not a room to be found anywhere in town," Kaylar answered. "The census has—"

"Yes, I know," Joseph said. He stopped and took a breath. "I'm sorry, but Mary is starting into labor and I have been all over town and I can't find a room for us and we are out of time and we can't go back out to the hillsides and there is no midwife and I need to find someplace for us to go and I can't leave her here while she is—"

"Joseph," Jessik said. His voice sounded calming—like a cool quenching rain on a wildfire. "Joseph, is there anything we can do to help? Perhaps we could stay with Mary while you go back out to find something?"

"Would you do that? That would be great."

"We would be honored to help. We will stay with her until you return."

Joseph turned to Mary. "You rest here for just a few more minutes and I will be right back." Before she could answer, he took off at a full run, muttering, "Oh, no. . . oh, no. . ."

Where do I go? Where do I go? His feet pounded against the ground, and something from within bubbled up into his brain. *The one place that had the roof damage. Maybe the man will let us stay in one of the damaged rooms.* At this point they didn't need anything fancy, just a place with some walls for some privacy. He ran straight there.

"Please," Joseph begged after the man turned him down again, "my wife is in labor. I have to find something."

"I would like to help you, but I'm afraid it is just impossible. I haven't cleaned up the mess in those rooms yet. There is rubble everywhere—you can't even see the floor."

"Something? Anything? I'm desperate! Don't you understand? My wife is in labor!"

"Look, if all you need is some walls and a roof, I do have a nice stable out back. I know it's not much, but it is better than being out in the hillsides. And I just cleaned it out today, so it is fresh—as fresh as a stable can be, that is. You will have to share company with our milk cow and—"

"We will take it! Now, how about a midwife? Do you know where I can find a midwife?"

"Oh. . . well, no. Sorry. We have not needed the services of a midwife in our house for many years. I'm sure you should be able to find someone, though. Just ask around town."

Joseph didn't have the time to press the innkeeper further. Just glad to have found someplace to bring Mary, he ran as fast as he could back to the carts with the intention of securing a midwife after he got Mary nested into the stable.

43

ALMOST TIME

Birth minus 7 hours

*E*lric watched Joseph scramble down the street. Time now to inspect the manger. Before him stood a small wooden structure, just big enough for two stalls for the cow and a few goats and chickens. The innkeeper herded the chickens out with his feet and led the cow out with a rope. Elric waited for him to finish.

This stable will provide sufficient concealment. He stood outside shaking his head. *This whole situation is unthinkable. The most magnificent palace on earth isn't worthy to be the birthplace of the King of the universe, and here I am preparing a livestock shelter. The King wanted a humble, unexpected entrance. This is as humble as it can get, and the enemy will never think to watch an animal pen for the coming of the conquering King.* He shook his head again and stepped through the entrance.

He crossed the threshold, and memories of the times he had crossed the threshold into the inner court of the throne room overwhelmed him. He wept at the sight of the earthy stalls. Instead of the familiar sweet fragrance of the heavenly courts, this place reeked of musky dirt, straw, drafty old wood, and animal excrement.

He is simply amazing. Even though I have stood before Him face to face, through the centuries I have continued to discover new facets and depths of the Lord's character. His awesome power and holiness cannot be rivaled, and His love and mercy are deep. But this demonstration of humility is a quality of the King's nature I had never imagined. I wonder if the men He is coming to save will recognize it. Probably not—there aren't even going to be any who will see it.

Elric pulled the cloak he had received from the King from his side pouch and folded it with care. He poked his head through the side wall. The innkeeper had gone back into the house. Retreating back into the stable, Elric unfurled his wings, wrapped them around his body, and translated into the Physical Realm. He wrinkled his nose and took reticent steps across the crunchy, mushy ground toward a shelf on the wall. He placed the folded cloak on an empty space next to a small pail on the shelf. He paused a moment, rubbing the smooth fabric with his finger.

A clatter at the door latch! Elric closed his eyes and translated back into the Middle Realm.

The innkeeper bustled in with a pitcher of water, an oil lamp, and some coarse linens.

We are as ready as we can be. This is it.

———

At the same moment in Egypt, Marr lifted his nose into the air, and his flared nostrils twitched. He closed his eyes and let the vibrations in the Middle Realm pulse against his skin. One of his attendants entered his court and bowed low. "Master, another report from one of our spies."

Marr sat back in his throne and looked across the Egyptian plain at the angelic stronghold. "Bring him in."

"Master, a birth within the palace is imminent. My sources in town say it is Rachael and Benjamin. And the angelic forces within the stronghold are posturing."

"Yes," Marr said. "The sense of expectation is thick in the air. Tonight is the night. I can feel it."

He sat up straight, positioned his arms on the throne armrests, and bared his jagged lower teeth.

"It is time to deliver my prize to our lord. Go, report this news to Satan and bring him here. Do it quickly."

The messengers disappeared like shooting vapors, and within only a few minutes, a fast-moving cloud of black billowed toward his location over the grey horizon.

"He brings an entire entourage, as though my forces would not be sufficient," Marr seethed under his breath.

He resented having to call him at all—he didn't need his help. But he didn't dare challenge his authority or orders now because there remained too many loyal to the dark cherub—if only out of fear.

Soon that would change, though. *Once the Child is born, I will personally lead the attack and slay the mortal flesh of the great immortal King before Satan can, thus winning the respect and loyalties of all the forces of darkness. I will then usurp Satan's throne and take my rightful place as lord over the whole earth. From there, with part of the Godhead destroyed, I will finish the job Satan was not able to complete and ascend to the throne of the great King.*

The blackness of the cloud of evil spirits settled over Marr's makeshift throne and boiled there for several moments. Then descending in a cloud of black mist and dark red flame came Satan himself. He alighted before Marr's twisted throne and crossed his massive arms. Marr lowered his head, stepped down from his throne, and watched with reviling eyes as Satan spun round and sat upon the throne with superior pomp.

"You have found the Coming One?" Satan said with a low and electric voice that shook the whole place like rolling thunder.

"Yes, my lord, the enemy has hedged in a young couple named Benjamin and Rachael behind a substantial stronghold. Rachael is about to give birth. I have surrounded the palace with a far superior force, and we are prepared to begin our attack once the child is born."

"You are sure this is the right couple?"

Marr scowled and turned up his lip. "The genealogies are correct. The location is correct."

"What about Bethlehem or Nazareth?"

Marr's tone revealed his agitation. "I have made an extensive search in both locations for months. There is nothing there. *This* location is correct. The enemy has been building a stronghold here for months. I saw the four cherubim descend before the presence of the King nine months ago. There have been additional signs that my spies have uncovered. And now, the time for His coming is upon us. All of creation in the spirit is heavy with labor."

"You are certainly correct about the time. The labor pains are obvious to us all. I hope you are correct about the place. Why did you delay so long to inform me?"

"I needed to be sure, my lord. I would not wish to present you with an empty gift. I have made all necessary preparations so you would not need to be troubled with them."

Satan snorted a fiery "hmph" through his flared nostrils and pierced Marr with his incredulous serpent eyes. "I am not as convinced," he said. "There are hidden things still. But I will stay here and see if you are right."

He sat back on the black throne and waited with indulgence. "I have anticipated this moment for centuries, and soon I will turn the King's weakness of love for mankind against Him and gain the advantage I have long sought."

44

THE BIRTH

Birth minus 6 hours

The fullness of time had come. The weight of labor bore down on all creation. From the deep darkness that hung over the land of Israel to the deep darkness of deep space, the crushing pain grew. The Creator of all things prepared to enter His own creation supernaturally through the natural course of the created. The omnipotent turned head-first into the birth canal of human frailty. The infinite began squeezing into the finite. The timeless One began taking on the heartbeat of a world bound by time. This would be no small delivery, and in the spirit the stretching ligaments and separating bones of creation made a way for the One long awaited.

From the lower back of the farthest galaxy to the ever–tightening belly of the earth, the waves of pain found a heated cadence. The waves started from the deep reaches of space and came screaming downward until the galaxy, the solar system, the earth, became completely gripped in breathtaking agony. For prolonged minutes, the dilating pain clenched the creation. Then, the waves receded, and creation breathed and rested and prepared for the next wave.

The angels in courts of the Great Creator watched as the searing waves emanated from the Throne and blasted through the outer court downward into the physical universe. The angelic warriors at their earthly posts dropped a reverent knee with every contraction. Even the dark forces of the enemy bent their shoulders and heads under the unyielding waves. They all became stone silent—partly for lack of breath, partly for anticipation, and partly for awe and wonder at the amazing thing happening in the Spirit.

Never since the beginning of time had anyone witnessed an event like this. They all knew the miracle happing around them, but even so, it remained too impossible to fathom. They could do nothing but endure the labor, rest between contractions, and wait for the delivery.

This Son would be born, and nothing could stop that now.

The natural world felt only a shadow of the labor. The race of man continued on, oblivious to the rending of the heavens. While some who lived more attuned to the Spirit suffered unexplainable fitful sleep, the rest of mankind didn't sense a thing.

The widow Hannah had sensed a strange kind of anticipation in the air all evening and went to bed with her mind buzzing over something exciting but elusive. She kept waking for no reason. Each time she felt strained for a few moments but then slipped back into a shallow sleep.

The great King Herod in Jerusalem, on the other hand, enjoyed a deep sleep. The heavy curtains in his slumber chambers stood like soaring stately sentinels beside the marble columns, blocking out all the light from the arched balcony windows. Covered with a blanket, weighty and warm, he rested in a comfortable, undisturbed place.

The animal kingdom sensed something stirring in the air. On the other side of the planet, a small herd of spotted deer jumped with spring–loaded legs at the beginning of a contraction and then watched with perked ears for some unknown danger.

A large flock of brightly colored birds burst to flight over an African jungle canopy from some unseen startle.

Dogs here and there throughout the towns in Judea barked sporadically at nothing in the darkness.

Shepherds on the hills outside of Bethlehem stood on sharp alert because their flocks seemed unusually skittish. Thick, fast–moving rain clouds rolled in, but the shepherds knew something more than the weather had their flocks on edge.

The milk cow of an innkeeper in Bethlehem twitched and turned her neck, stretching to see the source of the strained cries coming from within the backyard stable.

Elric had the unique perspective to see both worlds. He, Jenli, Jessik, and Kaylar stood inside the stable, overwhelmed at the honor of being at the center of this moment in history.

Elric tended to Mary, speaking words of strength and encouragement. Jenli did all he could to keep Joseph calm. The other two angels kept watch with wide eyes. Elric saw and felt the wave of each contraction reverberate through the heavens and then watched as Mary's contraction echoed the energy of the Middle Realm. The grip of a contraction released, and Joseph tried to help Mary rest and dabbed her sweaty face.

Outside, the clouds opened up, and a heavy shower of rain fell. Elric noticed a few leaky spots in the roof and briefly appreciated the cover of the stable. His thoughts were cut short, though, because Mary's water broke and sent Joseph scrambling. Joseph jumped and let out a distressed yelp, but Mary reassured him, and he went to work grabbing linens and cleaning and dabbing and looking out of control. In that brief moment of levity for the angels, they chuckled at the innocent inexperience of this young couple. But their smiles lasted only a few moments, for another contraction began to bear down.

The labor continued for hours. As the hours wore on, Elric became more and more concerned about keeping the newborn Son hidden. He had worked so hard over the last year to keep the time and location of the birth veiled from the enemy, and with every contraction he could feel his secret slipping away. He had no idea the Coming would happen like this. "This is no secret entrance," he said with a grimace under the weight of a contraction.

Every spirit in the universe knew that the Creator was entering the Physical Realm. Elric trusted that the Lord had a plan for all this, but he couldn't help but wonder if the enemy would be able to pinpoint the epicenter of this great shaking. He sent Jessik out to warn the rest of the team to be especially vigilant. "A full–out onslaught from the enemy is possible—in fact, likely—if this continues much longer," Elric said.

The rain fell only briefly, but the contractions became longer and the time between them shorter. The stars blinked beneath the pain, the moon winced under the pressure, and the winds on the earth lost their breath. Then, when the creation could take no more stretching, the final push began. Everything went numb, and the weight of the ages bore down on planet Earth. More pressure. More pressure.

He was almost there.

Then, from the very inner court came an enormous rush of wind. To the watching spirits it sounded like the unbridled fury of a hurricane. It raced across the galaxies and flared around the sun. It plowed into the earth like a swirling wave, and those who watched it from a heavenly vantage point wondered how it didn't send the tiny planet reeling off its axis.

At that same instant, Joseph found himself holding a tiny, naked, pink and bloody frail and helpless baby boy.

The Baby took His first breath of air and let out a tiny little cry.

Birth plus 0 hours

Elric fell to his knees. Jenli and Kaylar followed. The Great King had arrived. The King's overwhelming presence and holiness pressed in on Elric's body as strongly as it did in the inner court of the King's Realm. Elric remained still with his head bowed low. *Yes, Lord. Your servant awaits.* Unlike the throne room, the King didn't tell them to rise and then give them instructions.

Instead, a human baby cried with a thin, frail voice. After a few awkward moments of not knowing what to do, Elric lifted his head. Joseph wiped off the Newborn and fumbled through the cutting of the umbilical cord. He found a soft blanket on a shelf next to a small pail. He rubbed it between his fingers and touched it to his face. He then looked at the bloody mess, set the blanket back, and reached for a small pile of linen strips—probably burial cloths—from another shelf. He gingerly swaddled the Baby in them, and handed Him to Mary.

Elric rose to his feet, his mouth hanging open. Jenli and Kaylar followed. In the past, he had stood in the inner court, felt the rolling thunder of power from the Throne, and looked upon Him who sat on the Throne. Now, the utter frailness and smallness of what he looked upon in this dirty animal shelter left him dumbfounded. He stared, breathless, unsure what to do.

Jenli looked over at Elric as if to say, "What next?"

Elric's face answered as one who is wholly undone.

More awkward minutes passed, and Elric finally spoke. "This is all wrong," he said.

"It can't be—these were the King's orders," Jenli said. "Everything is as He planned."

"I know, but. . . look at us." Elric paused and surveyed the young couple and the tiny band of low–ranking angels. "We are the only ones in all creation to see this. Does that seem right?"

Jenli shrugged.

Elric continued, "I feel like I will explode if we don't tell somebody."

"We could sneak the rest of the team in one by one if we are careful."

"Yes," Elric said with an unsatisfied thoughtful tone, "we shall do that. But somehow, that is not enough. I want someone from the race of man to know."

"But captain, we do not dare give away our position! Everything we have worked for. . ."

Elric held up his hand. He needed time to think. The Baby had stopped crying and snuggled close to His mother. Joseph sat beside Mary, touching her arm. The night became completely silent. No dogs barked. No crickets chirped. Not even a whisper of wind dared to disturb the clarity of the quietness.

Jessik appeared through the stable roof and alighted on the dusty floor amid the quiet disarray. The unmistakable presence of the King drove him to his knees. And then, like the others, he pressed through the awkward moments and lifted his head when it had become clear that he would receive no acknowledgment from the King. He looked first to Elric, who stood like a silent pillar, arms crossed and eyes closed. The remaining angels stood or knelt, transfixed by the tiny bundle in Mary's arms. Jessik closed his gaping jaw and joined the rest in staring at the One in whom they had long awaited. After several deliberate minutes, Elric opened his eyes. The look on his face had changed to calm resolve.

"We must tell somebody. The Lord will give us success in keeping our location hidden."

"Who shall it be, sir?" Jenli asked. "The priests in the Bethlehem synagogue?"

"No, that would be too dangerous. It is not time for Him to be revealed to them."

"Someone in town then? Perhaps the innkeeper?"

Kaylar said, "There is a God–fearing family who are in town from the Judean countryside. They have finished their business here and are planning to leave tomorrow."

Each of the suggestions met with an unsatisfied wrinkle of Elric's nose and a contemplative shrug or nod. They offered several other ideas, but none of them seemed right. A brief pause filled the room with silence. Jenli flipped through his ledger.

Jessik broke the silence. "Captain, earlier while I was out, I saw some shepherds on the hills just outside town."

Elric lifted an eyebrow and cocked his head. "Any enemy forces accompanying them?"

"None that I could see."

Elric rubbed his chin and then dropped his hand down to the hilt of his sword. "I like it. And I think it will please the Lord. Jenli, I would like you to deliver the message. I will stay here with these two warriors. You go assemble the rest of your team and prepare for the herdsmen's movements. It is critical that they do not arouse any attention or pick up an enemy shadow. Once your team is in place and the timing is right, make your appearance to the shepherds and give them the good news."

Elric stopped and let a satisfied smile sneak out. "The Great Shepherd will have shepherds for His first earthly worshipers. I like this very much. Go. Quickly."

45

HERALD CHORUS

Birth plus 1 hour

The storm that blew in over the flocks outside Bethlehem proved to be strange indeed. It arrived as swift as a pack of wolves, dropped a brief shower, and passed on. The four men who held the flock together during the time of unexplainable edginess gathered back together and compared stories, trying to figure out what had happened. The flock rested peacefully now, but the men shivered with soaked clothes. They all agreed that something else besides the peculiar storm had spooked the sheep. None of them had seen anything. As they compared stories and wrung out their saturated clothes and hair, the sheep nearest them jolted backward and became jittery—again for no apparent reason. The men looked all around, straining to see the unseen disturbance. They saw nothing.

And then, as sudden and gentle as a snowflake, a tiny light appeared in front of them, hovering about eye-level and blinking like a distant star. All four men saw it at the same time and became captured by its intrigue. The sheep saw it, too, and became serene and motionless. The light grew in size and intensity. Within a few moments it looked like a large ball of pulsing energy. Within another few moments, it grew into the size of a small cloud, and it became clear that in another few seconds it would envelop the area where the men stood. They remained still, not sure what the light could be and not sure what they should do. Then, like a wave of unstoppable energy, the light swept through them, and they found themselves standing in the midst of a brilliant white cloud of light. It looked as intense as lightning, yet felt warm, restrained, and strangely peaceful. The entire outside world disappeared, and they could only see themselves and this thick, clear brilliance. When they thought the light could get no brighter, a dazzling flash blinded them. They strained through wincing eyes, and there in front of them stood another man.

The huge, muscular man towered a full ten feet tall. He looked intensely white from the top of his stubbled head to the bottom of his bare translucent feet. He wore a full–length tunic, fluid and functional, belted and edged with light. A single silver band woven into his sleeve shimmered in the light. A most formidable looking sword in a scabbard of exquisitely carved light hung at his side. And upon his head he wore a headband of interlaced cords of fine white ivy, glowing and pulsing with energy. The same pattern of living ivy leaves appeared along the inner edges of the tunic and sparkled around the wide belt. His eyes felt like they could burn through mortal flesh.

The four men panicked. One of them dropped down face first and covered his head with his hands. Another curled up into a fetal position. The third fell backwards and tried to scramble away, crawling on his back. The fourth tried to run but stumbled over the third man and fell on his face on top of the other man.

In a full but calming voice the angel called to the men, "Do not be afraid. Come. There is no need for fear. Come, that I may speak with you."

The four gathered their waning strength, stood, and inched toward the radiant figure. After only a few steps, they dropped to their knees and bowed face down.

The angel spoke with a quick and sharp tone, "Get up! Get up! Am I not merely a servant of the Lord of the Host? There is only One who is worthy of your worship. Get up."

They climbed to their feet and peered at the figure through the cracks between their fingers. Once they saw him eye to eye, they knew this was no dream. A real being—as real as they—stood before them, and he something important to say.

"Do not be afraid. I bring you good news of great joy that will be for all the people. Today in the city of David a Savior has been born to you; He is Christ the Lord. This will be a sign to you: You will find a baby wrapped in swaddling cloths and lying in a manger."

As the last words left his lips, the entire sky above them opened. Past the glory of white that surrounded them, layers of clouds billowed up in the sky. In each layer of the clouds were lines of beings—beings similar in form to the one speaking to them on the ground. The beings stood shoulder to shoulder and formed long ranks from one end of the visible horizon to the other. Each layer had a different color. The lowest clouds glowed red like blazing fire with the tongues of flame ending in shafts of angelic light. The next layer up had untamable orange that blasted with fervent passion. Next, a powerful yellow.

CROSS INTENTS: THE BIRTH

Layer upon layer. Infinite green. Soaring blue. Deep majestic purple. The top layer consisted of an intense violet, rich and glowing with energy. Thousands upon thousands of angelic beings.

The men collapsed to the ground—eyes wide, mouths open, and unable to move.

The angels in the upper terrace of clouds blew clear silver trumpets that melted the very marrow of the men's bones. The tone of the horns resounded so pure and full that the sound itself became visible to the men's eyes, blasting outward like waves of multi-colored light and echoing off every layer of the sky. They rang out a fanfare like none ever heard by mortal ears.

The trumpets joined in perfect unison, but the fanfare built, and they broke into intricate harmonies. Simple four–note arpeggios wove together and created soaring melodies that left the men weeping. Upward and upward the fanfare built. Soon the notes themselves transformed from raw tones and rolled up into understandable words.

Bouncing off the layers of the heavens, the trumpet blasts echoed as "Glory to God" and then "Glory to God in the highest!"— as though the sound itself was alive. The angels in the remaining terraces of clouds joined the song. "Glory to God!" climbed up from the bottom layer. "Glory to God in the highest!" bounded back down.

The spectacle had such exquisite perfection that the men thought this choir had practiced for a millennium. The fanfare continued for almost ten minutes until at the very peak of the music, the entire assembly joined together in a single melody and verse.

Glory to God in the highest
And on earth, peace toward men.
For the fellowship of Adam
Shall be restored again.

Glory to God in the highest
The Great One, the Ancient of Days
Has entered the world as a man
Let everyone join in His praise.

Men cry 'Hosanna, hosanna,'
And the King has heard their call.
With His foot on the neck of His enemies,
He delivers His children all.

The Christ, the Messiah, the Savior
Is born to earth this day
To sit on the throne of David
And remove Israel's dismay.

Glory to God in the highest
And on earth, peace toward men,
Glory to God in the highest
On whom His great favor rests.

They broke out into another lofty fanfare followed by several
more verses. They ended with an ever–building fanfare followed by a
finale of exploding light.

Each angel shot upward like an accelerating comet until swallowed by the depths of the heavens. It looked like a million shooting stars, more brilliant than diamonds shimmering in the sun.

The sight of the great company of the heavenly host and the breathtaking choruses of praise left the shepherds utterly speechless. They hadn't noticed that the angel who spoke with them and the cloud of glory that encircled them had disappeared, but now that the skies had become quiet, they realized that they lay flat on their backs, surrounded by darkness, out in a field with their sheep. They picked themselves up from the ground, their eyes streaming with tears, their clothes dry, and their faces glowing like the moon.

Dumbfounded and weak, they stared at each other. Their eyes sparkled, and tiny grins emerged. Like an explosion, they started slapping each other's shoulders and jumping up and down. After the initial excitement settled down, they said to one another, "Let us go to Bethlehem and see this thing that has happened, which the Lord has told us about."

Birth plus 1 hour

Across the valley on the hill adjacent to the shepherds, Daniel and his brother Jesse, lay on their backs and watched the stars. Daniel had just had an argument with his father and had left the tents to get some air. Jesse followed and tried to help Daniel see their father's point of view. Daniel wouldn't hear a word Jesse had to say but stared into the sky at the fast–moving clouds. All of a sudden, the clouds lit up and trumpets started blazing.

With all the fading breath he could muster, Daniel called over to Jesse, "Do you see that?"

"See what?"

"The angels! In the clouds! Can you not see them? Can you not hear them?"

"Daniel, there is nothing there. See—this is what father is talking about. You always have your head in the clouds and dreaming up nonsense. . ." Jesse continued with a speech of well–meaning father-like wisdom, but by then Daniel lost himself in the angelic chorus.

Birth plus 1 hour

Luchek skulked about in the field among a flock of sheep outside Bethlehem. *How am I going to get past the ring of warriors that turned me back at the gates? I'm fairly confident that the girl, Mary, carries the Promised One, but I can't get close enough to see for sure. And now, after watching the hours of labor pushing down through the heavens—I have to see if her child was really the One.*

Oh no! What's this? A warrior in white streaked his direction. *Need to hide! Need to hide!* He leapt into one of the sheep. The host sheep jumped, and the sheep nearby started fussing over his presence. *Not the best hiding spot, but it does provide some veiling. Hopefully, the angel won't see me or notice the restlessness of the flock.*

The angel landed in front of the four shepherds and made a careful scan of the entire area. Luchek held his breath and kept his sheep host perfectly still. *Don't see me. Don't see me.*

The angel, a lieutenant, proceeded to reveal himself in full glory to the four men standing there. *He's showing himself in the Physical Realm! I know what message he brings. It has to be a most important word to warrant a waking, face-to-face revelation of one of the host of heaven.*

The angel did not disappoint.

This is the confirmation I needed. I have, indeed, found the Son of God. I should fly straight to Egypt and report my finding. Marr will surely be surprised. Marr! I hate him. You know what he'll do—he'll swoop in and claim credit and receive all the glory. I hate him. No. . . he's the last one I would tell. But I can't go directly to Satan now. Not until I see the Child with my own eyes. Somehow, I need to get in close enough, verify it's Him, pinpoint His location. . . then I'll report to Satan. Or. . . what if I could be the one who destroys the Son of Man myself?

His head reeled with visions of glory and triumph. *I could do this. There are no cherubim surrounding Him. The Host have obviously posted minimal forces around the Child in order not to draw undue attention. Only a small team. And Captain Elric. . . Elric, who has already beaten me once. I can't get past him. But he doesn't know I'm here, and he doesn't know I know. I could build my own team. My own team. With me as their master. And we'll wait. And build our numbers until we have enough strength to overcome Elric's team. Yes. Yes. Just imagine the glory. Yes. The potential rewards far outweigh the risks.*

The angels above sang their predictable puppet song, and he winced from their painful melody. Blocking it out as much as he could, he devised his plan. He would stay hidden within this sheep and follow the shepherds into Bethlehem. Once he had located the Child, he would duck away into the shadows somewhere and start looking for other beaelzurim in town to build his task force.

He had a perfect plan.

———

At the first sound of the trumpets, Elric shot from his hidden location and blazed over the field and up into the clouds to the lead trumpet player, another captain.

"No!" shouted Elric as he flew upward.

In less than a blink Elric stood with the trumpet captain and called him aside.

"What are you doing!? You must stop this immediately!" Elric could see all their work of keeping the location hidden evaporating with every note.

The trumpet captain appeared unmoved by Elric's concerns. He gushed with excitement and joy. "Brother, this cannot be stopped. If we do not sing, the very stones of earth will cry out."

"But. . ."

"It is the Lord's will. He is smiling upon us."

"Then at least do this—send your host to Egypt and make the announcement there as well. It is crucial that we do not single out Bethlehem right now!"

The trumpet captain smiled. "This is already done. As we speak, this song is being heralded over the entire earth. Look, see for yourself."

Elric had been so focused on the host over the field outside Bethlehem that he hadn't even looked over the horizon. When he did, he saw the assembly stretched over the horizon and beyond. He breathed a deep sigh and placed his hand on the other captain's shoulder with a smile. "In that case, may I join your troop? I feel like I am going to explode if I do not let this out."

The trumpet captain smiled wide and snapped his trumpet back up to his lips and joined the lilting fanfare. Elric took a place among the singers and released his praise. Within a few moments, Jenli joined and squeezed in next to Elric. Together they melded their hearts and voices with the multitude and became carried away in the waves of exaltation.

The host enjoyed a grand night—the single most exciting event since time began.

After the song finished, Elric took a hidden way back to his post. Jenli descended to make a walk to town with four herdsmen.

46

BATTLE BEGINS

Birth plus 1 hour

Satan sat on the twisted black throne just outside the perimeter of the angelic stronghold in Egypt. The powerful but secondary Prince of Persia hulked close to the right–hand side of the throne. The two of them, along with dozens of generals and the hundreds of lower–ranking demons in the evil court, watched the announcement of the angelic host in the heavens. They sneered and hissed and shot hateful glances upward while holding their hands over their ears. The ostentatious display fueled their anger.

"Impressive display," a general growled, his ears pressed tight.

"Typical," Marr replied with a terse tone.

Another general approached the throne with his hands covering his ears. "Master, permit me to take my army and bring an end to this infernal noise." He had festering dark red skin with deep black cracks producing a permanent scowl. Stubby sharp spikes formed his angry eyebrows.

"Do not waste your time or energy," Satan answered with a low, cold voice. "This pitiful show will be over soon enough, and when it is, you shall have your chance to unleash your vengeance against our real target. Soon the Child trapped within this stronghold will be dead, and we will be ready to ascend to our proper place."

Hundreds of lesser spirits had already begun their assault on the citadel. After the rush of wind that followed the final labor pains, these demons—who had more bravado than discipline—started swarming the outer perimeter. Their attempts to break through proved ineffective, and as Satan and Marr watched from a distance, they looked like a swarm of inconsequential gnats being swatted away at every hand. Their lack of success brought no concern to those observing through the dusky smoke of the throne room, for they knew it would take much more force to break through the defenses, and they had not yet released the full power of their prepared armies.

Not since the original rebellion in heaven had Satan amassed so large a force in one place. Convinced they had the Son of God entrapped, every one frothed at the chance to drive their swords through the flesh of the Child.

Flesh!

Not an all–powerful, unapproachable being in the thundering inner courts of heaven—but a man with real flesh. Flesh could be reached by even the most insignificant of the dark forces, and that prospect fueled many glory–hungry fires. The angelic stronghold appeared well defended, but every creature in the battlement that encircled it had confidence that they had sufficient numbers to force a breach.

Once the angels' song announcing the birth finished, the evil court fell deathly silent. Every sinister eye in the room turned toward the throne. Streams of hot sulfur jetted from hundreds of flared nostrils and swirled around yellow fangs. Long black broadswords hoisted up and rested on spiked shoulders. Then without a blink or sound, the one on the throne of power lifted his right index finger, crooked, dark, and filthy.

Marr announced, "Prepare your forces for attack. Wait for my signal."

Like caged bats unleashed, a flurry of motion swirled around the demon headquarters, and within seconds, the court stood empty except for the few remaining attendants of Marr and Satan.

Once the demon ranks formed, Marr took a large ram's horn and blew a long low–pitched blast across the field. While unheard by the unwitting mortals at the center of the imminent contest, the blast rumbled across the very foundations of the Middle Realm and filled it with an awful, evil dread. Every demon warrior shouted a deafening war cry and clanged their weapons. Their thick, leathery skin twitched in hot anticipation.

The battle sound settled like an iron blanket over the entire region, and at the sound of the shouts, the attacking gnats pulled back and joined the ranks of the main force. Then, with a high–pitched sequence of three blasts from Marr's horn, Marr unleashed the forces of darkness.

They broke upon the stronghold like a crashing wave of reckless fury, but like stalwart stones set in a timeless beach cliff, the defending angels stood unmoved, scattering the wave skyward and backward in a swirling spume of disarray. The tide of demon forces curled around and formed a new wave to pound the fortress.

Wave after wave tried to break through. Wave after wave ejected back. Anger and hatred propelled every swing of their jagged blades. The blazing treachery in their wild eyes matched their ghoulish screams as they pressed the onslaught. They clawed over each other and kicked others back in an effort to reach striking distance of the wall. Impulsive and wild, they only formed into cohesive efforts when a tide of collective energy swept over them and overcame their individual pursuits.

The defenders remained calm, disciplined, solid as stone. They paired up in groups of three or four with their backs facing each other so each could protect the other from the rear. Their blades were straight and sharp and strong as light itself. Their darting eyes were bright and alert and full of composed wisdom. Some held positions at ground level while others hovered at various levels to create a canopy over the fortress. The front line of defenses held—although only barely. Occasionally some of the attackers breached the vanguard, but the even stronger inner line of warriors met them and sent them reeling. The captains in the second line, commanders in the third, and generals forming the very inner circle stayed prepared for the challenge of the larger, more powerful champions of evil which had not yet entered the battle.

None of the combatants knew how long this campaign would last, but considering the stakes, they all expected it to be prolonged and desperate. They could remain locked in combat indefinitely. The demons, bloated with pride and energized by treacherous ambition, believed a quick victory could be attained, but the defenders in white anticipated the siege to stretch out for months or maybe years. Even a dozen years of direct warfare would be inconsequential when measured against the backdrop of millennia of continuous struggles already fought and a future of eternity. This battle might decide the fate of all creation, and it would certainly not be decided in a single day.

"The battle is a good one," Satan said, "but so far their defenses are holding."

"Yes, but once I. . ." Marr's words cut short when a development captured their attention.

The demon horde organized into a swirling tornado that soared hundreds of feet into the air. More and more individuals left their individual duels and joined the boiling vortex. The shrieks and roars of the spinning demons split the spiritual air for miles. Soon they had formed a monstrous twister, black as black, and swirling with enormous energy. Then, as if on cue, it came crashing downward like an enraged fist and smashed into the citadel. Black shards spiraled off in a thousand directions. The defenses held again.

Marr continued his thought as the cloud of black spread back out over the palace. "But once I release the commanders and generals, this puny fortress will crumble beneath my will."

With a slight wave of his hand toward the last unsuccessful barrage, Satan sneered. "You would do well not to underestimate our adversary. They are strengthened with power from the Throne, and sheer force may not be sufficient."

Through gritted teeth Marr shot back, "Maybe not with this current siege, but once I release—"

"Yes, yes. . . your champions will breach the defenses and deliver our prize." Satan sat forward and looked Marr in the eye. "Forget not that there are many others of the host who could be called upon. If all summoned, we would be outnumbered two to one. Therefore, this is how we will proceed: keep your strongest forces back for a time. We shall let this battle run its course for a full season. The defenses may not tire, but they will get into a familiar rhythm and will be caught off guard when I do send in the heavy forces. For now, use these outer rim forces to ensure no enemy reinforcements are allowed to enter. Also, make sure none of the host are allowed to leave. I want them sealed off. No word comes in or out. And reinforce your rear lines just in case the enemy decides to attack from behind and hem you in front and back. In the meantime, continue efforts to get someone in through covert means. Walk in inside a human or an animal. Perhaps now that all the defenses are distracted by the frontal assault, we may be able to slip someone in unnoticed. We have the strategic advantage of position and mobility. We will execute this battle on my terms and on my timetable."

The two locked contesting eyes. Then, with all the defiance he could deliver with his eyes, Marr answered, "Yes, master."

47

FINDING THE CHILD

Birth plus 1 hour

When the angel chorus finished, Daniel, still flat on his back, wiped the streaming tears from his eyes and said, "Wasn't that amazing, Jesse?"

Jesse didn't answer, and Daniel looked over to find Jesse wasn't there.

He must have thought I was ignoring him, got mad, and left. How is it possible he didn't see and hear that? He lay still for several minutes trying to catch his breath and gather his thoughts. *Was all that real? Did I really see it? Am I going crazy?*

He sat up and stared across the valley to the hill where the sheep they had just sold were passing the night. Three of the four shepherds with several sheep were starting down the road to Bethlehem. The fourth shepherd ran toward him. *What is he doing?* Within moments the shepherd reached Daniel and stopped right in front of him. Still winded from his run, the shepherd didn't wait to catch his breath before asking his question.

"Did you see that?" the shepherd panted.

Daniel jumped up. "Yes! Yes! It was the most amazing thing I've ever seen!"

"I know! We were just. . . and all of sudden. . . I've never. . ."

Daniel nodded his head and bounced up and down. "I know! Me too! Me too!"

The shepherd took a deep breath and grabbed Daniel by the shoulders. "Young man, I know your master has sold us these sheep and that they are no longer your responsibility." He paused for a breath. "But we need to take a very important trip into town for a few hours. It is a most important errand. Only we can't leave the flock unattended. If you would be willing to watch over them—just for a few hours—I would be able to join my companions. I would really like to go, and I would be most thankful if you. . ."

Daniel looked back at the tents of his own camp. Tents where Jesse and his father slept. He turned back toward the shepherd. "I would be happy to. Go join your friends. Take all the time you need."

The shepherd patted Daniel on the shoulder. "You are very kind. Thank you."

Birth plus 2 hours

"Wait for me," the shepherd called to his three companions.

"Who is watching over the flock?" one called back.

"The son of Jeremiah." The shepherd caught up with others. Panting, he said, "He was out on the hillside and was eager to help. The sheep will be fine with him."

They didn't know what to expect when they got to Bethlehem or what to say or do if they could find the newborn King. They had no gift to bring to honor the King, so they selected three choice lambs from the flock. As they walked, they tried to recall all the things they could about the angel's message and the song delivered by the angels in the sky. They moved as fast as the little sheep's legs would allow. One of the sheep seemed eager to keep up. In fact, any time the shepherds paused for break, that one sheep would try to continue— as though it knew their special errand.

Luchek peered through the eyes of his sheep host. The elzur lieutenant walking in front of the four shepherds appeared to be the only angelic escort. *Hiding within this sheep was a brilliant tactical move. I am so close now to discovering the exact location of the newborn Son of Man. If only I can get close enough to see the actual house. If I am crafty enough, maybe I can even see the baby Himself. I wonder what the Baby will look like. Why can't these sheep move any faster? Just relax. Don't push too hard and raise suspicions of the angelic escort.*

Birth plus 3 hours

"How will we ever find a baby in this city?" one of the shepherds said when they reached town. "There are hundreds of visitors in town. And there are too many houses to search them all."

One of the others answered, "We know He will be in a manger."

"Do we wander through town and search every backyard stable?"

"And why a manger?" one of the others asked. "Does it seem strange to anyone else that the Messiah would be born in a manger?"

None of them had a good answer. They continued onward in silence and looked up and down the passing cross streets, trying to figure out where to start looking.

One of the shepherds, the eldest, said, "Father Abraham had a humble beginning. And so did Moses. And David. I rather like the idea that the Messiah would. . ." He stopped talking and walking and cocked his head to the left. "Wait, I think we should try looking up this street here."

"Why? Do you know something we don't?"

"No, it's just a feeling. And we need to start somewhere."

"I think you might be right," agreed one of the others. "We should try turning here."

They saw nothing noteworthy up that dusty side street. Two homes on the left. An inn. Another inn on the right. Several more homes ahead. Mostly dark, sleeping windows. A barking dog. One of the sheep of the troop wandered off behind one of the inns. One of the shepherds followed it to herd it back in toward the group.

———

Luchek spotted something interesting and turned in to investigate. He saw no cherubim or seraphim, but he did spot an imposing angelic captain standing watch outside a backyard stable. Luchek pressed his sheep host closer. *Elric! This has to be the place!* Like a soft puff of wind, Luchek whisked away from his host and melted into a neighboring house. The room Luchek stepped into contained a sleeping baby who awoke with a start and cried. The baby's mother rocked the baby, but Luchek turned without notice and spied with nothing more than the front part of his face protruding through the stone and mud wall at the backyard stable.

48

THE SECOND ADAM

Birth plus 3 hours

The stray sheep bolted. By the time the shepherd could catch it and scoop it up into his arms, he had wandered well behind the house and found himself standing in front of a stable. He saw a milk cow and two goats and several chickens in a small pen beside the stable. Something unusual caught his eye. A lamp flickered from the inside the stable, and he thought he could hear muted voices through the weathered wooden slats. Then he heard the soft cry of a baby. He scuffled to the street, still carrying the sheep.

"I think I may have found it! Come quickly."

The four shepherds gathered outside the stable and looked around. A light glowed inside, and they could hear people talking. They nodded to each other. The eldest shepherd tapped at the stable door. The door cracked open and a thin slice of a man's face appeared through the opening.

"Yes?"

"Sir, I know this may sound strange, but we are searching for a newborn King." The shepherd strained over the man's shoulder into the warm glow of the lamplight and caught a glimpse of what he hoped to find. "We were told we would find Him wrapped in swaddling cloths and lying in a manager."

"Who told you this?" The man's tone sounded curious and leading.

Slowly, almost apprehensively, the shepherd told the story of their experience with the angel. He didn't know if this stranger would believe such a tale, and he couldn't tell yet if they had found the right place.

The man seemed very receptive to the story and stepped outside where they could talk without disturbing the sleeping Child. The one shepherd began, but soon all four recalled their experience, interjecting details, and completing each other's sentences with excited inflections and animated gestures.

"And so here we are," one of them finished. "Please tell us, sir, are we in the right place?"

The man smiled—a tired smile that, on the surface, showed the weariness of a long journey and a hard day, and yet it hinted of a reservoir of energy bound up in a story bursting to be told.

"My name is Joseph. Now let me tell you my story."

Joseph shared his story. He told of Mary's visit by an angel and then about his vision. He told about the prophecies and all they had been through. When Joseph finished his account, all four shepherds' eyes were as large as the moon and their mouths hung wide open.

"So, it is true. . . the promised Messiah is born."

"The very Son of God."

"And He is lying right inside this stable?"

"May we see Him?"

"We will not die, will we? No one can look upon the Almighty and live."

"No, you will not die," replied Joseph, "at least I don't think so. Mary and I have seen Him. He looks like a typical newborn. Come."

Joseph opened the door, and the four crowded through and became transfixed by the newborn cradled in Mary's arms. They stood and gawked at the sleeping bundle. Then, almost as if on cue, all four fell to their knees with their faces to the ground and remained in speechless worship for several long minutes. Joseph and Mary looked at each other and shrugged.

Eventually, the shepherds knew they had completed their time and they needed to leave this young couple to rest. Before they left, they summoned Joseph outside with them.

"Thank you for letting us share this occasion with you," one of them said. "You are most blessed among men, and it has been our great privilege to look upon our Lord. If it pleases you, please accept these young lambs as a gift to honor the newborn King. We are simple men and do not have gifts worthy of the Son of God; however, these are the finest among our flock."

"This is no small gift," Joseph said. "I can't. . ." he stopped. Then he smiled. "Thank you. May the Lord bless you for your kindness."

They secured the sheep in the pen and exchanged farewells, and the four shepherds with beaming smiles and childlike skips in their steps began their journey back to the hillsides.

"Can you believe what we have seen tonight?"

"Yes, I can. I have no doubt about what we have seen."

"I know, but it is so just incredible! And why us? Why here?"

"I don't care why. . . I am just thankful we were chosen."

"It is amazing."

"When do you suppose He will overthrow Rome and establish His throne?"

"I don't know, but I hope we will be alive to see it."

"It matters not to me. I have already seen the King."

Birth plus 4 hours

Outside the stable, peering through the wall of the neighboring house, Luchek brimmed with excitement. Even though he couldn't see the Child inside the stable, he knew he had found Him. He heard all the conversations of the shepherds and Joseph. But the complete lack of fanfare in the Middle Realm still puzzled him. *Where are the cherubim? Where are the myriads of attending hosts?* He didn't mind their absence, of course, because with them missing—combined with his superior skills of concealment—he had gotten this close. Then it dawned on him. *This was the King's intent all along. He intended on sneaking into the world without notice.*

Luchek muffled a silent sinister chuckle. *But I did notice! I alone have seen through His plan. And now I alone am in a position to thwart everything.* He remembered Marr and sneered. *And to think, that the high and mighty so-called prince tried to banish me from "his" region. If he could only see me now. He will. He will soon enough.*

What next? I could attack the Child myself right now and be done with it. No, even as good as I am in a fight, I could not get past these two warriors. And there might be additional defenses inside. I shall have to wait. I will wait until they get settled into a house. Then, I will assemble my own team and surround the place. Then, when the time is right. . . I will do the job that Marr was not able to.

———

Elric stood at his post outside the stable and listened to the muffled conversation of the shepherds fading into the night. *They will be talking like this for days. I need to move Joseph and Mary out of this location soon just in case word from the shepherds make it to anyone who shouldn't hear.* He slipped inside the stable, and Jenli moved outside.

The Baby slept, and Joseph and Mary settled in to get some much-needed rest themselves. Elric took the opportunity to gaze upon the Child in wonder.

In most respects, this infant looked like any ordinary human. To other people, who could only see in the flesh, He would look quite unremarkable. However, to those who saw in the spirit, He had something too remarkable to escape notice. Elric had not seen a man like this since Adam. For when the Lord created man, Adam, He formed him into a multidimensional being. The man had a physical, biological body. The man had a mind, will, intellect. And the man had a living spirit. The spirit of this first man dominated the center of his being, and through it he could have fellowship with the Lord. Elric remembered what this looked like. A man—body, soul, and spirit—created in the image of God.

He also remembered when all of that changed. He pictured the day when Adam rebelled against the King's law and his spirit died. The light that used to be visible in the Middle Realm went dark.

After that, the man became controlled by his will and body, and a piece of him went missing. And then, every man born of Adam's seed carried this same condition. They all had a body and intellect, but their spirits remained dark and void. Cut off from the life in the Spirit, he became unable to commune with the Lord. Every one lived under the curse of sin, and every one would commit sin.

This Child, however, was different. Though born of a woman, His seed came from the Father Himself—so He did not come under the same curse. Not since Adam had Elric seen a human with a spirit alive to God. He looked at the Child in utter amazement. *The second Adam.* And for the rest of the night, he stood and admired the shimmering light of this living spirit.

———

And the rest of Bethlehem slept.

APPENDIX

References to quoted passages.

Chapter 16

Luke 1:13–17 (NASB1995): "Do not be afraid, Zacharias, for your petition has been heard, and your wife Elizabeth will bear you a son, and you will give him the name John. You will have joy and gladness, and many will rejoice at his birth. For he will be great in the sight of the Lord; and he will drink no wine or liquor, and he will be filled with the Holy Spirit while yet in his mother's womb. And he will turn many of the sons of Israel back to the Lord their God. And it is he who will go as a forerunner before Him in the spirit and power of Elijah, to turn the hearts of the fathers back to the children, and the disobedient to the attitude of the righteous, so as to make ready a people prepared for the Lord."

Luke 1:18 (NASB1995): "How will I know this for certain? For I am an old man and my wife is advanced in years."

Luke 1:19–20 (NASB1977): "I am Gabriel, who stands in the presence of God, and I have been sent to speak to you and to bring you this good news. And behold, you shall be silent and unable to speak until the day when these things take place, because you did not believe my words, which shall be fulfilled in their proper time."

Chapter 23

Luke 1:28 (NIV): "Greetings, you who are highly favored! The Lord is with you."

Luke 1:30 (NASB): "Do not be afraid, Mary, for you have found favor with God."

Luke 1:31–33 (NASB): "And behold, you will conceive in your womb and give birth to a son, and you shall name Him Jesus. He will be great and will be called the Son of the Most High; and the Lord God will give Him the throne of his father David; and He will reign over the house of Jacob forever, and His kingdom will have no end."

Luke 1:34–37 (NASB): But Mary said to the angel, "How will this be, since I am a virgin?" The angel answered and said to her, "The Holy Spirit will come upon you, and the power of the Most High will overshadow you; for that reason also the hold Child will be called the Son of God. And behold, even your relative Elizabeth herself has conceived a son in her old age, and she who was called infertile is now in her sixth month. For nothing will be impossible with God."

Luke 1:38 (NIV): "I am the Lord's servant," Mary answered. "May your word to me be fulfilled."

Chapter 27

Luke 1:42–45 (NIV): In a loud voice she exclaimed, "Blessed are you among women, and blessed is the child you will bear! But why am I so favored, that the mother of my Lord should come to me? As soon as the sound of your greeting reached my ears, the baby in my womb leaped for joy. Blessed is she who has believed that the Lord would fulfill his promises to her!"

Luke 1:46–55 (NASB1995): "My soul exalts the Lord, and my spirit
has rejoiced in God my Savior. For He has had regard for the
humble state of His bondslave; for behold, from this time on
all generations will count me blessed. For the Mighty One
has done great things for me; and holy is His name. And His
mercy is upon generation after generation toward those who
fear Him. He has done mighty deeds with His arm; He has
scattered those who were proud in the thoughts of their heart.
He has brought down rulers from their thrones, and has exalted
those who were humble. He has filled the hungry with good
things; and sent away the rich empty-handed. He has given
help to Israel His servant, in remembrance of His mercy, as He
spoke to our fathers, to Abraham and his descendants forever."

Chapter 29

Luke 1:60 (NIV): "No! He is to be called John."

Luke 1:61 (NIV): "There is no one among your relatives who has that
name."

Luke 1:62–63 (NASB): And he asked for a tablet, and wrote, saying,
"His name is John."

Luke 1:68–79 (NIV): "Praise be to the Lord, the God of Israel, because
he has come to his people and redeemed them. He has raised up
a horn of salvation for us in the house of his servant David (as
he said through his holy prophets of long ago), salvation from
our enemies and from the hand of all who hate us—to show
mercy to our ancestors and to remember his holy covenant, the
oath he swore to our father Abraham: to rescue us from the
hand of our enemies, and to enable us to serve him without fear

in holiness and righteousness before him all our days. And you, my child, will be called a prophet of the Most High; for you will go on before the Lord to prepare the way for him, to give his people the knowledge of salvation through the forgiveness of their sins, because of the tender mercy of our God, by which the rising sun will come to us from heaven to shine on those living in darkness and in the shadow of death, to guide our feet into the path of peace."

Luke 1:65–66 (NIV): "What then is this child going to be?"

Chapter 34

Matthew 1:20–21 (NIV): "Joseph son of David, do not be afraid to take Mary home as your wife, because what is conceived in her is from the Holy Spirit. She will give birth to a son, and you are to give him the name Jesus, because he will save his people from their sins."

Chapter 45

Luke 2:10–12 (NASB): "Do not be afraid; for behold, I bring you good news of great joy which will be for all the people; for today in the city of David there has been born for you a Savior, who is Christ the Lord. And this will be a sign for you: you will find a baby wrapped in cloths and lying in a manger."

Luke 2:14 (NASB1995): "Glory to God in the highest, and on earth peace among men with whom He is pleased."

Luke 2:15 (NIV): "Let's go to Bethlehem and see this thing that has happened, which the Lord has told us about."

NOW WHAT?

The primary angelic characters in this story are fictional, and the specific actions they carry out are the simple musings of a single man. However, the underlying battle for the throne of the universe and the individual souls of mankind is real. Whether we know it or even believe it, we are embroiled in a perilous struggle that stretches from ancient times to the present day. All around us spiritual forces struggle for the hearts of men. The good news is that the King is and always has been working His plan for the redemption of man. This is the amazing story found throughout the Scriptures.

Because of sin, man is separated from God and enslaved to spiritual forces of darkness. The only payment for sin that will satisfy the righteousness of God is death. This is the primary issue facing every person who has ever lived—how can we ever hope to stand before a holy Creator with any, even one, sin on the ledger of our life? If we were left on our own, our situation would be desperately hopeless indeed.

But God did not leave us in our impossible condition. According to His plan, He Himself entered the world, lived as a man, and lived a sinless life as only He could. Then, He took all the sins of all mankind upon Himself and paid the price to satisfy the law of sin and death. The spiritual forces of darkness did not win a victory by killing Him—rather it was always His intent to take our place in death so He could offer us life while still satisfying His holiness. This is the greatest story of good news imaginable. Instead of facing the eternal wrath of God, He has provided a way for us to be set free from the bondage of sin, enter His Kingdom as beloved children, and live with Him in glory forever.

So how do we step from darkness into light? The scriptures make it clear that there is no work we can do to earn His righteousness. Only His perfect blood can cleanse us. All we need to do is simply believe with our heart that Jesus' death and resurrection provide the way to God and confess with our mouth that Jesus is Lord, and we will be saved. When we put our faith in Him, our spirits that were dead because of sin become alive to God, His very Spirit takes up residence within our mortal bodies, and He transfers us into the Kingdom of light.

If you're not sure what you believe about Jesus, I challenge you seek the truth. Get a Bible and read it for yourself. Start with the Gospel of John and ask the King of Heaven to reveal Himself to you.

Angels are fun to think about, and hopefully my story provides a different view of Jesus' life and work on earth, but do not focus on the angels themselves. The real story is about how God Himself came to make a way for us to reach Him. He accomplished His intent. Now you need to decide what you are going to do about the cross.

ABOUT THE AUTHOR

Scott Wells' journey in His service began with missionary aviation—a private pilot license and some Bible college. It continued with an Air Force career, spanning twenty-one years, during which he earned a Masters and PhD in aeronautical engineering, specializing in feedback control theory. He taught aero engineering at the Air Force Academy, where he reached the academic rank of Associate Professor and served as an adjunct instructor at the Air Force Test Pilot School. In 2008, he retired as a Lieutenant Colonel and took a senior engineering position serving an aerospace company. His analytical and military background, combined with his lifelong studies of the scriptures, form a unique canvas for his speculative world of multidimensional realms and angel physics.

Dr. Wells lives in Arizona where he designs flight control systems and writes. He married his high-school sweetheart in 1983 and has three children. He enjoys playing saxophone on the worship team at church.

CPSIA information can be obtained
at www.ICGtesting.com
Printed in the USA
BVHW070712300721
613239BV00006B/78